IN CUSTODY

ALSO BY LUNDY BANCROFT

The Joyous Recovery:
A New Approach to Emotional Healing and Wellness

IN CUSTODY

A CARRIE GREEN NOVEL

LUNDY BANCROFT

RAISE THE ROOF
Books

Author photo by Natalie Goodman

Book and cover design by Wendy White Kniffen

InCustodyTheNovel.com

for Wendy T., Sue S., Cory T., and innumerable others

CHAPTER 1

Shane Kresge was not happy about being on reception booth duty. He swirled the coffee in his styrofoam cup, then tried to maneuver his lower back, hoping to get his mind off the persistent ache produced by an afternoon of relentless sitting. What he ended up thinking about instead was worse.

On his previous shift, he had come back to the station after a harrowing domestic call, relieved that it was over and that nobody had gotten killed. He and his partner pushed ahead of them a fuming male in handcuffs, thirty-two years old, clean-cut and full of justifications, he worked an important job, not the kind of lowlife they should be arresting. And it turned out that Lieutenant Herzog at least partially agreed; after Kresge reported in about the incident, Herzog ordered him back to the house to arrest the man's wife as well. The grounds? That she'd admitted to having thrown a dishtowel at her husband before he shoved her into the dishrack full of dishes. Therefore in Herzog's eyes she had struck first.

A day and a half later Kresge still couldn't stop circling it around in his head. "A dishtowel?" he said to no one, since he was the only staff in the booth. "A dishtowel??" If he had to keep working under Herzog, maybe he should go back to construction.

You would not call Kresge an advocate for women. His beef had more to do with wanting to be left alone to do his job in whatever way seemed logical to him, unencumbered by Proper Procedure. Unfortunately, that might have involved more latitude than was wise to give him.

Pursuant to those procedures, Kresge now had reports he was supposed to be writing during spare moments in the reception booth. But he couldn't concentrate. He was normally not picky about coffee, he could drink most anything, but this morning the convenience store brew rolled caustically through his mouth as if the beans had been pre-soaked in turpentine. He sat obsessively replaying Saturday's scene in the couple's kitchen and then Herzog grouching at him back at the station.

Then, as if the lobby itself had decided to relieve Shane of his mental looping, the front door to the station imploded, and standing before Kresge's booth window, as if deposited in that spot by a cyclone, was a white guy roughly the size and shape of a toll booth. His glasses were bent, lending a hint of comedy to his spewing anger.

Kresge found the man's rage hard to follow. At first he seemed furious at the police, but that turned out not to be true (though it would be soon enough). He was, however, in a lather toward pretty much everybody else.

"I've been telling people for *months*, no *years*, that this was going to happen!" he yelled into the glass. "Does anybody listen to me? No! What in hell do I have to do??"

Kresge told him to calm down and stop yelling, which had its usual effect of making the party get louder. The man's tirade continued, "She was supposed to bring my kid back *six hours* ago! She's not answering her phone, my kid's got her own cell, she's not answering either, I called her family, no one's heard a thing, *nothing!* I *knew* she was gonna run, I knew it. Why didn't anybody believe me? My own lawyer didn't believe me!"

Now tears were trickling down his face, two or three in little rivulets. His hands were trembling when he wasn't waving them around.

"All right, sir, have a seat," Kresge replied efficiently. "An officer will be out to speak with you in just a moment." He proceeded to shut off the microphone since he assumed, correctly, that the man would keep right on yelling and he wasn't in the mood to hear more of it. While the man's arms continued to wave wildly but now silently in front of the window, Kresge turned calmly to his switchboard and punched in the shift supervisor's extension.

When Sergeant Martinez came on the line, Kresge said to her, "There's a hurricane in the waiting area and someone should come out and take its statement."

Only no one was available, with the result that Martinez instructed Kresge to leave his cozy booth and circular ruminations to go talk to their visitor himself. In the meantime he could set incoming calls to forward to her.

The hurricane introduced himself, between epithets, as Kelly Harbison, failing to follow the rules for the naming of tropical storms. No, he did not want coffee or water, but was it okay if he smoked?

That wouldn't be possible, Kresge answered, he'd come to the station ten years too late for that.

Harbison gushed out his story. He had split up from his wife three years ago because he'd caught her cheating on him with one of the guys from his work. Since then his life had been nothing but court, court, court, as they battled it out over custody of their seven-year-old daughter, well now she was ten. The family court doesn't care too much what the father says or wants, it's pretty much all for the woman over there, so even though the kid wanted to live with him, she was still mostly at her mom's. The kid complained to him all the time about how Mom had a different boyfriend in the house every few months. Well, for the first time the court had actually put its foot down, saying she had to stop canceling Kelly's visits whenever she felt like it or face fines.

"And you'd think that was good, right? Except I knew that if she stopped always getting her way at hearings, she'd want to hit the road with my little girl. I told the court they had to take steps, make her leave a bond or take away her passport or something, but they didn't do squat. I swear, if one hair on my little girl's head gets hurt, I'll *kill* that bitch. You've gotta find them fast, you don't know how crazy this woman is. She'll jump in the ocean and tell my daughter they're going to swim to Europe, or who knows what."

He kept taking his pack of cigarettes out of his chest pocket, pulling out a cigarette, fumbling with it in his hands, returning it to the pack, and returning the pack to his shirt. He repeated this action four or five times as he sputtered out his words, like a puppet controlled by an invisible master.

Kresge had been taught back at the Police Academy, through endless hours of instruction and unbearable role plays, how to calm an emotional party and de-escalate volatile behavior. These lessons had been lost on him, however, and he'd retained his preference for winding angry citizens up further rather than settling them down. Seeing his chance, he declared condescendingly, "I know you're upset, sir, but you can't come into a police station and threatened to kill someone. That's illegal and I'll be recording the threat in the log. Pull yourself together, for the sake of your daughter."

Harbison now looked ready to kill Kresge instead of his ex-wife. "Everything I do is for the sake of my daughter," he snarled, emphasizing every word.

As the man continued to grow frighteningly in size and rage before his eyes, Kresge made the rare decision to behave maturely. "We'll do our best to help, sir, but you need to manage your emotions." Words he suddenly remembered, straight from the police manual.

Kresge left Harbison to settle down in his padded chair and went in to find Sergeant Martinez. She was unimpressed by the story. "The guy's ex and the kid are late by six hours and that's a major crisis? Give me a break. We're not going into a flurry of action over that. In the twenty-four to forty-eight hour range we maybe start poking around a little, maybe at seventy-two hours it's looking serious. In these custody battle situations the parents are on a hair-trigger, they treat everything like it's the biggest crisis since Cuban missiles. A few hours later everybody turns up and it turns out their car broke down and their phone battery died or whatever."

Kresge argued that the situation was out of the ordinary, in that the man's ex-wife had recently been threatening to flee with their child, and he had just won an important court victory that was exactly the kind of outcome that could make her decide to kidnap the kid. It wasn't that far to the mom's house, wouldn't it make sense for someone to just go have a quick look? He generously offered to make the drive himself; he was dying to get out of the station before Herzog came on duty.

Martinez, looking annoyed, paused and then said okay, he could go, as long as he got back quickly. She took the moment to assign Kresge two or three items she needed him to follow up on regarding other cases, but when he got outside he realized he'd already forgotten what she said.

~

After less than an hour with Harbison, Kresge's compassion, not impressive to begin with, was gone. The man talked like he was the only person in the world anything like this had ever happened to. And since he knew for certain his ex-wife had kidnapped their daughter—he just knew it—why the hell shouldn't that be good enough for the police, the FBI, and the network news?

They had driven in separate vehicles to the home of Harbison's ex-wife, twenty minutes north on Route 45 and then off into a kempt neighborhood of shade trees, stone walls, and tidy brick work. Not ritzy but homey. It took Kresge some work to extract his ex's name, since he insisted on calling her "the bitch." When he finally said, "Lauren Harbison," his face curled up as if the moldy accumulation from the bottom of a refrigerator had passed over his tongue.

Lauren's house showed no signs of flight. Not that it would. The front door was locked, as was a side door that entered off of a small deck. "They keep a key under that flower pot," said Harbison, pointing down at a three-foot rubber tree left of the door. "That's how Brandi gets in if her mother's not home." Harbison found the key in its usual spot and held it out to Kresge, who didn't accept it. Instead he moved across the deck to look in the windows, which irritated Harbison further.

"Why are you just peeking, for God's sake? The key's in my goddamned hand!"

"You ever hear of a search warrant, Mr. Harbison? I can't just go in there because I feel like it."

"Oh great, you have to have evidence that she's a kidnapper before you can go in the house—but that's where the evidence is! All right then, I'll go look. No one can stop me from going in there, that's my daughter's house, which I paid for." He put the key in the doorknob and unlocked it, but Kresge moved quickly forward to block the door so he couldn't pull it open.

"That doesn't make it your house," the officer said. "And if you enter, that casts doubt on anything we find later—you could have altered things while you were in there. You don't want that."

Harbison looked murderously at Kresge, then stormed ten paces away and stood fuming. "My daughter could be dying, but at least you'll sleep well tonight, knowing you followed your *procedures*."

Kresge circled the house, looking in from all angles. Nothing looked disheveled. No signs that people inside had been packing suitcases or hurrying. No indications—whatever those might look like—of a ten-year-old being dragged off on a trip she wasn't expecting and didn't want to go on. The kitchen, which Kresge could see into pretty well, looked tidy but not overly so, a few dirty dishes remained in the sink. In a word, normal.

Harbison's raspy voice continued to grate Kresge's ears. "Lauren's required to tell me everywhere they're going. If they travel up to her sister's in the Poconos for the weekend, I get notice. If Brandi has a soccer game over in West Virginia, it's on the calendar. I'm telling you, they're not stuck somewhere!"

Kresge turned from the house and fixed his gaze on the distraught father. "This is the fifth time you've told me these things, Mr. Harbison. I need to get back to the station, I left important work back there." He put a little weight on the word "important."

"Why aren't you issuing an Amber Alert?" Harbison spat back, "Every hour we spend dicking around here the bitch gets another seventy miles away."

Kresge outright laughed, not recommended in the manual. "Do you know anything about Amber Alert, sir? First of all, to trigger it I need evidence that your daughter was kidnapped. I'm trying to look for that if you'd just let me. Second, I have to know that the kidnapper is likely to harm her, and by 'harm her' I don't mean raise her up wrong."

As Harbison gave a hard kick to a stone on the ground, Kresge wondered which of them would hit the breaking point first. "Right," the big man said, lips protruding, "You have to wait until she hurts my kid before you can do anything. Sure."

Kresge was finished. "This house is telling me nothing, and neither are you," he said curtly to Harbison. "Call us if they haven't appeared by this time tomorrow." And with no further words he strode purposefully back toward his cruiser.

~

Harbison showed up back at the station an hour and a half later. Kresge was still stuck in the booth. The irate father handed over the description of Lauren's car and contact information for her parents, siblings, and a couple of old friends, whatever he could find around his house. He'd also written out a list of facts about Lauren's life: where she went grocery shopping, the building where she sometimes went to yoga classes, a fitness club where she'd belonged and might still.

Kresge took the information and—never one to miss the chance to tighten a screw—said, "You could have given me this stuff two hours ago when I asked you." Then he added with a smirk, "Better late than never."

As Harbison turned to leave, Kresge glanced up from the list and said, "You told me your ex-wife has had lots of boyfriends. There's nothing about them on here. Any names, or ideas how I'd find them?"

He shook his head. "But I'm sure her friends and relatives can tell you all about those guys."

CHAPTER 2

TUESDAY, AUGUST 24TH

It was a great day at the *Morriston Chronicle*. There wasn't a moment of peace and quiet, and the staff hated peace and quiet; most days in the newspaper's offices were as dull and uneventful as their sleepy, economically-depressed little corner of post-industrial Ohio.

Tempers had raged at the previous night's city council meeting over a proposal to build a hotel in the heart of downtown Morriston, where the only possible spot would be to squeeze it between a hundred-year-old elegant brick roundhouse and a reasonably maintained but glamorless apartment building. Marriot had agreed—with the mayor, apparently, though she publicly denied having made any deal—to build a six-story pillar of a hotel in the shape and footprint available between the two squat buildings. The owner of the roundhouse, a silkscreen artist who rented studio spaces to painters and sculptors, had commented famously about the planned project, "The mayor evidently thinks that the apartment building owner and I are two testicles in need of a penis." Many citizens were inclined to agree with her after viewing the official artist's rendition of the proposed new skyline.

Emotions among warring factions of the city council had reached an unprecedented pitch as they battled over this sea change to the image of the downtown area. At the previous night's meeting, an anti-hotel councilor had swept another councilor's extensive spread of carefully organized studies and reports onto the floor of the chambers, leading to a near-brawl.

The city council was divided at four in favor of the proposal and four opposed, with one abstention. The mayor threatened to invoke an archaic city by-law that empowered her to break a council tie in the event of an emergency. This maneuver led the roundhouse owner to stand up during the public-comment portion of the meeting and observe drily that, though she was accustomed to men thinking that their erections constituted an emergency, she hadn't expected this from the mayor.

The result at the *Chronicle* was that by late morning on Tuesday staff reporters and stringers were running in every direction, dropping their telephones and calling each other by the wrong names.

So when a report came across the City Editor's desk that a woman and her daughter had been missing since the previous morning, just barely twenty-four hours total, the editor, Marco Vinestri, shook his head and said to no one in particular, "I've got to get a job at a real newspaper."

Fortunately for Marco, he had an intern at the paper who was happy with anything he gave her. Many days he had to invent tasks for her, assigning her to copy edit an article by another staffer (which would nonetheless be passed on to the Copy Editor), proofread an article (before it went to the Proofreader), and similar busywork. He was happier on days when he could hand her a task that might actually help her learn real reporting, despite his sense that she had neither the insight nor the discipline for a future in journalism. Although, he thought wryly, she might have just the right level of skill to embark—or more like disembark—on a career right here at the "Martian Chronicle," as locals called the paper.

~

The intern in question was Carrie Green, a blindingly white twenty-year-old who looked fifteen. She'd grown up in Mormon Valley, an unincorporated part of the county between Middle Beaver and the Pennsylvania border. The nearly two thousand residents of the hills and vales she haled from largely shared her skin tone which, were it a color of interior paint, would have been named something like "Persistent Peroxide."

Historians debated the source of the Valley's name since no Mormons were known to have ever lived there. The residents of the region took little interest in this question themselves, needing to focus their energies on scraping food and clothing together for their children, fixing leaking roofs, and propping up sagging walls. If Marco Vinestri had been, say, one of Carrie's siblings, he might have understood why to her it was a big deal to be working at the

Morriston Chronicle, feeling like a break into the big time even for an intern's stipend.

Vinestri thought she was a pretty little fool who couldn't tell an insult from a compliment. When he grinned and said, "Here's an assignment that will put you to the test," and sent her out to find out why the fee at the landfill had gone up from five to seven dollars a carload, she was grateful for his confidence in her and raced off to the dump to ask the tough questions.

A little more than two months earlier she had finished her Associates degree at the Community College of Beaver County, across the state line in Pennsylvania. She was only the third among fourteen first cousins to get that far in school. Her professors found her "earnest" and "eager to explore ideas," even if they silently observed that those explorations tended to founder before she'd sailed far from the port.

So when Marco informed her that she was to put a short piece together about a mother and daughter who'd been missing for barely a day, he wasn't surprised that she reacted as though he'd handed her a prize assignment. She dashed out of the building in the fashion of her favorite detectives and sped away for the thirty-minute drive to the East Liverpool police station to collect information that, Marco knew, could easily have been obtained over the phone.

~

When Carrie presented herself before the reception window in the small police station, the officer in the booth didn't look up. She appeared to be deeply involved in a tense exchange with a citizen on the phone. When she finally disconnected and noticed Carrie standing there, she made an annoyed frown and sat closed-lipped.

"Uh, hi," Carrie said after an awkward moment. "I'm from the *Chronicle*. I'm looking for some information about a woman and her daughter who are missing."

The desk officer looked baffled. "*The Chronicle*? What school is that?"

"*The Morriston Chronicle*," Carrie replied, a bit snippily. "Not a school newspaper."

She looked Carrie over carefully, slowly picked up the phone, punched in an extension and spoke a few words to someone, then matter-of-factly told the reporter to take a seat. There was no apology.

After a few minutes a young uniformed man came through the door from the back offices, on his face already the hint of a smile which never left. Carrie picked up on his transparent efforts to come off as older than he was; he looked twenty-five, if that. He introduced himself as Officer Kresge and then, without giving Carrie a chance to say her name, asked how she'd heard about the disappearance. Carrie, already nervous, felt her head go foggy and said, "Oh, uh, I can't say who our source was." She immediately felt like a fool.

The officer bit his lip not to laugh, not bothering to hide it much. "Whatever you may have heard down on the corner, darling, it's not true. There's no cause for concern here. We don't even open a missing person case until 48 hours have passed unless it's a child lost alone. We put out a BOLO on the vehicle, that's routine, we just want to be sure they aren't somewhere needing help. Let's not make a mountain out of a molehill."

"That sounds good," the young reporter said, bothered by the overly eager sound of her own voice. "If anything goes in the paper, I'm sure it'll just tell people not to worry but to pass on any information they might have."

"Do whatever you newspeople do," he said, and disappeared back into the inner reaches of the station with barely a parting nod.

Carrie went from nervous to pissed. This young cop had more or less patted her on the head like a toddler. She wished she could pee on the floor of his lobby.

There'd been no reason to conceal her source, though. A man named Kelly Harbison had called the paper late the previous evening and again early this morning, both times deafening the receptionist as he ranted that the Morriston police weren't lifting a finger to pursue his ex-wife, who had kidnapped his daughter. Editors three offices away could hear every word he shouted. If ever there was the opposite of an anonymous source, this was it.

Carrie chewed her gum thoughtfully while skimming through all the meanings of "bolo" that came up on her phone.

Harbison had given the newspaper office both his address and his ex-wife's. Greatly overestimating how much time her supervisor intended for her to devote to this story, Carrie hopped in her car to embark on the drive up Route 45. It never occurred to her not to.

~

The cub reporter had quick eyes and quicker fingers. By age twelve she'd become a skilled shoplifter and all-around petty criminal, like most of her friends, having grown up with no allowance and the usual desires for candy bars, lozenges, eye-liner, five-hour energy boosts. She would have been willing to earn a few dollars babysitting but paid opportunities in Mormon Valley were rare.

Her neighbors had relatives around to look after their kids and little spare cash, as the peeling paint on their houses loudly announced.

Unlike her friends, though, Carrie rarely got caught. She was less impulsive and more strategic than the rest of her disreputable crowd, having learned from the arrests, pregnancies, broken noses, and school suspensions of her six siblings.

Not that the Green kids were a bad lot by Mormon Valley standards. Their teachers didn't cringe when they saw them coming the way they did when approached by, say, a Machado or a Banks, the Valley's notorious families of hoods, thieves, and predators. School personnel viewed the Greens as the future just-good-enough servers at Applebee's, equipment operators for construction crews, and sanitation workers for local towns.

They were only a little wrong.

~

Carrie had no idea what she was looking for on the property. Does the outside of a house look different when the dweller leaves for good than when they leave for a few hours? If she could find signs that they meant to be back soon—a kitten in the house, say—that could be revealing. But other than something obvious of that kind, what would tell her anything?

As she snooped, her eyes kept shifting back toward the roadway, watchful for Lauren and her daughter pulling into the driveway bursting to tell friends and neighbors the story of their misadventure. They might not take kindly to discovering a kid going through their trash barrels, poking her head under their back deck, and standing on their lawn chairs for a better view through their windows.

At the same time, she wasn't about to stop doing those things. She was an actual newspaper reporter. Well, not really, but the paper had given her a journalist ID, which she carried proudly in her pocket. She had a small notebook, a pen, and—yes—a pencil. She pulled this last item out of her bag and tucked it behind her ear; now if people appeared and asked her what the hell she was doing snooping around, she could just point at the pencil and hold up her pad, which would explain it all.

Carrie Green, investigator, found nothing interesting visible from outside the house. On the other hand, neither was anyone materializing from the neighboring houses to suspiciously confront her. So when she absent-mindedly jiggled the side door of the house and found it unlocked, she thought, "Isn't that handy?" and walked quickly and quietly on in.

Her first thought, rooted in old habits, was to glance around for small but valuable objects to pilfer. She gazed with brief longing at an expensive-looking (she had no idea why) bottle of red wine in a wooden stand, clearly too big to pocket. If she saw an easy-to-hide ring or necklace, however, her inner battle was going to be more challenging.

She kept low, walking like a stiff grandparent to avoid being visible through the windows. The downstairs was impeccably neat. No cushion was out of place on a couch, no newspaper was spread around in sections, no slippers on the living room floor. The kitchen looked clean as a whistle, not even clean dishes in the dishdrain, the counters clear except for canisters. Oddly, though, there were several dirty dishes in the sink, not fitting the rest of the picture.

She crept upstairs, where she was less likely to be seen from outdoors but would be trapped if the owners arrived. It was easy to tell which room was Lauren's and which belonged to her daughter, adult possessions being sharply distinct from a fifth grader's. Brandi's room was a total mess, a little island of actual living in this spit-shined house. Her bed hadn't been made, several items of clothing were strewn around on the floor, including a pair of pajamas. Trinkets were in a jumble on the small desk, drawers were left half-open on her dresser. What you'd expect from a ten-year-old's room, in other words.

Except it turned out not to be an island. Lauren's bedroom was in no better shape, perhaps worse. The bed clothing was open and askew, there were skirts and dresses on the floor of the closet, books and magazines and an old flip phone on the floor, a chair leaning at an odd angle against the wall near a corner.

Why would you scrub the rest of the house hospital-clean but leave the bedrooms in an uproar and dishes in the sink? She spun stories in her head for a minute, that they'd been about to leave and then had decided for some reason to go to bed instead, had at least partially unpacked, then decided to leave in a cloud of dust in the middle of the night because of a phone call or a bad dream or something.

Kelly Harbison certainly appeared correct that Lauren had snuck away with Brandi, and that the flight had been planned. But something in the plan seemed to have gone a little screwy.

This is gonna be good, Carrie thought.

The next words through her mind were, *I gotta get out of this place.*

~

Carrie needed a cover story to account for how she knew about the mysterious condition of Lauren Harbison's home. So she began knocking on doors, introducing herself as a reporter for the *Morriston Chronicle,* which caused people to squint at her as if they hadn't seen her quite right the first time. She asked the residents if they'd heard or seen anything unusual in the past few days, because a woman and her daughter down the street had gone missing. In less than half an hour she had virally spread the very overreaction she'd assured the local police department she would squelch.

As she expected, no one had noticed a thing. But that was beside the point. She succeeded in canvassing three individuals and one couple, a total of five citizens she could now hide comfortably behind. She wasn't even settled back into her rusty Dodge when the story took full shape in her head, a neighbor who had told Carrie that she (or he) had been told by Lauren that she was leaving town for the weekend and needed someone to stop by to feed the cats. Except there weren't any cats. So something else, check on a leaky faucet, it made no difference, just a story to tell her editor along with some reason why this person didn't want her name in the paper. None of the actual facts about the state of the house would be an invention; she knew she'd have to rise much higher in journalism before she could exercise that type of license.

~

Marco Vinestri had risen high enough in journalism to earn an office where he could sort of see out a window. It was not a large one, and his view was impeded by corners of filing cabinets, a ceiling fan, and a coat rack. Nor was there much out there to meditate upon: a parking lot, the building next store which stood close by, two or three tree branches and a small triangle of sky. Enough, though, to help calm his frazzled brain.

The past two days had been unusually fast-moving and pressured in the offices and corridors he frequented; he'd been tense and impatient, racing to meet deadlines, cursing his superiors, snapping at reporters while juggling phone calls. In short, the best days he'd had in years.

Now he hoped his periscopic view of the migrating clouds would help him respond patiently to the draft story his intern had handed to him twenty-five minutes earlier. He'd been expecting something like, "A local father reports being distraught about his missing ex-wife and daughter, but the police spokesperson told the *Chronicle* that these kinds of matters typically resolve themselves in a day or two." Which is to say no story at all, but adequate filler for two column inches.

Instead the Green girl had taken off in her car (was she really old enough to drive?) up to Lauren Harbison's neighborhood to play private eye. He hadn't told her *not* to go up there, but some things you shouldn't have to say. He stepped out of his door to call her name into the sea of cubicles.

The young intern materialized before him, as if popping out from a hiding spot under his desk. Vinestri blinked and asked her to take a seat. He felt slightly off-balance when talking to her—he was noticing for the first time—as if he were attracted to her, which of course he absolutely was not; she was twenty years younger, a little dim, and frequently annoying. She had adorable eyes, though, round and puppy-dog earnest.

Stop that, he said to himself.

"Carrie, I appreciate the initiative you showed on this story, you know, taking it upon yourself to inquire a bit." The intern cast her eyes down at his tone, distracting him. "But the thing is, people go missing for a couple of days in Columbiana County like a dozen times a year. It's early to be speculating, quoting anonymous sources, that sort of thing."

The intern responded softly, her voice a little raspy, a kid in the principal's office. "Yeah, but it's a scoop, isn't it? The police don't even know about it yet."

"Sure, every reporter wants that. But we aren't exactly experts in analyzing the condition of a house. Who was your source?"

Carrie looked up surprised. "But—I promised the person I wouldn't name them, they were anxious about that."

Marco smiled patiently. "Ms. Green, I'm not talking about putting it in the paper. Anytime you're going to use an anonymous source, you have to tell your editor who the source was, and we decide together how reliable that person might be. I assume they went over that in your journalism classes at CCBC, right?"

It wasn't ringing any bells. But Carrie wasn't that clear on what had been discussed in any of her community college classes; her practice had been to drift off to distant kingdoms of sadistic princes and lovemaking couples, males with massive chests and females with perfect round breasts, so that the clock would hurry along. She'd also frequently been pretty high.

The air leaked out of her.

Marco felt a tinge of compassion and told her not to worry about little mistakes, that she was doing a really good job at the paper, though it was an assertion he would have found hard to back up.

Carrie slunk back to her cubicle which she shared with two other interns, neither of whom did much besides surf the web and exclaim, "Whoa, listen to this!" Unable to shake her disappointment, she started seeking a second opinion. She soon stumbled upon a web piece about the *New York Times,* that bastion of journalistic standards, also the dullest paper in the world. The article stated that, two months earlier, the *Times* had instituted a new policy that a reporter was obligated to reveal the identity of any anonymous source to his or her editor before using that source in a story.

Two months ago? Why the hell was Vinestri making it sound like this was a time-honored principle that everyone in journalism knew but her? Not to mention that exactly *one* newspaper had adopted this policy.

She slipped to the women's room and sat on the toilet for twenty-five minutes reading *Fifty Shades of Grey,* which she carried neatly stashed in her pocketbook. She returned to her desk revolted by Christian Grey, disgusted with the pathetic Ana Steele, and furious at Marco Vinestri. She wrote her source back into the article, stuffed two sticks of Doublemint gum into her mouth, and pounded the "send" button. She then strode purposefully to Marco's office to tell him that the rewrite was now in his inbox.

He put aside some papers he was leafing through and glanced at the file he'd just received. Then he peered curiously at his intern. "So?"

"So, you said don't speculate. I cut it down so now it's only what the person told me, no conclusions." Carrie sucked on her gum and hoped it wouldn't squeak.

Vinestri was racing to meet multiple deadlines, already feeling drained from the long day of invigorating local drama. He replied irritably, "Okay, I'll let it this one time. But no more promising anonymity. Got it?"

Carrie cast her eyes down again, appropriately admonished. Then she went down the hallway, turned the corner, and pumped her fist.

~

Towards 6:30 Sofia Madsen found a tall uniformed cop at her door. He introduced himself as Officer Kresge, East Liverpool Police Department. He said he needed to speak with her for a few minutes about a situation involving Lauren Harbison, who he understood was one of her close friends.

Sofia's stomach knotted. She'd been trying to reach Lauren for three days, most recently just twenty-five minutes earlier. Lauren rarely took more than two hours to get back to her and more commonly was in touch within minutes. Sofia leaned on Lauren even more than on her sisters, all three of whom were pillars of her life.

She braced herself for the officer to tell her that her dearest friend was dead.

But the officer reassured her, as quickly as she could yank the screen door open to let him in. "Ms. Harbison appears to have left town unexpectedly,'" he explained, "and we're just trying to see what we can find out. Ninety-nine percent of these things come to nothing, but the little girl's father is worried about his daughter."

She felt a quick flood of warmth toward the young cop, as if somehow he'd saved Lauren's life by not announcing her death. As soon as she could bring her breathing to normal, she offered him a cup of coffee and a seat at her kitchen island.

But within five minutes she couldn't stand him. He looked about twenty-five but was already arrogant and full of himself, his voice machine-like though his words pretended to show concern for Lauren and Brandi. He was no doubt eager to punch the clock so he could go out for beer and darts, surrounded by posters of nearly-naked women, and focus on life's important concerns such as the grim state of the Pittsburgh Steelers' defense.

The officer complimented her coffee. "You wouldn't believe what comes out of our machine at the station," he rumbled. "I give it to suspects when I'm questioning them, I'm surprised some watchdog group doesn't come after me."

Aren't you just hilarious, Sofia thought.

Aloud she said, "Sorry, I need to cut right to how I can help, I've gotta get dinner together for my kids."

Kresge nonetheless asked his questions slowly and methodically, as if afraid the interview would end before he finished his coffee. How close were she and Lauren? Had Lauren said anything to Sofia about planning to leave town? Did she have any relatives that might have suddenly gotten sick? Was there anyone she was afraid of, say someone she owed money to? A violent boyfriend?

He wasn't half way through his questions when it hit Sofia exactly what had happened.

Her stomach churned; it should have dawned on her even before this prick came knocking at her door. She turned her back, walked to the kitchen faucet, and poured herself a glass of water she didn't need, buying time to yank all emotion off of her face. Then she returned to the island and said, "I have no clue. This is so unlike her. You've got me worried now."

She paused, playing back the sound of her own voice. It sounded like a confession. "Listen," she said, her voice edgy and rushed. "I've gotta get back to my kids, I was at work all day, they need me with them. I'll come down to talk to you at the station tomorrow, they'll be at their day camp."

The officer resisted being put off. "It's important for us to go over just a few more things—"

She fought to keep her temper in check. Walking to the door and opening it, she said, "I'll call first thing in the morning."

The officer finally got to his feet, said in a rehearsed tone, "I'm sorry we had to trouble you," squeezed his wide frame past her, and stood briefly on the front stoop before heading down the walkway.

Jarred and Kiara came running into the living room as soon as they heard the officer leave. "What's going on, Mom? Are you in trouble?"

Sofia forced a laugh. "It was nothing, kids, they're raising money. This town still has a Policeman's Ball, believe it or not. Come on, you guys come in the kitchen and help me pull dinner together, it's getting late."

The kids couldn't help but notice their mother's shakiness as she handled teaspoons and measuring cups, the skillet that slipped out of her hand and banged loudly on the stovetop, the words she occasionally got out of order. She must really hate the Policeman's Ball.

~

More than two hours passed before Kiara was firmly ensconced and reading in bed, Jarred having conked out much earlier. Feeling as though she'd held back a boulder from rolling down a hill into a crowd, Sofia finally let go. In came lurching thoughts and emotions, a landslide pouring over her filled with tree branches and plastic buckets and the bodies of small animals.

Daryl picked up right away when she rang his phone.

She started in without even saying hello. "Could you come over, like, immediately? Lauren's gone missing, I'm not kidding. I thought she was pissed at me or something because she hasn't answered my texts for three solid days. But a cop just came by to tell me no one knows where she is."

"Oh, honey," Daryl said, speaking through a noisy background of voices and music, most likely at The Dirty Truth where he loved to eat and drink and meet cute guys. "I'll be there in, like, twenty minutes, maybe not even. I'm on my way."

When he arrived he entered the house without knocking, ordered Sofia not to serve him coffee, and gave himself permission to go through her cabinets and refrigerator, assembling an endless collection of ingredients for a cocktail he called The Devil's Handshake. He didn't need another drink, it was evident to Sofia that his evening had already provided abundantly, but he moved with certainty, confident that Sofia would share his pleasure in the final product.

She didn't wait for him to finish concocting. "Listen, Daryl, I know you've hung out with me and Lauren a few times, but have you ever exchanged numbers with her? Like, would your info be in her Contacts? Or any other way you could be connected to her?"

Daryl made a squinty face. "Honey, Lauren and I were definitely just friends, whatever else she may have wished for."

She glared at him.

No, he assented more soberly, the police wouldn't find him on a list of Lauren's friends. But why would it matter?

"Because," she said, "I know perfectly well where she's gone. She's in fucking Columbia, with Brandi. That bastard Kelly has been hassling her non-stop ever since they split up, trying to take Brandi away from her in court, demanding more and more and more time with her. She's made a run for it."

Daryl's eyes were even smaller now, down to slits. "What the hell? Colombia?? Like South America type Colombia?! What are you *talking* about, girl?"

Sofia's eyes welled up. "That bastard drove her away from me. And now they'll be after her for kidnapping."

Darryl patted her arm several quick times, as if she were a hot ember that needed to be cooled before it burned a hole in the carpet. "Sofia, darling, she can't kidnap Brandi. Brandi is her daughter." He spoke in the tone he used as bank manager when reassuring customers it was fine to mortgage their lives away.

"You're so wrong! If there's a custody order, like from a divorce, leaving counts as kidnapping. I read about a woman who went to jail for months in Michigan for taking off with her children for less than three weeks." Tears then gave way to anxiety. "Oh, God, I can't believe I said the name of the country. Shit, Daryl, you've got to forget what I said, okay? It's Paraguay, it's Somalia, it's fucking Guam, okay? You got that?"

"Yeah, yeah, Guam, I got it. But Sofia, the cops are never going to find out I even know Lauren. They won't be talking to me."

She wasn't pacified. Her heart didn't stop pounding until Daryl shared a hefty pour of his esoteric cocktail with her, and then another and another.

CHAPTER 3

Sergeant Patricia Martinez entered the station through the personnel door ten minutes before the eight o'clock start of her shift, which she supervised. As occasionally happened, multiple cops wanted her ear right away, making her feel like a triage nurse. And her officers had a good feel for the kinds of situations she wouldn't want to be bothered with, so several of them clamoring for her attention at once meant it would be quite a morning.

The voice of Robert Myers, a crusty and slow-moving long-time officer, got through the noise first. *The Morriston Chronicle* was reliably dropped at the station by 6:45 each morning and Myers had sat reading it, typical of his contributions to the work of the department. "The newspaper says they have a source who went inside Lauren Harbison's house, and the bedrooms were a mess, like they'd been abandoned in a tizzy, but the rest of the house was picture perfect. Looks like they got out of bed suddenly and didn't come back."

Intrigued, Martinez lifted up a hand to silence other officers in the queue. "Since when does the *Chronicle* have a 'source'? I thought the kinds of things that got leaked to them were, like, secret recipes for key lime pie." She demanded a look at the paper.

Then she grabbed the phone to call Kresge, waking him up; he'd worked noon to 10:00 pm the past two days and was off.

"What's going on?" he rasped.

"When you went to Lauren Harbison's house Monday, did you check inside?"

Kresge, half awake, went straight on the defense. "Sarge, you know I couldn't go in there. Kelly Harbison doesn't own that house, he can't authorize me to go in. If I'd seen anything through the windows to give me probable cause, but there was nothing. What was I supposed to do?"

"Relax, Shane, I'm not saying you should've entered. The issue is that the *Chronicle* got some information from someone about the conditions inside the house, and I just wanted to make sure it didn't come from us. It's in today's paper."

"A girl from the paper came by the station yesterday, like a teenager or something, maybe she's the kid of someone on their staff. All I said was it's too early to worry."

"All right, don't sweat it. Sorry to wake you."

Kresge trusted that the Sergeant believed him, but this was the kind of thing that could leave even your buddies on the force with lingering doubts. He never got back to sleep. So after a while he called in and asked whether, since he was awake anyhow, he could put in a few hours. Martinez flipped through timesheets for a moment and then said yes, he could come in for a half day. "And as soon as you're in here, get right on the phone and pull Ms. Madsen down here. Looks like we've got more to talk with her about."

~

The insistent ringing of Sofia's phone pulled her out of a deep sleep on the living room couch. On the other end of the line was her dear friend Officer Kresge, taking her up on her kind offer to have a more detailed discussion to-day, now that her kids were at camp. Could she come into the station? Or did she need him to pick her up at her workplace?

"No, no, I'll be down there in thirty minutes," she stammered, not admit-ting that she'd called in sick to work after lying awake in bed most of the night.

~

The tone Sofia encountered at the station contrasted sharply with the polite introduction and cordial questions put to her by Kresge at her house the night before. Within just a few moments of her arrival at the station two cops came out to meet her, as if they were concerned that she might overpower a single officer and take his weapon. They guided her into a cold room with linoleum flooring, hard wooden seats, a formica table, overly bright florescent lighting. They indicated to her without comment which chair she was to occupy and then stepped out without saying how long she'd be waiting, or for whom.

Nearly fifteen minutes passed before Kresge himself appeared, accompanied by a sharply-uniformed, dark-skinned woman whom he introduced as Sergeant Martinez. Sofia was momentarily confused, thinking the new arrival was somehow connected to the military.

Martinez notably did not tell Sofia there was nothing to worry about, didn't say that they just wanted to ask a few quick questions. She did offer a cup of coffee, which Sofia made the mistake of accepting. The police department coffee, brewed more for propulsion than bouquet, would soon catapult her agitation.

Martinez and Kresge sat left and right of her, making it hard for Sofia to know what to do with her eyes; she felt she was acting avoidant no matter where she looked. Across the table from her was an empty chair, and on the wall behind that a plaque with small gilt lettering that Sofia couldn't make out except that it had been presented by the Kiwanis Club. Members of the Kiwanis Club were no doubt aware that police departments had Sergeants and Admirals and such, and knew whether you were supposed to address then as "madam" or "Your Honor," but Sofia had never been in legal trouble and preferred historical fiction to murder mysteries. She'd been to family court a couple of times with Lauren but that didn't involve any cops or ranks or formica rooms, in fact seemed hardly even to involve the judge, who just appeared at the end of the day to tell the parents that, whatever they wanted, they couldn't have it.

Sergeant Martinez was talking; Sofia might have missed some, she wasn't sure. "The situation has gotten more serious, ma'am. As of this morning Lauren Harbison and her daughter have now been missing for 48 hours. They may be in grave danger if they were taken against their will. And if Ms. Harbison fled with her daughter, that would be a kidnapping charge, a felony as I'm sure you're aware."

Sofia was still not following well, wondering what she was missing.

"It's going to be very important for you to tell us everything you know, ma'am," Kresge said from off to her left, causing the sensation that he'd just arrived in the room.

But, as she told him the night before, she knew nothing. *That's what's eating me up!* she wanted to yell.

"Ms. Harbison said nothing about any upcoming travel plans? Special outings she was going to take her daughter on? Unusual events in her life?"

Sofia said no to everything.

Sergeant Martinez took the interview over, her voice growing colder with each question she posed. Had Lauren ever talked about fleeing with Brandi, even if this happened quite some time ago? Did she ever make even passing references or seemingly lighthearted jokes about taking her daughter into hiding? Did Lauren want to remove Brandi's father from her life?

Sofia continued to reply in the negative to everything. She was aware of sometimes answering too quickly, before Martinez had quite finished the question.

Kresge stepped back in, cued by Martinez in some way that Sofia missed. His penetrating, insincere smile had the freezing power of dry ice. If only he would glare instead. "You understand, Ms. Madsen, that we are not prosecutors. We're not accusing anyone of anything—that's not our job. It is our job, though, to know the signs of someone who isn't being truthful. Helping someone who commits a crime—even after the crime has already been carried out—can make you an accessory. That would include concealing information about where someone is hiding, or denying having knowledge that you have. Any part of this not clear?"

"But I want, I mean—of course—to help in any way I can. If I hear anything, I'll definitely tell you right away. Why would I conceal anything?"

Kresge and Martinez glanced at each other. The Sergeant rose to her feet and said, "The officer and I need to attend to a couple of things. We're going to step out for a bit and then we'd like to speak to you a bit longer."

"But I've got to go," Sofia protested. "I can't miss any more work."

"We'll be as quick as we can," Martinez responded, without making eye contact. She and Kresge exited, closing the door carefully behind them.

Nearly seventy-five minutes ticked painfully by before police personnel finally came through the door of the little room. Different officers this time, both males. They questioned Sofia for nearly two more hours. It was not a friendly conversation, and she was asked a number of times whether she might want to have a lawyer present.

By the time she was finally permitted to leave the station and walk dazedly to her car, she couldn't get a tight grip on the steering wheel and fumbled aiming her key into the ignition. At home she stared for a long time at her phone, but couldn't figure out whom to call and what to ask. Eventually she fell back to sleep on the couch, not waking until a call came in from the day camp, asking whether she had any plans to pick up her children that afternoon or was she thinking that maybe they would like to spend the night there. The staff expressed a preference to head home for dinner themselves, if Sofia could be troubled to pop by.

CHAPTER 4

A little after 7:30 in the morning, the East Liverpool police department again had the pleasure of hearing from Kelly Harbison, perhaps the tenth time he'd dialed their number in the past two and a half days. This time he abandoned his disparaging, blusterous tone, opting instead for top-volume yelling, his words scrambled and echoing with rock-concert level distortion. The dispatcher had to repeatedly tell Harbison to calm down so that she might be able to discern what words he was saying, and from there perhaps their intended meaning.

She believed she heard the following words, with garbled or deafening sections in between: "IF YOU CEMENTHEADS HAD LISTENED TO ME BE—... SURE IT WAS HER, I... WHISPERING, I COULDN'T FUCKING... WORD 'VIRGINIA' PRETTY ... DROPPED IT OR THE BITCH GRABBED ... ALMOST AT... TURNING BACK RIGHT NOW... SHOW YOU!!"

The dispatcher attempted to speak, not sure what Harbison could hear. "Sir, sir, I can't help you if you ... Sergeant Martinez will need to handle this, she'll be here in less than half an hour..."

Suddenly Harbison heard her just fine. "HALF AN HOUR? ARE YOU OUT OF YOUR MIND? THEY WILL HAVE...," then more screeching and feedback.

"Call me when you're not in your vehicle, sir, so that I can hear you and get your location." She heard no response, and gave up.

Two minutes later he was calling again. "OKAY, I'M PARKED NOW DARLING. CAN YOU HEAR ME?"

She could hear him clearly, as could everyone on the continent. "Yes, sir, go ahead," she said politely for the recording.

"MY DAUGHTER JUST TRIED TO CALL ME, THERE'S A MESSAGE ON MY PHONE. SHE SOUNDS TERRIFIED. YOU'VE GOT TO SEND SOMEONE RIGHT THIS SECOND!!!"

"We'll see what we can do, but we'll need your phone with the message on it. How far away are you?"

"I WAS ALMOST TO MY WORK WHEN SHE CALLED. I'M HEADING BACK, BUT YOU CAN USE SIRENS, I CAN'T. SEND SOMEONE TO MEET ME!"

"I'm afraid we wouldn't gain any time that way. Drive carefully and we'll see you when you get here. I'm going to hang up so you can drive with two hands."

She hoped a guardian angel would watch over his driving.

~

A rapid examination of Harbison's phone led to an urgent official call to T-Mobile. The cell provider, after a quick check, informed police that the phone that had placed Harbison's last incoming call had stopped transmitting a signal a half hour earlier. The company provided a set of GPS coordinates for where the phone had last been. Since then it had either been destroyed or placed in a foil bag; if it had merely been turned off they'd still know where it was.

Martinez peeled out of the station with three other officers and two vehicles, lights flashing, heading south.

Twenty-three minutes later they found themselves in a section of woods past Collier, West Virginia. There was no one there, as they expected. They continued dialing Brandi's number, but the phone cut straight to voice mail each time.

Even in the best circumstances, cell tower triangulation can only approximate a phone's location within about a quarter-mile; in the remote and hilly terrain where the police now found themselves, twice that distance was possible. There was much ground to cover.

Nearly a half hour had passed when one of the officers came across a section of trampled bushes about sixty feet back into the woods, out of sight of the road. The crew gathered and poked under logs and bushes, crawling on their hands and knees and sweeping leaves aside. No phone.

They did come across fresh footprints in a muddy section of the otherwise dry area of pine and oak woods, a lucky find given that even the heavy boots they were wearing left few visible marks on the hard ground.

The prints were photographed and cast. Soon they were able to establish that there were two sizes of prints, a men's size seven-and-a-half or a women's nine, and a children's size five.

~

Martinez stood back at the station with officers Kresge and Arielle Mason, neither of whom had been out on the morning's race to empty forestland in West Virginia. Mason wondered aloud what Lauren and Brandi would have been doing out there.

"Making a connection, most likely," Martinez replied. "They pulled over in an out-of-the-way spot to be passed off to their next driver. Brandi probably said she needed to pee, walked into the woods, and then her mother realized she was calling for help and ran after her to grab the phone away. Which means she'll never let Brandi have the phone back. I'm sure she's furious that the girl tried to call the Evil Father."

"Anybody that lives around there see or hear anything?"

Martinez gave a wry half-smile. "Nobody lives around there, that's how the spot was chosen. Half a mile down Route 10 there's a gas station, that's the closest building in that direction. The other way there start to be a few houses after it crosses 27, but still very spread out. Brandi could scream at the top of her lungs out there and no one would hear."

"So?" Kresge asked.

"Since they've crossed state lines we should be able to get the FBI on board soon, especially with Brandi's phone call to confirm that it's an abduction. But for us, it's clearly time to search the house. I want you to put in for a warrant. We'll head out there the second we've got it."

Mason said, "I'm on it. Don't we also need to figure out which neighbor went into the house over the weekend?"

"Oh, yeah," Kresge muttered, "the *Chronicle* thing." He shook his head. "That newspaper squeaks by until it tries to get taken seriously. Then it just turns itself into an even bigger joke."

~

Sofia had been in law offices before, during her divorce, but three years had passed since that grim period and now she was at a firm that didn't even handle family law. The décor felt like a replay, though; the same tall dark bookshelves replete with gilded hardbound law guides and the same genre of overly large framed prints on the walls exhibiting vaguely experimental and vacuous paintings, swaths of dull color.

Across a large desk from her sat Barry Shipley, one of the more respected criminal defense attorneys in southern Columbiana County. Over the previous two days Sofia's solid, colorful life had gone dark and frantic. Shipley's voice was the calming antidote; forceful but not loud, clear, in charge.

He was answering her first question, regarding confidentiality. "Since I'm now your lawyer, anything you tell me about past behavior is privileged. Just don't tell me any new crimes you plan to commit, because I could be obligated to reveal that."

"Okay," she ventured, "and when I tell you what someone *else* has done, do you keep those things confidential too?"

Shipley hesitated, but only briefly. "Again, if it's about past acts, you're covered. Were you involved in any way in what this other person did?"

"No, but… some of the things I said to the police maybe weren't one-hundred percent true."

Shipley smiled but said nothing, waiting for the rest. Sofia gulped, but soon heard her voice spilling her story: how she and Lauren had grown close, then Lauren's nasty divorce, Brandi's increasingly frequent meltdowns, Lauren's periodic outbursts about going into hiding, Sofia's many lies to the East Liverpool police.

Then she waited for Shipley's condemnation to rain down upon her.

But he not only seemed uninvested in judging her, he showed no worry either. "Ms. Madsen, police commonly say that they can tell you're lying and you're gonna be in big trouble for that. But they can't, and you're not. It's part of their routine. To convict you of making false statements to them, they would have to prove not only that Lauren had talked to you about running away with her daughter, but that you *remembered it*. How could they possibly do that?"

Sofia felt some of the pressure ease out of her overinflated insides.

"The future is a different matter, however. Each time you lie to police you're increasing your vulnerability to getting charged with a crime."

"But there's no way I can tell them what I know! I can't do that to my best friend."

Again came the lawyer's calming smile. "You aren't obligated to tell the cops anything; it's only illegal to lie to them, not to keep your mouth shut. Don't answer questions or, even better, don't even agree to meet with them."

All right. That much she could do.

Shipley had an additional caution. "There's a wrinkle, in that Ohio has an unusual law which says that if you know a felony has been committed and you don't report it, you're committing a crime. But the thing is, you don't know that a felony has been committed here—no one does. So you don't need to worry unless you hear something from Lauren that confirms that she's voluntarily on the run. So best not to communicate with her at all; that will be safest for both of you."

Sofia's head moved lightly back and forth. "But I'm dying to hear from her, to know that she and Brandi are okay."

Shipley remained fatherly. "Say you receive a message from her, and then a while later the police ask you if you've heard from her. You can't lie to them, so your only choice would be to say, 'I'm not going to answer that,' which they would know meant 'yes.' And at that point they could make your life miserable until you cooperate with them."

The edge came back to Sofia's voice. "There's no way I'm blocking her number. Not until I at least know she's all right."

Shipley put up his hands. "Don't go blaming the messenger, this is what you're paying me to do. Remember also that your children need you to stay out of the slammer."

"Oh Jesus," Sofia blurted out, crossing her arms on her chest and leaning forward, "you're seriously going to lay that guilt trip on me? Have you ever had a dear friend go missing?"

The lawyer remained unflappable, as if debating nothing more loaded than the rules of a board game, his neutral gaze upon her. Sofia sat fuming until the steam was gone, then shrank into her chair. "I'm sorry," she said softly, " I'm not in the best shape at the moment."

Shipley's mouth formed its trademark half-smile. "Ma'am, in my line of work, that outburst didn't even score a two on a ten-point scale."

~

The crime scene investigators observed just what the *Chronicle* article had described; the downstairs of the house seemed to have been gone over with a fine-toothed comb, with the exception of the kitchen sink, while the bedrooms showed every sign of having been exited in a mad dash after both beds had been occupied.

It seemed indeed that Lauren and Brandi had expected to sleep, but then had arisen and rocketed out of the house with objects flying.

The not-sleeping could have been any of the three nights from Friday to Sunday; Kelly had dropped Brandi to Lauren's house at 10 am Friday morning and expected her back at the same time on Monday. Unfortunately no test existed that would be able to tell them which night the beds had last been used.

Detective Annika Ledbetter pointed at shoes placed in a neat row by the door. "Hurrying away doesn't have to mean the departure was unexpected. Maybe they were planning to take off over the weekend but had to wait for a particular moment for some reason, maybe a signal of some kind."

Detective Janet Wisneski concurred. "It looks like Mom was waiting for a certain opportunity, or waiting for a ride, or—"

Ledbetter cut in. "There has to have been a ride. Her car is here."

Meanwhile, Sergeant Martinez wandered in and out of the room the detectives were standing in, carefully overseeing the proceedings as evidence technicians pawed through every drawer and felt around on every shelf, placed fibers into plastic bags, dusted surfaces for fingerprints. But her ears caught the tip end of the detectives' conversation.

"Here's a question," Martinez interjected as she walked up to the duo. "Kelly Harbison is saying he and his daughter were so close, she adored him, etcetera, etcetera. So how does Lauren get her daughter to flee with her? Brandi is plenty old enough to understand exactly what's going on. Is there a struggle? Is Brandi fighting physically not to leave the house? We're not seeing any sign of that."

Ledbetter piped in, "Maybe Dad is a jerk, he sure seems like it. Maybe Brandi couldn't wait to get out of town."

Wisneski looked doubtful. "The key to being a successful jerk is to make everyone think you're a great guy. I bet Dad is mostly bark and not much bite."

"So?"

"Two possibilities. One: Brandi was given a story. A relative had died and they suddenly had to go across the country to a funeral, or who knows what. So she totally cooperates until it becomes clear to her that the story is B.S., and then she tries to call her father."

"Why do they have to jet out of the house in the middle of the night to go to a funeral?"

"So Mom came up with something better than that. Who knows."

"And your other theory?"

"The girl was drugged."

"Drugged, but she can still make a mad dash?" Martinez gave the barest hint of a grin. "Anyhow, doesn't look like a house that was riddled with drugs. I'll make sure the techs have that possibility on their radar, though."

~

Speculation remained the order of the day, because nothing remarkable—beyond the large and oddly localized messes in the bedrooms—turned up during the search. They were left to hope that test results would bring revelations.

CHAPTER 5

At 6:45 am, Sofia's phone played three notes from Beethoven's Fifth Symphony, her indication of an incoming text. She was not out of bed yet but should have been and, lunging for her phone on the bedside table, managed only to knock it off so it went skittering across the floor. She dropped after it and hit her head on a corner of the table. Her kids heard her swear loudly.

The text said

> Get Tor browser for your computer. Go to Protonmail and
> create an encrypted email address called MyPreciousFriends@
> protonmail.com. Don't give any accurate information about
> yourself when you register this address. Delete this text now.

The number the text originated from meant nothing to her.

She groped around for a piece of paper and something to write with, could find nothing, ran out of her bedroom and down to the kitchen, scribbled down the name of the account she'd been told to create, and deleted the text.

She could hear Kiara moving in the hallway. "Ma," she called out, "what the hell was that all about?"

"What was what all about?"

"I'm not deaf, you know. It sounded like you tackled someone in your room, then your door burst open and you flew down the stairs, then next you're trying to put out a fire or something in the kitchen. This is not normal."

"I… misunderstood a text I just got from Darryl, I thought he was saying it was an emergency and he needed me super fast. But that's not what he meant."

"Ma, that, like, makes no sense at all. You've been acting, like, weird lately? Like, it would be cool to know what's going on?"

Sofia couldn't believe this girl had nearly four years to go before she'd be a teenager. She already had the routine down.

"I'll explain everything tonight," Sofia said, adopting her best I'm-the-mother-and-I'm-in-charge voice, though with no idea what she'd say when the time came. "I overslept, and for now we need to focus on getting you and your little brother ready for school."

"Whatever," Kiara said. She rolled her eyes and went back into her bedroom.

~

Sofia couldn't skip work again, though she might as well have for all she accomplished. When she wasn't dealing with customers in the waiting area of the auto repair shop where she was receptionist, she was supposed to be handling bookkeeping and other paperwork. But today she smuggled her laptop in behind the counter and hoped that Jeremy, the owner and lead mechanic, wouldn't notice it if he popped into the front to ask her something.

The first moment when no one was asking for her assistance she started downloading Tor onto her Mac.

While she waited for the process to finish, her eyes drifted off into reading the front page of the *Morriston Chronicle*, which lay on the service counter for customers. The lead story was about Brandi's attempt to call her father the day before. A criminal justice professor from Kent State was quoted as saying, "A ten-year-old who was kidnapped by strangers would dial 911, as all kids nowadays are trained to do in an emergency. The fact that Brandi instead tried to call her father suggests strongly that she's with her mother, not with strangers. Fortunately, that greatly improves the odds that she'll be returned unharmed."

Sofia was baffled. Why in hell would Brandi try to call her father?

A couple of hours later she received some interesting answers from a therapist who specialized in the trauma of divorce. Corinne Fletcher had worked with Sofia's children three years ago when their own home was blowing apart. Fletcher had been following the recent news, and was happy to offer insights when Sofia reached her by phone.

"To begin with, Sofia, can you tell me how you're so sure Brandi hates her father?"

"Lauren talks about it all the time. She was constantly stressed about having to send Brandi over to his house, but his visits were court-ordered."

"Well, parents often leave their marriages with tremendous bitterness"—it was kind of her not to throw in *as you well know*—"and they start to read a lot of negativity into their children's statements about the other parent. So it can be more about the parent's bad feelings than the child's.

"Second, when a parent is holding onto bitterness, it can feel good to them—in an unhealthy way—when their child speaks badly about the other parent. This reaction can create a dynamic where the child starts to notice how happy they're making their mother by turning against Dad, and so the kid learns to play the complaints up. From there you can get this escalating loop where the child and the mother work themselves into a frenzy, and the child gets turned completely against the father. It's called 'Parental Alienation Syndrome.'"

Sofia fought the temptation to raise objections. *Just listen,* she told herself. *You didn't call to get into a debate.*

Fletcher had one more thought. "A young girl could get excited about running away with her mom, and then quickly discover that life on the run wasn't the adventure and glamor she'd pictured. For example, it would sink in that friends, teachers, home, the other parent, everything, was all gone for good, this was real life, not a movie."

She thanked Fletcher for her time. The therapist's framework made a kind of superficial sense, she supposed. But something wasn't ringing right.

~

At 8:00 that night, Sofia received her first Protonmail message:

> We're okay, things are working out bit by bit. Say nothing to anyone, please, I mean it. Could be a while before I can write again, don't worry about us. Love you.
> L.

CHAPTER 6

Gavin Neal felt like he'd stepped back in time to the day of his high school graduation. That event had turned out tolerable—better than that even— but only because of Sunni. She rolled up a stellar bud of Red-Headed Stranger to share with her boyfriend Param, and Gavin had spotted them ducking behind one of the countless minivans parked by Edgeworth Falls parents. Sunni and Param had waved him over and salvaged his day.

The speeches, however, had been awful. As was true again today.

At the moment he was stuck listening to an orator who was tickled pink by her own sense of humor, as she admonished them on, "Avoiding Bias When Reporting the News." Her pedagogical approach involved making fun of other writers and predicting a future of shameful subjectivity for all but a few of the young members of the audience. To make matters worse the audience was laughing at her smug, predictable jokes, which only served to encourage her.

The conference Gavin was enduring bore the title, "New Blood in the Ink: Young Journalists Changing the World." Though the changes they were making appeared to be primarily ones to their hairdos, their accents (subtly, they thought), and their erstwhile idealistic values ("maturing, becoming more realistic"). Few of the presenters were young journalists themselves—or young anything for that matter—and the few youth who did address the conference attempted to mimic the tone and wisdom of the older generation, which were bad enough in the original.

His coat pocket held a fragrant, crystalline collection of reddish-green Super Lemon Haze buds, tightly sealed in a plastic bag. He stood up and worked his way laboriously sideways across knees and feet, the rows too close together so the conference could accommodate all the future heroes of journalism, until he could squeeze into the aisle.

When he was close to emerging at the back of the mass of young sheep, his jaded eyes happened to land on a painfully cute girl in an aisle seat, chewing gum, bobbing her knee up and down, glancing at her phone, and looking around everywhere but at the speaker. She didn't look older than seventeen but no one that young came to this conference. He stopped abruptly next to her seat, smiled and leaned down as if recognizing her, then whispered in her ear, "I'm heading out to smoke a bud. Care to join me?" He tapped his coat pocket.

The girl pulled her head back a little, looked Gavin up and down through squinting eyes, then gave a smirk. "Oh, man, you're my savior," she said, perhaps more audibly than she intended to, and reached down to grab her bag off the floor.

~

They stood by some shrub-like trees, or tree-like shrubs, that grew in two rows along a walkway that didn't lead to the main conference area, pretending (for no one's benefit) that they weren't part of the proceedings.

The girl took a deep breath as Gavin pulled out his baggie. "Please tell me this conference is gonna get better," she said. She waited patiently, and then contentedly took a long hit off Gavin's blunt and handed it back to him. She held the hit in with discipline.

"What were you expecting?" he asked.

"I dunno, I didn't really think about it. My paper paid for me to come, why turn it down?"

"It won't get better. More like worse."

"Oh God, for real? Then why're you here? Somebody making you?"

He nodded. "My boss can't stand me. I had to come last year too. She keeps hoping this'll be the last straw and I'll quit."

"She can't fire you?"

"It's a long story, but I think she's afraid of my parents. Of my father, really."

"They own the paper or something?" She took another deep pull and held it tightly, as if waiting for the smoke to come out her eyes.

"No, but they own like a quarter of the county I live in and a couple of politicians. Maybe she thinks my father could get advertisers to leave or something. He probably could, actually."

"Nice," she said. "Job security."

He snorted. "I wouldn't go to him. But my editor doesn't know that. She'll get rid of me before long anyhow, though. She's totally full of shit and she can tell that I can tell." He'd been in his new job at the *Lincoln Republican* (a clever name, you have to admit) less than a week when Jody Carpelli had offered one of her authoritative pronouncements on a subject she knew nothing about—in this case it was males and females competing against each other in wrestling—to which Gavin made squinty eyes and said, "You're kidding, right?"

She looked at him as if he were a Corgi who had just lowered a wet poop onto her Persian rug.

It should be said, in the spirit of fairness, that Carpelli found him a spoiled, entitled brat who thought he knew everything. He was the kind of bullheaded kid who someday would make an error of such colossal proportions that it would embarrass every journalist in a 200-mile radius. She hoped that he'd be as far away from her as possible—working for a foreign bureau, say—when he shit the bed, so that she wouldn't be contaminated by it.

~

Though deep in his usual self-involvement, Gavin couldn't miss it: the girl he was getting high with already had a crush on him. *I doubt she's ever smoked weed of this caliber,* he thought. *She's so high right now she'd fall for the scrawny, wispy-bearded career cashier at the Stop & Shop.*

Carrie was her name. She said she worked for a daily paper in Ohio with a circulation even smaller than the *Republican,* an intern there, which Gavin thought of as something like being Special Assistant to The Busboy. Through her cottony mouth she began to tell him a series of events from three days earlier, confirming for him the backwoods nature of the paper she worked for.

~

Back on Wednesday morning, Tuesday's chaos not only still reigned at the *Chronicle* but had intensified. Clueless about the looming civil war in Morriston over the proposed hotel, the local Walmart had chosen the previous day to announce that it was donating $13,000 of *ammunition* (of all things) to the Morriston Police Department. The offer was instantly recognized as groundbreaking in the history of charitable giving.

A patrol officer, speaking on condition of anonymity, had responded, "I don't think we want ammo from Walmart. It was probably returned because it couldn't penetrate burlap." Citizens furiously debated the appropriateness of the gift, and a city councilor, already on fire from his efforts to block the hotel, asked caustically, "Can't they sweeten the deal by throwing in a few grenade launchers?"

The police chief, on the other hand, wished everyone would please shut up and allow her to accept the delivery before the offer got withdrawn. The director of a local non-profit protested that Walmart should instead be donating food, clothing, and medical supplies, to which Chief Brodsky was quoted as retorting, "Would you like me to send my officers into confrontations with terrorists armed with rubbing alcohol and rolls of gauze?"

So Marco Vinestri needed his intern to handle the Harbison matter again. He still felt sure it would amount to nothing, but the paper had to give a nod to the fact that the East Liverpool police were now saying it might be a serious matter, and that meant someone had to go get a quote from Kelly Harbison.

Carrie concealed her excitement at being sent out. "The guy sounds awful," she pretended to protest. "Can't I just talk to him on the phone?"

"No, I want you to meet with him. This is a good learning opportunity for you, Ms. Green."

It occurred to Marco that sending this teenage girl (she was twenty, really, but he kept forgetting) out to interview Kelly Harbison would make the man even more enraged than he'd already sounded on his half-dozen calls to the paper. Maybe Marco's intern and Harbison would be like the gingham dog and the calico cat, and he'd no longer need to worry about either of them after today.

~

Carrie left Vinestri's office slowly. But once she was out of his sight she made a dash for her small desk and punched Harbison's number into her phone.

He sounded irritated from the moment he picked up. "I'm on another call. What's this regarding?" When she explained, he said, "Listen, talk to the police, maybe they'll tell you something, they won't tell me squat. I don't have time to talk to you, I've gotta be looking for my kid." And he hung up without letting her respond.

Her disappointment was short-lived. In less than twenty minutes he called back to say he'd found a few minutes to speak with her. It would have to be quick, right at 11:45, at his house in Irondale. Carrie told him she was on her way, to which he barked, "Don't bother getting here early, I can't talk to you before then."

Carrie was parked outside his house in twenty-five minutes, more than a half hour early for their appointment. Ten minutes later Harbison came out and walked up to her car window. "You people don't listen, do you? Might as well come on in, no sense sitting on your butt in the car." He walked pointedly back toward the house and through the door, leaving it open for Carrie to follow him in but never looking behind.

When she stepped inside she found Kelly already seated at his kitchen counter, where he had returned to surfing the web on his laptop, talking on his phone, and making notes on pieces of paper of various colors and sizes. No offer of a chair was forthcoming, so she stood in the entryway, rocking back and forth on her feet and looking awkwardly around.

A few minutes later he ended his call with an annoyed salvo, looked up, and for the first time registered Carrie's youth. He shook his head disgustedly, as if the paper had sent a German Shepherd to interview him. "I hope people around here have their own child go missing sometime, then they'll see what it's like. Nobody's taking it seriously." He turned back toward his computer, simultaneously starting to punch another number into his phone.

"I understand your frustration, Mr. Harbison," she said, though she had no clue. "But can I ask you a few quick things for our story?" The "our" was deliberate, to create the impression that the paper had a whole spotlight team on the case. She officiously pulled out her pad and pen.

Harbison ignored her. After listening to his phone for a brief moment he barked into it, "I've already spoken to the National Center, they're the ones that told me to call *you!* You're gonna just keep shuffling me around like everybody else?" And he hung up emphatically.

Keeping his eyes on his computer and continuing to scroll through screens, he said, "What do they want you to ask me, kid? Let's get it over with so you can give your boss what he wants."

Carrie was distracted for a moment, wondering how Kelly knew who her boss was. "Did you speak with Mr. Vinestri, sir?"

"Vinestri?" he responded. "Who the hell is that?"

"Oh. My editor."

"No," he said, looking back at his screen, "I haven't spoken with any *adults* there yet."

Charming fellow.

Carrie fought the temptation to pat her hair and say, perhaps in a drawl, *Why, sir, I am so pleased that you appreciate my youthful good looks.* Instead, with an eye toward keeping her job, she asked, "They say you're concerned your daughter might've been abducted by her mother."

Harbison acted as though there was no end to the affronts. "Oh, I'm 'concerned she might have been,' am I? It's only the most obvious thing in the world, if people had a brain in their heads!"

Carrie waited, not sure what to say.

What then followed was a forty-five-minute torrent (perhaps longer— deep into Kelly's endless stream of words she lost her sense of when it had all begun) about his horrible ex-wife. The aggrieved father seemed to now have unlimited time to talk in the middle of a day that he'd insisted barely contained a spare minute.

Carrie scribbled notes as fast as she could, wishing for a voice recorder like the real staff reporters carried. Her notebook ended up containing the following:

> —wife pushed him away from baby, didn't want him to feed her, not his job, you'll do it wrong, etc.
> —then bitched that he didn't help. He asked what am I allowed to do?
> —started badmouthing him to the kid before she was three, Did Dad upset you?, Did he remember to give you lunch?, He didn't leave you in that hot car, did he?, brainwashing her
> —but Brandi still closer to him than her, realized her mother's paranoid, always thinks someone's trying to do something to her or Brandi, the poor kid grew up scared
> —after divorce, fought for him to have almost no time with B. after divorce, but he was the sane one. B. asking for more time at his house and less at Mom's
> —K. wanted to win at court but got nervous when he finally started to, thought L. would flee with kid for revenge, no one listened, look what happened

Even with all this she'd still gotten fewer than half of his points down on paper; there was no keeping up with him, he was a boulder careering down a hill.

When Harbison finally lost a little of his velocity, Carrie said, "Could I ask you a couple things?"

The father looked startled, as if he'd forgotten she was there or had imagined he was talking to someone else—someone a little older, for example.

"Does Lauren have friends who're divorced women? You know, spend their time hanging out complaining together about the old bastard?"

Harbison's eyes widened. "From the mouths of babes. You're the first person to come out with an intelligent question. Your boss tell you to ask me that?"

Carrie wasn't sure which answer he wanted (would he be offended that she was capable of thinking of it herself?), so she said nothing, instead leaning forward with pen poised, the eager intern.

"That's *all* Lauren does," he spat out bitterly, "play victim with her friends. Sometimes she brings 'em to court hearings, a cheerleading squad, mothers whose lives are so tough 'cause they have to live off child support that the fathers bust their asses to earn."

"You know their names, friends of hers I could talk to?"

"Not really, she dumped all her old friends, no one was allowed to question anything she did. After we split up, friends of hers, even one of her sisters, came to me and said, 'There's no way to talk to her anymore, she's off the deep end.' So I only know names I hear from Brandi. There's a Sofia, maybe a Delta or some weird name like that. But the person you really should talk to is Lauren's sister Hillary, she'll give you an earful. Anything else they wanted you to ask me, kid? I got to wrap it up."

Carrie was afraid of what her final query would unleash; but this one Marco had indeed sent her with so she didn't dare skip it. "You're not happy with the police response? What's going on with that?"

Harbison was so well refueled by this question that his stream of words didn't stop for nearly another half hour.

Carrie had been in Harbison's ranch house for nearly two hours by the time she was finally able to extract herself. Wrung out like a dishrag, she staggered to her car under the sheer volume of words the man had laid on her. She shuddered to think how long he would have held her captive had he not been so badly pressed for time.

~

Gavin took advantage of the pause in Carrie's account to glance at his phone. "The morning session's breaking for lunch, let's go back in and eat. Meals are the saving grace at this conference, they have surprisingly good food."

"Why are you here if you hate this conference so much?" Carrie wanted to know. "Does your boss have a way to check up on you?"

"Yeah, you have to sign in. You must have done that when you came in this morning."

"I suppose I did." Had she? "You gonna quit soon?"

"Oh, God yes," Gavin said. "But I need to have something lined up. Newspapers are a tiny world now, everybody knows everybody, with my editor's connections she could make sure I get mired in some backwater—no offense—for years."

"So you need a big story, right? Get other papers interested in you?"

He laughed derisively, she wasn't sure why.

The lunch was a colorful assemble-your-own taco display with fresh cilantro salsa, lime-green guacamole with tomato and mango, spicy ground beef or beans (take both if you want), cheddar cheese that looked freshly grated rather than poured out of a plastic bag, and a bottomless bowl of sour cream. The weedheads could feel their eyes shimmering, reflecting the palette before them.

"I don't think we should eat it," Carrie said, "It'll wreck the experience. I just want to stand here beholding."

"I think we can find a way to eat and behold at the same time," Gavin said.

~

Carrie continued her story over their tacos.

On Thursday morning Vinestri had sent her back out once more, this time to collect evasions and platitudes from the East Liverpool police department. But he simultaneously gave her the heads-up that by early afternoon he'd have a staff reporter available to take over the Harbison story.

It knocked the wind out of her. She forced out the words, "It's no big deal, I've got it, don't worry about it," thinking her boss was afraid of dumping too much on her.

"It's becoming a big deal. It's been seventy-two hours now, plus the whole custody battle angle. We'll handle it, you've got plenty to do."

What a crock. She had almost nothing to do, same as the other interns. And now she'd been cast back in among them.

~

As Carrie worked on the generous knoll of guacamole that formed the summit of her conference meal, she asked Gavin, "Can I make a complaint against Vinestri for age or sex discrimination or something? I was the one who broke the story on Monday, then he admitted the interview I did with Kelly on Wednesday was good. Now he dumps me off the story."

"An intern's got no rights," Gavin declared, with a light shake of his head and lift of the chin. "That's why they hire interns, so they can stick you with whatever no one else wants to do and call it a public service. Anyhow, the new reporter they assigned it to was a woman too, wasn't she?"

"Yeah. Like fifty years old, though. And she'll just write whatever the police media guy tells her."

~

Carrie had put in a call to Harbison from her car before aiming toward his house. He answered angrily, "Who is this??"

"Sorry to bother you, sir. It's Carrie Green. It sounds like something is—"

He broke in, "I can't talk to you, I'll call you later!" and disconnected. The intrepid young journalist sat in her car for another ten minutes, thinking, *All right buddy, you made your point about what a crisis you're living in, you already did that yesterday. Frickin' call me already.*

But he didn't. And when she got back to the office a half hour later he still hadn't called. When he finally got in touch it was almost two o'clock and Carrie had already been relegated to Boy Scout research, her carriage turned back into a pumpkin. "I'm not on the story anymore, Mr. Harbison. It's been assigned to a staff reporter, I'm sure that's good news for you, she's a little older. I'll get her for you, her name's Jenette Shelburne."

She wasn't "a little" older, she was more than twice Carrie's age, and her last name was Sherborn but Carrie wasn't sure and didn't care.

Kelly caught her off guard by snarling, "I'm not starting over again with another reporter, forget it!" and hanging up.

Carrie strolled down to Vinestri's office and informed him of this twist, half-heartedly masking the tone of triumph in her voice. His response was to act like an ant had just pulled a tiny gun on him. "Kelly Harbison's mission in life is to be a prick. He's not gonna dictate which reporters we assign. Anyhow, in another fifteen minutes he'll call here begging to speak to Jenette."

Which, to be honest, Carrie expected also.

But an hour and a half later there was still no word from him and time was pressing. So Marco told Jenette she'd better take the initiative, but when she called Kelly to introduce herself, he yelled into the phone, "Don't bother me, Ms. Shelburne!" and was gone.

Vinestri and Sherborn were snippy with Carrie, apparently seeing her as somehow the cause of Harbison's incalcitrance. "We don't have a story, the cops aren't telling us anything today," Marco said disgustedly. He turned to Carrie and said, curtly, "All right, he wins, get a quote from him and get it to Jenette right away."

But the battle of wills wasn't over yet. When Carrie called to say that she'd been reauthorized to interview him, Kelly said, "They've given you back the story?" She explained that, no, Jenette Shelburne (now she was getting it wrong on purpose) still had the story but Carrie would collect statements from Kelly to share with her.

"Nothing doing!" Kelly pronounced. Dead air followed.

When she reported this exchange to Vinestri, he erupted into the most pronounced irritation she'd ever seen in him, not that she'd worked at the paper that long. He called Sherborn over and said, "Harbison doesn't run our business, we've never allowed some jackass citizen to tell us what to do!"

~

"Of course not," piped in Gavin. "Only the paper's advertisers get to do that."

Carrie shrugged. "Anyhow, Shelburne's stories yesterday and today were stupid. The police haven't made any announcements, so without Kelly's outbursts there's nothing to write. "

"So do the story yourself and submit it to another paper," he said.

"Yuh, like anybody outside of Columbiana County cares about our four-day disappearance."

"I'm not talking the New York Times. Where's your closest urban daily?"

"Couldn't tell you. Youngstown maybe? Canton? But the *Chronicle* would kill me, I might as well start looking for a job this afternoon."

"Some job, Carrie, no offense." She curled her lip at him. "Look," he said, "It's a gamble, but in this business you need a stroke of luck that pulls you ahead of the pack. If this turns out to be a big story, you'll be the one with the angle, since the guy refuses to talk to anyone else. Pull your courage together."

Carrie wished she could pull her courage together to tell Gavin to go to hell, the arrogant prick. "Come on," she said instead, "how many kids disappear per year in the U.S.? In the thousands, right? This won't go anywhere."

"In the tens of thousands. But almost all of them turn up in a day or two. Look, this might never be national news, but what, you think your first story will go continental? Grab onto it. You don't have much to lose where you're starting from."

"Gee thanks," Carrie said. "Anytime I need an insult, I'll know where to find one." They both gave little laughs, but she was pissed. Who did this guy think he was?

CHAPTER 7

Carrie made no effort to find Gavin the rest of the day Saturday, her resentment amplified by how attractive she'd found him. But when she spotted him exiting the lunch room the next day in a stream of people drifting toward their final workshops, she decided to see about ending on a more pleasant note. He didn't deserve the courtesy, but her eyes framed that beautiful mouth, and the silky light brown hair that she would love to run her hand through, and he'd been kind of cool until the end. So what the hell. She strolled over.

"How's it all been?" she asked. "Any better than usual?"

He laughed. "I caught an okay panel on collaborative journalism, which is all the rage. Other than that, the same old crap... You kind of stormed off yesterday."

"Yeah, well, you started talking down to me, so I figured lunch was about over." But then, leaving no pause for him to respond, she said, "What's collaborative journalism? Two reporters on the same story?" *Like me and Shelburne,* she thought grimly.

Gavin started explaining the Panama Papers, a story where a hundred and forty journalists had worked together instead of competing for the big exposé. Carrie wasn't registering much of what he said, her attention on his voice, pleasingly gravelly, the sound of a stream gurgling through a bed of pebbles. His mouth was the best, she watched words form and unform on his lips, without much registering the content. It was cool that he knew facts but she didn't need so many.

It never occurred to her that he might be nervous.

Carrie would hit the road back to Ohio as soon as the closing workshops ended. "Glad we're almost done here, eh? Nice knowing you."

But as she turned to walk away, giving a quick little semi-humorous wave of her hand, Gavin, said, "Hey, I'm sorry if I seemed like a dick yesterday."

She was caught by surprise; he didn't seem like the type to apologize, or even notice. "Forget about it," she answered. "No big deal."

A bigger surprise was coming.

"You want to hang out sometime?" he asked, with a hint of awkwardness.

"Seriously?" She pulled her head back and squinted, trying to figure out where he was coming from. "I live, like, more than an hour and a half from here, you know." Which wasn't really the point, but...

"I'll drive out there."

Whoa, he was for real.

"Um, also,"—she put up a hand—"where I live isn't too much like what you're used to. We don't, like, have politicians who pull strings for us down my street. We're happy if a dog doesn't bite us."

She paused just briefly. Gavin hesitated for a moment. Then, just as he was about to say something, she gave a half-laugh and blurted, "All right, sure. You're on."

Maybe he wanted a glimpse of how the other half lives. She would do her best to rub his nose in it.

~

Gavin had not planned to ask the girl out. She was insanely cute but a lot younger, and not just in years. But when she had turned to leave an unexpected reluctance to say good-by had washed over him, and the words blurted out of his mouth. He had just agreed—no, volunteered—to spend three hours in his car, ninety minutes each way, to get together with a girl he had nothing in common with. He usually had better impulse control.

~

A notion was taking root inside of Carrie as she made the two-hour drive from the Bigelow Conference Center on the east side of Pittsburgh to her neighborhood on winding streets in Mormon Valley, Middle Beaver, Ohio. The sun was in no hurry to lower its way through the royal blue, and rich green hardwood forests rolled past her windows on both sides. September was coming, she no longer had to brace herself against mid-summer heat. The afternoon was perfect.

The growing seed had been planted by Gavin the previous day. And despite how irritated she'd felt at the time, it had germinated without her realizing it, and now was growing into a tree-like plant in her center, an avocado perhaps, a stem two inches thick and woody, ready to stay upright even in a strong wind.

By the time she pulled up in front of her childhood home—still home today—she was hungering for a fight. *I'm going to make my mark by fucking some shit up. Who cares, I'll worry in the morning about whether it was worth it or not.*

Not those words exactly, but that strain of thinking.

She would have stopped for beers except she remained four months short of her twenty-first birthday. Instead she bummed two PBR's from her sister Francesca's collection in the fridge, peeling them off the plastic connector, promising to give her money for a whole new six tomorrow, then announced authoritatively, "I've got work to do."

And with that she went to her room, shared with her younger brother Scoop, kicked out the retriever whom she normally welcomed in there, and saw to her amazement that Scoop wasn't there. Maybe he was getting a life, though she doubted it.

Kelly Harbison answered on the first ring. He started barking immediately before he even had the phone to his mouth, the tireless guard dog, so she missed his first few words. "...you that I'm not talking to you. Why are you bothering me?"

"I'm gonna write the story myself, Mr. Harbison."

"Oh, the bigshots took pity on you?"

"No, they didn't. I'm doing an end-run, the *Canton Repository* gave me the go-ahead to take the story to them. Could I meet with you this evening?"

Carrie could hear Harbison trying to hide how happy he was; he'd be thrilled to stick it to the *Chronicle*. He snarled, "This is seriously short notice. You think I'm just here on call for you?"

"I had to work in Pittsburgh and just got back. The Canton paper wants my article by 8:00 tonight, it's kind of a rush job."

He emitted more grunting sounds, like a pig rooting in a garbage pile. "All right, it's for the sake of my kid or I wouldn't do it," he said, as if making a huge concession. Then he added, "I have to see what you write before it goes in."

"No problem, Mr. Harbison. I'll be there in thirty-five minutes."

Now she had to move fast; the truth was that she had no idea how to get hold of anyone at the *Repository*, much less whether they would consider an article from her.

Her first try was the news desk, where she reached a recorded message instructing anyone with breaking news to leave a message at extension 4656. She doubted Mr. or Ms. 4656 would be in on a Sunday night but she proposed the story to their voice mail anyhow, claiming she could have it ready in an hour and a half. She figured twice that long was more likely.

Then she sat unmoving for several minutes, watching the seconds fly by on the wristwatch her friends made fun of her for wearing, nervously scratching her arms and legs. For all she knew the paper's drop-dead arrival time for copy had already passed, perhaps as early as the previous evening. She was up the creek.

No choice remained but to call Gavin. Fuck his connections, except now she needed them.

He picked right up, his voice curious. "Carrie, hey, what's up?"

"I need to get someone at the *Canton Repository* to talk to me tonight. Like pronto. Any strings you can pull?"

"Did the Harbison guy agree to speak to you?"

"In his own lovely and tender way, yes. Which means now I've gotten myself into something."

"My editor hates me, she won't be any help. And she wouldn't pick up a call from me on a Sunday night anyhow."

"How about your father? You said he knows everybody."

"Not in the whole country, Carrie."

"What do you mean 'the whole country'? Canton is like two hours away from you. If he's such a big shot, he's gotta know some people in eastern Ohio."

"Maybe. But any time I ask him for a favor he thinks that gives him the right to piss on me for the next three weeks."

"So, take lots of showers. This was your idea, Gavin, you've gotta go to bat for me here."

"Jesus. All right, I'll call you back. This may not go anywhere, though."

"Thanks, old man, you're a brick."

She disconnected, grabbed her reporter notebook, and dashed for the car. Tomorrow she was gonna borrow money from somebody and buy a voice recorder even if she had to pay it back double.

~

Harbison had intriguing information to share. The police were denying the existence of any new evidence on the case, but he had inside information that they had begun receiving crime scene analysis results that afternoon. Footprints had been found in the house that were much larger than Lauren's, ones that had to be recent because no other prints crossed them, impressions on rugs and in dust that had been revealed through sophisticated lighting and photography.

He wouldn't say how he knew these things.

Carrie glanced down at her own feet, too small to create the footprints he was describing. Good thing, because she'd had no idea she could be leaving discoverable traces.

Next, Kelly claimed to have uncovered a complex underground network that assists women to kidnap their children. They were fed by a mentality that vilifies fathers and blames them for every difficulty that children have, from ADHD to the common cold. With the assistance of a friend of his who was a professional computer hacker, they were learning about this clandestine world.

Carrie wanted to know how someone could be a professional hacker. "It sounds like 'licensed criminal' or something."

He answered, "Companies hire hackers to test their security, they're like double agents. The guy I know makes good money."

Next she asked if there was any reason to believe that Brandi's mother was connected to this underground. His response, with some irritation, was that "you can just tell," due to Lauren's mentality, the kind of people she hung out with, and now these footprints that showed someone had helped them run.

How could Carrie learn more about this underground?

He couldn't help her with that, everything he knew came from the hacker, who wouldn't want any connection to a reporter. "Get one of your nerdy college boyfriends to take you on a dark tour, they love to impress the girls."

As she was putting her notebook back under her arm and standing to leave, he ordered gruffly, "Email me the article when it's ready and we'll see, maybe I let you use it and maybe I don't."

Carrie pretended to be flustered. "They said I have to turn the story in by eight o'clock." She tried to remember if that was the same time she'd said before. "I'll need a quick decision from you."

"Your deadline is not my problem," he grouched. "You gave me your word I could approve the article."

"Of course," Carrie said, though she hadn't exactly agreed to that, and stepped out onto the cement stoop. He closed the door hard behind her, just short of slamming it.

Walking to her car she puzzled briefly over why Harbison wanted her on the story, since he dripped dislike for her and took offense at every word out of her mouth. Maybe it was all a front, maybe he was a hurting, lonely father who wanted her attention. And maybe he wanted to feel connected to a young female because he was so scared for his daughter.

Maybe.

~

When Carrie was about ten minutes back down the road toward home, her cell rang, the caller's number unfamiliar.

"Hello," said a smooth voice, friendly in an unconvincing way. "This is Katrina Schell from the *Canton Repository*. Is that Carrie Green?"

Carrie scrambled to gather her thoughts while peering around tensely for a spot to pull off the road. "Thanks so much for calling, Ms. Schell. I'm an intern at *The Morriston Chronicle*, I don't know if you've heard about the kidnapping down here, I wrote our first couple stories about it."

Schell said yes, she was aware of the case, people were following it even up in the huge metropolis of Canton (population 71,000).

"Well, I don't want to keep you," Carrie went on. "The short version is that the father, Kelly Harbison, has refused to talk to the woman the *Chronicle* put on the story."

"Yeah, he won't talk to our reporter either."

"But the thing is, he is willing to talk to me. I guess he felt some kind of rapport when I interviewed him a few days ago, don't ask me. Only the paper won't agree to let me have the story back, I'm just an intern, yeah, okay. So I got a really good interview from him tonight on my own time. I could finish writing it up in like an hour." She hoped Schell couldn't hear the cars whipping past her on Route 7, it would be a while before she was even home.

The editor wasn't interested. "Thanks for thinking of us," she said, a standard kiss-off. "We don't want to get in a pissing contest with the *Chronicle*, we make a point of keeping on friendly relations despite the overlapping territory."

Carrie knew otherwise. In her months at the *Chronicle* there'd been steady rancor over maneuvers by the *Repository* to put more nails in the coffin of Morriston's struggling daily. The *Chronicle* was the kind of paper that didn't last long in the current market no matter how long its history: no distinct urban center, no big conglomerate willing to buy them out, a less-than-solid advertising base. They were hanging on by their fingernails. So each time the Canton daily lured one of their key reporters away with a higher salary offer, or cajoled a major advertiser into getting more bang for their buck at the *Repository*, a stiff jolt was felt at the *Chronicle*. Perhaps what Schell meant by "friendly relations" was that the *Repository* wasn't yet sending thugs out to break the legs of *Chronicle* reporters.

"I can understand that," Carrie forced herself to say, "but it's not your fault that the *Chronicle* is dropping the ball here."

Schell sounded impatient. "Look, you don't want to start your career off by violating your non-compete agreement, you'll wreck your reputation in the business."

Carrie didn't know what the editor was talking about. "Interns don't have a non-compete agreement," she said, with barely a missed beat, "only staff reporters." For all she knew it could be true.

Schell was finished. "Pearth Hurlbert asked me to speak with you and I always want to assist his people, but this time it doesn't work for us. Thanks again for—"

Carrie didn't let her finish. "I'll find someplace else to submit the piece. But why not take a quick look at it before I do that, just in case?"

Perhaps concerned that Carrie would call Pearth Hurlbert to complain, Schell responded gruffly, "All right, send me something in the next sixty minutes and I'll read it."

Carrie couldn't have complained to Pearth Hurlbert, since she lacked the foggiest idea who he was. There was no telling how many links there'd been in the chain of favors extending from Gavin's father to Katrina Schell.

~

A little before ten o'clock, a call came in from Schell. Carrie's heart rate caught speed.

The editor's voice had warmed up several degrees. "I went over your article with our Managing Editor. We've decided to use it. And we're open to considering additional submissions from you during the coming week." They would pay her their standard freelancer rate. "I have to rush over now to the office, it causes chaos to add a story after the paper's already laid out. We'll touch base in the morning."

And Schell was gone.

Carrie tried to absorb what Schell had just said: they were moving stories around to make room for hers. This was a big deal. She couldn't remember the last time her chest had beaten such a contented rhythm. Time for another beer. Maybe a few.

CHAPTER 8

Chief Ari Tobias of the East Liverpool police convened a 9:00 am meeting of his newly formed investigative team for the Harbison case. Janet Wisneski was one of his best detectives. She'd be assisted by Annika Ledbetter, who could be ornery but was Wisneski's favorite person to partner with and it paid off to keep Wisneski happy. Sergeant Patricia Martinez brought strong practical, day-to-day judgment to the team, plus was often the shift supervisor. He rounded out the group with patrol officers Shane Kresge and Arielle Mason, both competent but not very experienced, perfect for handling whatever tasks the other members of the team needed done.

Wisneski read a mixed message. The chief was present himself, which sent a message that the case was serious. On the other hand he'd appointed only women to the team, with the exception of Kresge, as if putting the case in some "women's issues" category, which bugged her. Her concern was not about the individuals; Ledbetter and Martinez were excellent, and Kresge was a hard worker with good instincts if perhaps not the sharpest knife in the drawer. Mason she knew little about one way or the other.

Martinez took the lead. "We have good photographs of foot impressions revealed in carpets and in dirt on the wood and linoleum floors. Most of them fit Lauren and Brandi's sizes, based on shoes that we found in the home. A couple of them were in between those two sizes, perhaps friends of Brandi's who'd been at the house. However, three or four prints were men's size eleven and a half. We have some partials from the stairs and the second floor that could conceivably match this person, but we only know for sure that he was in the downstairs."

Kresge asked whether the footprints could be Kelly's; he'd seen the father's eagerness to enter the house and play detective, maybe he snuck in there during the three days that passed before police sealed the house on Thursday.

Martinez doubted it. "He's a size ten, he let us measure his foot and he produced a few pairs of his shoes. And the footprints aren't right for someone who was looking around the house; they're just in a few places, mostly close to the door to the outside."

She moved on. "The woods in Collier, West Virginia, show no sign of Mr. Eleven-and-a-Half, but the footprints in the mud are a perfect fit for Lauren and Brandi. If the man was still with them, he stayed close to the roadway or on other hard ground. Most importantly, we have no leads on where they went from there."

Finally, samples from Lauren's home could take anywhere from five days to five months to come back from analysis, based on the track record of Ohio labs. "But we're close to getting the FBI to come on, and then our lab samples would get fast-tracked."

"And we get pushed aside," Kresge grouched.

Tobias responded impatiently. "That's not our experience, Shane. When we've had the FBI on board before they've been nothing but helpful."

Kresge was unconvinced; but as he was even newer to the force than Arielle Mason, his opinions counted little. His teammates registered his facial expressions, however, and proceeded to needle him about his inability to get rolling "so early" in the morning (he usually worked late shifts), and his "issues" with having to work on a team with so many females. His considered response was to tell them all to fuck off.

The agenda moved to a discussion of news reports. The first was a medium-length piece from the *Chronicle* that rehashed old information and lacked personality. The second one, however, was a longer article from the *Canton Repository*, written by none other than Carrie Green.

"Carrie Green??" Kresge said, incredulous. "Isn't she like sixteen or something? And when did she start writing for the Canton paper?"

"It gets stranger. She quotes extensively from an interview with Kelly Harbison, while the *Chronicle* has no jewels of wisdom from him, and neither do the TV reports. This kid seems to have some kind of in with him, which is downright weird."

"Maybe there's some connection between the families," Ledbetter said. "I'll look into it."

"No, don't," overruled Wisneski, "we've got bigger things to spend our time on than worrying how a reporter gets her story."

"Well, yes and no," said the Sergeant. "There's a problem. The Green girl wrote in her article that we found large, almost certainly male footprints that were new. That's information the Media Relations Officer wasn't authorized to release. Now Mr. Eleven-Point-Five knows that we know about him, which stinks for us. How the hell did she find that out? Does she have friends everywhere?"

"Don't look at me," said Kresge, "I thought she was a lost child, I wasn't gonna tell her anything."

Tobias put up his hands. "Shane, no one would have suspected you if you hadn't denied it. Okay, we'll set up a meeting with the Green kid, I can throw a little weight around if necessary. But just so it's said, no one but the MRO or myself says *anything* to the press. Clear?"

The Media Relations Officer would, they knew, use the standard lines: "We're pursuing all leads. Evidence is at the lab. We expect to get mother and child home unharmed. Most cases of this kind are resolved rapidly." Follow-up questions would be handled by repeating the above phrases, varying the order.

Wisneski doled out tasks. Ledbetter was to dig harder into Lauren Harbison's history and lean on friends of hers to talk. Wisneski would coordinate with the FBI and Ohio State Highway Patrol. Martinez would follow up on each category of evidence, and look for ways (probably impossible) to pressure the labs to give the case priority. Kresge and Mason would hop when anyone said hop.

"All right," Tobias closed, "I have total confidence in this team. We hit the ground running this morning and don't stop until we bring that girl to safety. Give me your best."

And they were off, feeling like big-city cops.

~

Marco Vinestri hadn't taken ten steps through the front door of the paper's office building to start his workday before an administrative assistant approached him holding out a copy of that morning's *Repository*, looking funereal. "You'd better read this," she said, pointing to an article below the fold on the front page.

The byline read, "by Carrie Green."

Vinestri skimmed over the article in stunned disbelief. Not only had that little Green twit gotten Kelly Harbison to give her an earful (of great quotations, no less), she also appeared to have cozied up to someone in the East Liverpool police department because she had a scoop on evidence from Lauren Harbison's house that the police hadn't told the press about.

Vinestri's upper body grew two sizes larger. He would crush that kid like a bug and make sure no one ever hired her in this business again. Her name was gonna be cat turds. And they'd take legal action against the *Repository*, this time they'd hired someone who hadn't even given notice yet at the *Chronicle*.

Anyone in the path of his march between the lobby and his office moved quickly aside, recognizing a primed and oiled assault rifle when they saw one. As he stomped forward he simultaneously brought up Carrie's number on his cell and punched it in. The girl did not pick up, as he'd expected, and in a clipped, well-controlled tone he informed her voice mail that her internship had been terminated. Any belongings of hers at the office that she preferred not be thrown in the dumpster were to be retrieved before noon.

Marco, looking down, ran smack into his Managing Editor, Candace Pratt, outside his office door, though at the last minute she saw him coming and popped up her hand to brake his acceleration, softening the impact. He was glad she was there, though; he couldn't wait to add her (much greater) firepower to his.

Except that Pratt proved to be less convinced than Marco that the paper's emergency priority was to establish his dominance over a teenage girl. (Okay, she was twenty, and legally an adult, but to anyone with eyes still obviously a child.) "If we fire her, we hand the Harbison story over to the *Repository* wholesale, and with a couple of twists it might turn into one of the top stories of the year. We can't take that risk over an ego battle."

Now Vinestri was really pissed; before he'd just been warming up. "You're seriously saying we let her get away with this??" he sputtered, eyes bulging.

"We may well have to. You and I don't exactly work for a thriving paper, not to put too fine a point on it. If this disappearance is resolved in the next few days, you can send your intern packing as rudely as you wish. But until we're sure this isn't getting big we're not cutting off our noses to spite our face."

"How can we have someone here who thinks she can just ignore her noncompete agreement? She'd go from being an intern to the opposite extreme, having a special status."

Pratt decided to throw him a bone. "Call her to come to the office immediately. We'll read her the riot act like we're terminating her, let her sweat. Then we back off and tell her she can stay, but with a probationary period. She'll feel lucky to have it end there. Remember, she's a Valley kid, working here is a prize for her."

Marco didn't like it. Nor could he bring himself to admit to the message he's already left for his intern. He waited until the Managing Editor was out of earshot before calling Carrie to take it back.

~

Carrie had woken up scared to show her face at the office. But she hadn't had to dread it long; just after eight o'clock Vinestri's call came in, telling her she was fired and to pick up her stuff by noon.

She decided to wait until 11:45 to go in, when she'd run into as few people as possible because of the lunch hour.

At 8:47, Marco called again. Carrie gathered he hadn't vented to his satisfaction in the first message; this one would be a real howler, best to erase it without giving it a listen. But then it occurred to her how much she'd enjoy letting him start talking (just barely) and then hanging up on him. So she picked up.

He was audibly startled, the possibility that she might answer his call evidently not having crossed his mind.

"This is Marco Vinestri," he said. He sounded, well, stupid.

"Good morning, Marco." She couldn't wait to hear what would follow.

"My earlier call was premature. Candace Pratt, the Managing Editor, has decided the three of us should sit down and talk together. She wants you here for 9:30."

It was Carrie's turn to be caught off guard. Marco must have called in one of the Big Kids so they could beat her up together. She didn't even know who Pratt was, though she must have passed her at one time or another in the hallways.

"I'm not sure I can arrive that soon. Could we find a later time?"

"We'll wait for you, the sooner you get here the better." And he hung up.

The coward.

She hadn't even had the chance to tell Gavin the good news from last night, and now it was already not so good anymore. But what had she expected?

Gavin answered his phone with, "Well?"

"Well what?"

He was fighting his way across Pittsburgh to get to work, his regular morning commute except today traffic was moving much slower than normal, an accident he assumed. "So, what all ended up happening last night? I never heard back from my dear father."

Carrie gave a little laugh. "Your dear father came through in a big way, he'll be pissing on you extra frequently." She recounted the previous evening's events in ample detail, taking advantage of an audience that was trapped in rush hour. The story ended with her lying in bed for some three hours, unable to sleep but too exhausted to move, until she finally lost consciousness close to 4:00 a.m.

"You couldn't have sent me a text last night?" He had a point.

"I wanted to tell you on the phone, in person. Anyhow, this morning Vinestri wants to fire me, but he said I'm supposed to go in and meet with him and his boss. I have a feeling it's just so they can ream me out close up."

"You gonna go?"

"Might as well see what happens, I can always walk out. I could use a couple beers first, but it's too early."

"Listen, don't hesitate to play the card of, 'There's a child in danger in this case, getting the best possible information out there is essential, blah, blah.'"

"Mmm, I like it," she said.

~

Candace Pratt's office was large and sun-filled, at least by *Chronicle* standards. The view was the main reward for being Managing Editor; the job didn't come with an impressive salary increase, and the two additional weeks of vacation were a nice idea but she never seemed able to take them. Pratt determined that the meeting should happen here, rather than in Marco's office, to put the young intern face-to-face with the huge gulf that loomed between her minor-league self and the important, successful people in the world who worked by large plate-glass windows.

Carrie sat stiffly in an unpadded wooden chair that she'd been pointed toward, disciplining herself not to leap into a fighting stance, a position familiar to her. Vinestri sat well to her left and was facing towards her rather than towards Pratt's desk, demarcating the teams.

"We have a serious problem on our hands," Pratt opened gravely, playing high school assistant-principal. "You're in violation of the non-compete clause of your contract. This is a violation of a legal agreement, with large implications. We're taking steps to terminate your position, but in the spirit of fairness, this is your opportunity to persuade us that nothing like this will ever happen again and that we should take a chance on you."

Carrie said, "Can I see the agreement I signed for my internship? I don't remember it being called a contract, but anyhow I'd like to read it."

"The language is standard for everyone who works here," responded Pratt, and briskly handed her a sheet with the language of the non-compete clause on it.

"Yeah, but I'd like to see what I actually signed."

Pratt's tone hardened further. "That won't get you anywhere, Ms. Green, the wording's right here. But you're welcome to request a copy from Personnel, it will be part of your employee file of course."

"I'd like to have that now, before we continue the meeting," Carrie said, using the polite voice she held in reserve for times when she couldn't punch people.

Pratt wasn't about to let the kid take control of the meeting. "Ms. Green, as an intern you're an at-will employee, meaning we can let you go at any time without even having to provide grounds. The precise wording of your contract is therefore irrelevant; you know perfectly well that we're the ones who provided you with access to Kelly Harbison, and you turned around and used it for the benefit of our primary competitor—in fact, our exclusive competitor."

Carrie began to chew her gum, forgetting she'd promised herself not to let them see that it was in her mouth. "I don't really want to make the drive up to Canton every day, it's kind of a ways. I'd rather work here. But Mr. Harbison is the center of this story, and since he's only willing to talk if I'm the one covering it—"

Pratt cut in. "We're not going to have a citizen dictating which reporter we assign to a story!"

Gee, where had Carrie heard that pronouncement before?

"Yeah, you've got your principles, I probably don't understand them like I should, being so new. But this kid Brandi's life may be at stake here, I wouldn't be able to sleep if I knew I was turning down a chance to be talking to her father. I'd write the story for the *Weekly Advertiser* if they were the only ones who would print it."

The cool-and-collected Pratt now transformed into Vinestri's twin, bullets and tracers flying from her eyes. She left a deliberate, furious pause, then her words came out following evenly one behind the other in exaggeratedly measured beats like a talking metronome. "We expected a somewhat different attitude from you, Carrie; perhaps we were naïve. And thank you *so* much for raising our consciousness about the risk to the child, we of course never thought of that. You can go ahead and pack up your stuff."

None of this was raised a decibel above her normal speaking voice; her words traveled in one direction while their sarcastic meaning raced away in the other.

Carrie stood without hesitating and, hoping to match Pratt's unflappable tone, said, "This morning the *Repository* asked me to be a regular there. I was hoping to avoid that, though; the drive, you know. Oh, well." And she strode out the door.

~

Pratt and Vinestri sat off-gassing in silence, the air around them turning progressively harder to breathe. Either of them would have happily grabbed this little shit by the neck and squeezed the life out of her. The Managing Editor's compassion for Marco had grown, just a bit, now that she'd watched this Green kid in action.

"The mouse that roared," she said at long last.

Vinestri verbally raised his fists. "Let's call the *Repository* and find out whether they offered her a job. I so doubt it. What a liar."

"Marco," responded Pratt, in what sounded like a cough, "she's an *intern* here for Christ's sake. If they want to use her as a freelancer, or even go all the way and hire her on staff, that'll be viewed as totally legit by everyone except you and me. They would not in a million years tell us whether they're offering her a job or not."

"Then call her bluff. There's no way they hired her on after she wrote one stupid article for them."

"Yeah, well, bad luck for us, it wasn't a stupid article. It was surprisingly good. And it's not like they have to offer her much money, the girl lives with her parents."

Vinestri couldn't believe his ears. "Seriously, you're not gonna reward her for what she just pulled by letting her stay on here! Please!"

Pratt breathed deeply, struggling more with herself than with Marco. "It's worse than that, my friend…"

"Meaning what?"

She spoke almost without opening her mouth, scrunching the words. "I don't see any alternative to… making her a staff reporter."

"You what??"

"We can't have an intern on this story, and we can't take the risk of the *Repository* offering her a real staff position."

Marco came out of his chair. "You've got to be kidding! You do that and I quit!"

"Don't get my hopes up, Vinestri," Pratt replied, turning away.

~

As Carrie was packing up her office desk a call came in from the East Liverpool police, none other than Officer Kresge. Reception apparently hadn't been informed of her termination because they put him through to her. He was pretty much the last person she felt like talking to just then.

"Good morning, Ms. Green. We want to update you on weekend developments in the case, and we'd prefer to talk sooner rather than later. Can you come down to the station?"

For a moment Carrie couldn't figure out who or where she was. The police wanting to talk to her—as a reporter, not a street punk—was one thing too many to make sense out of in the twisted context of the past fifteen hours.

She told Kresge she had to finish up something she was in the middle of, which made her laugh even though it wasn't funny. She'd head down to East Liverpool in a few minutes.

She didn't have many belongings at the *Chronicle* anyhow; an emergency pack of cigarettes, a small makeup kit, a hairbrush, and some scattered Power Bars and bags of Goldfish.

As she headed out, it occurred to her that she was probably supposed to go to Personnel for an exit interview, whatever that was. (If you don't pass the interview, they don't let you exit?) Well, she'd have to come back to the paper some other day. Or not.

~

Carrie expected to be kept waiting at the police station, as she always had been previously. But almost as soon as she'd announced herself at the front booth Kresge appeared at the inner door. He thanked her for coming, odd enough in itself, and ushered her into a small meeting room, his tone now friendly and collegial. She sensed a trap.

He offered to get her a cup of coffee, which she accepted even though she didn't want it. He was out of the room only a few moments, and as soon as he returned and they were both seated he launched right in.

"We were interested to see your article in the *Repository* this morning. You working for them now?"

"Just on this story," she answered, rehearsed wording to a question she'd figured was coming.

"Kelly Harbison isn't saying squat to us when we ask for information, then he complains we aren't doing enough. It's good he's at least talking to you, it seems you're the only one."

She let the implied question hang in the air; it wasn't like she had any more idea why than anyone else did. She gave a small, unfamiliar smile in place of a response.

"Let me fill you in," Kresge resumed after an awkward pause. "First, we have indications that Lauren and Brandi were either assisted to leave or forced to leave by another individual."

"Male or female?"

"We believe it's a male but we don't know for sure yet."

"Not too many women wear a size eleven men's shoe. What's that, like thirteen in women's?"

Kresge raised his fingers off the table in an odd movement, his wrists staying planted. "Let's come back to talk about foot sizes in a few minutes."

"Okay. Your media guy hasn't been answering when reporters ask about signs of a struggle. Something you can say today?"

"We have no indications of a struggle. But that doesn't mean Brandi and her mother aren't in danger, there are ways to get people to cooperate, with enticements or threats. If anyone sees Ms. Harbison or her daughter, even if no other individual seems to be with them, do not approach them, for your own safety and for theirs. Stay a safe distance away and call the police."

Kresge had already given her enough for a decent article and most of the day still lay ahead of her. If only she knew what outlet she would be writing it for. She couldn't tell if her life was going great or terribly.

There was more. "The FBI is leaning toward joining the case, and the Highway Patrol is already assisting. Our situation is complicated by being on the Pennsylvania and West Virginia borders, we don't know which direction Lauren and Brandi are going, a lot of interagency collaboration will be required."

That was the end of the news. But this meeting had to be about something else. Carrie waited for the other shoe to drop.

Kresge paused for a moment, then said, "So, about those footprints." Here it comes. "They were eleven and half, by the way, not eleven, but that's minor. We specifically decided not to release that information, so we weren't happy to read it in the paper. In the middle of an investigation we make careful, strategic decisions about what should get out and what shouldn't."

"Because…"

"For two reasons. We don't want to get the public all stirred up, it just makes our job harder. I can promise you that today we'll get dozens of calls from people who saw a guy who they think had a very large foot. I'm not kidding."

"Yeah, I was gonna mention my dad, actually. He wears at least a ten and a half, you might want to check him out."

The officer peered at her for a moment, vaguely confused, then went on. "But more importantly, when we find information that points us toward a suspect, we don't want that person alerted to what we know, because that could spur them to start destroying evidence, or intimidate a witness, or flee, all of which interfere with our investigation."

Kresge put a cigarette in his mouth, but made no move to light it. "So we want to have the best possible relationship with the media, for your sake and ours."

Carrie smiled inwardly; suddenly she was "the media."

"We know you don't want to harm our investigation," he went on. "But obviously you have a friend or relative on the force who's passing tidbits to you. We're asking you to go over off-the-record information with us before you print it, so that we can tell you the parts that are going to hurt our efforts."

"You're saying I need the department's permission about what I write?"

"No, no. When we step in, we'll just be requesting that you use good judgment, and maybe delay a few days, before you go public with stuff. And the decision will of course always be yours."

Carrie didn't give a shit what the police requested. She'd spent her teen years being targeted, along with most residents of Mormon Valley, for hassling and humiliation by cops who seemed to think that keeping everyone in her neighborhood intimidated served the public good. The predictable result was that no one in Mormon Valley would call the police unless lives were literally on the line, which was precisely when you could most count on them not to show up.

Of course, if the cops got a call from a mansion in the Round Hill Estates, reporting that a raccoon was knocking over trash cans, they went diving into their cruisers and roared up there six minutes later, lights flashing and weapons drawn. *No raccoon's gonna ignore the law around here.*

Kresge filled the silence again. "In return, we make sure you have top-drawer access to all the best information from us without having to wait for that day's press conference. It puts you ahead of all the other reporters."

A few hours lead time on the TV stations each day would pay off big time. But the thought of making a backroom deal with the cops nauseated her. "It's been a pleasure," Carrie said, then gathered up her stuff and headed for the door, neither shaking the officer's hand nor responding to his offer.

"We look forward to working with you," he called out, as if believing some kind of agreement had been reached.

Carrie didn't know who "we" referred to, these people who looked forward to working with her, but it was obvious that Officer Kresge was not among them.

~

As Sofia Madsen drove to work on Monday morning, she was pulled over by a local police officer after crossing an intersection near the center of town. The grizzly-haired cop asked the usual, "Do you know why I pulled you over?" question, and when she had no idea proceeded to coldly report, "You rolled through that stop sign, ma'am. That not safe. You need to come to a full stop." He then went back to his vehicle and stayed there for nearly fifteen minutes, as if she were a stranger to town whose long criminal record he had just discovered on his laptop.

When the officer finally reappeared at her window, he said, "I let you off with a written warning ma'am," handing her what looked like a traffic ticket. "Drive carefully." With that he turned sharply and marched back to his vehicle, not allowing time for Sofia to ask how it could have taken so long to fill out a warning.

If what she'd done at that intersection counted as rolling through the stop sign, she'd rolled through hundreds in her life.

She'd also been pulled over on Saturday evening, that time by a young officer with a ponytail who informed her that one of her running lights—a little yellow one, not a headlight—was out. She'd handed Sofia a ticket-like form that gave her seven days to correct the problem and provide written proof. And on Friday she'd been contacted by the building inspector's office at Town Hall, inquiring about her failure to secure a permit for the shed she'd had built in her back yard three years earlier, the clerk quoting her the number of a city ordinance.

An actual subpoena wouldn't have spoken any more clearly than these three interventions did: these hassles would become her life until she told the truth about what she knew.

And at 11:30 am, three hours after the stop sign warning, a detective named Ledbetter was on Sofia's phone, asking her to come down to the station to answer more questions.

"I've already told you everything I know," Sofia protested. "I've been racking my brain for anything I might not have noticed, I haven't come up with anything."

"We have to pursue every possible avenue," Ledbetter said. "We won't take much of your time." Of course not.

~

Harbison was pissed. (Was he ever not?) "I thought you were different," he grouched into Carrie's ear, not exactly yelling but plenty loud, "like you gave a shit. So much for trusting your word, your article came out nothing like what you showed me."

It hadn't changed that much, but it wasn't worth arguing the point. "Mr. Harbison, what happens to my article after I turn it in isn't up to me; they don't even show me the final version before they print it. I did everything I could." Except, that is, to let him see what she was actually turning in by the time she'd finished working on it.

"Then you tell them they can't use it if they change it. You're a freelancer, you can do that."

I'm a freelancer all right. Don't remind me. So much for having the money to rent my own place.

"Well, whatever I am," she said, "I turn into the unemployed version of that if I try to tell my editor what she can do. She'd already be pissed if she knew I made changes based on what you wanted."

"Well, aren't you just the bravest girl on the planet."

Carrie pretended to take his rude comment as a good-natured crack. "Hey, you got that right, I put my neck on the chopping block. I'll check in with you late today for anything new I should know for tomorrow morning's story. When's a good time to call?"

Kelly snarled, more softly though, that it didn't matter when she called, he was very busy; maybe she'd reach him and maybe she wouldn't. She thanked him heartily and rang off.

Wisneski and Ledbetter invested an unexpected number of hours in tracking down the names of Lauren Harbison's current close friends. Following some leads from Kelly the detectives had tracked down a number of her friends from years back, but it appeared that none of those relationships had endured past her divorce, seeming to confirm Kelly's assertion that Lauren required people to be either for her or against her.

They came at last to focus on three women. First was Sofia Madsen, by all accounts Lauren's closest friend. She and Lauren had met while in the process of their divorces and Sofia's children had become friends with Brandi. Madsen had squirmed and stuttered, her eyes in rapid motion and her breathing uneven, during police interviews with her; they were eager to know what she was concealing.

The second was Delta Evans. Lauren and Delta had been Zumba class aficionadas at the local Fitness Frenzy. Delta was married, supposedly happily though the detectives wanted to examine that question more closely, with three children. She made her living doing academic research on a freelance basis, assisting college professors with grant-funded investigations.

The third was Rhapsody Stearns. It was not clear how she and Lauren had met, and she seemed young to be the missing woman's confidante, only recently turned twenty-eight to Lauren's forty-two. She was a second-year law student at the University of Akron, said to be specializing in civil rights.

The police were especially interested in Ms. Stearns. She had a background as a crusader, having become a student activist at Ohio University Eastern and the leader of an occupation of the administration building over the college's investments in sweatshops. If Lauren Harbison was good at playing victim, as Kelly asserted, Stearns might be just the kind of person she could manipulate into aiding and abetting.

In the detectives' brief initial conversations with the women, each had denied that Lauren had ever discussed fleeing or that she even spoke badly of Kelly as a father. They also all claimed not to know the names of any of her other friends. The detectives were skeptical.

~

Sofia arrived at the East Liverpool station at 12:50. She was surprised to see Lauren's friend Delta sitting in the waiting area. She walked quickly up to her and, sticking out her hand, said, "Hi, you may not remember me, Sofia Madsen. I'm a good friend of Lauren's."

"Of course I remember you," the woman responded, taking her hand and shaking it energetically. "Delta Evans. You came to a couple of classes at the gym with me and Lauren. She speaks highly of you."

Sharing this moment, the first time either of them had been with a close friend of Lauren's since she and Brandi vanished, caused tears to spring to their eyes. "Oh my God, Delta," Sofia said, "this is such a nightmare. I hardly do anything besides worry about them." She seized the other woman in a desperate hug, which was somewhat awkwardly received with pats on Sofia's back. She let go. "But, why are you here? Has something happened?"

Evans quickly put a hand back on Sofia's arm. "No, no news at all, it's okay. They asked me to come in to answer some questions. At one o'clock I'm supposed to talk to a Detective Wisneski."

"Odd, they gave me the same time. Detective Ledbetter, they told me."

"Coordinating their schedules. They must have dozens of people to talk to, that's why they have us come to them instead of vice-versa. Plus it saves us having a police car parked in front of the house."

"I've already been brought in, though. They kept me for hours. They're only pretending to be nice, don't be fooled. They grilled me like a murderer."

"Honey, no more for now, okay? This isn't the place to talk." She pulled out her phone. "Give me your number, darling, let me put it in here."

A third woman, young, came through the station doors. Neither of them recognized her, though Delta looked at her a little hard as if trying to remember something. The girl went up to the reception window and they heard her introduce herself as Rhapsody Stearns, arriving for a 1:00 appointment. The booth officer instructed her to take a seat.

Sofia's eyes squinted a little, and she leaned toward the girl. "Excuse me, did I hear right, you have an appointment with Officer Kresge?"

"Yes," replied the girl uncertainly, looking askance at Sofia, ready to defend against invasion.

"We're both friends of Lauren Harbison's. Are you here about her?"

The girl straightened in her seat, startled. "Yeah, I know her." They made introductions, studying one another. This was not a person Lauren had mentioned to Sofia. "I only met Lauren a short while ago," the girl said. "I don't get why the police want to talk to me, or how they even found out about me. Lauren was looking into the law school at University of Akron, that's where I go.

I'm one of the volunteers that reach out to prospective students to talk about the program. She's very nice, but I mean, I barely know her."

Another blow struck Sofia's formerly solid world: Lauren had said nothing to her about law school. Why had she shut her out of such a major life decision? And how was Lauren planning to pay tuition, plus manage the piles of schoolwork while single-parenting Brandi most of the time?

The sinking feeling from several days earlier—that the closeness of her friendship with Lauren had been an illusion, that she'd had a whole life that Sofia was excluded from—rolled back through her, an earthquake's aftershock.

In her swirl of emotions she almost blurted out that she knew both mother and daughter were okay. Then she felt heartless for not saying it, for leaving Delta and Rhapsody burdened with worry. Everything she did seemed wrong.

Rhapsody wondered aloud, "Why would Lauren be working on getting into law school around here if she was planning to leave the area?" Sofia, pretending to speculate with her, said half-seriously that perhaps Lauren had a secret life, maybe she'd been forced to flee because of money she owed drug dealers.

Delta poked around in the periodicals on the low coffee table where visitors, left impatiently waiting, put up their feet. "I'd love to talk to you both another time, but I'm going to read now." She looked meaningfully at Sofia and turned slightly away, the message to shut up clear. All three women took to perusing vapid stories from four-year-old Home & Garden magazines.

~

Visitors left to wait in police station lobbies can be seen studying walls and corners, trying to figure out where the security cameras are. Sometimes cameras are visible and sometimes not, but they've got to be somewhere. What the public is less commonly aware of is that the cameras are fitted with sensitive microphones. Even a low whisper, when magnified through this listening system, is audible on the video recording that will be kept for months. Visitors may speak softly to avoid being overheard by people on the other side of the room, but to an officer watching the tape it will sound as though it came from one seat over.

It was no accident that all three women were scheduled for the same hour and were left waiting in the lobby until their conversation died out, some twenty minutes after they had trickled in; Wisneski and Ledbetter wanted to hear what they would say to each other privately.

A number of observations stood out. First, Delta Evans could be seen at least twice trying to discourage the others from talking. Her discomfort had been most noticeable when the other two were spinning out possible scenarios about what had happened to Lauren and Brandi.

Second, Rhapsody Stearns had emphasized and reemphasized how little she knew Lauren, understandable given that she was talking to two of the missing woman's close friends, except her tone sounded forced.

Last was the visible shockwave that went through Sofia Madsen—followed quickly by her efforts to cover it up—when the young law student claimed that Lauren had been preparing to apply to her program. How could this be news to Lauren's closest friend? Rhapsody's story wasn't adding up.

One point went in the women's favor: it appeared that they indeed hadn't known each other before, at least not enough to remember names.

~

Around 2:00 in the afternoon, Vinestri looked up from his desk to see that his Managing Editor was back. She walked into his office and closed the door behind her.

"I've gone over the situation with Peralta." She was referring to the paper's Executive Editor. "He agrees we can't let this one get away. Personnel is calling to make her an offer."

Marco's skin went ghoul-colored. His day, his month, was ruined. And the Green kid was going to be a disaster.

~

Carrie's phone rang at 2:20. She saw the *Chronicle's* exchange, but it wasn't Vinestri's extension. Perhaps Personnel calling to insist on that exit interview. She let it go to voice mail, then listened.

"Hello, Ms. Green," an unfamiliar female voice said, "I'm calling from Human Resources at the *Morriston Chronicle*. We'd like to discuss a job offer with you, please call us back at your earliest convenience."

A job offer? Did they want her to wash off the grime caked on the exterior windows?

Forty-five minutes later, Carrie found herself in a conference room at the paper, sitting with Candace Pratt, Marco Vinestri, and an HR person named Alexa something or other. The Managing Editor did the talking.

"We've decided that we underestimated the value of the work you did in building a trusting relationship with Kelly Harbison. So we're making an offer to bring you back on as a staff reporter."

Vinestri must have been dying inside, eating a whole pieful of crows.

Pratt went over the salary and benefits they were offering, with corrections and amplifications from Alexa X. Then, in a tone that took on an edge, she reviewed the non-compete clause in fine detail, leaving no room to mistake any part of it. But she also chose to end on a diplomatic note. "This clause is rarely relevant to interns, so I doubt anyone went over it with you; that's our mistake."

Carrie noticed they still hadn't shown her what she supposedly signed.

It was now her turn to offer some apology, however insincere it might be; but she'd never apologized to anyone in a position of authority and couldn't bring herself to do it now. "Thanks for the offer," she said simply. "Since it's a big step for me, though, I need a couple of hours to go over the deal with my parents. I'll get back to you." She shook hands all around, as if she found herself in situations like this all the time, and made her exit.

Benefits?? she thought, her facial muscles releasing their tension as she walked away. *Lord God!*

~

As soon as his (former) intern was out of earshot, Vinestri erupted. "We're hiring a staff reporter who still reviews documents with Mommy and Daddy?? Does that create misgivings for anyone besides me?"

Pratt emitted a cold laugh. "You're nothing *but* misgivings, Marco, they didn't just arise. Anyhow, she's not heading to her parents."

"She just said so."

"Any fool knows she's running straight to the *Repository* with our offer." Any fool other than Vinestri, that is. "She's hoping they'll top it. And we're hoping their budget is too tight."

"Or that they have a policy against child labor," he snarled.

~

The Harbison case team met again briefly in the late afternoon. Martinez asked, "Any new information before we call it a day?"

Ledbetter had some. "To our surprise, Rhapsody Stearns' story checked out. We called the law school, and sure enough she's on a student committee that contacts potential students, talks the program up, and offers them a friendly campus tour. Plus the school makes records of all contacts from prospective students—recruitment is intense these days—and they confirmed that Lauren had expressed interest in the program and Rhapsody had volunteered to reach out to her."

Kresge sat shaking his head. "Something is off here. She just didn't sound believable when I was questioning her. My gut is speaking loudly on this one."

"That's because all you ever eat is greasy french fries," said Ledbetter. "I can hear your gut speaking from across the room."

CHAPTER 9

"To what do I owe the pleasure of your visit, Detective?" Annika Ledbetter squinted her eyes just slightly and shifted in her seat as Dr. Robert Kinzer gazed majestically across his wide and shining cherry desk, his reflection in the surface visible down to the impeccable Windsor Knot in his tie. "I'm here to learn what you know about a family that's the subject of a police matter," Ledbetter explained. "It's our understanding that you and your colleagues performed a forensic evaluation of the Harbison family."

The detective was posturing; not only did she know that Kinzer had performed an evaluation, but it was one of the most-discussed issues in the divorce documents she'd pored over the previous evening. The report itself, however, was not in the records. On the previous afternoon, when Kelly Harbison had provided Ledbetter copies of a pile of legal papers, he told her that the court hadn't allowed him to have a copy of Kinzer's report.

Dr. Kinzer smiled affably and lifted his chin. "Ms. Ledbetter, I'm sure you're aware that I'm bound by strict professional rules regarding confidentiality. I can't discuss the content of any interviews we performed."

Ledbetter knew something about Dr. Kinzer's standing in the region. He was coordinator of the renowned Children In the Law program, performing evaluations of children in legal cases where they were the objects of custody fights, the victims of child abuse, candidates for adoption, or the perpetrators of juvenile crimes. The program was based at UPMC Children's Hospital, the top facility in the Pittsburgh area. Kinzer was known as the most relied-upon forensic child psychologist in the western part of Pennsylvania and took cases from nearby parts of Ohio and West Virginia as well.

Ledbetter mustered her mildest tone, still far from heart-melting, and said, "But you interview people for reports you write for courts. So what do you mean that your work is confidential? Anyone could read your reports."

"Well, actually, no. Nowadays courts typically impound custody evaluations, which means the parties have to read the report at the court and can't show it to anyone. Often the court order says that the parties can't even *discuss* the contents of the report with anyone other than their lawyer, and even the lawyer has to read it at the courthouse. So you see, confidentiality is taken very seriously."

Ledbetter was intrigued. She'd been told that custody evaluations were hard for investigators to get their hands on, but she hadn't heard that sometimes the lawyers themselves weren't allowed to have copies. Was this the family court or the National Security Administration? It sounded like being tried with secret evidence, Saudi Arabian style.

"Well, let me cut to the chase," the detective said, shifting into an aura of authority that she could turn on and off. "Lauren Harbison and her daughter Brandi have been missing for more than seven days. The indications so far point to a likely abduction of the girl by her mother."

Dr. Kinzer's eyes widened at this pronouncement. He pushed his chair back several inches from his desk and made himself taller. "I... I assumed that you were here to ask about allegations of... excuse me, I can't say what I assumed you were here to ask about. This is a great shock to hear. Do you know if the girl is okay?"

"I'm afraid we don't. She was alive and okay as of a couple of days ago, that's all we know."

The psychologist shook his head back and forth several times, his eyes dark. "This is extremely worrisome. That poor girl. She has an over-involved, helicopter mother who was determined to alienate her from her father. This must be a painful and frightening time for him, in addition to whatever the daughter may be suffering."

Now Ledbetter's tone reached for nonchalance, just making conversation. "What sorts of things did Lauren do to harm the girl's relationship with her father?"

But Kinzer noticed his error. "Ms. Ledbetter, I may have been unwise to share my opinion. Your news shocked me. But in any event I certainly can't provide factual details, that's another matter from sharing impressions or opinions."

"Consider your comment forgotten," Ledbetter replied collegially, knowing she'd carefully record his words as soon as she got back to the station. She added, "And we would never ask you to go beyond what you thought was ethically appropriate."

She went straight to wondering whether they had a way to get a judge to force him to talk.

~

Kelly Harbison had handed that same collection of divorce documents to Carrie on Monday afternoon. She'd sat reading in the nylon chair in his small study, periodically looking up to ask him questions, while he carried on his usual furious dialogue with the internet, in writing and aloud, making her a party to his debates and frustrations.

Custody battles weren't a prominent feature of life in Mormon Valley; no one had money to wage them with. Couples there didn't so much divorce as blow apart and more often did neither, instead staying together while accumulating bitterness, making frequent threats to leave, and periodically storming out of the house and not reappearing until the next day. A wife or a husband wasn't that different from an infuriating sibling; you didn't divorce your brother or your sister. People didn't view life as all that changeable and were largely right.

Kelly's documents had been Carrie's introduction to how couples outside of the Valley parted ways. She felt like she was reading the personal theatrics of movie stars in a tabloid, except the characters had neither glamor nor bottomless bank accounts, though the money they did have still seemed like a pile to her.

She couldn't figure out what the hell these people had to whine about.

Accusations went endlessly back and forth through the pile of *Harbison v. Harbison* documents, mostly camouflaged in language such as "I have it on faith and belief that..." and "pursuant to" and "aforementioned" and "ref. *McClintock v. Lacasio,* 2014-Ohio-278, 985 N.E.2d, #1058" (perhaps a street address in a Cleveland apartment building?).

At times Carrie despaired of her ability to unearth the story from this morass unless she attended law school.

But by digging deeply for her very limited supply of patience, the young staff reporter (!) managed to extract the essential plotlines:

1) Ms. Harbison insisted that Mr. Harbison (their first names didn't exist in this shadowy world) was a selfish individual who had taken no interest in their daughter—or in anything other than himself for that matter—for the first six years of Brandi's life. When it became clear that Ms. Harbison was preparing to leave the marriage, Mr. Harbison swung to the other extreme and wanted to be with their daughter all the time, striving to convince the girl that her mother was the reason her cherished home life was blowing apart. His only reason for pursuing court-ordered time with Brandi was to punish Ms. Harbison for having left him, and to see if he could work his way up to joint custody and thereby get out of paying child support. He never met with any of Brandi's teachers, didn't come to medical appointments, was always too busy to help his daughter with homework or changing a bike tire. Brandi frequently begged her mother to reduce her visitation time at Dad's house.

2) Mr. Harbison, on the other hand, described how badly he'd wanted to be a father and how ecstatic he was when their daughter was born. But Ms. Harbison had been controlling from the outset, convinced that he was going to kill their child by giving her spoiled milk or dropping her on her head. She would block him from parenting, then criticize him for not helping more. Ms. Harbison was paranoid, constantly convinced that nefarious people wanted to harm her and Brandi. Mr. Harbison got along well with school teachers, parents of Brandi's friends, and soccer coaches, unlike Ms. Harbison who was always in conflict with everyone. Brandi frequently expressed reluctance to go back to her mother's house after her time with Dad and complained about Mom's many boyfriends.

Carrie began asking questions about the pieces she hadn't understood, Kelly at first giving his usual clipped, impatient answers. But before long details were pouring out of him with color and flavor.

And emotion; she was startled to realize that this brute who so annoyed her was *crying*. Not loudly, no sobs, but two or three thin streams that ran steadily down his cheeks.

There was no end to the surprises.

That had all been the previous day. This morning Kelly called her yelling furiously that she had humiliated him by describing his tears in her article. "You reporters just want a sensational story for your career! You stripped me naked in public!"

Carrie held the phone several inches from her ear and nervously popped her gum. "That's the whole point, Mr. Harbison, the human element. I want people to know you have a heart."

"Up yours, Green," he spat back. "I'm not interested in being your display." And he disconnected.

But three hours later Carrie was the first person Kelly called with big news: he'd just heard from Brandi again.

~

Officer Mason was working front booth when the phone rang. Her screen showed that the caller was Kelly Harbison. "East Liverpool Police," she said, bracing herself.

Harbison's volume was reduced a little from his previous calls to the station, but the words came rapid-fire and his emotion was boiling. "Brandi just called me! You've got to *believe* me this time and get someone out there fast. She used a different number this time, obviously her old phone got taken away." And he spat the number out much faster than Mason could record it, she had to make Harbison repeat it two more times to get it down correctly.

The department swung into action—not that they'd failed to the time before.

The cell phone number belonged to a burner phone from T-Mobile on their "PayGo" service. The purchase was tracked to a Target in Cambridge, Ohio. But the buyer had paid cash for the phone and thirty days of service, so no identifying information was available. Ten minutes later they were given the phone's location, GPS coordinates in Athens, Ohio.

Athens police responded quickly, seeing the name Harbison on their alert list, as did the Ohio State Highway Patrol.

The GPS coordinates led them east of town to Pushcoat Lane, then through fields, across a stream, and into the woods. At some point they crossed the boundary into Strouds Run State Park. They had walked more than a mile from their vehicles by the time they started to approach the location, at which point they slowed, spread out, and moved cautiously, weapons at the ready.

Their path led them down into a hollow, where the trees thinned and a number of large boulders were scattered. When they were about two-hundred feet from the lowest point in the gorge, they saw that three huge boulders were piled on top of each other to form a small enclosed, cave-like area. From their position they couldn't discern whether they were seeing the only way in and out of that den or if a person could crawl out through another passageway.

The officers drew a wide circle, checking for hidden people while moving closer as safely as possible. Cell tower triangulation doesn't offer precision, only marking a spot within roughly three-quarters of a mile in such hilly, broken terrain. Approaching the cave would be highly dangerous unless they could find some fissure in the back that would allow them to see inside; to move close enough to see inside from the front would expose them to weapons fire at close range.

Two officers, trying not to make a sound and ready to hit the ground if they heard anything, painstakingly circled behind the pile of boulders. They found no alternate entrance and no view into the depths. The opening in front could open into a den that was four feet deep or fourteen feet deep; there was no telling from the back side.

Next police called loudly, eventually using a bullhorn though it seemed unnecessary; the boulder pile couldn't create an enclosure deep enough to be out of earshot. Repeated attempts over a ten-minute period elicited no response.

The team leader then said loudly, "Regroup! The area is clear, no one's in there!" and they all walked twenty or feet further away, heavy boots crunching loudly in the leaves as though they were leaving. They then crouched in position and waited silently. Twenty minutes passed and no one emerged from the cave.

Their commander declared they couldn't afford to wait any longer; if something happened to Brandi they'd all be wearing the guilt for the rest of their careers. So three of the most crisis-trained members of the group gingerly approached the mouth of the cave, rifles raised. From a safer distance, other team members shined flood lights toward the opening. No one was visible in the twelve or so square feet of enclosure they succeeded in illuminating. There was no choice but to enter, which would involve creeping close up and then stepping downwards into the small hole where the cave began.

The three stepped toward the mouth of the cave. Simultaneously, deafening reports exploded and bullets were flying everywhere.

All officers, whether close up or distant, hit the ground. The crew fired their weapons but deliberately off-target to avoid killing any hostages, mostly notably Brandi herself. In the terror and surprise of the moment, however, a few hurried shots did enter the cave or hit near the mouth and bullets were ricocheting wildly.

The shooting stopped. For some time nobody moved. Then they slowly risked rising to see if there were injured.

There were. Two of the three advancing officers had taken bullets and two other officers farther back from the cave mouth had also been shot. The third member of the lead trio had been perched right at the lip of the depression in the forest floor when the shooting erupted and thus had pitched forward into the cave.

As they were attempting to assess the seriousness of the injuries to their personnel, simultaneously listening anxiously for a new round of shots to explode, the officer who had fallen into the cave stumbled back up and out, holding his head. He dazedly examined himself to see if he'd been shot.

Then he yelled out, "There's no one in there! The cave is empty!"

Personnel scattered in every direction.

One of the injured kept saying "in the back, in the back," as if he had seen people, but the only "back" he could be referring to was behind the boulder pile and that area had already been cleared.

Then the person assisting him realized that he meant he'd been shot in the back. The gunfire hadn't been coming from the cave. It had come from behind them.

They'd been led into a trap.

The commander called frantically for reinforcements, medical personnel, and a helicopter search. They had no guess how many shooters there were, and only a general idea where the shots had come from, behind them and to their left judging by the positions the downed officers were in when they took fire.

The two advancing officers who'd gone down didn't show life-threatening injuries. Their flak jackets were pulled off of them; one of them had a bullet penetrating his shoulder but not deeply, and the other one had taken two bullets but they had both stuck in her jacket, likely cracking ribs but apparently nothing worse. Another officer had been shot in the leg and was in pain but insisted he was not in danger.

Their fourth casualty was a state trooper, the one who'd been shot in the back. He was an undeniable emergency. He'd stopped responding to questions, was not moving, and was bleeding profusely. While they were hoping a helicopter would get a bead on the assailants, it wouldn't be worth squat as a rescue vehicle in these dense woods. They would have to attend to the trooper themselves until a rescue crew could arrive with a litter.

~

Wisneski, Ledbetter, and Kresge drove screeching up to the Jeep dealership where Kelly Harbison was manager. The salespeople said he wasn't there, that he was constantly in and out since his kid and her mom had disappeared. He would almost certainly be home.

Wisneski said sternly, "You are not to tell him we're on the way, that would scare the shit out of him that something bad has happened to Brandi, which isn't true. Any call to him will be considered interfering with the police. Is that clear?"

The employees didn't care, whatever; it wasn't like they adored their warm fuzzy manager.

~

The real reason for Wisneski's order of silence was that the officers wanted to observe Harbison's reaction when they gave him the news. They raced to get to him before he heard of the events from another source.

Harbison's car was in his driveway. The officers approached the house quickly but warily; the events in Athens sounded so bizarre that they feared what might be waiting for them here. Peering in the windows they could see Harbison at his desk, keeping an eye on his computer to his left while scrolling his phone to his right, electronics in stereo. He looked agitated, but he always looked agitated. No one else appeared to be in the house.

He appeared rapidly and angrily at the door in response to their knock, then drew back in surprise when he saw who it was. "Oh my God," he cried, "Brandi! What? What?"

"No," Wisneski said quickly, hands up as if to keep Harbison from falling over, "there's no bad news about Brandi. But we have to talk. Can we come in?"

"Yeah, yeah," he said, breathing loudly, and he turned toward the living room, which they took as a cue to march through the door and follow him. "You didn't find her?"

"No," Wisneski said. "Personnel went to the location, but she wasn't there."

Harbison scowled and looked at the floor.

Wisneski went on. "Mr. Harbison, the phone's location was a trap. Our people were lured into a forest depression so that a sniper could fire on them from higher ground. Four law enforcement officers are down, one of them in critical condition."

Kelly jerked his head up, his face distorted as if in a cubist painting, eyes pointing in one direction, nose aimed off in the other, his skin suddenly gray, his lips red and protruding like a camel's. He appeared possessed. He burst out of his seat, turned away and, launching a sliding glass door out of the way with a violence that nearly shattered it, erupted into his back yard and began throwing whatever he could find, a barbecue grill which he knocked over, cinder blocks he threw against the side of the house, then a metal trash can that he torpedoed against one of the back windows, sending splintered glass spraying like a fountain. The bin bounced back and almost hit him.

The shattering window appeared to bring Harbison a cathartic climax. He took several agitated paces further but attacked no more objects. Then he walked over and sat down on the porch steps, pounding his right fist into his left hand slowly, methodically, the full violence of his rage having passed.

Ledbetter reached for her radio and reported a mental health emergency, triggering the mobilization of a crisis team.

After a couple of minutes of Harbison remaining more or less stable, Wisneski stepped out onto the deck and asked him to come back inside. He waited another minute, because even now he (of course) had to show them they couldn't push him around. Then he entered with his head down and resumed the stuffed chair he'd occupied briefly before.

The officers pulled up chairs forming a semi-circle in front of him, leaning in, alert.

"What can you tell us about what happened in Athens today, Mr. Harbison?" Ledbetter asked, her tone clinical, as if inviting him to unburden himself.

"What can *I* tell *you?*" Harbison replied incredulously, as if the detective wanted him to explain how to breed moose. "*You* explain this to *me!* All I know is my daughter's gonna be dead soon, if he hasn't already killed her."

"Who would that be, Mr. Harbison?"

"What's the hell's the matter with you? One of Lauren's boyfriends, obviously! She goes through men by the dozen. And she picks some real doozies."

You can say that again, Kresge was thinking.

"It wasn't Lauren firing at your people, come on! She couldn't shoot, she's never touched a gun in her life."

"Mr. Harbison, I know you've had a bitter divorce, but at this point we have to consider the possibility that your wife didn't run, that both she and Brandi may have been kidnapped. Can you think of anyone who might want to harm them? Or harm you by harming your daughter?"

"That's total bullshit," Harbison said acidly. "Don't give me that shit! You know perfectly well Lauren took off on purpose. And anyone else would ask for ransom!"

"I know how much you love your daughter," Wisneski replied, her hard tone not matching her words, while moving her face subtly closer to his to signal that she wasn't intimidated. "So give some thought to what I'm asking. A parent who cares as much as you do doesn't want to leave any stoned unturned."

Wisneski stood abruptly, motioned Ledbetter and Kresge toward the door, and shepherded them quickly out. She wanted to leave her last words ringing in his ears.

"In other words, the police are gonna keep wasting time instead of catching Lauren and her latest man!" he called down the walkway, always sure to have the last word.

~

On the return drive, Ledbetter said, "If he was faking it, that's the best performance since Leonardo DiCaprio played that retarded kid."

"Yeah, except all Harbison has to do is act naturally," grumbled Kresge.

"And sacrifice a window." Ledbetter was driving, she didn't take her eyes off the road.

Wisneski cast the tiebreaker. "That man's rage was real. My eyes were glued to his when we first gave him the news, and a shock wave went through his body like a tsunami hitting the beach. Too hard to act out."

Kresge gave a hint of a nod, reluctantly conceding the point.

"Besides," she went on, "what would be in it for him to set that trap? If he's got something to hide, that sure wouldn't be the way to hide it. The law's gonna be paying a hundred times more attention to this case now."

Kresge said, "Shit, if you were trying to share a kid with that crazy asshole, wouldn't you run away?"

"Shane, he just learned his daughter's in the hands of a killer. You so sure you wouldn't put something through a window if that happened to you?"

~

Gavin was alert for opportunities to slip out of work early. Today looked good; he'd worked three hours late on Monday evening following up on the story of a high school football player who'd suffered a serious concussion during preseason practices. Six days later the injured kickoff returner, seventeen years old and 210 pounds, could still be seen in the halls walking a little off true and stuttering, neither of which he'd done before. The result was a raging debate in the community over whether three or five was the correct number of times to let this happen to kids.

Around three o'clock he went to his editor's office and asked if he could leave, since he was owed time. And though she was opposed in principle to anything Gavin was in favor of, she growled, "Okay," and kept her eyes on her screen.

He found Carrie's number in his phone and punched it. "Hey, I'm free soon," he said when she picked up. "How's tonight as a time for me to make the drive out to Ohio?"

"Go for it," she said. "Should be a great evening. I won't be there, though."

"What? Where are you going?"

"Athens. Not as in Greece. Turns out we've got one in Ohio."

She proceeded to spill out the latest dramas. The upshot of it all was that her paper was putting her up in a hotel tonight. She'd drive back home mid-day tomorrow assuming she managed to get a couple of good interviews and that nothing new blew up.

Well, then could he come see her tomorrow night instead?

"No, Gavin, I can hardly focus as it is. I don't know whose life I'm living, it's definitely not mine."

He didn't give up. "What if we call it a working date? I've been doing a little research for you, and you might be surprised by some of what I learned." He explained that he'd seized on a detail from Carrie's *Repository* article: Kelly Harbison's belief that an underground network was involved in his ex-wife's flight. "Turns out he's not crazy to think so."

Carrie took a loud breath. "Okay, what the hell. I don't know what time I can get out of here tomorrow, I'll text you."

Gavin felt the giddiness start up again in his midriff. The pull he felt toward her, mysterious though it was, showed no sign of letting up.

~

Kresge, Mason, and the two detectives gathered around a little excuse for a conference table in one of the meeting rooms and listened to the recording of Brandi's call that they'd copied from Harbison's phone. It was mostly noise, she couldn't have had much service, unsurprising since she'd placed the call in the middle of a state park.

"Or was forced to make the call, more like," Ledbetter pointed out.

Only occasional words or phrases were audible. "Hello there … Can you believe… No way… Jesus…"

Harbison could be heard asking Brandi if she could hear him and where she was and whether she was okay. She presumably heard at least fragments of what her father was saying or she wouldn't have kept talking—unless her captor was ordering her to do so, perhaps whispering to her exactly what to say.

"Audio experts will analyze the recording," Wisneski said. "They may be able to pick up clues to what was happening in the background."

After the other three returned to their duties, Kresge sat listening to the recording play through a dozen more times. He kept feeling on the verge of capturing some message that Brandi's voice was trying to get across.

~

Over the previous three days, Sofia had disciplined herself to open the Protonmail account only when the children were asleep or at school or outdoors, to keep them from getting stressed and mystified by her reactions to Lauren's messages. So it was close to ten o'clock on Tuesday night before the coast was clear for her to enter her little study and punch in the dual passwords to her encrypted email. By that time many hours had passed since her last opportunity to check it.

There in her inbox was a message from the mystery address, the first to arrive since Friday night:

> Sofia:
> Things have taken a turn for the worse. Today was not good. I
> need money, it's an emergency. Could you get me $500? I hate to
> ask you, but you're the one who gets how serious this all is.   L.

Instructions followed for how to transfer money to her online in a way that wouldn't be traceable, a mysterious set of steps that involved going to Western Union with cash, then downloading a VPN (she had no idea what that was) and buying BitCoin for Lauren.

Keeping secrets was one thing. Sending money through the dark web to a—could she bear to say it?—kidnapper was another matter altogether. But she knew too much about what Lauren and Brandi had been through before they fled; not doing whatever her friend needed was out of the question. She looked desperately around the study as if hoping to wake from a grisly dream.

CHAPTER 10

A search team with dogs scoured the relevant portions of Strouds Run State Park on Tuesday afternoon. They followed a scent that went in and out of streams, eating up time as the dogs kept losing and regaining the trail. Hours had passed when the team reached Strouds Run Road, where the scent vanished altogether. The shooter had either stashed a car there or met a getaway driver.

That evening's local news shows offered a precise description of where a vehicle would most likely have been parked, and some two dozen callers reported having seen a blue sedan there, some said specifically a Ford Fusion. It was one of the most common makes in the state.

Carrie spent Wednesday morning interviewing the residents of Pushcoat Lane, who spoke colorfully about watching the dogged march of armed officers heading into the woods the day before, the rapid claps of gun fire a half hour later, a dozen shots or more, then the removal of the severely wounded officer. She got enough to fill the whole front page. In the early afternoon she collected whatever recent details she could drag out of the media spokesperson for the Athens police. Then, since she had no idea how to start unearthing the connection between the Harbisons and this part of the state, she undertook the three-hour drive back to Morriston.

She hadn't had this much fun in as long as she could remember. A list formed in her mind of all the pinheads, doomsayers, and bullies in Middle

Beaver whose noses she couldn't wait to rub in the news of what her life had become. *Eat your hearts out, you assholes.*

~

When Carrie was passing through the center of Morriston, less than a half hour left in her long drive home, she perceived what seemed to be a fight or an accident ahead on the left. Upon closer examination it turned out to be a protest, a dozen or so men and a couple of women walking in a slow-moving oval, carrying signs and yelling chants. Morriston was not a land of peaceniks, nor was any part of Columbiana County for that matter; it would take a major war to turn out this many resisters. Carrie wondered what she'd missed by not listening to the news on her car radio.

She pulled to the side of the road to check it out, developing a reporter's nose for a story wafting in the wind. She hoped it involved corruption.

The marchers' placards rang out with, "The best parent is both parents!" and, "Dads matter!" Two of the protesters carried posters pasted with blown-up photographs, and as Carrie climbed out of her car and walked closer she saw that the face portrayed was Kelly Harbison, of all people. Were the employees of his car dealership picketing him for some reason?

A man spoke through a megaphone, looping back over a set of themes like one of those endless videos in a museum that allow you to arrive any time without missing anything: Mothers win ninety-five percent of custody battles. Fathers are barred from seeing their kids if the mom says anything about abuse, even if there's no evidence and he's a great dad. Fathers are just seen as cash registers to provide child support and otherwise are told to get lost. It's time for kids to be divided fifty-fifty in divorces.

Periodically the man declared loudly, "We need Fathers' Rights!" which the crowd would echo back to him and was the turnaround tagline as the loop restarted.

Carrie's curiosity was piqued. These guys looked nothing like the young, messy, colorful marching and chanting demonstrators she'd watched on national news shows. And it appeared that they'd adopted Kelly Harbison's plight as their cause.

~

Carrie and Gavin sat in a crowded Italian restaurant in Morriston where no one would pay any attention to their conversation. A noisy bar would have been even better if only Carrie had reached the legal drinking age.

"The thing that Harbison said about an underground network ferrying his wife and daughter along—turns out it isn't that far-fetched. In fact, there are individuals and even organizations that are open about the fact that they help parents run with their kids."

Carrie scrunched her face up. "They don't jail you for helping kidnappers?"

"You'd think. But here's what happens. First off, parents are rarely prosecuted for running with their kids. They mostly give up in a few days or weeks and return the children to the other parent."

"And that parent doesn't file charges?"

Gavin shook his head. "There can't be a prosecution unless the kids testify, and what parent wants to put their kids through that? Plus what kid wants their mother or father to go to jail? So if the kids aren't harmed district attorneys don't push it."

"So the parent totally gets away with it."

"Well, not exactly. The usual punishment is that the family court gives full custody to the other parent, and it's a long time before the one that ran even gets to have visits with the kids. That's considered enough of a disincentive in most cases."

Carrie, incredulous, proceeded to burn her mouth with too large a slug of coffee, which came spitting out onto the table. "Fuck, they set their coffee machine to 'Firebomb.'" She got a server's attention and asked for an emergency cup of ice water so she could suck on ice cubes. Her tongue felt like it was already swelling and blistering.

Gavin paused two seconds, maybe three, to demonstrate his compassion and kindness, then dove back in. "And here's the key thing for the underground: you can't prosecute someone for abetting a crime if you don't prosecute the criminal."

"Ah," said Carrie, getting it now. She continued icing her painful mouth. "So what's in it for these undergrounds to help kidnappers?"

"They say they're helping parents get kids out of horrible cases of abuse, where the family courts have refused to protect the child. Usually mothers running when the kid has an abusive dad."

"These networks check the parent's story out?"

Gavin drummed his fingers on the table. "In the articles I read, they claim they investigate cases carefully. But then you have the other parent saying, 'I was totally innocent, this underground was a bunch of reckless zealots, with the slightest effort they would have seen my ex-wife was lying about everything.'"

Carrie's heartbeat accelerated pleasantly; the story was taking on even more exciting dimensions, distracting her from her inflamed tongue. "You're a first-rate research assistant," she said. "Want to come work for me?"

Gavin gave his signature smirk. "So, they not only made you a staff reporter but reworked the budget so you can hire a team?"

"They gave into every one of my demands," she said. "Just wait 'til you see my new vehicle."

When they'd finished dinner they strolled back out to the street. Gavin squinted, then pointed out that Carrie's new vehicle bore a striking similarity to a fifteen-year-old Dodge Charger with a mounting rust problem and a bit of a list.

"Well," she said, digging in her bag, "you have to look at it through these special glasses. It's a Beemer when viewed correctly."

~

Twenty minutes later they were still standing talking on the sidewalk. The question of what would come next started to hang in the air.

Carrie finally addressed it directly. "You remember I live with my parents, right?"

"Yeah," he said regretfully.

"After the eighth of November I won't need my sister to buy beer anymore, and I can get my own place. Hey, I've got a real job now, I could actually do it." The thought had just struck her, emerging from the swirl of recent events.

Gavin wasn't sure what to say. He didn't feel at all ready to say good night and head back to Edgeworth Falls, but he also got why Carrie wasn't going to bring a guy home to her parents on the first date. If it even was a date; so far it had been all business.

He groped for something. "Can I come see you on the weekend? Are you around?"

She laughed, not at him. "I don't know where I'll be tomorrow morning, much less three or four days from now. I feel deranged."

Gavin said nothing, though there were words wanting to come out. Carrie picked up on the awkwardness. "Hey, sure," she said. "We can talk about something besides kidnappers and methheads next time."

Her dose of encouragement was enough to unlock Gavin's brain. It was a warm summer night, it hadn't even gotten fully dark yet. "Any place around here to go for a dip?"

"Uh, people don't have pools where I grew up, sir."

"No, like a swimming hole or a pond or something."

Carrie's face lit up and she punched him in the arm, not exactly what he was hoping for though not the worst thing either. "Fuck, yeah," she said, "I know a place we could go." She turned around and started walking. "It's a ways, but not too bad. Where's your car?"

He had apparently just been appointed driver.

"You got a flashlight?" she asked.

"No, the light on my phone is fine for walking in the dark."

"Where we're going, mister, we don't want to run out of battery, we'd be groping our way home on hands and knees." She popped over to her car and returned properly prepared for nighttime forests.

~

Annika Ledbetter sat at the kitchen table in the comfortable and modern home of Annabelle and Kaleel Marshall. Joining her nervously at the table was their nine-year-old daughter Aisha, who had just finished dinner. The parents sat on stools at their dark-blue formica peninsula, trying to fade into the background while nonetheless listening for every nuance.

The detective began with a set patter. "You understand that you're not in any trouble and Brandi hasn't done anything wrong, so you don't have to worry about anything you tell me. This is just to help us get ideas about what might have happened to them."

"Okay," Aisha said, uncertain.

Ledbetter could see little tremors. "Take a couple of deep breaths for me," she said, consciously producing a big smile, not part of her normal repertoire. "This isn't gonna be any big deal."

"Brandi never said anything about leaving. If she had I would've told somebody."

"Sure. But what you and I are going to look for is things that aren't obvious. Sometimes people tell me the most silly-seeming details and they end up breaking a case for us." Ledbetter led the girl forward, striking a light tone.

Aisha and Brandi had known each other throughout primary school, but became friends during the summer between third and fourth grades and started to hang out a lot. Both girls were a little rough-and-tumble, liking to wrestle, play soccer, go to the town pool. Neither was big into Instagram or video games, and preferred to head outdoors.

Brandi's head was full of intrigue: secret weapons, betrayals, magical powers, time travel. But her playful, fantasy side was mixed with a heady tendency to ignore rules set by adults, especially when they were out of sight. "My parents weren't always so psyched about us being friends, they thought Brandi was kind of a troublemaker."

The two girls ended up glued at the hip for the first half of fourth grade. But Brandi was changing. "She started to get bossy, worse and worse, it was bugging me. And now it's gotten, like, she's kind of mean some days, she'll start saying I'm stupid or calling me short, things like that. A couple months ago she said... well, something racist. I didn't tell my parents about that one, they wouldn't have let her come over anymore."

Her parents stirred, but said nothing.

"So you've had a falling out?"

Aisha gave a distinct shake of her head. "No, Brandi's still my friend. We're good. I just wish she'd be more like she was before. And..."

"What?"

"No other kids will hear what I told you?"

Ledbetter held up her hand as if swearing an oath. "You have my word."

"Brandi's really smart, you know, so this is weird, but she started to cheat on stuff. I don't agree with doing that."

"Cheat? In fourth grade? Like how?"

"Like math quizzes, she'll look at what other kids are writing, but she's good at it, the teachers don't see. Or say we're supposed to make up a story and write it, she'll take an idea from a book or steal an idea from another kid and say she thought it up herself. Oh, yeah, that's another thing... Last winter she started to take kids' stuff sometimes. I caught her with my gloves last winter, which I thought I lost..."

Ledbetter asked whether Brandi's moods seemed to vary with which parent she was staying with at the time. Aisha had to ponder that one. "Not sure. She says her mom is way strict, at her dad's house she can pretty much do what she wants and eat what she wants, he doesn't bug her about stuff. He lets her watch, like, movies that no way my parents would let me watch. He sounds pretty cool."

"Do you hang out with her at her dad's house sometimes?"

"No. She says her dad complains about how few days they get together, so he doesn't like her to have friends over, like, 'This is our time.' I've been over there maybe twice."

"You like Brandi's mom?"

"Yeah, she's pretty cool. She makes these warm sandwiches that are great, she puts this awesome dressing on them that they should use at D'Angelos. She is kind of strict, though, as bad as my parents, maybe even worse. She's nice, though."

Nothing stood out for Aisha regarding the last few weeks before Brandi disappeared: she hadn't seemed unusually tense or secretive, she hadn't looked bad or anything. And Aisha insisted that she still liked Brandi when her friend was in a good mood; those times just came less and less often.

Ledbetter was left pondering Aisha's portrayal of Brandi's growing volatility over the past year.

~

After they'd traveled some twenty-five minutes and taken a convoluted series of turns, Carrie pointed Gavin down a dirt road. He'd only driven another minute when they reached a locked gate. "From here we walk," Carrie said, and hopped out of the car.

The moon was due to be bright that night but was just coming up and the woods were dark. The dirt road continued beyond the gate, soon becoming deeply rutted and full of large rocks; they had to stay aware of where they stepped and would have sprained an ankle or smashed a tailbone without a light. The road dwindled to a path after a few minutes and they passed four forks where choices of direction had to be made. There were no signs, but Carrie turned confidently each time, on familiar ground.

"How do people find their way out here?" Gavin wondered.

"Unless you have someone bring you who's been here, your chances aren't too good. Kids get way lost out here trying to meet up with friends to swim, especially at night."

The breeze was sleepy but so were the mosquitoes, and the worst of the summer humidity had broken a week earlier; the air felt cozy around them but not sticky. A slight lightening of the sky called to them and they came out into a clearing with a pond, the water so black you could walk across it.

"Popular summer spot?" Gavin asked.

"For sure. No way to haul a keg out here, though. I know 'cause we tried."

When they had walked within a few feet of the water's edge, Carrie turned and moved just a few feet away and went straight to pulling off items of clothing, first shirt, then pants, then bra, then underwear, without hesitation. She had her back to Gavin and in the dark he saw only her form, but his blood rushed and his head went light.

She walked into the pond and was instantly up to her waist in water, then turned around to him with her arms across her chest. "Are you just gonna stand there? I didn't bring you here to lifeguard." And she turned and dove under the black water.

Gavin came out of his trance, stripped, and dove in after her. They swam out into the middle of the pond, which turned out to be larger than he'd made out from the dark edge, it had long arms to the left and right that curved forward around the trees like dragonfly wings. In a couple of hours this hollow would be shimmering magically in the moonlight. Behind the sound of their swim strokes ran a backing track of crickets, peepers, and cicadas.

When they'd waded back through the shallows and walked up on the shore, Gavin expected Carrie to slip on her clothes as smoothly as she'd escaped them. But instead she stood half facing him, shaking water off of her arms and legs and hair, showing no hurry to cover up. "Until a couple of weeks ago I had a towel in my car all summer," she said, "but I needed to take it in the house to wash it, it was filthy, and then I forgot about it." Even in the dark Gavin could make out her adorable small round breasts jiggling lightly as she danced the drops off of herself.

When she had shed as much water as she could, she casually put her clothes back on, not even turning her back, as if out with one of her sisters. Gavin, divided between reluctance and relief—he'd felt that at any moment his body would have a visible and embarrassing reaction to how attracted he felt to her—pulled on his pants, which were tighter now. They sat for a while on a wide flat rock that looked out across the dark pond, seeing the occasional bat but otherwise no movement. He took Carrie's hand and braced himself for her to pull it away, but she didn't.

She did go back to talking about work stuff, though. "Kelly Harbison started crying the last time I met with him," she said. "I can't figure the guy out."

"He wants you to feel sorry for him. Pull the young girl's heart strings."

Carrie shook her head. "He was ashamed of crying and tried to fight it off. Not like in school plays where people's eyes get all red and they rub them or whatever, he had real tears running down his cheeks in little streams."

Gavin wasn't buying it. "I doubt he's so innocent. His wife and daughter didn't take off for no reason."

"What if there was a reason, and it was revenge? Even if he's kind of an asshole, this is his kid we're talking about, he doesn't know if he's ever gonna see her again. It's not like he's a monster, he's got no record, the cops didn't even know who he was before this."

Gavin continued to shake his head.

She stood and brushed dirt off her butt. "Let's head back. God only knows what's gonna happen tomorrow."

The moment had slipped away, Gavin didn't know why.

As Carrie turned the flashlight back on and they started back into the woods, he asked her, "The case is getting to you?"

"Um, ya think?" she replied, impatient. "Ten-year-old kid, the war between her parents isn't her fault. And she's obviously trying to escape from her mom, she called Dad for help. And now, to top it all off, it turns out they're with a man who's crazy violent."

"But this is the kind of shit reporters have to deal with all the time. Reporters and cops, that's what we have in common, the nastier side of life. This is reality."

Carrie stopped walking, turning pointedly toward him and dropping back on one foot. Her eyes narrowed. "Did you come down to Ohio to explain life to me, on a church mission or something? I'm not an idiot, you know."

Gavin's stomach sank, he scrambled, not sure what he'd said wrong. "I don't think you're an idiot, not at all."

"So don't lecture me. You don't exactly work for the *Chicago Tribune* yourself." She turned and they strode on, the silence awkward. He flashed to how she'd walked off angrily after Saturday's conference lunch; he seemed to have a knack for setting her off.

But then, to confuse him completely, she took his hand. He gazed foggily down at their interlaced fingers. She continued next to him, and they started to talk about nothing in particular, just being together in the night. As they got closer to the gate where they'd had to leave Gavin's car behind, the moon emerged from behind a small cloud and cast them in a milky glow.

Midnight was fast approaching by the time they stood by their cars in the center of Morriston, preparing to say good night. No one else was out on the streets. He took Carrie's hand as she was pulling her keys out of her pocket, and she leaned in and kissed him warmly on the mouth. "I'm not a little kid, okay?" she said.

He nodded, pretending to get it though he didn't. What he knew was that he was flooded with feelings for her.

~

The Fathers' Rights rally was covered on the local news at 11:00. The NBC affiliate in Canton also managed to get Kelly Harbison on camera at his home. This was a small miracle because, despite the lengths Kelly went to each day to make himself the center of attention, he had until now angrily side-stepped television reporters. But that afternoon he'd stood on his walkway as the TV-5 talent, microphone in hand and every hair on her head in place, asked him crisply to share his reaction to the rally carried out in support of him that day.

"What happened to me would never have taken place if the custody courts took fathers seriously," he said. "My daughter would still be here, safe."

The reporter asked Harbison if he was connected to the Alliance for Child Rights, the organization that put on the picket. "No," he said, "I'm not a joiner. And these kinds of groups can get a little extreme. I just want my girl back home."

This version of Kelly had none of the bluster and brimstone Carrie expected from him. The pressure of being on camera must have softened his cutting edge.

CHAPTER 11

As Detective Wisneski entered the East Liverpool station, she was greeted by Officer Mason in the hallway. "You need to read Carrie Green's latest work of literature," Mason said. Wisneski rolled her eyes but headed straight to her desk and opened her laptop.

The story had gone up on the *Chronicle* website a little after 11:00 the night before and was now on the front page of the morning's print edition. Green wrote that the police had found Brandi's phone call on Tuesday largely inaudible. The article also revealed that the police had begun interviewing children who might have insight into Brandi's state of mind prior to the disappearance.

Neither of these facts had been released to the media by the police.

Wisneski put out an alarm and convened her investigative team (making Kresge drag his butt out of bed and drive erratically down to the station, hoping he'd remembered to put on a belt). Chief Tobias postponed his meeting with the union steward. Martinez was the only one missing; the sergeant was in an important meeting with a toxicology expert at the college.

"Carrie Green's got a mole in the department," Wisneski began. "I was concerned last week when she reported that unreleased information about the footprints, but I hoped it was just careless station gossip that got out to the public. This time, though, there's so much detail that someone has to be passing it to her on purpose. We have to close some gaps. In the mean time, can we take action against her?"

Tobias shook his head. "There's no way to stop a journalist from writing anything except national security secrets. Talking to an irresponsible source is entirely legal."

"Any chance she's got someone hacking our computer system?"

The chief continued doubtful. "We have some of the best computer security in the country."

Mason rubbed a palm against her jaw. "Jesus, Green is just some junior college kid, how does she manage to be such a pain in the ass?"

Ledbetter had a brief report. "I dug into her background a little bit to find a connection to our department, but no luck. I did learn that she was a troublemaker as a teen, so she's continuing with that."

"What kind of trouble?"

"She was in court once on possession of weed and once for Minor in Possession of Alcohol, and twice for beating other kids up pretty bad."

"Fights over boys?" Martinez asked.

"The kid she did the most damage to *was* a boy. He wasn't a major bully, but not a pushover either. She broke the guy's arm."

"Jesus, how does she end up being a news reporter?"

Tobias thought for a moment and then laid out a plan. "Two steps. One, all discussion of the case is team-members-only from now on, except for the Media Relations Officer. Second, I'll have the tech people create a closed realm on the computer system for the team, no one else sees emails between us, interview notes, photos, nothing. We've done this with sensitive matters in the past."

Wisneski asked if the MRO himself could be the leak. Tobias said no way. "Gregorius has been in that position for eight years. He's never messed up once."

~

Kelly fought with Carrie daily over the questions she asked and the requests she made for inside information. But the spats always ended the same way—with him telling her what she wanted to know. He seemed to just need a battle first, a sense of power. Or was it that he craved Carrie's company, wanted to drag out his time with her?

He looked worse with each passing day. By yesterday the bags under his eyes had been bulging, his hair sticking out in various directions, his clothes gathering wrinkles. He showed signs of losing weight and his skin was pallid. "I don't know how much longer I can go not knowing what's happened to her. This is killing me." He sat hunched in his chair.

"To Brandi?"

He looked right up. "Of course to Brandi! I don't give a shit what happens to her mother, she should rot in hell for this!" Waving his arms around, and blood rushing to his face, he looked a little less death-like.

Harbison gradually allowed what he knew to trickle out to Carrie: the police had been stepping up the pressure on friends of Lauren's to talk, especially a woman named Delta Evans. He'd even gotten an address and phone number for Evans from his mysterious window into the department, and he shared those with Carrie.

He also knew that police had interviewed a child the night before, though he didn't have a name. Carrie's curiosity surged.

On Thursday morning she tried to reach Delta Evans by phone, without success. So she drove to her house in Columbiana, on the route to Youngstown, and found her home. Evans scowled when Carrie said she was a reporter but invited her in politely, sat her down in a comfortable armchair in the somewhat chaotic living room, and offered her coffee.

The woman was, unsurprisingly, insistent to know how Carrie had learned her name and address. She replied, "At the paper we're always monitoring a police scanner, that's how we find out about breaking news." This was true, though it had nothing to do with how she'd come to be in Evans' living room. "I understand you're a close friend of Lauren Harbison's. What's your take on what happened?"

Evans squinted. "I already talked about this with the police, I don't know anything useful. They're blaming Lauren but I don't believe she ran, she gave no hint she was considering that."

"But she pretty much hated her ex-husband, right?"

"Listen, girl," Evans said, not sounding particularly unfriendly despite her words, "I've got a family, I work in academia, I have responsibilities. Whatever poison Lauren's gotten herself into, I can't have it spraying around me."

"That's fine, I won't use your name or anything else that shows who you are."

Evans emitted a hard-edged laugh that managed to be both derisive and good-natured. She studied the girl for a few moments, looking her up and down like one of those color consultants. "How long you been a reporter?" she finally asked.

"Long time," Carrie answered. "All the way back to Monday."

Evans snorted. "And they've got you covering this disappearance?"

"Yeah, well, no one else was available."

That was a good one.

But, to Carrie's surprise, the fact that she was so new worked in her favor rather than against her in Evans' eyes. The woman dropped her guard, as if there'd been a sheet on a line between them and a gust of wind had raced by and vacuumed it away.

"All right, as long as my name goes nowhere."

A bell rang in Carrie's head. "It won't be in the paper. But I do have to tell my editor if he wants to know."

"How long's he been in the business?"

"The editors at the *Chronicle* were pretty much born at their desks. Looks like they're planning to die there, too."

Evans gave a hint of a smile, then her face went grave. "Lauren's been in a tough situation, and she's hardly told anyone. Kelly was scary as hell when they were married. His face would turn red and swell up like it had its own air pump, he'd yell so loud Lauren thought she'd go deaf, threatening, 'You keep effing with me you're gonna be sorry!' And he's a big guy."

"You knew her back then?"

"No, I met her in a Zumba class, they were divorcing by then. The class was stress-management for her."

"So you never saw stuff like what you're describing?"

"No. Good thing I didn't, I would've put my fists into that man, probably got myself killed."

"He hit her?"

"Not that she ever said."

Carrie picked up on a shift in Delta's tone, the edge was gone from the matter-of-fact way she'd been dropping words onto the table. "You think there was more," she said.

"No, I think she was truthful about the past. But sometimes her voice drifted off a little and she wouldn't finish what she was saying, or she'd seem super careful about how she was choosing her words. I'd say something new was eating her."

Like that she was getting ready to run with her daughter, Carrie thought.

"Any guesses what it was?"

"No."

On a hunch, Carrie asked, "You said a couple of other people know what Lauren's been through. Who else?"

Evans shook her head. "It's not my place to tell you that, honey. There were two or three of us, that's all I'm gonna say."

"You spoke with each other about Lauren's situation?"

"Yeah, maybe a couple times. Wishing we could help her, sure."

In other words, Lauren had recruited a team. Gavin had read about this precise dynamic, how in a hostile divorce the parents tend to form cheering squads around themselves and strive to get that group's sympathy—and loyalty—by playing up how bad the other parent is. A kind of Groupthink results, with team members getting revved up against the other side, like football players tearing up the locker room before a big game. A war camp mentality.

From there Carrie's thoughts went to Evans's earlier observation that Lauren seemed to carefully craft her statements about Kelly.

"But you didn't tell the police any of this stuff. Why not?"

Evans looked annoyed for the first time. "How would you know what I told the police?"

Carrie thought fast to cover her error. "Well, you said you hadn't had any useful information for them."

Evans looked hard at the reporter for a moment, then said, "I'm not going into what I told or didn't tell the police."

"Sorry," Carrie said. "None of my business."

"You got that right."

The young reporter awkwardly moved on. "Do you know if Brandi gets along with her dad?"

Evans was emphatic. "She hates that man. She would have loved to have nothing to do with him."

Carrie wished Gavin were present to hear these words. He'd quoted to her from divorce experts, explaining how a parent's bitterness toward the other one can lead to losing all perspective, the ex becomes evil. The parent then describes their kids as having nothing but resentment toward the other parent; the children's mixed and conflicted feelings get blown aside like oak leaves scattering into bushes. Evans had just spoken straight from Gavin's script.

Watching this play out before her, Carrie wondered why Gavin had sounded so lacking in sympathy for Kelly Harbison that night at the pond.

Before leaving, she raised one more issue. "You think Lauren was keeping something from you, but you also don't believe she fled with Brandi. How does that add up?"

"Well, for one thing, she was applying to law school. You go through all that when you're not even planning to stick around?"

~

At 3:15 on Thursday, shortly after the elementary school let out, Ledbetter arrived at a small white but graying house where her first interview of the day was to take place, an eleven-year-old girl named Gabbi Stolnik. Gabbi had made it onto Aisha Marshall's "Brandi-can't-stand-her-anymore" list, and Ledbetter was intrigued to see what might emerge.

The girl radiated anxiety and asked at once, "Is Brandi okay? You have news?"

Ledbetter answered honestly, "We don't know. There's no bad news, but we haven't had much good news for a few days either. We need to find her as rapidly as possible."

Gabbi nodded. "Everybody at school is upset, especially the girls. A lot of the boys try to make like it's no big deal but the girls are, like, obsessed. Even kids who don't get along with Brandi are worried about her."

"Are you one of the kids who doesn't get along with her?"

"No. Well, yeah. We kind of avoid each other now."

"Did you ever hear of anyone wanting to hurt her?"

"Hurt her? Not really. I mean, there were two boys saying they were going to kick her— I don't want to say it. But they were just talking."

"You know what it was about?"

"They said Brandi was making racist comments, one of the two boys is black, the white kid's his best friend, they supposedly were gonna teach her a lesson…"

Ledbetter apologized for leading the girl into unpleasant territory, then continued in the same direction. "What happened between you and Brandi?"

"How's that gonna help find her?"

"The thing about being a detective, Gabbi, is that half the time we don't even know what'll help. We find out everything we can and, if we're lucky, some key piece comes out."

"Huh… Well, she like has to have her way all the time, like she's the boss. And if you stand up to her, she starts spreading bad stuff about you. And she does this poking thing, always poking you with her finger, you tell her to cut it out and she stops but pretty soon she's doing it again. And… she does other stuff, it's kind of embarrassing." Her voice trailed off.

"It's okay, whatever it is, I'm sure I've heard it all before, being a cop."

"I don't want to say it… She just… says a lot of gross stuff, kind of disgusting."

Ledbetter tried a couple more times, but no details were forthcoming.

As had been true with Aisha, Gabbi knew nothing, not even rumors, about any plans Brandi had to go away. She said Brandi would talk badly about both her parents, but then would get super mad if anybody else said anything negative about either of them. "She's gotten touchier and touchier," Gabbi said.

~

Carrie had a scoop on her hands. Since the Athens shooting, the police had been leaning toward the theory that Lauren and Brandi had been sequestered by a third individual, a violent male on some nefarious mission not yet determined. But now she had a source in Delta Evans who, inadvertently, was making it look likely again that Lauren had disappeared by choice. Though Evans hadn't shed any light on the Athens events.

~

In keeping with Chief Tobias's orders, Wisneski laid a trap on Thursday afternoon. Three officers were identified as the ones most likely to be pipelines to Carrie Green, based on a few hours of research into the reporter's history, including connections to the Community College of Beaver County where Green had somehow attained an Associates Degree. Those officers, each separately, were led to believe they'd accidentally overheard about a twist in the investigation: new evidence was supposedly leading police to turn their sights on Kelly Harbison himself as the most likely culprit.

If this "major development" turned up in a Carrie Green article, they'd know the leak was one of the three. Plus it would be a lovely burn on Green, who would be publicly embarrassed for having trusted a bad source and for humiliating the already-traumatized father.

Since all three of the suspected officers were outside of the team, though, Wisneski would still be left with the question of how they were getting access to the team's information, now cordoned off within the computer system.

~

The detective had no idea that the leak to Carrie Green went by way of Kelly Harbison. She thus had no way of knowing that she'd invented the worst possible story for the test leak, one that Kelly would under no circumstances pass on to the media.

~

Wisneski raised another possibility privately in the chief's office. "What if Kresge is the one who's talking?"

The chief, surprised, asked her to say more.

"I think Shane's a good officer, I do, even though he acts pretty immature sometimes. But he's been so weird about this case. He has these mysterious reactions to things during meetings, and he's distracted or annoyed all the time. Something's up with him."

Tobias's interest waned as quickly as it had arisen. "He's done a solid job for us, on this case and in general. Put him to the test if you have to, but don't let him find out you suspect him."

Wisneski said she'd feed Kresge a correct piece about the case but not tell it to the Media Officer for another 48 hours. "We'll see if it turns up in the *Chronicle* before the press has been informed."

CHAPTER 12

Results from labs finally started to trickle in Friday morning. Wisneski had originally told the team they could be waiting as long as two or three months; in line ahead of them for lab work had been murders and rapes with the assailant still out loose, arsons in which children and pets had lost their lives, point-blank assassinations of key witnesses in upcoming trials. But with the FBI's entrance into the case, and now even more significantly the officers who went down in the Athens shooting, the Harbison case had jumped to the head of the line.

The first finding was that scrapings from the kitchen counter tops had revealed trace amounts of a powerful sedative, flunitrazepam, more commonly known as the date-rape drug Rohypnol. Traces can come from people cutting pills, to give half doses for example, or can result from invisible powder on the surface of the pills that gets on the hands of people handling the drug.

No one, not even Kelly, had alleged that Lauren was a drug user, and the search of the house had turned up no sedatives or psych meds; it appeared they had the answer to how Brandi had been prevailed upon to leave the home without a fight. And to why she might have started to resist later, when the drug wore off and she realized she was being kidnapped by her mother.

"They had to find a source of the drug and procure it, so this was not an impulsive flight," Martinez noted. "Lauren had been making her plans."

"This contradicts the idea that Lauren and Brandi were abducted," said Ledbetter.

The bullets from the Athens shooting had been identified as 6.5mm Creedmoors and were believed to have been fired from a Savage Arms Axis rifle. So far they hadn't been matched to any weapons used in a previous crime, but that was a virtually endless database.

Wisneski left a pause, taking a sip of coffee, stalling out of reluctance to share the last piece of news, which was bad. "The audio analysis of Brandi's call to Harbison the morning of the Athens shooting—well... they don't think she was really calling. They think the caller made recordings of Brandi's voice and then played pieces of them over the phone to Harbison. That would explain why he didn't think she was hearing him when he responded to her; he said she would be quiet for a moment after he spoke, and then would say words that seemed unrelated. Brandi may be hurt or sick, or even no longer alive; the caller might've saved recordings of her voice to create the impression that she was still living."

Kresge sat with his usual furrowed brow. "Could Harbison have made this recording himself? What if he's done something to the wife and kid?"

"The audio analysis was able to confirm that it was indeed Brandi's voice—whether pre-recorded or not—that was transmitted over the phone, and we know the phone was in Athens. And we know Harbison was here."

Kresge shrugged non-committally.

Wisneski hoped Kresge would never become a detective. He reminded her of investigators she'd worked with before who didn't like to be held up by the actual facts of a case once they'd spun out an exciting theory, and who as a result ended up embarrassing themselves and their co-workers.

~

Georgia van Scoy, an advocate for A Safe Path in Pittsburgh, sat across a small table from her new client, Maria. The young woman pushed her short, almost spikey dark auburn hair backward, as if to get it away from her eyes, and turned her large, sheepish, chestnut eyes toward Georgia.

"He gets his rocks off by torturing me," she was explaining. "He'll take me hard so it really hurts, or he'll choke me—he loves that one. Day before yesterday he attached these huge binder clips to my boobs, it killed!" And she abruptly pulled down her t-shirt from the neck, exposing both of her breasts, and there were disturbing purple and red splotches, large ones covering half or more of the surface area of each one, centered. "How can that turn him on, me screaming out in pain? He's fucking insane."

The advocate was familiar with the disturbing topic of abusers who enjoyed sexual torture. "Do you think it's dangerous for you to stay there?" she asked, as she'd been trained to do, despite the obviousness of the answer.

"Fuck yes," Maria said. "He's gonna kill me, though it'll probably be by accident. He'll have his stupid orgasm and then it'll dawn on him that I'm not such a good color, plus I'm not breathing. And guess what, then he'll feel sorry for *himself* that I'm dead."

Georgia asked if Maria was considering leaving him.

"Are you kidding? I think about it every day. But I'm stuck here. A year and a half ago I started divorcing him, I wanted to move, like, thousands of miles away. But the divorce judge—Bloom, she's a mean lady—said I couldn't leave the area with Mila, who was two and a half then. I told her the things Carlo does, and she didn't believe me, she said Carlo's just angry about me cheating on him—which I hadn't, but whatever. She ordered me to stay living here so that the father could get"—she made air quotes—"'plenty of time with his daughter,' meaning plenty of chances to kill us both."

"But you're back together. You withdrew the divorce action, I assume?"

Maria scrunched up her face, embarrassed. "No, we never got around to it… So, the reason I got back with him is he said he was gonna kill me for leaving him, and since I wasn't allowed to move away I had to make him happy to save my ass. But now I'm gonna die anyhow."

The advocate followed her protocol, taking the client through a list of danger signs. Did her partner have weapons? Was he a drunk? Was he sexually violent? Did he talk about killing her? (The last two had already been answered.)

She covered fifteen lethality indicators in all. Maria said yes to eleven of them.

When the hour was almost over, the advocate asked Maria to wait for a few minutes while she went to consult with her supervisor. She reported the dire results of the lethality assessment, but then explained that the client had a family court order that would subject her to kidnapping charges if she moved away. "Should I pressure her to come to shelter? This case is about as dangerous as they get."

Her supervisor grimly shook her head. "If she comes to shelter, she'll have to let her daughter go on visits with the father, believe it or not, since there's a custody order. And God knows what this guy will do to their kid to get her back for leaving him. For now just persuade her to come to support group as soon as possible, tomorrow's group if she can, and then we'll strategize where to go from there."

Georgia sent Maria off with the most encouraging words she could muster, quietly worrying whether she'd live to see the weekend.

~

Carrie walked five blocks to her car, which she had deliberately parked far away. She settled into the driver's seat and turned the rearview mirror downwards so she could remove the chestnut-tinted contacts she'd bought the day before and had learned with some difficulty to put in. Her vision had always been fine, she had no experience poking objects onto her eyeballs.

Other aspects of her "Maria" disguise were harder to remove. She wondered how the world would react to her suddenly deep red-brown hair color and close crop. She'd have to use the excuse that she wanted a new and sharper look to match her rising job fortunes.

The real reason for the change was so her face wouldn't match the photo that accompanied all her articles on the *Chronicle*'s website. People in Pittsburgh, where A Safe Path was, weren't likely to be readers of her small-town Ohio paper, but she couldn't risk it; especially given how widely news about the kidnapping had spread in the wake of the Athens shooting.

~

In the mid-afternoon, following multiple attempts, Sofia succeeded in getting Attorney Shipley on the phone. The waiting area of the auto shop was empty, typical at this time of day when it was too late to drop cars off and too early to pick them up, so she was able to talk.

"I'm losing it," she declared. "I'd run away myself if I didn't have kids. The police aren't letting up on me, they're doing the opposite, they're all over me."

"You have the option to cooperate."

"I'm not sure I do anymore… There's been new stuff since we met in your office. Lauren's been sending me messages."

Shipley switched from his supportive voice to pointed directiveness. "That was not a good thing to say over the phone, and even less so while you're in a public place. We need to meet in person."

"Barry, I have no money left."

"You can pay it over time."

He was such a mixture of bluntness and kindness.

Sofia was conscious of her shakiness. "Maybe what I tell them won't help them find her anyhow, maybe I should just get it over with. Can you look into what kind of deal they would give me?" The sound of her voice rang in her ears, a person trying to convince herself of what she wanted to believe.

"Not until you're sure, Sofia. Once they know you do indeed have important information—which is what my call would tell them—they won't let up on you until they find it out."

"So then what's in it for them to make a deal?"

"Every day counts for them. They don't want to spend weeks hassling you, they want your information today. That's what we work with to get you protected."

She told him she'd think about it over the weekend. Maybe some other answer would emerge for her in the coming days.

~

Kelly Harbison was in a short-tempered mood (as if that had to be said). "There's really important stuff to talk about, you need to come out to my house right away!" he blared into Carrie's ear.

She couldn't imagine undertaking the drive to Irondale, she was deeply tired and juggling so many balls at the moment that casting one more into the air could bring them all crashing down onto her head. "I'm sorry, Mr. Harbison, I'm swamped this afternoon. But I can talk on the phone, I can do that right now."

"I read your article, the one that just went up."

"Yeah."

"So the police are saying that call to me was faked! In other words, Brandi could be dead!"

Carrie waffled. She was starting to sense that Kelly was relying on her company, an awareness she bristled at. On the other hand, she was learning how to play him, reminiscent of a couple of unstable and intermittently scary men she'd grown up around in Mormon Valley. Interactions were a sort of contest, you had to bob and weave, know when to duck and when to poke, when to be accommodating and when to return rudeness with a crude if perhaps humorous response of your own, playing for respect.

She'd developed good skills to join a bomb squad.

Now he'd gotten the news that his daughter was in real danger—if she was still alive. And his reactions to this latest blow would, of course, be big news. So despite her reluctance she soon found herself dragging her ass to her car, mentally and physically wrung out but putting one foot in front of the other.

The reward was a great Kelly Harbison quote, guaranteeing Carrie another above-the-fold byline: "If they can't find my daughter before it's too late, I'm gonna quit my job and go find her myself. What the hell is law enforcement up to?"

Every day someone managed to stir up a new dust storm just when she needed it, a big splash for each article, making her the closest thing Columbiana County had to a home-grown NFL quarterback or Oscar nominee.

~

Wisneski and Ledbetter, ending their workday back at the station, evaluated their efforts to find the leak. It was the end of Friday afternoon and nothing about the "major development in the kidnapping investigation"—the false story they had attempted to plant about suspicion falling on Kelly—had appeared on the *Chronicle*'s website. There was no way the pipeline, or the reporter for that matter, would have allowed a story this big to pass. So the mole couldn't be any of the three officers they'd put to the test.

Nor had the mini-leak to Kresge turned up in the news.

So if the mole wasn't one of those three guys, and wasn't inside the team, Chief Tobias had to consider seriously the disturbing possibility that the department had been hacked. The investigation would never get anywhere if every move they made was being passed on to the very people they were trying to apprehend.

~

A message popped up on Sofia's Protonmail Friday night:

> We've had a series of people transporting us, one person passes us off to the next. They were good people until the last one, who turned out to be totally insane, we're lucky to be alive. We're far away now, we'll be on our own soon, everything's okay. Could really use another $500, sorry.   L.

Lauren was looking to Sofia to be the best friend she'd always claimed she was. Sofia needed badly for the police to leave her and her kids alone, but she had to stay strong. Recent news reports indicated that the Athens shooting was making the police lean toward the theory that Lauren and Brandi had been kidnapped together by a third party, a belief that could throw them off the track for a long time. She absolutely could not be the one to put them back on course.

She reached for the half-empty (mostly full, really) bottle of Oxycodone left over from a paralyzing back episode she'd suffered three years earlier, probably triggered by the stress of her divorce according to the doctor. At the time she'd been unable to move for almost seventy-two hours and remained in mind-numbing pain for ten days. The opiates had been a life-saver and the doctor's office permitted her a refill. But then the pain had abruptly broken and she'd taken only a couple more. Now she'd find out whether those tablets had lost their power from three years of residing in her dresser drawer. She simply couldn't manage more days, and more felonies, without their help.

CHAPTER 13

Gavin Neal was perhaps the only product of his hometown who did not have a therapist. Though Edgeworth Falls was the third-wealthiest town in Pennsylvania and cast an enviable image, behind closed doors its citizens were troubled. They suffered from insecurity about their neighbor's better-designed mansions, they worried that their children were growing up with no work ethic (as if the adults knew anything about toil), they were wounded by their spouses' affairs. Above all they carried burdens of guilt about the contrast between their luxurious lives and the hardship of those around the world less fortunate—and, of course, less intelligent—than they were.

When Gavin was only sixteen, he had observed to a friend, "Therapy is where you go to work out the stress caused by your hypocrisy."

With no professional voice to rely upon, however, Gavin felt adrift on the ocean as he tried to untangle his feelings for Carrie. His only recourse was to send an SOS to his high school friend and heartache, Sunni, who was not exactly a soft shoulder herself.

Sunni had moved to New York City. She worked for a concert promoter with a split personality, an energetic, generous man who turned into a flaming self-centered asshole any time his stress level went above a 7 or an 8, which occurred at least twice a week. Sunni had learned to say, "Fuck you, Bill, fire me." He had indeed fired her multiple times, but her longest period of such unemployment hadn't lasted even four hours; there was no way he could keep his empire growing without his fast-thinking, judicious assistant, and he knew it. She loved her job.

Gavin had been listening to Sunni's tales about her boss for near on half an hour when it dawned on him: the longing in his gut, an ache that awakened every time he'd talked to her since first meeting her six years earlier, was gone.

He didn't see this development as altogether good news. It could only mean one thing: he was falling hard, harder than he'd ever fallen for a girl before. And for Carrie Green of all people, God help him.

Sunni, on the other hand, was thrilled. She loved Gavin but was also very done, had been for years, with his pining away for her. "This girl sounds super cool, Gavin. Sure, she's a little young, but so what, she knows a lot more about life than you do."

He took offense. "Are you kidding? She grew up in a little isolated bubble—a swamp more like—of narrow-minded people, that she thought was the whole world. She's smart in a way, but it's amazing what she doesn't know."

"Jesus, Gavin, don't be such a dickhead."

He didn't appreciate her word choice, not least because Carrie had used it on him at least twice now.

But Sunni stuck to her guns. "What do you think we learned in that la-la land we grew up in? The heart-wrenching pain of a bad call by the line judge in a tennis tournament?"

It had never been Sunni's style to tell people what they wanted to hear. That was a big part of what Gavin had always liked about her. Until today.

~

Maria dutifully walked through the front door of A Safe Path at five minutes to ten on Saturday morning to attend a support group, as she'd been advised to do on her previous visit. Her demeanor had softened; the other six women who showed up for group found their new young member endearing and vulnerable, like a wide-eyed, spotted puppy who stumbles with a gashed leg into a campsite of strangers and squats down whimpering. They tripped over each other in their eagerness to take her under wing.

The stories the women shared were startling. One told of her boyfriend yelling vile words at her because she didn't want to have sex with him a few hours after she'd received her breast cancer diagnosis. Another described her husband pinning her to the bed with his knee in her back, then pounding her repeatedly in the head with his hand, then scratching and pounding his own face, and when the police finally came they arrested her and offered him emergency assistance. A third recounted having informed her psychiatrist-husband that she was leaving him, only to have him force her into the car, drive her to a different hospital from the one he worked at, and inform the emergency department that she'd been threatening suicide. She was then held in the locked ward—"pink-papered"—for seventy-two hours.

Maria's story fit right in. Group members remained sympathetic even when she said she was considering fleeing with her daughter.

After the meeting, she hung around on the sidewalk acting anxious and unsure of what to do. An older woman, fiftyish, who'd been at the meeting noticed her on the way out and stopped to ask how she was doing.

"I'm all right," Maria answered, not sounding it. "I gotta go get my kid from her friend's house. But then what? Go put my neck on the chopping block?"

The woman stuck out her hand. "I'm Natalie, I'm sure you couldn't remember all of our names. Listen, first off, don't mention taking off with your kid again, it could get back to the wrong person." She looked around, then spoke more softly and less sternly. "I've heard about guys who are into that sex choking thing. I've seen in the news where people have died from that."

"Yeah, but, the judge said if I take my daughter, it's kidnapping. I'd rather die than leave her with him."

Natalie looked around again. "Keep your voice down a little, okay? Look, I know people who can help you. I don't want to talk here." She gave Maria the name and address of the Carrick branch of the Pittsburgh public library. "Meet me there in ten minutes, it's not far."

Maria said okay, she had to head home soon but she could talk briefly.

~

When Maria pushed open the tall glass doors of the modern library building, she saw two or three librarians and several parents with their kids reading books aloud or pawing through the stacks. She wandered for a minute before finding Natalie waiting in an alcove with benches that served as a small art gallery for the library. Natalie was studying a blue-gray-brown watercolor of birds and cattails in a reedy marsh.

Maria stood near her and joined the gazing. "Seriously," she said, nearing a whisper, "I couldn't do that to my kid, leave her behind."

Natalie nodded gravely. "There's people who can help you flee with her, if they believe you. You got anything you can show them? Court papers and stuff? Records from doctor visits?"

Maria thought fast. "Court papers, yeah I got lots of those, it's already a big friggin' pile and we barely started the divorce. Doctor records, I don't know, I… I went to the doctor after one of the recent times, I thought something in my brain popped when I couldn't breathe, but I lied about what happened, I made stuff up."

"That's okay, we've all lied to a doctor one time or another. Go to the office and get a copy that shows you went there and documents whatever story you made up."

"Oh, geez, okay. They'll let me have it?"

"You've got rights to your own medical records."

"Okay." She gulped. "Give me a second." And, acting overwhelmed and in need of a few moments to pull herself together, she wandered randomly looking at watercolors. Then she walked close again and said, "I really gotta go get Mila. And I have to think, my head's kind of spinning."

"Believe me, I know what you mean. You met with an advocate?"

"Yeah, Georgia something. We made a safety plan. It won't help."

Natalie became Stern Mother. "You follow that plan even if it seems pointless, got it? No one from the group has died in the year I've been coming, despite a couple close calls. Every little thing you try helps."

She assented. "All right. Shit… Is there a way I can call you?"

Natalie shook her head. "We're not discussing anything on the phone. You can call, but only to set up a time to meet, some place private."

Maria had entered the realm of cloak and dagger.

~

Carrie had difficulty squeezing her enlarged body back into her car in front of the branch library. With one leg still half way out the door, she saw she'd received a call from Gavin. He hadn't left a voice mail but he'd followed up with a text asking her to get back to him when she was free.

She took several minutes to collect herself and find the route out of the city, meanwhile pondering how much she could tell Gavin. She was dying to get it all off her chest. Who better to hear it than someone who lived a good two hours away from the real Maria Friberg, whose story Carrie had stolen— and greatly embellished—from among the case files she'd perused back at her home courthouse.

So as soon as Pittsburgh started to fade behind her, she rang him.

He hadn't been trying to reach her about business. "I'd like to see you again," he blurted a little shakily, not his usual blustery self. "I know you were kind of pissed at one point, but... "

"Forget about that, it's over," she said.

He breathed. "I could drive out to Ohio tonight, or even late this afternoon, I mean, whatever would work."

His uncertainty made him sound even more luscious.

"What are you doing right now?" she asked.

He was startled. "Right now? I'm home. Well, but I'm going on a bike ride soon with a friend of mine, Sam. Why, something up?"

"Yeah, what's up is I'm in Pittsburgh, just outside." She saw a veterinarian's office and pulled off the highway.

"What are you doing here?"

"It's a long story, plus I'm not sure I can tell you about it."

"Uh, all right..."

"But I will anyhow. Can I come over?"

"Shit, hang on, let me call Sam. I'll call you right back."

She pulled back out toward Route 22 and negotiated a left turn back toward the city, gambling that Gavin would find a way to make time, that her mysterious reference to her morning expedition would act as an aromatic but covered platter that he wouldn't be able to resist getting a look at.

And, indeed, he called to report that he and Sam had stalled their ride off for a couple of hours. She felt a surge of energy, then winced to remember that her new look might come as a shock. "Uh, Gavin, I cut my hair short and, um, kind of spiked it, not really, but... And it's, like sort of red."

He forced a neutral tone, covering disappointment. She could understand it; when she had a brand new crush—like now, for example—she wouldn't want the person to suddenly be wearing someone else's face.

"Also," she added, "I've gained a fair bit of weight."

His surprise grew. "You've gained weight in the past three days? How exactly did you pull that off? Steroids?"

"You'll see. And I'll show you how quickly I can lose it, too."

She navigated briskly to his Lawrenceville apartment, her Dodge zipping as if retrofitted to run on nervous energy, no gas required.

Judging by the unit numbers she guessed his apartment must be on the second floor, up a steep but solid flight of exterior wooden stairs, not rickety and rotting as they would've been in her neighborhood.

As she came up on the high porch, Gavin stood looking her up and down through the screen door. "Nice of you to come up, kid, you're very attractive," he said. "But this girl Carrie's arriving any minute from Ohio and she won't be happy if she finds you here."

"You're a frickin' riot," she said and, not waiting to be let in, flung the screen door aside and went straight to kiss him on the cheek and pull him close. "You're kind of attractive yourself."

"You're puffing like a track star," he observed. "Is that just from walking up twelve steps?"

"More like thirty." She leaned back and took her turn performing a visual once-over. "Wow, you're looking even better than usual. Did you comb your hair or something?" And she kissed him again, this time on the mouth.

He looked happy, though his next words were, "I have the damnedest time figuring out whether you like me or not."

"That makes two of us," she retorted, and after glancing around started uninvited down the hall. She peered into the bathroom (not especially clean but not gross, the best you could hope for from guys), the kitchen (in need of attention), the small living room (tidy, actually, and there were pictures on the walls, which for some reason a lot of guys couldn't figure out how to hang, so this was a good sign), a bedroom (not Gavin's she hoped, the walls were bare and there were socks and pants and wrappers all over the floor), and a second bedroom (a puffy, colorful, crafty-looking quilt on the bed, kind of an overly ornate mirror, a couple of cool posters, decent-sized windows, a pretty okay room all in all, please tell me this is his).

Gavin stood with his arms crossed. "You have a checklist for this inspection? Need to look in my drawers? Take samples from under the bed maybe?"

Oh good, it was his room. She plopped down on the bed like a kid in a bouncy house, and as quickly flew back up into the air and over to gaze out one of his windows, overlooking a small but lush backyard.

"You're hyper as a honey bee," he observed. "And what's up with the new identity? You testifying against the Mob or something?"

She sat back down on the patchwork quilt and reclined. "I'm going under-cover."

"No, seriously."

"For real. I'm weaseling my way into this supposed underground railroad of yours. Only it doesn't look so 'supposed' anymore, I've got someone offering to hook me up, I just need to pull documents together."

"You've got to be kidding me." He looked amused. "What does your editor have to say about this?"

"Geez, Gavin, think I'd be stupid enough to tell him? Me and him have troubles enough."

"He and I."

"Fuck you, whatever. So, what do you think of my hair?"

"Honestly? You look like you're in a high school musical. Very cute, actually, but not really you. Or at least it would be cute if you weren't hidden behind five layers of foundation and mascara and what-all."

She didn't care what he said because he kept looking and looking, she could tell he was intrigued. She lay across his bed on her side, obviously not going anywhere, so he sat on the floor with his back against his dresser and put his feet up on the mattress.

"So who's your roommate?" she asked. Really she wanted to know whether they could count on him being away for a while.

"He's a guy who was at Penn when I was there. The young professional type, but he's okay. We got this place like two years ago. You might get to meet him later, I'm not sure exactly when he's gonna be around."

Good, he wasn't expected back soon.

Gavin peered at her expectantly, and she finally dove into the story of the past few days: the great Harbison quotes, the latest leaks from his police source, her revealing meeting with Delta Evans, her transformation into a mother whose life was in danger.

While spinning out this account she peeled off her sister's leather boots, which had been blistering her feet, kept running her hands through her hair as if endlessly surprised to find so much of it missing, and fiddled repeatedly with three silver bracelets she was wearing, finally removing them and leaving them to the side.

"If I seem tense, it's cuz I am. I've been faking everything for two weeks. I feel like I keep adding another rusty car part to a shaky junk pile I'm standing on, and then climbing up even higher. I'm gonna end up bloody and my bones all broken."

She started rubbing Gavin's feet through his socks. He didn't pull them away, in fact he even closed his eyes for a minute.

"You got a blunt?" she said.

It was Gavin's favorite question, a need he was always ready to fill.

As he pulled his little magic cloth bag out of a dresser drawer, Carrie said, "I'm so friggin' hot," and tried to hold the top of her sweater away from her neck.

He lit a joint and they each took a hefty hit, Pineapple Trainwreck.

She couldn't take the hot clothes anymore. "So, you want to see how I got chubby?"

He laughed. "Sure. You buy some of those stage muscles or something?"

"You'll see," she answered. "Get up here." She indicated to him to sit up at the head of his bed. He went and cooperatively sat with his butt on his pillows, his back against the wall. She rubbed his feet for a moment in their new configuration, took another deep hit, passed the joint back, then stood up.

"Okay, here's the Carrie Green signature Lose-Twenty-Pounds-in-Two-Minutes Program, call the 800 number flashing on your screen." She peeled off her generous corduroy pants, revealing blue jeans underneath. She removed the jeans to uncover sweat pants. The sweatpants were rolled down to expose long underwear, skiing in January variety, almost unbearable to wear in August.

"Am I beginning to look somewhat normal size?"

He shrugged. "A little, I guess."

"I kept sweating during the support group, I had to claim it was from stress. Probably just made me more believable. Now you'll see what it was really from." She proceeded to take off her overshirt, under which she had a sweater that she'd just barely been able to keep from being visible. That she pulled over her head, revealing yet another long-sleeved shirt, and then, remarkably, a t-shirt under that.

Gavin said, with a stupid grin, "I still don't recognize you with all those clothes on."

It was meant as a deliberately juvenile joke; there was almost nothing left for her to remove. But Carrie, never one to let an opportunity pass, pretended to take it as a serious dare. She pulled off her long underwear, stripped off her t-shirt and bra, and lay lengthwise next to Gavin on the bed, pushing herself up against him in nothing but panties.

"Recognize me now?" she asked brightly.

"You're kind of familiar," he said, trying to act nonchalant but failing; he'd gone electric. Carrie ran a hand down his front side to further gauge his interest. The results were good; so she pushed her hand down inside the front of his pants, and a whoosh of air rushed from his mouth. She was pleased to see she'd succeeded in surprising him.

Then she was burying her face in those sensuous lips, an image she'd been obsessing about for two days. She wished she could take a shower, she'd been sweating, but the situation had become an emergency, it was too late. So she started to fiddle with his buckle and he quickly took over and squirmed himself out of his lower garments.

And since he'd doubled over to pull his pants over his ankles he took the moment to return Carrie's surprise attack; those magical lips found their way between her legs. Her dream the past two days had been exactly this, but it had seemed too much to hope for.

Even better, he stayed for as long as it took. She was blissed out.

Afterward she lay unmoving, drinking in minutes of delicious relaxation, purring, occasionally lightly running her hands over him.

Then, when she could sense him at the limit of what he could endure, she asked him where to find a jimmy, and he pointed to his top dresser drawer.

"See?" she said, as she pushed his underwear aside. "I did need to inspect in here."

She found a box, pulled a condom out and tore it open, wrapped him up in it, and in one smooth motion was up on top of him and had him inside of her. His face contorted, he was beautiful, she felt like she loved him, ridiculous of course, she barely knew him.

And in seconds he had burst, typical boy.

They lay peacefully for what seemed like an eon for two young people who were both talkers, both believing, rightly or wrongly, that this was the happiest they'd ever felt.

Just when Carrie was thinking Gavin had done the guy thing and fallen asleep, his lovely voice started to rumble as if in a half-awake rasp. "You came here to use me for stress-reduction sex… I'm just a vehicle for you."

"It must be awful to be taken advantage of like that," Carrie commiserated, holding him close.

"Just miserable," he agreed. And he spooned his back into her, the two of them at last drifting off.

~

Light slanted through the windows, shimmering on Carrie's eyes. She became dimly aware of lying on Gavin's quilt, one of her arms over him, his back still formed against her belly. From somewhere amidst her pile of clothes on the floor she could hear her phone vibrating. She so wished it hadn't woken her; she felt cast down from heaven onto rocky ground. But sleep was willing to accept her back into its green valley, she danced on the edge as if trying to grab hold of a cloud.

In a minute the phone started vibrating again, dragging her back down.

"What is up with that person?" murmured Gavin, not necessarily consciously.

Carrie tried to reach for her clothes without standing up, half climbing over Gavin, who groaned. Then someone started knocking loudly, it sounded like the front door of the apartment. Carrie felt dimly that the phone call and the knocking were connected, coming almost together as they had; people trying to warn them, a fire maybe.

The caller turned out to be Marco Vinestri. Carrie's screen informed her that this was her editor's third try over the past forty-five minutes. The first one she had no memory of. She started pulling on her underwear. "Gavin, wake up, someone's pounding on the door."

"Oh, shit! Sam!" he said and, erupting clumsily from the bed, started to throw on the first garments he could grab, which fortunately turned out to be his. Then he was out the bedroom door, still with no shirt.

Carrie finished dressing herself, with a single layer rather than her previous four, because talking to Marco while standing naked would have felt too strange.

"Where *are you?*" he shot out with irritation as soon as she dialed him back.

"It's Saturday. Where am I supposed to be?"

"You've been unreachable for almost an *hour,*" he scolded, a modern equivalent in irresponsibility to, say, handing a scalpel to a six-month-old. He barked at Ms. Green to get her rear in gear right away, arriving two hours ago would have been preferable.

The issue, when he finally got around to saying it, was that local law enforcement was in a mad tizzy. Brandi had been spotted.

As Carrie moved dazedly in the direction of her rusty sedan, the young reporter absorbed for the first time that her job was now 24/7. Good thing she wasn't one of those people who need forty-five minutes to reach orgasm, it could be months before she next had that much uninterrupted time.

~

A few minutes past eight o'clock that morning, the Ohio State Highway Patrol had contacted the East Liverpool police department to inform them that Lauren Harbison's debit card had been used at a supermarket in Highland, Tennessee, a town in the northwestern corner of the state near the Kentucky border. The card had been used at 6:15 am, shortly after the store had opened, to purchase $150 worth of food (much of it frozen), toiletries, plastic containers, sunglasses, and a couple of knives.

An update came for Wisneski over an hour later with helpful and not-so-helpful news. It was now known that the card had been used again at 7:20 am, this time to withdraw cash in Cherokee, Alabama, giving them a beam on the fugitives' travel direction. The Alabama Highway Patrol and a parade of local police agencies were keeping an eye out for them moving south or east.

The only problem was this: Cherokee is fully a three-hour drive from Highland. How could the fugitives have possibly covered that distance in sixty-five minutes?

The answer was that law enforcement had the wrong Highland, Tennessee. The second one was found in the south-central part of the state, twenty miles from the Alabama line. They'd raised the alarm 140 miles off the mark.

Highland #1 didn't have a Kroger's. But there was one in Dyersburg, twenty-five minutes down Route 51, and in the heat of the moment officers had assumed that must be the location and had torn off southbound. Close to an hour was lost sorting out the confusion. By the time police from Highland #2 had been rousted from their desks and whipped toward the correct Kroger's, the trail was long cold.

The manager of that store assisted officers to pore over footage from eight different surveillance cameras. Watching the time stamp, they could see that a young girl had made the 6:15 purchase. They then backtracked to her entrance into the store and followed her movements through the aisles, watching from a range of angles. She was never seen speaking with anyone, but she did glance frequently toward the front of the store as if looking out the windows at a person keeping an eye on her.

Video from the parking lot cameras showed the girl emerge from the store, glance around nervously for a moment, then spot a car pulling up to the curb. A door opened and she passed shopping bags in, climbed in the back, and was driven rapidly away. The car was a silver Nissan Sentra and the license plate was visible in the video, though blurry and distant. A tech team might be able to come up with the numbers. It looked to be an Illinois plate.

~

Wisneski yanked her team together. Kresge was not scheduled to be on duty but arrived at the station without complaint, accepting that days off were becoming rare. This time the stress showed most on Mason, who was still struggling to adapt to the long hours.

"Local Tennessee police are now saying that the girl in the supermarket is not a good match with the photos of Brandi that were zipped down to them," the detective announced. "Something strange seems to be up."

Kresge's brow furled in disbelief. "What, Lauren traded her kid to someone for a girl the same age? She's, like, Theo Epstein, building a new ballclub with a different set of skills?"

Martinez backed Kresge up, for once. "They probably changed her hair or whatever, colored it, who knows. As soon as we have the footage, we'll tell Kelly to get down here to look at it."

"Except he's gonna demand that we deliver it to his house, with popcorn," Kresge grouched.

Nobody laughed.

Ten minutes later the team had the videos, examining the girl from every angle, close shots and distant ones, while they looked back and forth at their extensive collections of photos of Brandi. They were left with doubts.

Except for Kresge, of course, who always had to buck the rest of the team.

Ledbetter kept pointing out details. "Shane, look at this moment on the video… Okay, now look at this photo from, what, only about three months ago… You're prepared to go on the stand and swear that these are the same person?"

"They look almost identical."

"Almost identical? That's crap. They look like just maybe they could be related."

Wisneski said, "Everybody knows there's cameras in a supermarket. I wonder if we were supposed to see this."

Ledbetter took that in. "Meaning they could be a thousand miles away with the real Brandi?"

Martinez shook her head. "It's not like we're closing in on them. So why would they feel the need to pull a major stunt to get us off track?"

Especially with some hacker keeping them up to date on the details of our investigation, Wisneski thought bitterly.

Ledbetter shifted to another concern. "This girl is glancing out the window from time to time but she's not looking scared. She could flee into the back of the store and get an employee to call the police, but instead she's intent on the shopping list in her hand. If this is Brandi, she's got to be traveling with her mother, not some mad kidnapper."

Kresge tried to share a not fully-formed thought. "What if both things are true? What if this kid really is Brandi, but there's still some reason they wanted us to see it?"

The room was quiet, each individual waiting for one of the others to do the honors. Good thing Kresge wasn't the brains of the operation, logic seemed to escape him.

~

Twenty minutes later, Kelly Harbison was ushered into the conference room. His face was red, his throat tight. "Is it Brandi? Is she okay?"

The chief responded somberly. "I'm afraid there isn't cause yet to get our hopes up. We're going to show you some videos and see whether you think this girl is your daughter."

Hands were quickly but coldly shaken all around, the now long-standing tension between Kresge and their guest particularly noticeable. Harbison was steered to a chair facing a screen on the wall.

He gripped the table, his breathing rapid, and glued his eyes to the screen.

The first segment showed the girl entering the store. Harbison's face brightened uncharacteristically.

Ledbetter, controlling a laptop, switched through a series of segments of the girl in various grocery aisles. In the first segment she was looking at a landscape of cereal boxes, trying to find specific brands from her list. Harbison's face tightened, serious and intent.

The next selection showed the girl choosing apples and grapefruit from tall slanted piles. The father's face wrinkled further, his eyes darkening. Then the girl was before a dairy case, opening and closing refrigerator doors. Harbison's face fell.

Harbison sat with hunched shoulders, looking down at the table in front of him, then turned to look out the window as if to hide his face. Small tremors were visible pulsing through his shoulders, his breathing strained.

"That's not her." He spoke slowly. "At first I thought Lauren just changed her hair and isn't giving her enough to eat. But when I can see her walking, that's not Brandi, that's not how she moves... They can fake her look, but they can't fake the whole way she is." Then he erupted. "She is the most revenge-driven person I've known in my whole life! This was designed to torture me!"

He stood and glanced around the room without focus.

"Let me ask a few things," Ledbetter said.

But Harbison cut her off. "I can't right now. I just can't do it." And he exited briskly and noisily from the room.

The team sat in silence, uncharacteristic for them, eyes downward or out the window. After a moment Wisneski said, "His last comment makes sense. I bet it's not that we were meant to see it, but that *he* was meant to see it."

Martinez said, "Then we better dig deeper into Lauren Harbison's story. If she has this much of a dark side—severe, deliberate cruelty—she'll have a past where that shows."

Both of the detectives nodded.

"What a vicious bitch," Mason injected.

Kresge as usual appeared deep in thought, but Wisneski knew that was giving him too much credit.

~

Wisneski called the Eastern Ohio Field Office of the FBI. Her contact, agent Jennifer Zink, was unavailable. She left a detailed message about the team's review of the video footage and Harbison's reactions when they showed it to him.

It was close to noon when Zink called back. She had news of her own. The Alabama state police had gotten access to video from the ATM in Cherokee, Alabama; the user of the credit card wore a brimmed hat, with his or her hair either tucked up under the hat or tied back, a scarf, and sunglasses. If it was a female she was exceptionally tall, and in any event was certainly not Lauren Harbison, who was only 5'5".

At one o'clock Wisneski decided it was time to release news of the morning's events to the media. Media officer Gregorius convened a press conference for 1:30. Carrie Green's absence from the corps of reporters was notable.

~

Carrie scurried into the *Chronicle* at ten minutes before 3:00 and headed directly for Vinestri's office, where her editor informed her that he'd attended the press conference himself.

"Couldn't Shelburne go?" Carrie asked.

"Her name is *Sherborn*. And no, Jenette wasn't available, her children have all kinds of activities today."

Carrie was pissed. Marco's tone made it sound like she'd failed to show up for work. Was she on parole, not allowed to leave the state without permission? For that matter, she'd gone to Pittsburgh to work on the damn story, though she couldn't tell Marco that. And as for stopping on the way home to get laid, that had been an absolute necessity. Weren't her professors at the junior college always going on about how, in a stressful job, it's so important to practice good self-care?

~

The best way to atone for having missed the press conference was to extract another eye-catching headline from Kelly Harbison's impulsive mouth. She called and asked if they could talk, and he said okay, come over if you want.

This time he didn't come to the door when she knocked. She found him in a back bedroom with belongings strewn all over the place, and she now registered that she'd passed several items tossed in the living room and hallway as she'd worked her way through the house. Kelly was packing.

"You heard what happened today?" he asked.

"Yeah."

"I can't sit here anymore while my kid is out there somewhere. The FBI, this state police, that state police, how can it be this hard to find them? When they consider a case important, suddenly they can track the culprit down fast. Notice that?"

"What's your plan?"

"I asked for time off work. They said I could take a week off, maybe a second one too but they're not saying yet. I can't afford to lose that job."

"Heading south?"

"I'm not saying. But off the record, where else is there to head?"

She said, "Listen, my editor wants me to ask you this," now her standard preamble whenever a question of hers seemed likely to piss Kelly off. "What can you do that the police and FBI can't? Won't you just be in the way?"

"To them it's a job, to me it's my life, that's the difference. When you care, you get things done. And no, I won't be bothering them, they won't even know where I am."

As reliable as the dawn, he'd handed her three beautiful lines to build an article around. The man was a gift.

"You still say the police aren't doing much?"

"Don't put words in my mouth," he snapped, rejuvenated. "Look, this local team that's investigating, they're coming apart at the seams. There's huge tensions between the detectives, the chief, the team members, they're barely on speaking terms with each other. That's why nothing's getting done, it's all ego battles and personality clashes."

Carrie went alert as a lynx. "Where did you hear this?"

"The same way I know other things from inside that building, meaning none of your business. Look into it for yourself."

"I will. And I appreciate the information."

"Oh yeah, you're so grateful. You care maybe five percent more than the rest of 'em do. All you want is a big story."

Carrie squinted her eyes, then turned to go. "It's always a pleasure working with you, Mr. Harbison. But I better get back to the office, so I can get rich writing newspaper articles."

He ignored her. As she was exiting the bedroom, she looked back long enough to say, "Keep me up on what's happening. All off the record, except when you tell me otherwise."

He grunted, but she knew he'd do it.

~

Maria Friberg's story was documented in a Columbiana County divorce file, a public record several inches thick. She did report that her husband had threatened her repeatedly and four or five times had outright hit her. But there was no mention of strangulation or sadistic sexual games; Carrie's imagination had crafted the necessary details to cast him as a killer.

Carrie would have to return when the court opened on Monday to make photocopies at the coin-operated machine. The desk staff appeared to pay no attention to people who were going through the records, hadn't even reacted the previous time when she'd ended up requesting and returning five different files, one at a time, choosing which ones to try based on the scant details about each case available on the court's website. They probably assumed she was a family lawyer's paralegal.

The greater challenge was the underground network's desire to see Maria's medical records. But Carrie found surprisingly detailed and practical DIY instructions at FakeDoctorLetters4u.com. There was nothing left in the world that you couldn't just look up on the internet.

She called Gavin to entertain him with several choice lines from the fake documents website. Her insides purred contentedly from hearing his voice. Then she told him the latest headline-making pearls from Kelly, and started thinking aloud about how she'd weave them into a news story.

"Hang on," Gavin said. "You're planning to write this stuff about infighting in the police team?"

She thought he was daft. "Well, duh. It's huge news. They're squabbling like little kids while a ten-year-old gets dragged around the country."

"How do you know these conflicts are affecting the investigation?"

"'Cause that's exactly what the pipeline said."

"But did you get any examples? Your editor's gonna ask why the team's dynamics are anybody's business—a small-town editor doesn't want to piss off the police department. You'll need to be able to say, like, 'They dropped the ball on such-and-such a key issue because they'd been arguing all day,' something concrete like that."

"Right, Gavin, like I could possibly get access to those kinds of details."

"I'm not saying you could. But you've got everybody impressed with the job you're doing, don't go and blow it by writing something that makes you sound like a gossip columnist."

"A gossip columnist?? Fuck you, Gavin!" And she hung up on him.

She sat fuming for half an hour, getting nothing written. Gavin was jealous of how things were taking off for her, that's what was happening. Fine, he felt stuck at his job with a jerk of an editor, he didn't have to take it out on her.

She cranked the article out and submitted it to Vinestri at 4:30. It should be up on the website before 5:00, another big splash for her. Then she could start working on a version for tomorrow's print edition.

Except at 4:45 her phone rang, Marco on the line.

"Carrie, we can't print a story this inflammatory based on a single anonymous source and nothing else. We need it backed up, and we need evidence that it's affecting the investigation."

Carrie breathed deeply to not scream. "Then how come this source was okay to use about the footprints they found? That turned out to be spot-on true."

"Because that leak didn't point fingers at any individual, and it certainly didn't accuse the police of fucking around while a ten-year-old's life is in danger."

Wow, he was seriously pissed, worse than he'd been about her *Repository* article. Or maybe that was still what it was really about.

Carrie left a long pause, going flat like a punctured tire. "Okay, I'll rewrite the article to leave that out. Maybe later I can get another source to back it up." But she knew that wouldn't happen.

"It's late now, Carrie. I need your article fast."

~

Even worse than accepting that Vinestri was right, she now owed Gavin an apology. Best to just get it over with, as had always been her style. Schedule the dentist for tomorrow, not for three months from now. If you're in trouble go find Mom and Dad, don't wait dread-filled for them to find you. So as soon as she'd submitted her defanged article, she called him.

"Listen," she said, "I lost my shit. I'm a bitch... Sorry."

"All right, apology accepted... Care to tell me what set you off?"

"It felt like you were raining on my parade, I was psyched about the leak so I didn't want to hear it."

"But I was just—"

She cut him off. "Gavin, don't start on me, okay? You were right, I get it."

She wasn't about to admit that it had taken her editor to force her heels out of the ground.

They were quiet for a few beats, then Gavin started to speak, cautiously. "Something happened at my paper when I was new here that I think you should know about."

"Okay," she said reluctantly.

"One of our reporters had a buddy high up in the Harrisburg city government, and when that scandal happened about the mayor's art-collecting habits, you remember that?, there was a—"

Carrie cut him off. "No, I don't remember that, dude, and I didn't forget it either. First of all, as far as we're concerned over here Pennsylvania is another country except for Pittsburgh, which is part of Ohio. Secondly, who the hell cares if the mayor is an art snob?"

"You'll love this. Mayor Reed was taking city money and buying weird, expensive stuff. A suit of armor, a vampire hunting outfit—whatever that is—a $15,000 theater program from the night Lincoln was assassinated, piles of stuff like that. He was planning to start a Wild West museum."

"They wore suits of armor in the wild west? I musta missed that."

"Yeah, and we missed it when those cowboys were hunting vampires."

"Harrisburg must be the laughing stock. Some dinky little village?"

"It's the state capital, Carrie."

"Oh, yeah? My little brother Scoop memorizes all that shit, state birds, flowers, capitals..."

Gavin went back to his story. "So this reporter was getting inside dope and we were the star newspaper for a while. But the mayor and his cronies got a hunch who the leak was in their office, and they started feeding that person false information, hoping that it would turn up in the *Republican*. And it worked; our reporter fell for a juicy tidbit of B.S., his friend in the mayor's office got canned, and the newspaper got humiliated."

Carrie was too exhausted to discern the moral of the story. Her day had been a bulging suitcase that she was sitting on the lid of, there was no way to stuff a single additional pair of underwear into it, not even a pack of cigarettes. She was going to roll off that lid and collapse to sleep on her mattress. "Wait," she mumbled, "are you saying this war-in-the-department story might be to sucker me?"

"The police obviously don't like you too much. But no, I was more thinking they're doing it to catch their pipeline."

"Except I doubt there's any such person. Who the hell would want to do favors for Kelly Harbison?"

"Then how's he getting this inside stuff?"

"He won't say. But he made a reference once to a friend of his way back who was a hacker, and I bet the guy isn't really so far back."

"The hacker would have to be a wizard. You don't get much higher computer security than a police department."

"In East Liverpool? Don't make me laugh."

CHAPTER 14

Sofia enjoyed her weekend. Her patience with her children was back, they relaxed together and had fun. Saturday evening they cuddled up and watched a PG-rated movie, a thrill for the kids. They were happy to have their mom seeming more like herself, though she made unusually crass jokes and kept a running commentary going through the whole movie, "Ooh, this part is nerve-wracking," "Oh, that's stupid, people wouldn't really do that," and so forth, until Kiara finally observed pointedly, "Ma, it's not a basketball game, we don't need an announcer," a line so appreciated by her little brother that he repeated it half a dozen times over the next half hour.

Sofia didn't mind. She was looped.

She'd slept seven hours Friday night, her first slumber longer than two and a half hours since Lauren disappeared. But immediately upon awakening Saturday morning she remembered Lauren's urgent need for another five-hundred dollars, putting Sofia in a financial pinch but more importantly dragging her deeper into abetting.

So she located the bottle of Oxycodone that she'd dipped into Friday night and took another sample. When the first pill didn't do that much she took a second; that was three total now including Friday night's, but that was a different day so it didn't count. When she found herself still lacking the courage to reenter the shadowy world of untraceable money transfers, she slipped herself a quick glass of wine (or perhaps two) to fortify her.

She continued to sip throughout the day. Just sip. She mentally referred to these sips as "booster shots," just there to give a little extra push to the pills. These, given their excellent effects, she decided to take every four to six hours as instructed on the bottle; she was using the medicine just as directed.

By ten o'clock Saturday night, following the movie, she felt brave enough to go through with the last step in sending the money to Lauren.

On Sunday night she read Jarred a story at bedtime and said a warm goodnight to Kiara at the door to her room. Maybe this new life would work okay. When her magic bottle ran out she might have to fake another back crisis, but with a full three years since the last episode, what doctor would be suspicious?

She made a last check for messages before falling asleep, and immediately regretted it.

> Sofia:
>
> Mixed news. No choice but to use credit card yesterday, no cash left, so police probably know where we were. They won't guess where we've gone now, but close call. Good news is we have a way out of the country (alone) in just a few days. Have to put up a lot, though, could you send $2000? So sorry, it'll be the last time.
>
> Much love, Lauren

Holy shit. Two thousand bucks, on top of the thousand total she'd already sent? Where the hell would she come by that? She could borrow it, but that would leave a paper trail that could send her straight to jail. Daryl didn't have that kind of money, plus what would she tell him?

And was helping them leave the country an even more serious crime?

Plus she couldn't fail to notice the not-so-subtle message behind Lauren's words: If Sofia had gotten it together to send money on Friday night, Lauren wouldn't have had to use her debit card on Saturday and almost get nabbed.

It took a pill and a half with three glasses of wine to ease her to sleep.

CHAPTER 15

Maria spoke in a raspy, barely audible voice. She was coughing intermittently and blowing her nose. "My husband's mother went in the hospital on Saturday, she had a stroke. So he figures that's a good reason to see if he can put me in the hospital too."

Natalie asked if she was okay.

"I don't know. I feel like something popped again in my face when he was choking me, a blood vessel or something."

"He tried to choke you again??"

"No, he didn't try, he fucking did it, the worst one ever. I gotta—"

Natalie cut her off. "Not another word. Find me where you found me before. Leave your phone at home, it's important. Half an hour?"

It would take Maria three times that long to drive there. "I gotta get my friend Maddi to look after my kid. I can make, like, ninety minutes?"

"I'll be waiting for you. Bring whatever you have."

Natalie was referring to Maria's documents, which was fine; she'd assembled an impressive collection at the courthouse that morning, then created fairly believable medical records with the assistance of her (well, Carrie's) little brother and roommate Scoop, whose technical know-how, and signature as the doctor, had come at the expense of a substantial bribe.

~

Sofia squinted into the morning sunlight as she exited the side door of her house to walk down to the school bus stop with her kids. The sun was unnecessarily bright; if it weren't for Oxycodone, plus a morning glass of wine, she would have started yelling at it to go the hell back down.

Kiara made it all a lot worse by saying, "Ma, look, there's a police car parked in front." It would have been blocking the main walkway to the street had they come out that way.

Sofia told the kids to hang on for a second while she walked around to the driver's side of the cruiser. The window was open. "Can I help you, officer?" she asked.

"No thank you, Ma'am," the young officer said very politely. "Just handling a few phone calls. We're not supposed to drive and talk now—new regulation."

"Any reason you're parked right here?"

"No, Ma'am, this is just where I ended up."

"Could you park somewhere else? It scares my kids when you park here."

"It does? What would they be scared of, Ma'am? Anyhow, looks like they're off to school. I'll be out of here before long."

Sofia was shaken up and pissed. She yanked it together to take the kids on down the block, telling them, "It turns out to have nothing to do with us."

Neither Jarred nor Kiara believed her. Given her mountingly peculiar behavior over the past two weeks, a police car there to meet them in the morning seemed like a natural next step, the improvement in her over the weekend notwithstanding.

Sofia passed the cruiser again on her way back to the house. As she was leaving a half hour later to head to work, she saw that the cop was still there. She strode up to his window and let it fly. "I know you're here to harass me, I'm not a fucking idiot! I'm calling my lawyer!"

At work she was stuttering, dropping papers, calling long-time customers by the wrong names. Jeremy squinted his eyes at her two or three times during his several passings between the office and the shop, but it wasn't his style to say anything aloud unless things got even worse.

~

Maria found Natalie once again in the stacks of the Pittsburgh library, Carrick Branch, and was handed a slip of paper with an address. "This house is about five minutes from here. I'm leaving now. You make yourself look busy for a good ten minutes here, then you head over to meet me. Take extra turns on the way, and don't park near the house."

"Jesus," Maria said. "Serious shit." She looked around as if checking for who might be able to see them. "Okay, I got it."

Twenty minutes later they were sitting at a table in a cramped, run-down kitchen.

"Isn't it a little hard to make meals in here?" Carrie asked.

"This isn't my house," Natalie said, offering no explanation. She sat reading through the stack of documents, saying nothing for quite a while.

Maria waited tensely for signs that Natalie wasn't buying the story. But the documents appeared to be persuasive.

Next came the cross-examination. What hospital is your husband's mother in? Why did you marry him in the first place? Did you go before the same judge each time you went to court? Why did you come all the way to Pittsburgh to attend a support group when there are groups in Ohio? What kind of relationship does your daughter have with her father? Do you realize how extremely difficult it is to live permanently in hiding? You realize you'll have to never talk to any of your friends and relatives again? Are you sure it's worth it?

Maria did well. Most of the facts she'd memorized from the file, and everything else she invented without too much of a hitch. Any time she had to stall for time to think of an answer she would happen to be hit by another coughing fit, caused by having been strangled the day before.

When Natalie's questions ran out, Maria asked, "What happens now? I feel like every day could be my last."

Natalie nodded compassionately. "The people I'm connecting you with, they only say yes to maybe one or two people a year, the cases they consider the absolute worst. And they don't make decisions fast. Follow your safety plan and be careful."

Maria slowly nodded her head, accepting the harsh reality.

Natalie left her with instructions for setting up an email account with an encrypted provider, and told her what to use as the account's address. "No more calling my phone, that's done, okay?"

~

Lauren had instructed Sofia not to send any messages, but tonight she had to.

> Lauren,
>
> The police are closing in on me, and if they catch me that's gonna help them catch you, no? I can't send the rest of the $$ unless you're certain to get out of the country fast. I love you.   Sofia

An hour later she heard back:

> **We're totally solid, it's a sure thing, situation's way better than it was. Please, if there's any way to get it to me, it'll make the difference for setting B free.**
>
> **Your BFF**

Lauren had always made fun of people who said "BFF." But fear can, strangely enough, trigger people's sense of humor. Sofia had seen it happen in herself sometimes.

At midnight she sent Lauren's secret account $2000. To do so she had to lie to two of the people she most cared about in the world; she hoped they would forgive her when the time came to tell them the truth. In the meantime she hoped she'd sounded believable, lying not being among her strengths.

CHAPTER 16

Detective Wisneski's days were not getting any easier, or more encouraging. After hitting the ATM in Alabama, the possessor of Lauren Harbison's credit card—who they assumed was male because of his height—and the young female with him had vanished back into the ether. The man had used Lauren's pin, though, so unless he tortured her into revealing it she was still part of the picture somewhere. But police had no new clue where any of them had gone.

To further darken her morning, Carrie Green's story in the *Chronicle* once again included a fact she wasn't supposed to know—that the Alabama police had done a thorough dusting and swabbing of the ATM and had recovered potentially significant prints and DNA samples, including a full handprint on a low shelf that was believed to be from the tall man leaning on one hand while punching keys with the other.

Law enforcement did not want their quarry to know they had these leads on his identity. So Wisneski was not only upset about Green's article interfering with the investigation but knew her phone would soon be ringing with irate callers from the FBI and the Alabama Highway Patrol, blasting her department for letting these facts out.

To make matters still worse—if that was possible—there was no hint in Green's recent articles of either of the stories Wisneski had planted with leak suspects within her department. Nothing about the supposed growing suspicion toward Kelly Harbison, nothing about the soap opera of bad blood within her team. The inventions that were supposed to get out were staying in, and true facts that needed to stay in were escaping.

~

At quarter after ten, Carrie found an email in the new Tutanota account:

> Hello Ms. Friberg,
>
> Have you ever considered applying to law school? I think Duquesne could be a great match for you. How about calling the law school and arranging an informational tour? They have group tours, but they also offer the option of a private tour with a student volunteer. I recommend that you do the second option. One of the volunteers, a girl named Amy, is especially knowledgeable and could answer all of your questions. The school doesn't like people to request a specific volunteer, however. So if you'd like a tour with Amy, it's best to keep finding conflicts in your schedule until she's the one they set you up with.
>
> Best wishes,
>
> Professor Folsom

For a moment Carrie thought she'd been spammed. Then it hit her that the email was addressed to "Ms. Friberg"—Maria. And upon reading it more carefully she saw that it wasn't a promotion for Duquesne Law; rather, it contained an oddly specific set of instructions.

She looked up the faculty list at Duquesne, and there was a Professor Folsom listed there; however, this email hadn't come from his address. This was worth checking out.

She reached the law school (as Maria), and was offered a tour appointment for the next day with a student volunteer named Kirk. She called again in the early afternoon to say she'd learned of a new work meeting and would have to reschedule. They offered her times late today, still with Kirk, tomorrow morning with Leila, or Thursday morning with Amy.

In a striking coincidence, it turned out that Thursday morning was the only time Maria's boss would let her go.

CHAPTER 17

Carrie was restless on Wednesday, eager for the next day to come so she could return to undercover work. In the meantime she needed to pursue the more mundane aspects of her job, included a follow-up call to Delta Evans.

The cub reporter opened by asking, "Do you feel we adequately protected your identity?"

"Yeah," Evans answered, "no complaints. Why?"

"I was wondering if I could ask you a couple more things."

"I ain't gonna say much over the phone, darling, but go ahead."

"You mentioned that Lauren Harbison has been applying to law school. Do you know where she's thinking of going?"

Evans's voice relaxed, as if she'd feared that Carrie would push in a different direction. "As far as I know, the only one she's considering is University of Akron."

"She told you she was applying there?"

"No, somebody else told me."

"Who was that?"

"Well, now, I can't be saying her name, Ms. Green. But this person is a student there, and she told me she took Lauren on a student-led tour of the school."

Carrie could have fallen over. She'd been fishing for hints of a student-led tour at Duquesne, and instead she'd landed one at Akron. Moreover, no one seemed to have any guess why Lauren had taken this sudden interest in studying law.

~

The news from Lauren wasn't good.

> My dearest Sofia,
>
> We didn't make it out. The plan looked rock-solid but wasn't. When we finally saw the documents that had been prepared for us, they were obvious fakes. We're forced now to travel over land and not use a legit crossing point. It's an unbelievable ordeal. Could you please send us help one more time, $2000 again? I promise this will be the last time. You are an amazing friend.
>
> Lauren

Sofia, wrote back quickly. "It may take me some time, I'll figure something out as fast as I can. Believe me, I'll give it my all."

But half an hour later, and despite the increased strength of character provided by an Oxycodone, then a second one, then a glass of wine, then two more of those, she knew she couldn't do it. There was simply no way to come up with any more money except by taking out a loan in her own name at the bank, in which case she might as well go straight from there to turn herself in at the jail.

And even if she could make the money materialize from thin air, she just didn't have what it took to continue further down this path. She'd already been to the doctor with an invented back crisis to get more painkillers. Her children's teachers had been calling her to express concerns about the kids' uncharacteristic mental absence in class. And Jeremy, the most easy-going boss a person could hope for, was starting to snap at her.

She lay awake, eyeballs burning, until 3:30 in the morning despite the precarious level of soothing agents in her bloodstream.

The last half hour of her wakefulness was propelled by a new preoccupation. This last message from Lauren contained a disturbing undercurrent. She could feel it: her friend was in greater danger than she was letting on. The dark thought came to Sofia that Lauren had fallen into the hands of the wrong people.

CHAPTER 18

"So, what makes you interested in coming to law school at Duquesne?" The question caught Maria unprepared; she had no desire to go to law school here or anywhere else. Were they truly going to play this game?

It turned out they were. She had to think fast. "Uh, I'd like to become a judge," she said randomly. "Except I'm not so sure about the robe." They were walking through the halls of the law school classroom building, supposedly on their way to the law library. There was hardly anyone around to overhear their conversation; Maria wondered what audience they were putting on this show for.

But the show continued. Amy pointed in every direction and explained what they were seeing, as if the hallways were wired with microphones. And even when they entered the cafeteria, where the din was close to deafening¬ – they couldn't possible be overheard in here -- Amy chattered on about the delicious features of breakfasts, lunches, and dinners at the dining halls on campus and bought big meals for both of them.

Maria would not have been willing to eat her meals in here if they guaranteed her a seat on the Supreme Court. The only days she'd been able to stand lunch at her high school cafeteria were the three times she'd gotten into fights.

After they ate, Amy finally, blessedly, led them to a bench in a large courtyard between three dorms, at least ten minutes walk from the law school. The young law student took one last careful look around them and said, "I understand you're in danger."

Maria launched into her whole story. For a girl who used to think all the Drama Club kids were pretentious and pathetic she proved remarkably able to leave heavy pauses while pretending to think things over, strain as if calling up forgotten details, make her eyes well up with something close to tears, all the while remembering her lines. When she was through studying law she'd move on to acting school.

"I was stupid to get back with him. Now things are worse than ever."

"No, you weren't stupid," Amy responded. "Since the judge was forbidding you to protect your child, what were you supposed to do?"

She asked for the documents that Maria had shown Natalie, and after flipping through them briefly said, "I'll need to read these carefully. Are these copies I can keep?" Maria nodded.

She then proceeded to talk, in greater and darker detail than Natalie, had about life underground. "We're here for you if you're ready to take this leap, but I don't want you to have illusions about what you're getting into. The women we help have to be mentally prepared, and their children have to be able to handle it."

Maria reflected on the implications. "I... don't see how I have any other choice. My kid's gonna be the daughter of a man who killed her mother. Probably by accident, but what difference does that make to her?"

"No difference at all. Plus you deserve to live."

Maria nodded her head slowly.

Amy pulled two phones out of her bag. "These are both burner phones—one for you and one for me. Today is the first and last time you'll see me. I'm a law student so I can't be involved in anything illegal. You and I will talk a couple of times over the next few days, then not again. I just connect you to other people. They will need several days, and probably longer, to get things in place. I get how stressful that uncertainty is, but it's the nature of the situation. I'll call you, probably tomorrow, and tell you exactly how to prepare."

She reached into her bag again, and this time pulled out a sheet of paper showing a list of websites. "You need to spend two or three hours today—really, today—getting familiar with these sites. The top one is the most important—it tells about a case that's incredibly similar to yours."

Maria started glancing down the sheet, but none of the website names meant anything to her. She was reaching to grab her sunglasses out of her shoulder bag when Amy said, "Maria?" She looked up, and Amy, already in position, shot an iPhone photo of her. It was as close a portrait as she could have taken without holding the phone against Maria's cheek.

"Wait, what?" Maria blurted out, suspicious and angry.

"Your helpers are going to have to know how to recognize you, Maria. Once you're safely far away from here, I'll delete it, and so will they."

"Yeah, yeah, of course… Sorry, I'm just tense. You caught me by surprise."

"Hey, I'm the one who owes the apology. Some people hate having their picture taken, so I figured a candid shot'd be easier. Bad idea." She smiled. Maria's pulse gradually went back to normal.

~

As Carrie settled into her car, Amy's words echoed in her head: *"The women we help."* Women, plural. There it was. The underground network was real.

It appeared that its gateway was a group of law students. She wondered how many law schools were represented, and how the students had connected with each other.

~

Sofia was spreading an exceptional meal across the kitchen counter. She'd gone all out this morning, fried eggs with bacon, pancakes, scalloped potatoes, fresh orange juice. She'd only slept a couple of hours, coming wide awake not long after three o'clock in the morning. She'd swallowed two Oxycodone from her new bottle, three glasses of wine (slowly, carefully monitoring the effects), then half of a third Oxycodone (just a half, see how careful she was being?).

She was looped again, this time at a whole new level. Breakfast with her delightful kids would be a blast.

Except that Kiara wandered past the living room windows on her way to the eat-in kitchen and could scarcely have failed to notice the long shiny blue and white cruiser parked in front of the house. She figured it was best to warn her mother so she wouldn't get caught by surprise later and blow up like last time.

So instead her mother blew up right away.

Sofia rocketed out the front door as if shot from a Howitzer. She marched furiously around to the driver's side door of the cruiser and began to yell with the imperious force of a queen. "You fucking assholes!" screamed Sofia, waving her arms around like a juggler. "Get the fuck away from my house! Leave me the fuck alone! I'm going to sue your ass so fucking royally, my lawyer's gonna carve you into little bits!" Her voice was already loud enough to fell trees and she was just getting warmed up; an impressive eruption of misbehavior from Sofia, a perennial Good Girl, at least when people were watching.

The officer did not roll his window down. He pointedly grabbed his night-stick in his right hand, opened the door of the cruiser, and commanded, "Move away from this vehicle, ma'am."

Sofia didn't miss a beat. She turned expertly on her heel and plowed her way back toward the house without ever stopping the barrage of words firing over her shoulder. "You cocksuckers! You motherfuckers! You Nazis! We're gonna kick your ass in court, just you fucking wait!!" And she disappeared around the side of the house.

Kiara and Jarred sat frozen at the kitchen counter, mortified. Their mother burst back into the house and headed straight to the bathroom to splash water on her face, calling out, "I hope you kids didn't hear that!" as she marched down the hall.

"They heard you in Cincinnati, Mom," growled Kiara.

By the time she came out of the bathroom, the kids were half way down the block toward the bus stop, twenty minutes early, hoping not to be associated with the crazy lady.

Sofia had been in her nightclothes the entire time. She only now registered this fact.

She dressed sloppily for work, didn't put on makeup, flattened her hair enough to not look freshly rolled out of bed, downed another glass of wine with a chaser of grapefruit juice to mask it, and drove off toward work.

She hadn't covered three blocks before colored lights flashed behind her. A butch-cut young woman in uniform approached her car. "Ma'am, you're driving erratically and you entered the last intersection dangerously. I need to ask you to take a Breathalyzer."

"You know what you can do with your Breathalyzer," Sofia said, though suddenly not feeling so tough anymore.

She proceeded to refuse a mouth swab as well.

The officer then asked her to stand on one foot, walk on a straight line putting one foot in front of the other, touch her finger to her nose, and other humiliating gymnastic tasks, while (Sofia dimly became aware) another officer recorded her nearly-random efforts on video. She was then arrested and booked for DUI.

~

Two dozen TV and newspaper reporters gathered at the press conference announced by the McComb, Mississippi police department. The press liaison welcomed everyone, and then Officer Justin Quinn approached the microphone and read from a prepared statement.

"Shortly after 10:30 last night, while driving on Delaware Ave., I observed movement behind the McComb Market grocery store where the dumpsters are. I assumed it was an employee but I drove around for a routine check, and could soon see that the individual was a girl of nine or ten, an odd spot for her to be. There was no adult around. I called through my open window to her, 'Do you need help with something, young woman?' She looked up at me, startled. The rear of the store was brightly lit and I'm sure she saw right away that I was in a police vehicle.

"At this point the girl dropped some items she was holding and ran in the opposite direction from where I was. I pursued on foot, but the girl ran across the street and disappeared between houses on Oak Street. Other officers joined me and we combed the area but didn't find her.

"I have studied photographs and there is no doubt in my mind that the girl I saw is either Brandi Harbison or is the look-alike girl that was seen in Tennessee. She looked somewhat more like the latter. That's all I have for now. Thank you."

Officer Quinn made his exit, and the police chief and press officer took over to field questions. Two additional salient points emerged. First, this was unquestionably an accidental spotting, the girl was not meant to be seen, so they were proceeding on the assumption that this was Brandi herself. Second, the things the girl had dropped were all food items; she'd been dumpster-diving for things to eat. The adult or adults she was traveling with were either out of money or afraid to be seen in public.

~

Wisneski's team sat to digest after watching the Mississippi press conference on livestream. "It doesn't make sense that this kid is the real Brandi," Martinez offered. "She'd be running toward the officer, not away from him, right?"

Wisneski's long experience suggested otherwise. "Kidnappers can brainwash and terrorize their hostages, and even more so with a child. By now they could have Brandi believing her father's trying to kill her or God knows what. There've been famous cases where hostages have refused to cooperate with law enforcement—that's what 'Stockholm Syndrome' is all about. But there's some good news here. First, it looks like this is the real Brandi, which means she's alive. Second, if they're sending her dumpster-diving for food, they're approaching the end of their rope. The typical end of parental kidnapping cases is that the parent gives up."

An urgent message sounded on Wisneski's phone. She asked the team to give her a few minutes and stepped from the room.

When she came back in, she said, "This is interesting. That was Agent Zink from the FBI. They just got results from some lab, I've never heard of this, that specializes in analyzing people, body and face, from still photos and video, and gives mathematical results. They're reporting an eighty-three percent likelihood that the two Brandi's are the same person."

Martinez was dumbfounded. "Could Kelly Harbison have been wrong about his own kid?"

"He seemed sure," Mason replied. "But still, you gotta wonder."

Kresge, who was saying less and less at team meetings and today hadn't spoken at all, finally opened his mouth. "The officer in McComb was black."

The team sat gaping at him, waiting—hoping—for the other shoe to drop.

"What I mean is, Brandi is supposedly this super racist kid, right? So maybe that's why she ran away from him."

Ledbetter shook her head in disbelief. "You're telling me a ten-year-old is such a fanatical bigot that she'd rather stay with her kidnappers than be rescued by a dark-skinned cop?"

"It's not like you have any great explanation for why she ran," Kresge retorted, reddening.

~

When their meeting broke up, the officers came out to learn that Sofia Madsen was in the holding cell, under arrest. Since they had succeeded in getting nothing further out of Delta Evans or Rhapsody Stearns, this might be their big chance to pry some information loose.

~

Attorney Shipley strode confidently into the East Liverpool Police Headquarters. The officer in the booth asked him to sit down, and a few minutes later Lieutenant Herzog came out to shake his hand.

"You represent Sofia Madsen?" Herzog asked.

"Yes, I do, Lieutenant, and I'm very concerned. She's been the target of a mounting pattern of questionable, dare I say unethical, harassment by your department. I will have to consider taking—"

Herzog cut him off. "Don't get on your high horse until you watch the video of the arrest."

The video was a shit show. Madsen could barely stay standing. She had played perfectly into law enforcement's hands.

To make matters worse, when he was permitted to meet with Madsen in a small interrogation room she was still talking like a drunk. "They set me up! This is entrapment!" she said furiously.

"Yes and no, Sofia," her attorney said, his patience finally worn thin. "They did piss you off, but you weren't arrested for being pissed off, you were arrested for being severely impaired."

"I was driving badly because I'm an emotional wreck from their harassment!"

"Nice try; you can't refuse the Breathalyzer and then claim that something else was impairing your driving. You'd have to argue that you weren't impaired. And you have zero chance of that, I watched the video. Plus in a few minutes they'll be taking a blood sample from you for drug testing."

"What?? I refuse, that's an invasion of my privacy!"

"I'm afraid they have the right to do that after a DUI, especially with the severity of your impairment. Do you have any drugs in your system?"

"Just prescription medication! That's totally legal!!"

"Yes, but driving while ripped on medication is not. Is it an opiate?"

"Oxycodone."

"Which you were drinking with? The arresting officer says you smelled of alcohol."

"No, I wasn't drinking with it! What do you take me for??"

"I take you for someone who'd better start negotiating with the DA's office. You will not win on the DUI, believe me; I've defended many dozens of them and this one's a loser. And you've been deteriorating noticeably through the past two weeks. We need to see if we can get you a deal before it's too late."

Sofia hung on stubbornly for another quarter of an hour, reality seeping into her addled brain at the rate of one concept every five minutes. By the time a knock came on the door to take her down to have blood drawn, she was staring darkly at the floor. Her last words to Shipley were, "Go ahead, go ahead."

~

Shipley was able, over more than two hours that he could not afford to spend, to negotiate a deal for Sofia, thanks to the police department's eagerness to gain any possible leads on Lauren's whereabouts. Lieutenant Herzog persuaded the district attorney to grant Sofia immunity regarding any assistance she had provided for the missing woman, in return for telling them everything she knew. The D.A. was not willing to drop the DUI, however; his offer was to continue it for now, on the condition that Sofia complete a drunk driving prevention class and go twelve months with no new arrests.

Shipley left the meeting believing that Sofia would sign the deal, now that she'd had a few hours since the arrest to clear her head. But there were two catches. First, the agreement required her to meet with police by eight o'clock this very night to tell all. The second and more serious one was that she had to agree to "cooperate to the fullest extent possible with all efforts by the police to gain information leading to the apprehension of Lauren Harbison and the recovery of Brandi Harbison."

As expected, Sofia's initial reaction was to say she couldn't possibly agree to a document stating she'd help the police catch Lauren. But Shipley persuaded her that "gain information" is not the same thing as "participate in apprehending," and that the alternatives for her were bad. Sofia had already spent the past three hours facing the reality of her choices, meaning their absence. She signed the deal.

~

Carrie decided to begin researching her web article for that afternoon by reading the materials Amy had handed Maria, regarding a mother named Katie Tagle in southern California.

The madness of the past two and a half weeks soon paled in comparison.

Katie Tagle lived in Yucca Valley, California. She had a son named Wyatt, fathered by her boyfriend Stephen Garcia. Wyatt was born in April 2009 and by August of that year Katie and Stephen had split up. The cause of the breakup, Katie's relatives would eventually tell news reporters, was that Stephen had punched her in the face and knocked her unconscious.

A few months after the split Katie attempted to start a new relationship, and Stephen escalated in response. She ended up in court in Joshua Tree on December 15th, trying to get a restraining order to protect Wyatt and her. She told the judge, "He had sent me text messages before that if his son was around certain people… that he would kill him…And that if I wasn't where I was supposed to be, he'd find me and kill me."

For reasons that aren't clear, Katie was not able to get access to the texts on her phone, but she told the judge the texts were there. With a baby's life on the line, you might expect that the judge would say, *Hold everything, how do we work it out so that I can see those text messages?*

But that wasn't Judge Debra Harris' response. Instead, she denied the restraining order and told Katie to come back on January 12th—almost a month later.

When January 12th of 2010 came, mother and son were both still alive. This time Katie was before Judge David Mazurek, and Stephen was there too. Katie told the judge that there had been a new assault since the last hearing; on December 31st Stephen had asked her to marry him, and when she refused he pushed her to the ground. Katie gave the judge the police report from that assault, but Stephen said she'd made it up.

Katie then handed the judge an email in which Stephen admitted to having hit her previously. The judge asked him about it, and he admitted it to the judge, though he called it a "slap." But then he went on to say that it was Katie's fault because of her "pushing and pushing and pushing until she could get something from me."

Well, gee, thought Carrie, *any guy would of course hit a pregnant woman if she kept trying to get something from him (whatever the hell that meant), right?*

Yes, Tagle had been pregnant at the time. Nine months pregnant, as she proceeded to inform the court.

Judge Mazurek then said, "I kind of get an idea of what's going on." But what he "got" turned out to be the opposite of what Carrie thought the judge would conclude after hearing Stephen admit to hitting his very pregnant girlfriend—for the crime of annoying him, no less.

The judge proceeded to say, "I get concerned when there's a pending child custody issue and one party claims that there's some violence in between. Based on my experience, it's a way for one party to gain an advantage over the other."

These statements were in the transcript.

How suspicious indeed, that the mom would accuse the father of committing violence that he admitted to having committed.

Judge Mazurek denied the restraining order. Strike two.

Carrie read on, cast in a morbid spell.

The next day, January 13th, Stephen Garcia sent Katie a story he'd written called "Necessary Evil." His tale told of two lovers, a man and a woman, except it was simply a recounting of their actual relationship, including details such as fights they'd had over his addiction to video games, their breakup the past

August, her recent decision to start a new relationship, and that day two weeks ago when he'd proposed marriage to her and she'd turned him down.

The story then split into two possible endings. In "Happy Ending," the woman sees the wisdom of getting back with the man. In "Tragic Ending" she stays away from him, so he takes their son to a lake, puts him to sleep with Benadryl, and the baby dies. The father talks to God, saying "My boy will have a better life with You than we can give him here." Then he kills himself.

Katie was petrified. She called 911, and the Deputy who responded immediately went to court and obtained an emergency restraining order on her behalf. (Ironically, Judge Mazurek was the one who signed it.)

But an emergency restraining order is temporary, only valid until a hearing can take place. So the next day Katie had to go to court again, this time before Judge Robert Lemkau in Victorville, CA. She was well-prepared with documents, however. She submitted Stephen's "Necessary Evil" literary work, and, even more startlingly, she submitted texts Stephen had sent to her and her relatives *in the past 48 hours* in which he made specific reference to the story's fatal ending.

Bizarrely, the hearing followed the pattern of the ones before Judge Harris and Judge Mazurek. Once again, the focus was on whether Katie could be believed.

Carrie felt as though she were trapped inside a spinning kaleidoscope.

Judge Lemkau said to Katie, "One of you is lying, and I'm very concerned. There's insufficient evidence in my mind. Mr. Garcia claims it's a total fabrication on your part. I'm going to deny the order, ma'am. If you're lying about this, there's going to be adverse consequences. My supposition is that you are lying."

The only one who got warned and threatened by the court was Katie. Lemkau refused to issue a protective order. Strike three.

Ten days later Wyatt was dead, murdered by his father, who went on to kill himself, just as he had made it clear, in writing, that he would do.

In what created the perfect epilogue to the "Necessary Evil" story—as if wanting to fulfill Stephen Garcia's creative ambitions—Judge Lemkau later stated that there had been no way to predict that a killing was imminent and that he was deeply sorry it had taken place.

Ah yes, what can anyone do? You can't expect us to actually look at the evidence just because lives are on the line.

Carrie tried to shake off the clouds plunging her into deep shadow.

She deciphered a message scrawled in pen, presumably by Amy, on the margins of the last page. "This case is no anomaly. There are dozens more like it all over the U.S., urban and rural, blue state and red. Nothing ever happens to the judges."

Carrie's article for the *Chronicle* website was due soon. Which meant she had to write one. The day had been long and emotionally depleting even before she'd read the news reports on the Tagle case.

She drank three beers from the refrigerator, none of them hers, wondering what the hell an "anomaly" was. Then she assembled what she knew about Brandi's (or pretend-Brandi's) dumpster-diving appearance and rapid escape the night before, and sent the article in. But she felt disconnected from the words she'd written, her sentences went in and out of making sense to her. She couldn't shake the image of Wyatt, Katie Tagle's baby boy.

~

Sergeant Martinez and Officer Kresge, Sofia's old pals, sat with her in a familiar room at the station. Martinez made the routine announcement that the interview was being recorded. Barry Shipley was present, missing an evening with his family and not happy about it. But he had to be on the lookout for questions that would lead Sofia outside of the terms of her immunity. He wasn't sure when he'd ever see the thousand-plus dollars that Sofia owed him, but he had to see the case through this last step before washing his hands of it.

No one said anything for quite a while, as if each person in the room considered it someone else's job to introduce the process. Shipley recognized the strategy, the officers out to make his client feel off balance and vulnerable. He stepped in as if it were his interview.

"Tell the whole story, Sofia, beginning when you first knew that Lauren was preparing to flee. Just relax and speak fully." Before the meeting he'd told her the rest, which was that he'd be on the alert and would seize the reins if he saw her gallop off at a dangerous tilt.

By this point Sofia wanted nothing but to be done and out of there; she barely hesitated, only taking a quick glance at Shipley for reassurance. "I never knew that Lauren was getting ready to go; her disappearance caught me completely by surprise."

And that fast Martinez and Kresge thought she was lying.

Sofia ignored their expressions and plunged on. "There were other things I didn't know. It's clear to me now that Lauren was afraid to tell people what was really going on with her and Brandi. There were times when she made references to going into hiding, yes. But never like she was serious about it, she was just blowing off steam. Or that's how she made it sound."

Shipley asked what the issues were about Brandi. The officers looked annoyed that he was continuing to run their show, but said nothing.

Sofia explained how upset Brandi was before and after time at her father's house, and how rude and attacking she would be toward her mother at those times, as if it were her fault. She also talked about the violent and at times racist references the girl would make, which Brandi would say came from movies she had watched. Either her father was showing them to her or he was making no effort to supervise her. Lauren was afraid for herself as well, because Kelly had been violent when they were together and it sounded as though he was escalating again."

Martinez said, "Hang on. No one, including you, has said anything to us to suggest that Kelly Harbison was a bad father or that he and Brandi were anything other than close. Where is this suddenly coming from?"

Shipley jumped in, addressing Sofia. "It's not your job to address what anyone else might have said or not said. Speak only for yourself."

Sofia nodded and breathed deeply. "I didn't want to see Lauren caught and jailed. I was hoping that it would look like she and Brandi were both victims of a kidnapper. So I didn't want to say anything about the reasons why Lauren wished she could flee."

Martinez said, "There's no mention of domestic violence anywhere in the divorce record, Ms. Madsen, and this case has been in the courts for some years."

"She, well... her lawyer told her not to bring up domestic violence at court. He said family court judges retaliate against mothers who accuse the father of abuse. Better to just say you're splitting up because you can't get along."

Martinez rolled her eyes. "This is ridiculous. Women use domestic violence allegations to get a leg up in their divorces all the time."

"That's exactly how the judges think, Sergeant," Sofia snapped. "That's why Lauren had to run!" Fury had driven away her fear of the cops, she wanted to bite their heads off.

Shipley stepped in once again. "Unless I'm mistaken, we're not here to debate the biases of the courts. Could we please get back to my client's story?"

Now it was Martinez's turn to look furious, while Kresge's appeared something closer to amused. The room was quiet for a few moments. Shipley then nodded toward Sofia, prodding her to continue.

"So... well, a few days after Lauren disappeared, I... started to hear from her." She described the text message, the instructions to create the encrypted account, the beginnings of requests for money—and how she had, in fact, sent the requested amounts. Until the most recent message, that is.

Martinez made no effort to hide her disgust—Kresge remained poker faced—but neither officer condemned her aloud. The sergeant pulled out her laptop, however, and went right to work. "What is the user name and password for your Protonmail account?" she asked.

"That's private information!" Sofia protested.

Shipley's mind was racing. But given the terms of the immunity deal he couldn't see a way out for his client. "Sofia, you've acknowledged that you created the account at Lauren's behest, for the purpose of communicating with her while she's in hiding. Under the terms of the agreement we made, I think you're stuck. I apologize that I didn't see this coming."

Sofia made huge deer-caught-in-the-headlight eyes. "I... I'm sorry," she said, "I have to step out and think for a few minutes, take a walk or something."

Shipley knew why, and so did everyone else in the room; she wanted to warn Lauren that any future messages under her name would actually be from the police.

"Ma'am," Martinez said, "If you go out of our sight the deal disappears. You agreed to give us all relevant information you had access to."

Sofia broke into hard crying. An irrepressible dam had burst.

Martinez became rapidly impatient, as if this show of weakness in a female would reflect on them all. "We have serious work to do, every hour counts on this case, pull yourself together ma'am."

Shipley snapped hard. "It is nowhere close to the eight o'clock deadline yet, you have no cause to tell my client she can't show emotion. She is cooperating fully, and you can be human with her."

There was a brief staredown between attorney and sergeant. Kresge broke the tension by saying, "I'm stepping out for tissues." In a moment he was back, handed a box to Sofia without comment, and resumed his seat next to Martinez.

Sofia, dazed now and speaking as if controlled by a machine, gave the officers the specifics about the Protonmail account. Martinez logged in successfully in case Sofia was lying.

Shipley's client looked as defeated as a wrongly-charged defendant pronounced guilty by a unanimous and angry jury.

The sergeant poked around in the account and then said, "There are no emails in your Inbox or your Sent folder, and only one in your Trash."

Speaking haltingly, her voice occasionally breaking, Sofia said, "I've been erasing each email as I got it, and emptying the trash right away... Except I wanted to look at the last one a little more."

"Because you were still planning to send this last amount?"

"No... Something about the email made me feel that Lauren and Brandi are in grave danger, and... I wanted to come back to it and see if I could figure out why." Sofia started to cry again, but quietly.

She answered questions for two more hours. Her voice became softer and softer, her skin greener and pastier. She looked broken.

~

On the sidewalk down the block from the police station, Sofia said to her lawyer, "I can't believe what I've done. I'm a worthless piece of shit."

Shipley responded, "Avoiding jail is not a cowardly act for a parent. Your kids need their mother."

Sofia nodded without conviction. "I just handed them the means to catch her. So she can be in jail instead of me."

"Lauren's gotten this far, she must not be so easy to catch."

"Thank you, Barry. Really, I mean it, you've been great. But I don't believe in a happy ending for this one anymore... I'll start making payments to you right away, but they may be kind of small. I'm really sorry."

And with that they said a cordial goodnight.

She resolved to keep in mind what a decent and smart man Shipley was. Maybe Lauren would need him some day.

The instant Shipley was out of sight she grabbed her phone and tried to get on the Protonmail account to warn Lauren. But the password had already been changed.

~

In the late afternoon, the police in McComb received a call from a woman on Rawls Street, near the medical center. She'd just been in her back yard with her Scottie and the dog had started intently rummaging in some papers scattered in low, dense bushes at the back edge of the lawn. Her property bordered on a small area of open land and a parking lot belonging to the medical center. The items turned out to include photographs, frequent-shopper punch cards, and a gym membership card. She would have thrown them away except that her neighborhood had been crawling with police all day asking neighbors whether they'd seen anything the night before.

So she coaxed her Scottie away and called the station.

The photos turned out to be three wallet-sized pictures. A couple of hours of communication between law enforcement agencies, with some help from relatives of Lauren's, led to the identification of a photo of Brandi at about age seven, another of their family dog who had died when Brandi was little but to whom Lauren (and Brandi) had been very much attached, and a snapshot of Lauren's parents.

These were not items that a ten-year-old girl would likely carry, but her mother very well might.

Lauren was the one person there had still been no sighting of in this drama. But law enforcement could feel that they were drawing closer.

~

Carrie got Gavin on the phone. "Listen," she said, diving in abruptly, "can you call in sick tomorrow?"

"Jesus, not really. I have a lot of work to do and I'm already on my boss's permanent shit list."

"Hey, if it's permanent, why get into a lather trying to work your way off it? Save your energy for better things."

"Like unemployment?"

"I'll keep you employed."

"Yeah, and volunteer work doesn't get much better than that. But I happen to also need to be paid. Care to tell me what this is all about? Is tomorrow supposed to be a beautiful day?"

"No. I mean, I didn't look at the forecast… My head is kind of spinning. I think we may have been messing up."

"What? How?" She could hear fear in his voice; he thought she was about to break up with him.

"About the Lauren and Brandi story."

He exhaled, relieved. "How could 'we' be messing that up? It's not my story."

"I'm trying to wrap my head around some stuff… Look, the deal is, I need to research a bunch of stuff tomorrow, it's kind of dark, I'm not down for doing it alone. I need someone to work on it with me."

"Hey, if that's what this is about, I can head your way now."

"Gavin, I'm serious."

She proceeded to tell him the sordid tale of her day as an undercover agent, then the news about Brandi's cameo appearance in Mississippi the night before. And last her disturbing dive into the Katie Tagle story, which had sickened and disoriented her.

But when she'd only given him the barest outline of that case, her phone signaled an incoming call. It was from Amy.

Carrie did a double take; this didn't make sense. Why was Amy calling her on her regular number, after telling her that she was under no circumstances to call Amy from anything other than the burner phone she'd handed her?

She told Gavin to hang on for a moment and switched over to the other call.

"Hello," she said. "Amy?"

Amy's voice was curt and cold, sharpened to a fine edge. "We know who you are. Don't ever contact us again. We'll be making a complaint with your paper." And she hung up.

Carrie tried to call her back but it went to voice mail.

A bay-full of f-bombs erupted from her, and she kicked Scoop's desk chair over with a loud bang.

She connected back to Gavin, swears continuing. "They already fucking figured out who I am! My little spy project is over as soon as it started!"

"What? How the hell did they know it was you? I hardly recognized you myself."

She explained about Amy's candid shot of her. "I'm sure they—whoever 'they' may be—were passing my photo around tonight, and it must have rung a damn bell for someone. I've been on local Pittsburgh TV twice now. But even more likely it's 'cause of the head shot of me on the *Chronicle* website. They probably sat studying the 'Maria' picture and comparing it to mine until they were sure. Shit, shit, shit!"

"But Carrie, how much more were you gonna find out anyhow? You've already got your main story, which is that this underground is real and operating."

"So much more. I could have learned how they move people around, gotten a sense of how wide a network it is, what their survival strategies are, how they keep from getting caught, inside of a whole secret world."

"But you couldn't have done any of that. You had no way to show up with a daughter."

Carrie was quiet for a moment. "Oh, yeah." In the rush of events she hadn't thought that far ahead. "But, Jesus, they're gonna complain to the *Chronicle*. Vinestri already looks at me like I'm a bundle of fireworks smuggled from

Tijuana, ready to explode at the wrong moment and take someone's face off. They're gonna kill me for this."

"Except this Amy person won't actually go through with telling them. What's she gonna say? 'Your reporter lied to us while infiltrating our kidnapping system? She took advantage of our illegal work for her own purposes?'"

"They'll come up with a way to say it. Fuck. What time can you get here tomorrow?"

Gavin didn't answer.

"Is your paper covering the Harbison story?" she asked.

"They print some of your articles, bought from the *Chronicle*. They don't have a person of their own assigned to it."

"Okay, so how about our meeting tomorrow leads to an original article from you?"

"You'd be okay with that?" he asked.

She wasn't so sure. But whatever it took to get him to get his ass next to her.

"I'll see if that works to get Carpelli to let me leave the office. I think it might." He sounded energized.

Carrie looked around at her room, which wasn't holding entirely still. She needed to muster the energy and focus to spice that afternoon's web article into a paper-selling version for tomorrow's print edition, with a magnetic headline. That was her job, as she knew; it was no secret that her dispatches were selling the paper, helping bring it back from the edge of destruction.

"I've gotta yank my head together," Carrie told Gavin. "Call me as soon as you know about tomorrow."

CHAPTER 19

Marco Vinestri settled at his desk to eat lunch after a reasonably merciful morning. Ahead of him was the prospect of the first calm Friday afternoon he'd had in weeks.

His phone rang. "Mr. Vinestri," said the caller, "My name is Marianne Somers, I'm the Executive Director of A Safe Path, a domestic violence program in Pittsburgh. I understand you supervise the reporter Carrie Green?"

With a sinking heart, Vinestri confirmed that he did.

"Well," the woman continued, "your reporter came to our program twice, pretending to be an abused woman. She told stories of being nearly strangled to death. Not only did she take advantage of our counseling services, she attended a support group where numerous other women were traumatized by her story, and—"

Vinestri cut the caller off. "Ma'am, I'm not sure why you assume a newspaper reporter couldn't be a battered woman. I would think as director of a program you'd know that. You're telling me things about my employee that are none of my business and violate her confidentiality."

Though right away he doubted it.

Somers left a pause, designed to add impact to the words that would follow. "Green's been here under a false name—Maria Friberg. And she's been wearing a disguise. It was brought to my attention by one of our support group participants, who got us to look at Green's picture on your website and pull up one of her TV appearances from last week. If you like we'll send you a picture of her in her disguise, our participant happened to take one."

It hit Vinestri like a tank: the hair cut short and restyled, the sudden change to dark brunette, Green's excuses about "a new job makes it time for a change."

"Ma'am," Vinestri said, making a last desperate try to save the *Chronicle* from disaster, "the fact that Green is now well-known in this region is all the more reason why she might have to go to large steps to protect her privacy. It sounds like she may be in danger."

"Well, Mr. Vinestri, if she is in danger, then she's a married woman with a four-year-old child and she's in the Ohio courts divorcing a man who nearly strangled her to death."

There was no place left to go; Marco knew that there couldn't be any such child and that Green still lived at home. His reporter had infiltrated a program for domestic violence victims. She could scarcely have chosen any action that would make the newspaper look worse.

What the hell would drive her to such a hare-brained move? The girl was either reasonably clever or the stupidest person on the planet, depending on whether it was a north or south wind day. Well, this time he was finally going to have the pleasure of firing her. That might even be adequate compensation for the fact that his peaceful afternoon had just gone to hell.

He changed his tone on a dime. "I can understand why you're upset, and I'm very sorry. Please send us the information you have and we'll start an internal investigation immediately."

Somers replied, "You'll have it right away. And I'm afraid there's one additional serious issue."

Vinestri could hardly wait.

"Your reporter appears to have impersonated a real person, using her real name and her court documents, in which case she has committed a crime. I should be able to find out this morning whether that's true or not."

Oh, joy.

~

Gavin arrived at Carrie's house a few minutes before ten, his lips the first part of him to cross the threshold. Carrie met them immediately with hers. She then managed to adequately reassure him that they were alone and would stay that way, such that he put up no fight as she pulled him to her room and removed his pants—not that he would have resisted anyhow.

Motion seemed to be accelerated, her approach to lovemaking this morning was abrupt, an edge of desperation to it. He showed no sign that he minded getting ravished, though, undoubtedly having had worse things happen to him.

Carrie lay holding Gavin for a while, wishing that her life, which only yesterday was so dazzlingly thrilling, would go away and leave her alone. But her stress level came down several notches, the magic of orgasm.

When they felt that they'd hidden away as long as they could, they got up and sat side-by-side with their laptops and cups of coffee and got to work.

Carrie first led Gavin back through last night's internet tour of the Katie Tagle case. When they arrived at the appalling and tragic end, she asked. "What do you make of this?"

"Not sure. But I've known plenty of judges who were total jerks."

Carrie squinted at him. "What do you mean, you've 'known plenty of judges'? Like, what, back when you were Governor?"

"Friends of my father's. One time there was even some kind of fancy dinner for judges at my house. They're pretty much like my parents' other friends except even more full of themselves, which is saying something."

Carrie sat shaking her head, peering at Gavin without being able to get his face entirely into focus. "You might as well've been raised by penguins for all we have in common," she said.

"What I find most remarkable," he said, hopping on ahead (like a good penguin), "is that a judge can make life or death decisions, no jury or anything, and refuse to be bothered with the evidence while he does it, calling her a liar while the proof that she's telling the truth is in his hands but he won't read it. Was he removed after the murder?"

"No. The outraged locals had to run a candidate against him and beat him in the next election. That was the only way to get rid of him."

The young lovers then sat for over two hours, as if possessed, researching case after case. It appeared that Katie Tagle was just the beginning of a gruesome litany.

~

They had just started to consider what to assemble for lunch when "He's the Boss" by Kohl and the Gang resounded through the room. It was Carrie's recently-chosen ringtone for calls from Marco. At least this time he was calling when she and Gavin had most of their clothes on and were breathing at a normal rate.

"I need you to come in and meet with me," Vinestri said ominously.

Uh-oh, she thought, *the shit's hit the fan.*

It was a mistake to answer the phone in her normal voice; she should have rasped and talked through her nose. "I'm sick," she said belatedly, "my throat is killing me. What's going on?" As if she didn't know.

Vinestri's tone was sarcastic. "Your escapade in Pittsburgh with your new hairdo has been brought to our attention. The Executive Director of the domestic violence program there is ripshit. It looks like you didn't absorb the message we tried to get through to you about professional conduct."

She took a fighting stance, her only option. "They're arranging kidnappings out of there. Not only that, I found a big-time similarity with Lauren Harbison's disappearance." She described the law school connection.

Marco demanded every detail, right this second. Carrie spoke with a strained voice and stopped periodically to cough. He was not likely buying the sick routine but there was no way she could stand to drive down to the paper right now.

When the whole story of her infiltration was told, Vinestri still had no trouble reaching an instant verdict. "Your lapses in judgment are astounding. Head this way immediately."

"I just can't do it," Carrie moaned pathetically. "Let me sleep for a couple of hours and I'll muster it somehow to come down when I wake up."

"Your job may be gone by the time you get here," he snapped.

~

Wisneski and Ledbetter strategized about the shape Sofia's next email to Lauren would take. They resisted the temptation to try for quick and dramatic results; it wouldn't take much to raise Lauren's suspicions. They went so far as to read the transcripts of their interviews with Sofia and then worked her characteristic ways of speaking into the wording they chose:

> Lauren:
>
> I'm worried sick about you both and I'd do anything in the world to come up with the money you need, but I swear I have no place left to get it from. I can't send much more than a tenth of what you need, I feel awful. KH has gone off hunting for you, thought you should know.
>
> I got a message from Brandi. Is it okay if I respond?
>
> Love, Sofia

The mention of the supposed message from Brandi had two goals. First, it seemed likely to elicit a response; Lauren would want to know why Brandi communicated with Sofia and what she had said. Secondly, they sought to sow tensions between mother and daughter; when Brandi denied sending the message Lauren would think she was lying, especially since she'd already caught Brandi trying to call her father. Conflict and tension between them could lead Lauren to make mistakes that might help police apprehend her.

They followed up the email with a $250 transfer. As long as money was still making its way to Lauren, even if it was less than she'd hoped for, she wouldn't drop out of touch.

~

Gavin's eyes were scrunched up when Carrie finished her call with Vinestri. "You told me the meeting you went to in Pittsburgh was for divorcing women. You mean all the women there were being battered by their husbands??"

"And boyfriends, whatever. It's a domestic violence program."

"You didn't tell me that."

"Yeah, I know. I didn't."

"Jesus, Carrie, you can't go using a real service and playing on people's heartstrings like that."

"Gavin, don't start with me. You think I don't know? Be useful, help me figure out what I'm gonna do."

He tried but came up with nothing. She was the one with a lifetime of surprise maneuvers under fire, tactical retreats, and renewed campaigns. So she worked out, in a dialogue with herself, the tack she was going to take while Gavin gaped in disbelief at what she was planning. The most he could do was propose a couple of strategic phrases she might use.

To further his amazement, only a few minutes had passed before she was punching the number for A Safe Path into her phone, demonstrating again her hatred of leaving dark clouds looming.

Carrie identified herself, then asked to speak to Marianne Somers. The receptionist asked what the call was regarding, and the young reporter answered, "It's about an article I'm writing this afternoon on your organization's involvement in an underground kidnapping network."

She figured that would get Somers to the phone. And, indeed, an executive-sounding and enraged voice soon boomed in her ear.

"What is this??"

Carrie reached for a friendly tone but due to her nervousness didn't nail it. "Hi, this is Carrie Green from the *Chronicle* in Morriston, Ohio. I've been informed about your complaint against me to my paper."

"I have nothing to say to you," Somers replied icily. "I'm in shock that you would misuse our life-or-death services in pursuit of a sensational story. You're welcome to speak to our lawyer."

"It's fine if you have nothing to say to me, I'm sure you'd love to kill me. But you might want to hear what I have to say. The reason I was there was because there's a kidnapping ring running out of your office, and I got proof of that while I was there."

"A kidnapping ring??" Somers virtually yelled into the phone. "What the hell are you talking about?"

The infiltrator responded with an account of meeting Natalie at support group—she didn't give Somers the name, of course—then being vetted by her, and finally meeting a student at Duquesne Law School for a supposed tour that in reality was part two of the vetting process. "And I think you should know," Carrie added, "that Lauren Harbison was instructed to call a student at the University of Akron law school and pretend she was applying there, and this was just before she kidnapped her daughter. It looks like a network of law students are the contact points for these cases."

Carrie was claiming more than she knew, and Somers could sense that she was overplaying her hand. "None of this has a single thing to do with my agency, and if you write anything that suggests that it does, your career will come to an early end due to our lawsuit. Whatever happened in private conversations between you and one of our clients—whom you fraudulently met in group—is your business, not mine."

"Actually, I talked to at least one member of your staff who assists this network. How could you miss this happening right under your nose? It doesn't look so good."

Natalie had, indeed, told Carrie that someone within the agency helped connect women to the underground—that's how Natalie had gotten involved—though she hadn't said who it was. For all Carrie knew it could have been the counselor who met with Maria, though she seemed straight-laced.

"Who is the staff person you're accusing??" Somers snarled.

"Listen," Carrie continued, talking fast to keep the director from hanging up, "you and I have the same interests here. I'll be writing about this kidnapping network, that's my job. I won't mention your agency, that's not the point of the story, I'm sure you do good work. The wording in the draft is 'a domestic violence program in Eastern Pennsylvania.' But if you make a complaint against me, then that becomes legitimate news in itself. You'd be putting me in a position where I'd have to tell the public everything I know, otherwise I'd look like the biggest asshole on the planet."

The last two lines were rehearsed, the first step in the nascent journalistic collaboration between Carrie and Gavin.

The program director was silent. A good sign. Certain aspects of what Somers had said to Vinestri indicated that she'd done some research on Carrie, which meant she would have to realize the size of the audience Carrie had built up over the past three weeks, including her appearances on Canton and Pittsburgh news shows. Somers was no doubt weighing the implications of the young reporter's popular reach.

Several seconds passed with Somers remaining silent. Carrie thought it best to plunge on. "I'm not even saying these mothers shouldn't run; they may be justified. My colleague from the *Lincoln Republican* and I"—another phrase from Gavin—"have been looking into cases all across the country where the courts sat there and let kids get killed."

Somers finally spoke. "I have no reason to trust you, given what you've proven about your ethical level. Moreover, I've read your articles. You make it sound like abused women are hysterical exaggerators, the courts are stacked against fathers, and false abuse allegations are rampant. You want me to believe you're suddenly Ms. Sensitive on these issues?"

Somers had a point. But Carrie, never one to go on the defensive, kept instead to her comfortable and familiar path, which was to lie. "Those were never my views, Ms. Somers. As a reporter, I keep my own opinions out of what I write. I've been reporting what people are telling me in interviews. Now I've started to hear some alternate opinions for the first time."

"Bullshit. You're no friend of ours."

Carrie abandoned the effort to build trust. "Okay, then let's put an agreement in writing. I treat you and your whole agency as sources, which in effect you are, so no one ever hears your name or location. If I don't keep my word on that, you can go ahead with your complaint and sue me too."

A tense negotiation ensued. The program director's voice lost none of its hostility, but she audibly shifted toward a grudging willingness to do business. After what seemed an interminable struggle, they finally agreed that Carrie would come to the agency in the morning; they'd go over specific wording which Somers would review with her agency's lawyer, and if all went well they'd sign binding forms.

Somers's "good-bye" dripped with resentment, but the uncontrolled fury was gone.

"Whatever," Carrie said after disconnecting. "If she wants to hate me forever, that's fine, long as she doesn't shoot me."

"And shoot herself in the process," Gavin added.

Carrie was instantly on the phone to Vinestri, not even having made it out of her room yet. "A Safe Path is withdrawing their complaint against me," she informed him. "They no longer want you to take any action about it. They'll be in touch tomorrow to say this formally."

The editor reacted as though Carrie were claiming to have proof that Santa Claus was real. "You've got to be kidding me!" She couldn't tell which one he was feeling more, disbelieving or disappointed.

"No, it's for real. They said they'll call you mid-morning."

They hadn't really, but with luck she could finagle an agreement by then.

Marco took on the tone of a lawyer opening a hostile cross-examination. "Carrie, what the hell is going on? Are you connected to the mafia or something? How do you get all this inside information from the police that the TV stations can't even get, Harbison refuses to talk to anyone but you, and now this agency withdraws a complaint they made only three hours ago? I smell a rat the size of a woodchuck."

She wasn't sure how much her paper should know, if anything, about the deal she'd just struck. She needed a lawyer of her own, or more like one of those reputation consultants. "I gave the Somers lady a serious apology, and then explained why I went there incognito. I said I shouldn't of done it, it was stupid, I'm brand new in my job. And, well, she ended up saying she'd overreacted, she doesn't want to interfere with my reporting, she's been following my articles on the case."

Carrie's skills were better matched for fiction-writing than journalism.

Though Marco really wasn't buying it. "You can't write anything in tonight's article about this supposed underground, not until we've gone over it with our legal department." And he went on to assert that there would still be an HR process at the paper regarding Carrie's conduct.

So she was gonna get an official scolding. *Make all the red marks you want in some secret file,* she thought. *Knock yourself out.*

~

Close to ten o'clock that night, Wisneski heard a tropical birdcall from across the room, meaning she had a notification from Sofia Madsen's Protonmail. The detective dropped the magazine she was reading on her living room couch, the closest she'd come to a successful breather in over two weeks, and went straight to her laptop.

> Hi Sofia,
>
> Please don't apologize, I'm grateful for whatever you can do. You're a great friend, I appreciate today's transfer so much.
>
> Brandi almost got nabbed the other night, you probably heard.
>
> Brandi didn't send you a message, she has no device to do that with. Be very careful, must be an investigator posing as her. Don't respond, please, if you get caught it's bad for all of us.
>
> I don't get a lot of chances to be on this account but for now it's still the only safe way to be in touch.
>
> Lauren

So much for their first attempt. But since Brandi had tried to call Kelly the second day after they fled, it made sense that Lauren would be keeping her on a very short leash. Maybe the reason why Brandi had run from the officer in McComb was that her mother had been nearby, keeping just out of sight.

~

"I can't read any more of this shit," Carrie said, massaging around her eyes and wishing she could massage her brain. "It's awful. And none of it makes any sense."

Like everyone else, she'd heard all her life that custody courts were all for the mother, a father didn't have a chance. Tonight she felt as though she were looking at an inverted world, like a baby trying to make sense out of shapes and movements that have no context, no history.

She wished she'd taken a law class in junior college. At the time she'd considered it total crap. But suddenly it was crap that mattered, the difference between a dogshit you pass in the woods and one that appears in your medicine cabinet, defying all reason.

There was Kathryn Sherlock, whose seven-year-old daughter Kayden was murdered in Pennsylvania during a court-ordered visit. The girl had been complaining of feeling scared of her father, that she'd seen him punching the dog and punching himself in the face. He was known to be suicidal. He had previously bitten a man's ear off, which he admitted to. He'd been banned from Kayden's school for rude and aggressive behavior. But, with all this known, the court, in its infinite wisdom, still ordered the mother to turn her daughter over for unsupervised time with him, and he murdered her and then killed himself.

There was Hera McLeod, whose baby son Prince was murdered after the Virginia court required her to send him on unsupervised visits, despite her pleading to the court to take seriously the extensive evidence of the father's involvement in prior sexual assaults, frauds, and murders. (He was eventually charged in the murder of an ex-girlfriend, but only after he'd murdered Hera's baby.)

There was Amy Hunter, whose two daughters, aged nine and twelve, were murdered by their father during a court-ordered unsupervised visit. Amy had told the court, including in writing, that the girls' father had been violent to her, had threatened to take the girls permanently out of the country, and had used other terror tactics. He had new criminal charges for violating his restraining order, but the family court didn't consider that adequate cause to suspend his visitation.

There was Jacqueline Franchetti, who repeatedly told the judge that her two-year-old's father was violent and rageful, and had made suicidal threats. But the forensic evaluator dismissed claims of domestic violence and marked the father "low risk." The New York judge told Jacqueline to "grow up" and ordered that visits go forward. The father, Roy Eugene Rumsey, then murdered little Kyra during one of his visits.

Gavin stood up and started kneading Carrie's shoulders. She leaned into it. "Fine with me to close up for the night," he said.

They were both silent for a while, digesting their long day's work. No part of the country seemed exempt. Evidence that would persuade any reasonable person that a murder was imminent made no impression on the judges in these cases. And in almost all of the fatal cases they found, it was the mother and her children who bit the dust, not the father. When had the divorce courts made this swing to the other extreme?

A life-long sore spot of Carrie's had just gotten rubbed worse. "I've always thought of judges as assholes, but *competent* assholes at least. Now it turns out they might as well be shitfaced drunk, they're so out of it."

"They're not incompetent, Carrie."

She rolled her eyes. "Are you seriously gonna give me that 'they're doing the best they can' crap?"

"No, the opposite. They know perfectly well what they're doing and do it anyhow. They wring their hands and whine, 'Oh, these cases are so complicated,' but the evidence is right in front of them, everyone else can see it just fine."

"So what is it? The judges are on the take? The abusers' lawyers are buying them off?"

"I'd like to know. I kind of doubt it's literal bribes, though. That would eventually get the attention of the FBI and DOJ."

"DOJ? There's a Department of Judges?"

Gavin explained.

Maybe some judges are just plain evil, Carrie thought. Except she didn't altogether believe in evil, it had a religious sound to it that had never been her thing. But it was hard not to feel the devil's mark on the accounts they'd been absorbing these many hours.

"I need to head home," Gavin said. "It's gonna be midnight by the time I get there. I've got an early-morning bike ride."

"Lord, I wish I had the strength to drive to Pittsburgh and stay at your place, I'm not down for being alone. But I'm shot, I can't muster it."

Gavin's face formed an expression she hadn't seen on him before, almost shy. "Listen, you said I should write an article about this case. How about I start researching these fathers' organizations, find out what they're all about?"

Carrie shrugged her shoulders and answered distractedly. "Yeah, go ahead, maybe they can put us onto cases where the judges do the same crazy shit to fathers." Then her sleepy eyes widened as if jolted by caffeine, and she bounced up abruptly. "Actually, forget general research, I want you to check out a specific group. Those Fathers Rights guys up in Canton, the Alliance for Child Rights. They've been all over the Harbison case—I stopped at their picket on my way back from Athens."

He nodded agreeably. "Sure, I'll go talk to them."

"No, not like that," she answered, eyes sparkling, hands up. "It's your turn to go underground."

CHAPTER 20

A young guy who had presented himself as "Percy Robicheau" sat in a circle with eight other men and one woman. They occupied folding chairs on the back deck of a house in a Canton suburb that belonged to group member Mark Chambliss. Three of the men, including Percy, were attending a meeting for the first time.

The group's leader amiably introduced himself as Nathaniel Holsheen. He explained that he always opened meetings by asking new participants to briefly tell their stories. Percy was a timid, soft-spoken character, angry but quietly so, and quite unsure of himself. He was also younger than all the rest. He said he preferred to go last.

Percy noticed similarities to the accounts of the two guys who spoke before him. Their partners had found fault with everything they did. Any time the man tried to stand up for himself, he would get labeled "abusive." Their partners found other rage-filled women and they fed off each other. When it came time to split up, both men had been nervous because they knew there was no fair shake for fathers in the divorce courts, and sure enough, they were being treated like terrible fathers. One of the men was only allowed to see his kids with a supervisor present. He cried as he spoke about it. "I can't even take my kids to the bathroom, the supervisor has to take them." The other father had his kids nearly half time, but was bitter that he hadn't won primary custody, since the cause of his divorce was his wife cheating on him. He was also enraged about child support. "She should have to account for how she spends the money I send her, it's obviously not going to the kids."

When Percy's turn came, he shared his carefully rehearsed tragedy. "My girl—we're not married—she's my ex now—she just wasn't cut out for the mother thing. I had to pretty much look after the kids. She kept partying like a teenager, and I just couldn't have that around the kids. I called the police on her a couple of times, but they didn't do anything—well, except one time they arrested me, even though I was the one to call. So then she started to tell the kids lies about me and try to turn them against me."

Group members showered Percy with supportive outrage. He acted uncomfortable with their cheerleading. "Well, she's got a problem with drugs and alcohol, it's not like she's evil or something. I just wish the court would listen to me about the kids."

His conciliatory stance was part of the script. He wasn't ready yet to "face reality," but over some days or weeks he would allow group members to "get him to see" how nefarious her strategy was. They'd have no reason to doubt his story if it took them a lot of work to win him over.

The next item on the agenda was the Kelly Harbison case. Percy was able to gather that, since Lauren and Brandi's disappearance, the Alliance for Child Rights had devoted most of its energy to publicizing the role the divorce court had played in letting the kidnapping happen. They'd recruited several new members in the past three weeks; the case was serving as a vehicle for building the local Fathers Rights movement.

Percy pretended ignorance. "Is this the one where the father was on the news?" He proceeded to describe Kelly.

"Yes," Chambliss said. "Just once, though, the night after our rally. He doesn't care for publicity."

Yeah, sure, thought Percy. "But isn't that guy kind of a jerk?" He tried to sound a little shaky as he posed the question.

"He's been through hell, you'd be pissed too."

"Kelly Harbison's not coming tonight?" he asked innocently.

"Absolutely not," Holsheen said peremptorily. "He's not in this group. He doesn't like us, he called us extremists on the news. That's the thanks we get for fighting for him."

They returned to discussing ways to protest the Harbison disappearance, bad feelings toward Kelly laid aside for the moment. Holsheen and Chambliss pressed members to write letters to newspapers and politicians, and it became evident to Percy that Chambliss was the group leader's sidekick.

The remainder of the meeting consisted of updates about their own legal cases. One man had gotten a temporary order for joint custody that he was cautiously happy about, another had won a reduction in his child support, another reported that his ex-wife had a new lawyer who was making himself difficult.

A couple of guys asked around to see if anyone had heard from a guy named Denny, who'd stopped showing up for meetings and wasn't returning phone calls. The one female present, who hadn't spoken until then, there to accompany her boyfriend in the fight against his vindictive and jealous ex-wife, said, "I think Denny just couldn't take it anymore, hearing after hearing went against him at court and he lost his will to fight."

As the meeting broke up, a few members asked Percy if he'd be returning next time. Exhibiting ambivalence and a generally weak character, he stuttered, "Oh, I don't know, I'm not sure this is for me. I learned a lot, though. Thank you, guys."

As he'd hoped, a few men stuck around for a few minutes to persuade him to keep coming. He indicated that he'd think about it. He was rewarded with a couple of friendly punches in the triceps that he could have done without.

~

It was around 4:30 when Carrie, having driven a little over half an hour northwest from Mormon Valley, arrived at the Youngstown home of Hillary Rogers, Lauren Harbison's sister. She found herself entering her precise image of perfectly-kept suburbia, with two-car garage, an actual white picket fence (she didn't even know that was a real thing), stunted young maple tree in the front yard, and an unusable amount of space both inside and out.

Rogers looked like something the house itself might have given birth to, after mating with a shopping mall. Her hoop earrings and her smile were too large for her smallish face, her voice a little husky like a long-time smoker (but of course she wouldn't dream of smoking in that neighborhood), a cocktail in her hand to smooth out the raspiness of her throat and of human interactions. The clothes did not look like Saturday-wear; either the lady had guests coming for dinner or she just never eased up.

Back when Carrie had first started covering the story, Kelly told her to talk to Hillary, saying she'd learn an earful about his ex that way. At the time it had seemed like trivial backbiting and Carrie hadn't pursued it. Now she was curious to see what she'd hear.

Rogers put the reporter at an ornate oak kitchen table so heavy that it made Carrie feel that the rest of room would float away, then took a seat across from her. She offered the reporter a drink, which the girl very much wanted but declined, though she wondered if she could ask for a vodka and tonic after the interview was over, in a to-go cup.

Hillary and Lauren had been very close as kids, she said. "We were practically inseparable." But their connection soured after Lauren got married and had Brandi, by which time Hillary already had two kids (of course) of her own. "I was surprised to discover a new side to my sister. First, she announced that she wasn't going to be taking her daughter to church. I was shocked. I'm not saying I'm the most religious person in the world, but you have to give your children a Christian education."

Carrie nodded in feigned agreement, though her parents had been strictly Christmas and Easter churchgoers and even that had been too much for her.

"Next, she started to distance herself from a lot of people, cutting off friends she goes way back with, getting rude and snippy with our parents."

"What do you think it was all about?"

"It seemed like she started to think she was better than the rest of us. Like she needed new friends that would be up to her caliber or something… And then she started cheating on Kelly, and that's something you just don't do, that's unacceptable."

"She admitted to an affair?"

"Affairs. Plural. No, I didn't know about those flings until after she and Kelly split up, when I learned about them from Kelly."

Carrie asked whether Lauren's affairs had caused the breakup of the marriage.

"Yes and no. It was part of a whole bad trend in her life. She started to hang around with women who hate men, the kind where anything a man does is harassment or something. Before long she was accusing Kelly of being abusive."

"She was? That's interesting. The police said they didn't find any hints of Lauren accusing Kelly of abuse."

"Well, he came to me the first time that word got thrown at him, he was practically crying. If you've been the regular reporter on this case, I assume you've gotten to know him some."

"A little, yeah."

"Then you know he's not an easy person. He's short-tempered, he can be hard to reason with, and stubborn. But he cares about his daughter, and he's been a good relative to all of us. It's not fair to take someone like that, who has some sharp edges, and start making out like he's a batterer or something. He's just not like that."

This last had a certain resonance for Carrie. She kind of enjoyed her sparring matches with the crotchety dictator and he clearly liked talking to her, though he'd never admit it. And he'd been the one to make her career take off, even if he'd done so unintentionally.

She asked what Lauren had accused him of.

Hillary shook her head back and forth, disgusted. "I barely paid attention by that time. But let's see… I can remember her saying he yelled a lot, which I'm sure is true, and that he'd call her the 'c' word, which I totally doubt. Then she said he was humiliating her sexually, making her do stuff in the bedroom that she found revolting. Her word was 'pornographic,' if memory serves me well. And that's just so not Kelly, I mean, he's stayed much closer to the church than she has. Sexually twisted stuff would have been more likely to come from her."

Carrie continued to nod as if deeply understanding.

"Any accusations of violence?"

"No. I'm sure she realized no one who knew Kelly would buy that one for a second. She was more into playing the 'cry rape' game."

"Rape? Lauren said Kelly raped her?"

"Yes, that was the kind of smear she resorted to."

"Did she say what happened?"

"Well, I asked her, 'What, did he fight you, or hold a gun on you?' She admitted it was nothing like that. She said he wouldn't take no for an answer, kept her awake demanding sex when she was trying to sleep, and then she said he went ahead and did it. That's bullshit, pardon my language. And even if it's true, I wouldn't call that a rape between husband and wife, he didn't force her."

They sat in uncomfortable silence for a few moments, Carrie needing to digest before deciding what next to ask.

She decided to switch directions. "What do you think happened to Lauren and Brandi?"

"Isn't kind of obvious? She took off with Brandi because she didn't want Kelly to be the dad. She decided he was Evil Incarnate. She probably has a boyfriend that she wants to make into Brandi's father-figure, I bet that's who has been traveling with them and helping them."

Maybe, though it was hard to see why a man in that position would lure officers into a trap and gun them down.

Before closing the interview, Carrie wanted to understand more about Rogers' friendship with Lauren's then-husband. "So you and Kelly managed to be tight even though their marriage was falling apart?"

Hillary nodded. "Kelly and I connected from sharing how upset we were about the ways Lauren was changing. And since she got more hostile toward both of us as time went by, that kind of pushed us toward each other. Kelly also realized that the church was important for his well-being and for Brandi's, so he became a regular presence at services around the same time that Lauren was getting scarcer and scarcer there. I wouldn't call us close friends, but we understand each other, and we both want what's best for Brandi."

~

Carrie and Gavin began their evening in a pizza joint. Carrie hadn't yet received her first paycheck as a staff reporter (which would double what she'd made as an intern), but she probably would have been eating pizza anyhow out of habit; she'd rarely had more than a few dollars in her pocket.

She couldn't take her eyes off of Gavin's beautiful yet casual-looking shirt, woven in mountain colors with odd homemade-looking buttons and a thin little collar. Maybe it came from India or someplace; probably his dad bought these things for him at street markets as he traveled around the world in his private jet.

(The shirt was from Guatemala, ordered online.)

Gavin had recounted his escapade as Percy Robicheau, and now was reacting to Carrie's report on her interview with Hillary Rogers. "She sounds like bad news. What kind of person cozies up to her sister's husband after being told he raped her?"

"She didn't believe her."

"Did she have any reason not to believe it? No, she just didn't feel like it."

"She's saying Lauren's accusations don't fit who Kelly is, and they came out of this whole process of Lauren turning bitter toward the world and shutting people out of her life."

Gavin's agitation was growing. "How do you know it's not the opposite? That Kelly and Lauren's sister bonded because she wouldn't take shit from either of them anymore? I mean, look at this: Kelly suddenly starts going to their church all the time right when Lauren stops going—gee, what a coincidence. And he bonds with her family about how tragic it is that she's not attending services anymore, when he never gave a good goddamn about religion before.

So manipulative. You can't just be taking what people say at face value like that, Carrie."

She felt that rage at Gavin starting to bubble up again. "Look, I get it that Kelly's a jerk, all right?. That doesn't make him a rapist, or... You see him as so *calculating*. His wife was cheating on him in a big way, so they break up, then she disappears with his daughter who could turn up dead any day. You don't have a drop of feeling for him? Bad things can happen to jerks too, you know."

"You don't have any information about Lauren's supposed affairs. And neither does Hillary; she admitted to you that she heard all that from Kelly. A journalist looks for evidence."

Carrie fought to keep her thoughts straight, as if slogging through thick mud that would barely allow her to lift her feet. She couldn't stand to sit here anymore listening to this pompous asshole.

"I've got to go home to bed," she said, rising to her feet. "I'm beyond maxed. I'm sorry you drove all the way over here, I'm a fuckup." But it sounded more like an accusation than an apology.

"It's fine, we don't have to talk about work anymore."

But suddenly she couldn't stand another minute around him, much less a couple of hours. Her voice was sharp. "I can't listen to you talk down to me right now. I can't handle it. I'm sorry." She sounded even less sorry now.

Gavin had hit that detonator button of Carrie's again, though he wasn't sure how. But he was too caught up in the fireworks to back away. "You can't handle me disagreeing with you," he snorted. "I'm just supposed to say 'yes, yes, yes,' and nothing else."

She shot a withering look at him, started to say something, thought better of it, and steamed off to her car.

~

By the time she walked into her bedroom and closed the door, Carrie's spirits had sunk the lowest she could remember in ages. Scoop was already asleep as was everyone else in the house. She lay on her bed still dressed, staring at the ceiling. Then she got to her feet without deciding to and wandered around the house like a specter. She made a snack in the kitchen, didn't register what she was eating and later couldn't remember what it had been, and sat back on her floor leaning against the bed, staring off.

She was faking her way through this case, a little girl playing at being a news reporter. She was putting on a good show but she was lost. This was real life, children were dying by order of the court, it was no place to play charades.

Any day now it would all blow up in her face, the whole fraud would be exposed, she'd be queen loser of Mormon Valley.

It made absolutely no sense to defend Kelly Harbison. And Hillary Rogers had revolted her; Jesus Christ, she'd said that if a man won't let his wife sleep and then fucks her while she lies there, that's not rape. Why the hell was Carrie sticking up for these people to Gavin?

Because something about him made her need to argue. Why the hell did he have to turn into such an arrogant prick?

She eventually crawled into bed, feeling defeated, and slept darkly.

CHAPTER 21

By prior agreement between the detectives, Annika Ledbetter took a few minutes break from a late morning whiffle ball game with her family (which messed the game up) to take another try at sowing suspicion in Lauren. Ledbetter sent out their carefully crafted second email:

> Hi Lauren:
>
> I got another message from Brandi. But it was really her, I asked her to give a detail about something at my house that only she would know. She really wants to talk, can I call her at the number she left?
>
> Praying for you all day every day.
> Sofia

~

Some time after ten o'clock that morning, police in Merrydale, Louisiana received a call from a man who said he could hear people in the empty house next door. It belonged to a landlord who lived across town; the previous tenants had left abruptly because of a crisis involving an elderly parent in New Jersey and the landlord, whom the caller was friendly with, hadn't found new tenants yet.

He reported that he'd heard odd rumbling noises the previous evening and once thought he heard a young girl yell angrily from inside the house, but there had been no lights on and he doubted what he was hearing. But this morning he could hear unquestionably that there were people in there, including a child. It couldn't be a burglary; they'd been in there since the night before, and anyhow there was nothing in there to steal.

With this strange report of a girl yelling from a vacant basement, combined with the recent sighting of Brandi Harbison less than a hundred miles away, the local department chose to notify the Louisiana State Police who in turn contacted the FBI. The feds completed the circle by instructing local police to watch the house but not betray their presence. They were to simultaneously start sweeping nearby streets for out-of-the-area vehicles, including a couple of specific ones for which descriptions were provided, but otherwise should hold tight until FBI personnel arrived to direct the response.

Vehicles screeched out of the station as quickly as officers could understand their instructions from the shift supervisor and hit the road. There was to be no use of sirens, however, so as not to put the occupants of the house on alert.

The order not to use sirens ended up making no difference. Not long after the first few police vehicles and officers on foot entered the vicinity, gunfire rang out. The patient waiting for the staties and feds was never to happen. The individuals were either trying to shoot their way out or were suicidal and wanted to die in a gun battle with police.

Police vehicles screeched to a halt and their occupants ducked down. Those on foot hit the ground or dove behind bushes and electrical boxes.

Minutes passed with no further shots, so officers started nervously moving from covered spot to covered spot, trying to get the house encircled. But before they could set a solid perimeter, two individuals were seen streaking away from the back of the house. They disappeared between two houses on the next street, emerged from bushes on the other side, dashed across the road, and disappeared between houses again. The two had a good lead on all the personnel pursuing on foot. One of the two officers who had gotten the closest look put out a call describing them as a tall male and a small female, probably a child. It was possible that one or more additional people had fled ahead of them without being seen, but there was definitely no one behind them.

Officers threw themselves back into cruisers and went racing up and down streets in the westward direction. As one of the units turned hard around a corner three blocks west of the house, the officers witnessed a silver vehicle launch wildly from a parking space almost a quarter mile away. The car, originally facing them, performed a screeching U-turn and jetted off in the opposite direction. The officer at the wheel turned on lights and siren and flew off in pursuit while her partner yelled information into his radio. Their quarry turned a sharp left at the next intersection, but by the time the cruiser got there and made the turn there was no longer any sign of a car moving westward on Glen Oaks Drive. It had vanished down one of the many side streets.

Phone calls started to come into 911 from individuals reporting a silver Nissan Sentra rocketing dangerously down residential streets. Nobody got a look at the license plate. One of the callers, however, said he'd had a clear view of the car as it flew past where he was walking his dog, and he could see that the driver was a tall male. No one else was visible in the vehicle, though perhaps someone was lying down in the back seat. Or locked in the trunk.

The possibility that Brandi might be in the trunk added to the dark mood among law enforcement personnel, not least because if the crazed driver crashed the car, a highly possible outcome, the trunk would be the worst place for her to be.

State police vehicles in the area raced to block the entrance ramps to I-110 and to cover both sides of Route 67. But a report of the terrorizing driving soon came in from Pembroke Street, which put the car beyond the Interstate, to the west.

Law enforcement went up and down every block of that area. Nothing. Calls from residents stopped coming in. The man thus had to have entered the airport, there was nowhere else he could have gone. This was potentially good news; police would have plenty of time to corral him before he could get on a plane and off the runway.

But he turned up nowhere among the travelers. Twenty minutes of combing led them to locate the Sentra in the airport parking garage, empty. Later that afternoon they were able, through meticulous interviewing of dozens of cab drivers who came and went from the airport, to find a fare that fit Mr. Tall's description. The cab had taken him down to the center of Baton Rouge, where he had paid in cash.

He had not had a girl with him.

~

The officers who stayed behind to guard the house were soon reinforced by Louisiana State Police and two FBI agents. The house appeared to be empty, but they needed to clear it and were wary of an ambush. A state trooper spoke through a bullhorn, instructing anyone inside of the house to come out slowly with their hands on their heads and warning them that if they remained inside they risked being harmed when law enforcement entered the premises.

Entering a hostile building is dangerous work. The risk to officers was compounded by the fact that they couldn't go in with rifles blazing, due to the serious possibility that Brandi or Lauren—or the mystery girl—could still be inside, perhaps drugged or bound, since only one female had come out of the house.

After a half hour, the FBI declared the time had come. State police and federal agents surrounded the house, checked all windows, and began the risky entry process through the side door, six officers in at once.

The door opened into the kitchen toward the rear of the house. No one there. They then began to clear the first-floor rooms one at a time with officers covering each other. The first floor had a small split to its level, a flight of three stairs leading up to a hallway, a bathroom, and two bedrooms. All empty. Three officers then started tensely upward to begin the sweep of the second floor.

The one in the lead, Louisiana state trooper Ilya Taylor, stopped when he was only halfway up the stairs. "There's a person on the floor up here!" It was neither Brandi nor Lauren; the trooper could see that it was the body of a large man, apparently unconscious. He barked, "Don't move! Our weapons are on you!" The man didn't stir.

The trooper remained wary of a trap. But when he was almost to the top of the stairs he saw that the man was lying in a pool of blood. He was breathing but not deeply, and his respiration made a horrible rattle. "We need medical!" Taylor called loudly. "Badly wounded man up here!"

The two trailing officers raced upstairs and cleared the rest of the second floor. They found nothing other than a Ruger LCP handgun which was four feet from where the wounded man lay, presumably his weapon.

Simultaneously officers descended the basement stairs. Here they finally found indications of previous human activity: two sleeping mats, empty food and drink containers, pillows and blankets. There was also a pile of feces in a corner of the basement with toilet paper strewn around; they had been doing their business without going up to the bathroom, apparently afraid of being seen.

Yet one of them had gone all the way up to the second floor. Why? And how had he happened to take a bullet?

The basement revealed no papers, credit cards, ID's, nothing that could have identified the individuals involved. They'd left in a panic but had also managed to grab their most crucial items.

EMT's arrived and went straight to blocking the man's blood loss and putting him on oxygen while police took photographs, including clear shots of his face which did not have visible injuries.

Once the EMT's had the man on a stretcher and into the ambulance, officers began examining the interior of the house. They found indications of gunshots in the walls of the second-floor landing and in the living room walls below. Judging by the angles it appeared that shots had been fired in two directions, up toward the landing and down from there. Their immediate thought was that the man had fired up the stairs before running up—perhaps there'd been someone above, or he'd thought there was—and then when he reached the top he'd turned, started firing downward, and been hit by law enforcement fire.

Except it was impossible to find any officer, whether local cop, state police, or FBI, who had fired a single shot. The gunfire had all occurred before arriving police could get established in their positions and distinguish what direction the shots were coming from.

They were forced to conclude that individuals inside of the house had been firing at each other. Solidarity among the kidnappers must have broken down.

Soon they had to evaluate anew; the FBI was able within minutes to provide a positive ID of the critically injured man. It was Kelly Harbison.

In less than an hour he was undergoing emergency surgery in Baton Rouge.

~

At 6:10 that evening, just minutes after local news broadcasts began, Merrydale police received a call that put the most peculiar finish to an already inexplicable day.

The caller, who provided his home address on Cedar Grove Drive, said that he'd just seen pictures of Brandi Harbison on the news and that he and his family now realized they'd been with her earlier that day.

Arnulfo Teodoro told a remarkable story. He'd been out for a Sunday stroll in the late morning with his wife Bella, their daughters six-year-old Pilar and three-year-old Linda, and their baby boy Arnulfo Jr. whom Bella was pushing in a stroller. They were walking along Blue Grass Drive when a girl suddenly appeared behind them, said a shy "hello," and started walking along with them.

They asked how she was, in usual conversational fashion, but received an unusually serious response. "I'm okay," she said somberly. "Well, not really." She was breathing hard. "My mom and my aunt are fighting, yelling really loud at each other. Whenever we come visit here, they always end up getting in a big thing. I ran out of the house."

"Do you live nearby?" Arnulfo asked, concerned.

"No. Well, my aunt and uncle do, but we live up in Pennsylvania, we come like every year or something."

His wife spoke compassionately. "It's upsetting when relatives scream at each other, isn't it? Are you scared to go back?"

"No, no," the girl said, shaking her head, "it's nothing like that. They stop after a while. I just hate it, I wish they wouldn't."

At about this time a state police vehicle came flying down the block they were on. The Teodoro children watched raptly as it went by, as kids will do. But the strange girl looked away, turning her head. Mr. Teodoro didn't give it a thought at the time; the kid was already shaken up, it made sense that a rocketing car would startle her.

But when he saw the girl's picture on the news, it dawned on him that she had been avoiding being seen.

Another police vehicle sped by as she wandered along with them, and then they began hearing sirens off toward the freeway. They speculated together on what it might be about, and the girl said, "Maybe a fire or something."

She stayed in step with them a good fifteen minutes. She was friendly with the Teodoro kids, though her manner seemed forced; she talked to the kids almost like she was a third adult on the family outing. Come to think of it now, everything she said had sounded a little theatrical. She was *so* struck by how adorable the baby's cheeks were, she was *so* impressed by how much the three-year-old knew about dog breeds, she was *so* enjoying being on this walk with them.

At one point Bella asked the girl if she was happy to see her cousins, and she said yes, and that she was happy they were all there this year. When Bella asked what she meant, she answered that last time they visited here a teenage cousin of hers had run away from home because of a fight with the parents, and had gone missing for three days. The girl then asked Bella and Arnulfo two or three questions related to that incident, such as where a teen shelter would be in the Baton Rouge area, where a hungry runaway might get food, and where her cousin might have gotten the burner phone she bought that time. The Teodoro parents had changed the subject, but only because they were uncomfortable having their children hearing about teens running away; it never occurred to them that the girl might be fishing for plans of action for herself.

About ten minutes into their stroll she asked if she could borrow a phone to call her mom and tell her she was out walking, so she wouldn't worry. Bella said sure and handed the girl her smartphone. The girl punched in numbers, and then when the call was answered she said, "Hey, it's me. I'm walking out on my own. I'm okay. I'll call again soon." And she hung up.

"My mom didn't pick up," she told them. "She actually has two phones. Can I try her other number?" They said sure. The girl fumbled with the phone for a minute, then dropped it, picked it up apologizing profusely, and handed it to them saying, "I can't remember her other number, it's her work phone."

Bella asked her what she had meant in her message about calling her mom again soon, but the girl laughed and said, "Oh, I didn't mean to say that, I meant I'd be back soon." They laughed with her.

At the corner of Apperson and Packard, the girl said she'd better head back to her relatives' house. She made a decisive turn to the right on Packard, waved good-bye, and went crisply off.

Teodoro mentioned to the police that the girl's hair was nothing like the style shown in the photos on the news, and that she looked thinner. But they had no doubt it was the same girl.

The police asked Ms. Teodoro to bring her phone to the station. While dropping it off she commented, "When the girl handed my phone back, it wasn't on the home screen. It was like on Settings or something. I thought it was an accident, but now I'm wondering—did she maybe want to mess with my phone for some reason?"

The cop speculated. "Maybe she was trying to erase the number she called, so it wouldn't show on your phone." The girl had failed, perhaps unfamiliar with the Samsung.

That night police dialed the recovered number. Their call went straight to voice mail, with a system greeting. They then investigated the source and found that the number was in a sequence that goes with wireless-based phone service. The techs said there was no way, at least in the short term, to find out who the number belonged to or where it was based.

Police were left wondering what Brandi's spoken message had been intended to convey. And where her mother was.

~

Kelly was in surgery for nearly two hours. The bullet could easily have killed him, narrowly missing key arteries. After the operation, though, the surgeon reported that there had been no danger of losing him while he was on the table;

the situation had been under control because they quickly located the sources of vascular bleeding and got them clamped. The operation had been time-consuming because the patient had multiple tears to both his colon and small intestine, and a smaller number of tears to his kidneys and liver.

~

Wisneski's team gathered at the East Liverpool station on Sunday evening, to the dismay of their families. The case seemed only to escalate on its danger-ous and cryptic trajectory, and the spouses and children of team members had stopped believing it when told that life would go back to normal soon.

The team sifted through the reports from Louisiana, with new informa-tion continuing to arrive every fifteen or twenty minutes. Brandi's slick escape was a maneuver well beyond her years; either her ordeal had caused her to grow up rapidly or she and her mother had rehearsed the act in case it ever became necessary.

Was Brandi aware that her father had been in the house and had been shot? They assumed not, since they couldn't picture her smoothly pulling off her flight with the Teodoro family if she knew her father might be dying.

Ledbetter's thoughts were embroiled in a different but equally salient question. "It doesn't make sense that this whole incident was able to play out with no trace of Lauren Harbison. Police down there found only two sleep set-ups in the basement and no sign that anyone slept elsewhere in the house. She must be traveling separately from Brandi and Tall Guy, though she was with them only a short time ago—all that stuff of hers in the McComb bushes. Figuring out why she split off might be our key."

Chief Tobias saw it differently. 'It's more likely that the tall guy took Bran-di away from Lauren and fled, probably to make a ransom demand. My guess is he was a supposed helper who turned out to have his own plans. That would explain why Brandi ran the other way when she saw her chance."

"Okay," Wisneski assented. "We'll pursue that angle. I still sense, though, that Mom is behind it all."

Kresge said, "No offense, but—"

Ledbetter cut him off. "The next thing out of your mouth after 'no offense' is guaranteed to be something offensive, Shane."

"Look," he said stubbornly, "If Mr. Tall is a bad guy, why isn't Brandi going straight for help as soon as she manages to break away from him in the chaos? How come instead she takes cover with this Theodore family?"

The lead detective responded, "Teodoro, not Theodore. She could be afraid the guy will find her and kill her if she goes to the police. But more likely she wants to be reunited with her mother and believes that if she goes to the authorities she never will be. I bet she's been frequently reminded by Lauren, 'If they catch us, I'll be in jail for a long time.'"

As had become the norm, Kresge continued shaking his head, conceding nothing. "How the hell does Harbison find out they're in that house? And why does he go there himself instead of letting law enforcement handle it properly?"

"Because he was hoping to be the big hero," Mason replied.

"Yeah, well, he's the reason they got away."

"We know that, Shane."

Kresge sat fuming, as if the team were somehow to blame for the incident having spun out of control.

CHAPTER 22

Shortly after ten o'clock Monday morning, the police officer stationed outside of Kelly Harbison's hospital room approached a nurse who had been in and out of his room a number of times over the past three hours. "Any sign of him waking up at all?"

Javier Reynosa (according to his badge) responded in heavily accented English, "He has moved around a little bit, and some muttering. He has not opened the eyes."

"Has he said anything intelligible?"

"Several curses. Intelligent, no, not really."

"I mean anything you could understand?"

"Once—no, two times—he said a name or something, sounded like 'Carrie Green.'"

The officer called in to report this to his supervisor, whose response was, "Who the hell is Carrie Green?"

~

Carrie Green (if he really wanted to know) was a brazen, uppity, some would say rude young news reporter from a disreputable settlement between Morriston, Ohio and the state line. At that particular moment she was in the *Chronicle* offices attempting to negotiate travel to Louisiana for herself. Her supervisor, Marco Vinestri, perched in his office chair, seemed uncharacteristically off-hand about the decision. "If you want to go, do it," he said, barely looking up from what he was doing.

But when Carrie said she'd go research airfares and get back to him, Vinestri said, "Wait. I didn't realize you meant for us to fund your trip. We can't do that, my friend, we don't even have a solid budget for ink here. Last-minute airfare, hotels, cabs, food... not happening. The *Chronicle* is happy to have you do your research on the good old telephone." Combined with the ancient tradition of web surfing.

Carrie had not expected an easy yes, but neither had she foreseen an immediate and outright no. Some way to treat the reporter who has brought your limping daily paper back from the brink of bankruptcy.

In a rare moment of restraint, however, she opted not to say those words aloud.

~

Harbison's Ruger LCP proved to be duly registered and he was licensed to carry it. The crime scene crew was able to find three bullets in the downstairs walls that were almost surely discharged from his weapon, and the lab would provide proof soon. But it was nonetheless going to be difficult to charge him with a criminal offense, given that he was the only person available to tell the story of what happened there and appeared to be the only victim. For his illegal presence in the home all they were likely to be able to conjure was a charge of breaking and entering, since no one lived there and the house contained no belongings. Even "Malicious Destruction"—for the bullet holes in the walls—would require them to prove bad intent. He'd crossed no police lines and disobeyed no orders.

Law enforcement wanted something to hold over his head when he came to consciousness, to help them extract information. It looked like they would be forced to invent scary-sounding charges. As they had plenty of practice in that area, though, it caused them little concern.

~

The day-shift surgeon saw Harbison mid-morning. He met with police briefly afterward and reported that the patient was stable and had been conscious for a brief period. The wounded man knew who and where he was. It might be possible for him to speak to police in another five or six hours.

The agitated officers went to great lengths to impress upon Dr. Hoedstetter that the information they needed to learn from his patient was getting less valuable by the minute, and that the survival of a ten-year-old child was at stake. The doctor smiled placidly, as if patients who were crucial witnesses in life-or-death matters were part of his daily routine, and told them he'd meet with them again around three in the afternoon with no promises even for that time. Then he was gone, busy prying other people from the jaws of death.

~

Only shortly after this, a woman standing with three or four other people at a bus stop on Foster Road in Brownfields, another Baton Rouge suburb, was approached by a young girl. "I missed my bus and my mom will be upset when I'm not on it," she said. "Can I use your phone to tell her I'll be on the next one?"

The woman happily handed the kid her iPhone. The girl punched in numbers, waited a minute, then said, "Hey, it's me. I'm at the corner of Foster and Saint Francis, the bus stop here... Yeah, okay... Uh, hang on a second." She took the phone away from her ear and said to the woman, "Do you know what corner we're on, like north or east or whatever?" The woman, who traveled that bus line every day, gave only a quick thought before telling her they were to the southeast. The girl relayed the information into the phone, then hung it up. She kept punching things into the phone as if starting to make another call, but then abruptly returned the phone.

"My mom said to wait here instead of getting on the next bus. She's gonna pick me up."

Seven or eight minutes later the bus was overdue, so the woman was still standing there when a red sedan came driving "scary fast" to the corner and braked heavily to a stop. The girl grabbed the passenger door and hopped in, the driver took the girl's hand for the most fleeting moment, and then the car sped off down Saint Francis, a short side street, rather than continuing on Foster.

The woman digested these events for a few moments until her bus finally arrived. Once aboard and seated she looked at her phone, curious to see what number the girl had called, only to find her call history erased.

She pondered the way the driver had taken the girl's hand. Don't you kiss your daughter, or at least put your arm around her? Or maybe you're angry that you had to come pick her up, but in that case you don't touch her at all. It was an odd gesture for a parent. And where is a girl who looks nine or ten taking a bus in the morning except to school? But she had nothing in her hands, no book bag or backpack. Plus she'd said that her mother had been expecting to pick her up on the other end, which made no sense.

Then it struck her that the woman driving had looked quite a bit too old to have a child that young. Flashing in her mind were public service ads about human trafficking, including one that said victims can become compliant with their captors due to trauma and threats. She dialed 911.

~

Local officers came out to take the woman's description of the girl at the bus stop, which they relayed to the Louisiana State Police. The details fit Brandi's appearance well. The woman behind the wheel of the red sedan had definitely not been Lauren Harbison, however; the driver described by the witness was the wrong height, build, and age.

In other words, Brandi was now traveling with neither her mother nor Tall Guy.

The news of Kelly Harbison's vigilante attempt to free his daughter, and of the near-fatal bullet he took in the process, was everywhere; it couldn't be much longer before Brandi knew about it. Maybe then she would reach out for rescue.

~

At four o'clock that afternoon the surgeon permitted the police ten minutes with his patient. Dr. Hoedstetter would remain in the room to monitor Kelly's reaction and would end the meeting early if he became concerned about the patient's stress level. The police told the doctor it would be better not to have him present during the questioning, to which he replied, "What a shame," before entering the room ahead of them.

Harbison looked horrible. His skin was a moldy gray and his eyes looked like fish broth. He was hooked up to multiple tubes and devices dripping liquids into him, collecting them back from him, and graphing his levels of oxygen, carbon dioxide, heart stress, and, who knows, moral development. The screens indicated that he wasn't doing very well, but the officers didn't know how to interpret the signals and so assumed he was right for grilling.

"Hello, Mr. Harbison," said the lead trooper. "I'm Jacoby Titelbaum from the Louisiana State Police, and this is my partner Mr. Kaplansky. We're glad you're doing better, we understand you're going to be fine."

Harbison said nothing.

"We don't have your daughter, I regret to say. An adult male escaped with her after the shooting occurred, before law enforcement could get into position. We want to learn anything from you that might help us find them."

Titelbaum was not free to share with Harbison the fact that his daughter was no longer with that man, having taken off on her own; the FBI had decreed it strategically desirable not to let the public in on this fact for now, and Harbison was the world's poorest bet to keep anything to himself. "Can you tell us what happened in that house?"

Harbison's lips began to move. Titelbaum leaned his ear close to the man's face as his words were inaudible from even two feet away. The surgeon moved in close as well, watching alertly.

Titelbaum said, "I believe your words were 'I waited all night in the house.' Did I hear you correctly?" Harbison made a sort of nod.

The officer then asked, "What happened this morning?"

"Shots," Harbison squeaked out. "A few. He got me." Then he closed his eyes.

"How did he get Brandi out of the house?"

But Harbison appeared depleted by the handful of words he'd forced out. Titelbaum tried two or three other questions, with no result. Suspicious that the patient was malingering, the trooper said, "Sir, you face serious charges regarding this incident. You can best avoid those by giving us your cooperation in apprehending the individuals involved."

Doctor Hoedstetter reacted to this tack by waving his arm emphatically to drive Titelbaum back from the bed. "That's all for this afternoon, gentleman. The patient must rest."

But Harbison suddenly was speaking, through still-closed eyes. The surgeon leaned over, listened, then asked the patient to repeat himself. Looking puzzled, he straightened and said to the officers, "What I'm hearing sounds like, 'Only talk to Carrie Green.' Most likely I'm not getting it right." He then ordered the troopers firmly from the room.

When Titelbaum relayed the meager results of the interview to the FBI, he was informed that Harbison's words actually made sense—though at the same time not really. With his daughter's life in danger, and his own swinging on a thin cord, why did Harbison want to speak with a cub reporter who was a thousand miles away?

~

Kelly's odd rasping words were transmitted to the East Liverpool police department, and from there to the *Morriston Chronicle*. Less than an hour later Carrie was in her rusty Dodge bound for the Pittsburgh airport, all expenses paid.

CHAPTER 23

C arrie arrived in Baton Rouge close to midnight on Monday, having driven an hour and a half north from the New Orleans airport, marveling over her rented Mitsubishi.

By seven o'clock Tuesday morning she was at Baton Rouge General Hospital, being denied entry. She punched the contact number she'd been given for the Louisiana State Police, and a trooper who identified himself as Jacoby Titelbaum said he'd tell the front desk to let her right in.

The surgeon allowed her into Kelly's room a little after nine. He told her that she would need to be brief "as the patient is still extremely vulnerable," the word "vulnerable" containing at least two extra syllables while nonetheless being pronounced with sharp distinction. Carrie took the doctor to be from Russia, guessing one hemisphere out of two correctly. (Later someone would tell her that Dr. Hoedstetter was from Macedonia, serving only to further confuse her; she could dimly remember from school that Macedonia was between the Tigris and the Euphrates.)

"Hi, Kelly," she said as she walked toward him.

His response was a raising and lowering of eyebrows. No other muscle moved. Conversation wasn't going to be easy.

Kelly proceeded to attempt to tell Carrie his story, four or five words at a time. She figured they'd get to the end by Veterans Day; at times she thought he'd fallen asleep. She kept having to ask him to speak up, because even with her face practically touching his, which she was finding unpleasant, his volume would fade to unintelligible.

After about twenty minutes a nurse came in to check on him and ask him if he wanted to continue. He nodded. But before she went back out, she said, "I can only give you about another fifteen, even if the patient would prefer longer. Doctor's orders."

Carrie did her best to make sense of Kelly's labored recounting. When he'd left Ohio, he went first to Tennessee and tried to retrace the likely path that Lauren and Brandi would have taken from there to Alabama. He made inquiries every few miles along the way, trying everything from starting random conversations in bars to talking to elected officials, covering ground slowly. He also used some connections he had through a "secret friend" who is involved in "the fatherhood movement." He was referred from person to person to person who might have leads for him.

When law enforcement finally released a detailed description of the tall man, based on his appearance at the ATM in Alabama, Kelly sent out an alert to fathers' groups all over the country, asking, "Does anyone recognize this guy? Has he worked with the mothers' underground on stealing other kids from their dads?"

In response he started to hear some theories about who the guy was, including one name in particular that started to come up repeatedly.

Carrie asked for the name.

Kelly took an even longer pause than was typical of his speech that morning, then said, "Chester."

A series of connections led him to speak with a particular father in the southwest. (Kelly said, "Let's call him Joe," refusing to say his real name.) Joe infiltrated the mothers' underground three or four years ago, posing as a man who wanted to help, but secretly passing information to fathers that helped them recover their children. But then he got exposed, and mothers' groups around the country spread his photo widely to keep him from doing any more "volunteering."

But Joe had infiltrated with a compatriot, Chester. Only that guy did the opposite of getting exposed. "He turned against us and became a real part of the mothers' underground." And Joe had recognized Chester from the descriptions of the tall guy in the news.

So Joe had somehow been able to find out for Kelly where Chester had been heading next with Brandi and Lauren, the basement in Merrydale?

Yes, Kelly said. But he was too tired to go into that now, it was complicated, he'd tell her that part later.

When Kelly obtained the address he was a hundred and fifty miles away in Mississippi. He drove like a madman for three hours, found the house, and got inside before they arrived.

He hid in the attic crawlspace. It wasn't floored, so there was no way to find a comfortable position; he was perched on rafters, stooped. He would have been found if they'd checked the attic, but why would they? And no one did, though eventually he heard someone walk around on the second floor, presumably to make sure it was empty.

After three or four hours cramped in that space, no way to stand or lie down, he hit his limit of pain endurance; every part of his body hurt except for his head. Forced to gamble that they wouldn't have reason to come up to the second floor again, he dangled his legs into the bedroom closet which the attic hatch emptied into and dropped down as quietly as he could.

He tiptoed across the wide hallway to use the upstairs toilet, which he didn't dare flush, and then positioned himself on the landing. He remained awake all night. He could occasionally hear voices and movements coming from the basement. No one came up again even as far as the first floor (which fit what police observed about feces in the basement).

Around 10:30 the next morning he sensed an abrupt increase in movement from the basement, and suddenly their voices were loud. They sounded upset and rushed, abandoning efforts to be quiet.

Kelly took a kneeling position where he could see if anyone entered the kitchen through the basement door. Within just a couple of minutes, Lauren and Brandi burst into the kitchen. Kelly's view was partially blocked but he could see enough to know they weren't carrying suitcases, they didn't look ready to travel anywhere. But they raced toward the door.

Kelly yelled as loudly as he could, ordering them to stop and pointing his gun at Lauren. Lauren pulled Brandi in front of her as a shield; he couldn't shoot, and they backed out the exterior door.

He was scrambling to his feet to run down the stairs after them when the tall guy came flying in from the top of the basement stairs, weapon extended. Kelly hit the ground on the landing and began firing downwards, getting off a few shots, he had no memory how many. Nor did he remember being hit by a bullet; his memory was blank until he came to consciousness in his hospital bed, hours after the surgery.

"He had no angle," he croaked. "One of the bastard's shots must have ricocheted and hit me."

Carrie told him that bullets had been found in downstairs walls from his handgun, but evidently he hadn't hit Chester at all; there wasn't a drop of blood in the downstairs and the man had sprinted away on solid legs.

Hearing this news Kelly proved able to swear impressively despite his weakness.

The nurse, most likely having heard the outburst, appeared at the door. "I'm sorry, time's more than up. You'll need to leave the room, ma'am."

"Two more minutes," the reporter said. "For real. You can stay here." Then she turned to Kelly, ignoring the nurse who came briskly toward her. "Why did you go in there instead of sending the police?"

"They've screwed up everything they've done. I wanted to do the job right."

Irony was absent from his voice. Carrie couldn't wait to see this quotation in the news side by side with the account of how he'd made it possible for the kidnappers to escape.

"So are you going to give police the real name for your 'Joe' guy, so they can track Chester down through him?"

Kelly, his tone sarcastic, said, "No, I'm not gonna feed Joe to the police in return for the help he gave me."

"Even with your daughter's life at stake?"

"He won't be able to get Chester's location again, Chester will know that Joe's the one who burned him this time. He'll be out for blood."

Arguing the point further would go nowhere. So on to her last question, the kind that Vinestri loved. "Would you change your choice if you could do it over again?"

"Ma'am," the nurse interrupted, "you must—"

But Kelly cut her off, expending his last ounce of strength. "Fuck no! At least Brandi's still alive. They probably would have ended up with her dead!" His eyes popped shut the instant the words were out of his mouth, and didn't open again for many hours.

~

Vinestri couldn't believe the scoop Carrie had just gotten. This could be the biggest boost to the paper—and to Vinestri's reputation as an editor—in ten years. And all he could feel was appalled. This ignorant punk reporter was going to be the center of it all.

As if informing Carrie of a death Marco stated grimly into the phone, "This will be a huge exclusive. Once your article is on the website you'll be spending the whole rest of the day on media interviews. All the national networks will want you on camera." He wanted to puke.

Carrie's stomach lurched too, though for a different reason. Did Marco mean, like, CNN, NBC, FOX? The big kids? Jesus, what would she wear? What if she accidentally dropped an f-bomb? Would they use terms that all journalists except her knew? People would be watching her in, like, Alaska?

Going on the local news in Canton had been stage fright enough for her. Doing the Pittsburgh stations had been worse. She would need a few beers and a spliff to get through. But she wouldn't know how to get them around here.

Playing at being a grownup was no game anymore.

"Marco, I have nothing but Kelly's word for anything he told me. You seriously mean I'm gonna repeat this shit? To Lester Holt, Robin Roberts, whoever else, fuck me, and it's national news? How do I look when it turns out Kelly made the whole thing up?"

"You've been pushing for the idea that Harbison's not as big a jerk as he comes off. Now suddenly he's a total liar?"

Carrie groped for an escape route. "So I was wrong, okay? Sometimes a guy who seems like an asshole turns out to be an asshole, I get it."

Who said that? Freud or Roosevelt or somebody.

Vinestri plunged on, business-like. "Write your piece as fast as you can and then I'll prep you for the TV interviews. When you're on network camera all you have to do is make your voice deeper and channel one of your community college professors. You're just all about the facts, like, 'Well, Anderson,'—like you and he go way back—'we don't have corroboration at this point, all I can report is what Mr. Harbison said to me. The public should keep that in mind,' blah blah. You'll handle it fine."

He didn't at all believe that she would. Neither did she.

~

Wisneski and Ledbetter, who had heard nothing from Lauren since Friday night, finally received a response to Sunday's second volley:

> Hi Sofia,
>
> I assume you've heard, Brandi and I got separated. I'm scared out of my mind for her. This time it might really be her contacting

you. Find out where she is and tell her I'll find a way to get to her. Tell her I love her and it's all gonna be okay.

Lauren

Here was the opening they'd been hoping for. Time to craft a strategy— and they needed to come up with a stellar one—to get Lauren to reveal where she was.

~

Gavin spent his evening channel surfing. He caught appearances by his girl-friend (assuming he hadn't blown it irreparably this time) on four different networks, and there was no telling how many others he missed. The interviews were all live, which he found harrowing to watch knowing Carrie's speech patterns. The networks had no alternative but to put this loose cannon on the air, it was a story they couldn't afford to miss.

She did okay. There were a couple of grammatical errors but they were quick and overshadowed by the magnificence of the account. She managed to avoid vulgarities, though Gavin saw her catch herself a couple of times. He could tell someone had coached her to skip past questions she couldn't answer, to just give a quick feint with her head and go back to talking about what she did know. She was not smooth at this maneuver but pulled it off.

The only part that didn't work was that the same (he assumed) coach had evidently told her to use the anchor's first name when responding, which would have been fine except that she did it over and over again and ended up sound-ing like a salesperson. ("Well, Craig, I see you have a huge grease problem in your warehouse, Craig, and if you'd just try some of what I'm selling in these five-gallon tubs, Craig, it would soon all be spic and span.")

It occurred to him, though more dimly than one might hope, to perhaps not share these observations with Carrie.

Her outfit was below the fine cut that TV personalities adorn themselves in, and she looked small, not one of the imposing figures that national audi-ences expect. But her round hazel eyes were so cute on camera it was painful to look at them, and if you put your fingers on those white cheeks you could feel their cotton softness right through the video screen. The entire country would have a mad crush on her by morning.

CHAPTER 24

Kresge woke up early, uncharacteristic for him, and couldn't get back to sleep. His sense of humor had been dimming for three weeks and was now gone, a dark slick left in its wake. Cops are rough with each other, a coping mechanism that comes with the territory. Shane had pretended to be fine with it, he considered himself a tough person; but he no longer felt sure. He didn't feel like being the butt of the Harbison case team anymore.

He wasn't on the schedule for today. But he expected to go in around noon anyhow, he'd been working six or seven days a week and had been told he could use unlimited overtime until Wisneski said otherwise.

Feeling stressed but too somber to focus on anything else, he sat at his home laptop reading over case notes. Everybody on the team had access to all the members' write-ups and any documents that had been scanned into the system. His only defense against the team picking on him was to keep up on every detail.

He was reading through Ledbetter's notes from her interview with Gabbi Stolnik and found himself stuck on one section, reading it repeatedly. Gabbi had made reference to "other embarrassing stuff" about Brandi but declined to say more. Ledbetter had pressed gently, but the girl hemmed and hawed and then said that it was just that Brandi would say disgusting things.

But Gabbi had at first referred to these unmentionables as things that Brandi had *done*. It seemed to Kresge now that the girl had just wanted Ledbetter to leave the subject behind.

How could he get the detective to put enough weight on his intuition, already the target of jokes, to persuade her to go back to the Stolnik kid and find out what the missing piece had been? He decided to call Ledbetter from home; perhaps away from the rest of the team the banter could be laid aside and she'd hear him out.

The attempt failed. He caught the detective in the middle of responding to the drama in Louisiana and she had no patience for any other theme. And, in a pattern that recapitulated previous interactions, she pressed him on what he thought the Stolnik girl was holding back and he was forced to admit that he had no idea; all he could say was he sensed some crucial piece hidden there.

"Well, then, I'll get on it right away," Ledbetter answered, an openly insulting kiss-off, and hung up.

He considered calling Chief Tobias next but couldn't see anything coming of it.

So having run out of other ideas, but with great reluctance, he punched in the digits to reach Carrie Green.

~

When Kresge interrupted Ledbetter she and Wisneski had been in the middle of finalizing the wording for their next Protonmail attempt. They settled upon:

> Lauren,
>
> Brandi says she's at a house a couple hundred miles from Baton Rouge. She says the people she's with won't let her give the actual address until they're sure it's you. What should I tell them?
>
> Sofia

Their strategy was to turn the tables by demanding that Lauren prove herself. If they could put her enough on the defensive, they might divert her from insisting on speaking directly with Brandi.

A response was back in less than an hour, not typical for past communications with Lauren. Her eagerness to be reunited with Brandi was going to lead her to make mistakes; they could feel it coming.

> Hi Sofia,
>
> I can't express what it means to me to hear that Brandi's okay. Send her so much love.

Here are things you can tell her. She used to have names for all of her toes. She calls my dad Grampapa but everyone else calls him Grandad. I have a birthmark on my waist in the back shaped just like a heart. She knows no one else knows these things.

Please, please, we'll be there as fast as we can drive once we know where she is.

Lauren

We'll be there. So either Lauren and the tall guy had been able to reconnect, or Lauren had a new handler.

Wisneski and Ledbetter looked each other in the eye, daring to get their hopes up that this would work. The senior detective said, "The FBI's bound to have a house we could use for this supposed exchange. Lauren may be afraid to come herself, though; maybe she'll send someone else, say the tall man, someone with firepower just in case it's a trap."

Ledbetter responded, "Hey, if we end up nabbing Tall Guy, that's almost better than catching Lauren. Especially since he's probably our Athens shooter."

~

The Charlotte airport was a chaotic roar, between the blaring repetitive loudspeaker announcements and the roar of conversations in the overcrowded gate area. Carrie was waiting to change planes and felt her phone vibrate though she couldn't hear it. The call was from an unfamiliar number. There couldn't be a TV station left to talk to in the whole fucking country, and anyhow her voice was gone from yesterday's marathon. She answered out of habit but immediately wished she hadn't; she could tell neither who the caller was nor what he wanted amid the deafening din.

After a few back-and-forths, she made out that the caller sounded something like Officer Kresge. *Seriously? Him?* She continued attempting to hear and be heard while she struggled through the crowd with her suitcase, phone tucked under her chin, until she was finally able to reach a less crowded zone two gates down.

Here she could almost hear the caller, at least during the brief respites between grating announcements reminding her for the fiftieth time not to share the extra space in her suitcase (there wasn't any, she had a jam-packed carry-on bag) with terrorists unless they were immediate family members.

The last phrase of something she'd missed the beginning of was, "… meet to talk."

"I'm in Charlotte," Carrie yelled into her phone, before realizing she didn't have to be that loud anymore. "I won't get back to Ohio until four-thirty or five."

Then it registered on her frazzled brain that he wasn't calling her from an East Liverpool PD number; those all started with the same area code and exchange, only the last four digits varied. "What's this phone you're using?" she asked.

"It's my personal cell."

"Uh, gee Kresge, you asking me out on a date?"

She was pretty sure they hated each other. On the other hand she'd also heard that Kresge was single, and he was a cop so God knew what went on in his head.

"No, I need to talk to you about the case. But away from the station. In fact out of town would be best."

Now he had her attention.

"You mean, like, tonight? Meet you in Morriston or something?"

"Are you flying into Pittsburgh?"

"No, Kresge, I'm flying into a cucumber field in Middle Beaver."

"I'll meet you in Pittsburgh."

This was pretty strange. On the other hand, compared to her day yesterday just about anything would seem normal.

~

Kresge and Carrie sat in a chain restaurant outside of security at Pittsburgh airport. Kresge spoke slowly, unusual for him. Carrie could see his effort to choose words cautiously. "I'd like to see us take a step toward joining forces. I can tell that you know a lot more than you're telling us, and of course we know more than we're telling the public. It might serve mutual interests to each show our hands a little more. Can I get you to consider that?"

"Wait, first, why are you being all secretive? Why aren't we talking at the station?"

He took a while to respond, as if trying to make a decision. "Look… People at the department don't trust you, I'm sure that's no surprise to you. You don't always follow what's considered proper for reporters. I'm not saying you're dishonest, maybe it's just from being new."

"You're saying I'm just a kid, I hear it loud and clear all the time, it's nothing new. You didn't answer my question."

"I'm getting to it. What it comes down to is that I'm gonna go out on a limb here and hope you don't saw me off. Okay?"

"Have I screwed anybody over yet?"

"What they would say in my department is that you went awful fast from intern to nationally famous reporter. In other words, you know how to maneuver."

"I don't give a shit what 'they' say. And just so you know, all of what's happened, me being on the networks and everything, it's been a series of bizarre accidents. If I knew how to make shit like this happen I'd be a millionaire, not working for less than my brother makes fixing cars."

A lot less, in fact.

"What I would say is I'm worried about Brandi, same as everyone else, so let's put whatever issues we have aside and see if we can work together."

"There's a non-answer for you... Okay, explain what we're doing here."

"And my name doesn't turn up anywhere?"

"Give me a little credit, for Christ's sake."

He paused and steeled himself. Carrie sensed that whatever he had to say first might be the hardest part.

"I'm on the Harbison case team, as you know. But I'm also kind of not. They just assign me stuff but they don't give a shit what I think. I'm the team's gofer, no big deal, except Arielle Mason gets higher status in the group than I do and she's truly dim, so that sucks. But whatever. The thing is... I think some mistakes are being made. I know I'm not the smartest guy in the world, I pretty much tanked in school, but I'm not an idiot either. Something's wrong with this picture."

So they had one thing in common: they'd both hated school.

"Don't stop now," she said. "It's just getting good."

"Okay. Well, first of all, Kelly Harbison is a total asshole."

Carrie guffawed. "No offense, officer, but I hope that's not your breakthrough discovery."

Kresge rolled his eyes. "I'm not talking about what a pain he is, it's way beyond that. Look, I was the first one to meet the guy, back when he blew through the door of the station to tell us Brandi was missing. And everything was all about him, right from the get-go. He's supposedly so upset about his daughter going missing, yet he's hardly had a word to say about her the whole time. It's all been about how this has affected his life, his stress, his job, how unfair it all is to *him*. What about what his kid is having to go through?"

He had a point. "Okay, what else?"

"This look-alike kid from Mississippi, right?"

"Yeah."

"It's Brandi. I never thought for a second it was a different kid. And now the FBI came back with some kind of statistical photo analysis, don't ask me, but they said it's more than an 80% chance it's Brandi."

"They did?"

"Don't write that, we didn't release that. And we can also tell, from what the guy said whose family she walked along with in Louisiana, that she's gradually going back to her regular look. Back when we showed Harbison the video from the store in McComb, you could totally see on his face that he recognized her. Then he quickly started acting like they'd fooled him, like he'd realized it wasn't her. Everyone bought it. But he knew it was her the whole time. So why the hell is he pretending it wasn't?"

"Got a theory?"

"Only that the tall guy wanted Kelly to know it was her but wanted us to think it wasn't. I couldn't tell you why. Okay, two more things."

"The more the merrier."

"First, if he cares so much about his kid, why does he go off vigilante style and hide out in that house? You want your kid to be safe and come out of this alive, you don't pull a stunt like that."

"He's a hothead and he doesn't trust the police."

"That seems like reason enough for you?"

Carrie thought about it. "Maybe not. He seems kinda crazy, but not that crazy. But what other reason would there be?"

"We'd love to know."

The gears in her head kept grinding. "And your second thing?"

"We interviewed a bunch of kids, trying to find out whether Brandi dropped any hints ahead of their flight. Her friends all say no. But then they talk about how strange and different she was getting over the past year or so. And one kid hinted that Brandi was doing things she wasn't ready to tell us."

"Like what? Stealing stuff?" A bit of shoplifting was good for a kid.

"Yeah, from stores and from other kids, but that's just the beginning. She was turning mean, no one wanted to be her friend and she'd been popular before. And turning racist at ten years old, for Christ's sake. And since this stuff is bad enough, what the hell is the part that's too bad to tell us?"

Carrie's mind jumped to the cases she and Gavin had been researching. "I know what they say kids have the hardest time telling grown-ups."

"Which is…"

"Sexual stuff."

Kresge made a face. "The girl didn't seem to be talking about things Brandi was saying, but things she was *doing*."

"Like, doing sexual stuff?"

"I wasn't thinking along those lines."

"Isn't Lauren known for having a stream of boyfriends since the divorce? God knows what Brandi has heard and seen at home. I had a couple of friends growing up who had to hear, like, every sound while their mom was making it with some guy. They hated it."

Kresge looked uncomfortable. "Actually, there's still one more issue on my mind," he said.

"Whoa there. We skipped past that last one kind of fast."

He ignored her. "Brandi worked hard not to get found by police in Louisiana. That's twice now. This time she didn't even meet back up with her mother, she took off with another woman, older, red car. Why is she going to these lengths to avoid us?"

"Because these people will get her back to her mother, or she thinks they will."

"Yeah, okay, except now it's been all over the news that her father was shot and barely survived. Wouldn't she be desperate to see him and see that he's okay? She supposedly loves him so much."

Carrie nodded, watching another piece fall, disturbingly, into place.

She cautiously told Kresge about her attempt to go undercover, changing the story so it had all happened in Cleveland. "I'm starting to think these people may have good reason to help mothers run. That's not what I thought at first, but…"

Kresge scowled. "People can't go taking the law into their own hands, it'd be anarchy. That's what police are here for, and the courts."

"Well, you would think that, you're a cop. Except in your job you must see how messed up the courts are."

He chose not to respond to that one.

"So, sir, I've got to ask you something. Are you the one who's been passing me information from inside the department?"

"No!" he said, feeling accused. Then he did a double-take. "Wait—you don't know who it is? How do they get the leaks to you?"

She thought for a moment, then remembered that, whatever else was going on, Kelly was still a source. "Sorry, can't tell you that. "

"I can tell they suspect it's me, so I'd love to find the real culprit."

"Yeah, well, me too. It may not even be a cop, but that's all I can say. Next question: what do you want me to do with all this stuff you're telling me?"

Kresge opened his hands and made a *You really have to ask?* face. "I can't go after this stuff independently, I'd lose my job." He paused. Carrie said nothing, waiting for the rest. "I want you to see what you can find out. I don't buy it that Harbison's just a hot-headed asshole; I think it's worse than that."

~

Kelly Harbison was the overnight poster boy coast to coast for the Fathers Rights movement. Tuesday had been Carrie's moment of fame, but Wednesday belonged to Kelly, beginning early that evening when the surgeon gave the green light for him to talk to a gang of reporters with cameras who had accumulated like a fan club at the hospital.

He started making brash declarations sooner than he could stand up. This time he took a break from decrying the bungling actions of law enforcement, instead spewing his wrath at the custody courts. "If family law judges were doing their job, fathers wouldn't be in the position I found myself in. Fathers are totally second class in court, nothing we say gets listened to. I've been telling the judges on my case for more than two years that my ex-wife was going to run away with my daughter, and they never lifted a finger to prevent it."

NBC's Lester Holt asked him, "Do you believe that your daughter would have been freed if you had allowed law enforcement to handle entering the house in Merrydale?"

Kelly's response was, "One person with the element of surprise can do better than a big system with all its required procedures. I wanted to surprise the kidnapper unaware and get my daughter out of there without anybody getting hurt. And I would have succeeded if the police hadn't come to the house. The kidnapper would have been leaving the house slowly and carefully and that's when I would have gotten him. Unfortunately he was alerted that the police were on their way—it turns out he had a scanner—and since he was clearing out at racing speed I missed my shots. And, too bad for me, the kidnapper didn't miss all of his."

Holt followed up. "You've been saying 'the kidnapper.' But didn't you say there were two kidnappers in the house?"

Harbison could be seen rolling his eyes. "I don't know if my ex was armed, but in any case I didn't have to worry about her being much of a shot." And he gave a small, bitter smile.

Holt again: "Wasn't the gunfire a danger to your daughter's life? Wouldn't it have been much safer to let law enforcement surround the house and force the kidnappers to come out with their hands up?"

Harbison said, "That's a dream scenario you're painting, not real life."

The interview was the focus of dozens of segments on national and local news broadcasts that night. Fathers Rights activists were ecstatic. The next morning groups all over the country would take to the streets with blown-up photographs of Kelly, underscored with his words, "If judges were doing their jobs..."

~

Lying on the living room couch awake but in a catatonic realm beyond exhaustion, Carrie heard her phone playing "Tell Me" by Who's Calling. It was her ringtone for unrecognized numbers. *It's still early, I should answer it.* But her limbs wouldn't move.

Ten minutes later she was aware of Francesca walking through the room, and she asked her to pass her phone over. "It's, like, eight inches away from you," her sister said, but did it anyhow. "Had enough to drink tonight, kid?" she tossed over her shoulder as she went on her way.

Francesca was one to talk.

Carrie apathetically punched in her voice mail passcode.

The caller's voice was female and a little shaky. "My name is Sofia Madsen. I'm Lauren Harbison's best friend. I'd like to talk to you."

Carrie's mind leapt up out of the near-sleep she'd sunk into.

~

By invitation, Carrie drove to Madsen's house. It was close to 9:30 when she arrived; she'd stopped being sleepy and crossed over into ragged, assaultive consciousness, her head aching and her legs unsteady.

They sat in Sofia's kitchen and sipped decaf coffee, after Carrie had declined a cup of tea (who the hell drinks tea?) and then a beer (which she wanted desperately but knew would leave her curled up on the kitchen floor given how sleep-deprived she was).

Madsen appeared in no mood for formalities, which was fine with Carrie. She went straight to business. "I made a deal with the police, so I can't get in trouble for what I say to you. But I still can't have you use my name because of my kids, okay? They've already been through a lot with all this, Brandi's a friend of theirs."

"You're, like, the fourth person who's told me to keep their name out of it. Not a problem." She pulled out her voice recorder and turned it on.

Madsen looked uncertainly at the device, then started unloading a weight that was clinging almost visibly to her chest. "I've read all your articles, and seen you on TV, it's always on at the auto shop where I work. So I can tell how people have been describing Lauren Harbison to you."

"Which is how?"

"That she was out to take Brandi away from the father, that she was a hysterical overreactor surrounded by women who hate men, embittered and looking for a scapegoat. That picture is total bullshit. And that divorce expert you quoted a while back, Corinne Fletcher, I've realized she's monumentally full of it. Funny thing is, she was my kids' therapist during my own divorce."

"Was she a good therapist?"

"Not terrible, she helped them in some ways. But she could have done so much more for them if she hadn't been in a camp that blinded her."

Carrie was intrigued about Fletcher's "camp," but Sofia was burning to talk about the missing mom. "Lauren has been such a great friend to me, the best one I've ever had, generous and supportive even when her own life is hell. This stuff about her being someone who loves to play up being a victim—that's so not her, she's the opposite, she puts a good face on day after day."

"Weren't her friends mostly other divorcing mothers?"

"Yeah, maybe. But look, I've been through a tough divorce myself, it gets hard to be around smiling happy couples, out in the yard with their perfect kids who look photoshopped. So yeah, you're drawn to people who get what your life is like. But we didn't sit around hating men, that's such a crock. And Lauren has other friends too, like Delta, happily married, great job, the whole nine yards."

"It sounds like Lauren wasn't someone who ever had relationships that worked, though."

"What? What are you talking about?"

"Well, she's had a parade of short-term boyfriends since her divorce. It sounds like that's why Brandi was fighting all the time with her mom."

Madsen laughed, looked carefully at Carrie, then said, "Oh my God, you're serious."

Carrie furrowed her brow. "I thought I was."

Madsen shook her head slowly back and forth. "I assume this comes from Kelly."

"He's not the only one."

"Let me guess—Lauren's sister Hillary, right?"

"Yeah, in fact. That was quite a guess; what made you think of her?"

"Because one of Kelly's abusive specialties is turning people against each other. Just to give one example: He had zero interest in church, not a religious guy at all. But when he learned that Lauren's family was upset that she'd stopped attending services, what does he do? He immediately becomes Mr. Christian. And—gee, what a weird coincidence—he starts attending *their* church. Which, by the way, he'd been to maybe twice ever up to that point, and only because Lauren wanted him to go with her. Now suddenly he's bonding with her relatives about Lauren's church attendance fading, saying how upset he is about her 'drifting from the faith.' Oh, and how important it is for their daughter to have a Christian upbringing, which he never gave two shits about before."

Carrie could hear Gavin's voice ringing in her ears.

"Next he discovers that, although Lauren's relatives are conservative and anti-gay, which she isn't, they don't like racism because their church is quite mixed. So he's suddenly all about harmony between the races, even though he's actually one of the most racist bastards I've ever met."

"Kelly Harbison? Racist?"

She nodded emphatically. "Like you wouldn't believe. He got so bent out of shape about Brandi having black and Spanish-speaking friends, especially since there was a year or so when her best friend was black."

"Do you know that girl's name?"

"Aisha. She and Brandi were connected at the hip. Kelly wouldn't admit he was bothered that she was black, but he never had anything good to say about her. And all of a sudden he had this thing about how Brandi 'leans on her friends too much.' A ten-year-old girl leans on her friends too much? What, she should be training for the military or something?"

"This is all from Lauren's side of the story, right?"

Madsen rolled her eyes and responded with a sharp edge. "No, I know Brandi very well. To pick an example from a year or so ago: Brandi was over here on a Thursday night to hang out with Kiara, Lauren wasn't here, and I asked Brandi if Aisha would be spending any of the weekend with her over at her father's house. She answers me, 'No, my dad doesn't like me to hang out with Aisha, he says she's not smart enough for me.' And she rolled her eyes.

Another time she said to me, 'My dad says bad stuff about black people sometimes, like people on television and stuff.'"

"Any chance she was trying to get in good with her mom by saying bad things about Kelly to you?"

Madsen responded pointedly, "There were at least two times when Brandi told me bad things about Kelly but said *not* to tell her mother." She left a pause. "I gather I'm wasting my breath. You've already made up your mind about this case."

"No I haven't. Well, maybe before, but not anymore. But I'm trying to write articles that'll hold up, I've got a lot of people breathing down my neck now."

She asked Madsen to go back to explaining about Lauren's boyfriends.

More sputtering, disgusted laughter. "Lauren has seen exactly two guys in the past three years. One relationship lasted four months, super-nice guy named Dante, but he turned out kind of dull. Lauren said later she guessed she'd tried too hard to find someone who was the opposite of Kelly. The second guy she dated for maybe four or five weeks but it just wasn't happening between them, they agreed to be friends instead. Justin something or other. They've stayed in contact, they even go out for a drink once in a while. That's it. That's the whole 'parade.' If you're waiting for more floats to come by, you're standing around for nothing."

"Other dates? One-night stands?"

"A few dates. No one else she brought home. And when she went out with guys it was on weekends when Kelly had Brandi. The accusations are laughable. Kelly's the type who throws mud and calls it artwork."

"Lauren's sister told me she was with lots of different men."

"But Hillary didn't give you any details, did she? Of course not. Go ask her what these supposed guys' names were, where Lauren met them, how long they saw each other, what the guys did for work, stuff like that. And ask her how she knows. You'll see right away she has no clue, she just hopped on Kelly's bandwagon."

"So where does Kelly get this stuff? Is he insanely jealous?"

"Not really, I don't think he believes his own accusations. He picked it up from his Fathers Rights buddies, they're all into saying what whores their ex-wives are."

Carrie shook her head. "He doesn't like the Fathers Rights crowd, he's gone to some pains to not be part of them even when they've tried to make him their big cause."

Madsen squinted. "That doesn't add up. Brandi even complained once, 'He doesn't spend any time with me when I've over there, he's too busy with his fathers' group, always talking on the phone or on his computer about their stuff.'"

"Well, there are fatherhood groups that aren't part of the whole Fathers Rights thing. I've been looking into the difference. Maybe he was involved in that kind of thing, something positive."

Madsen laughed yet again, grating on Carrie's nerves. "Think about it. If you were so upset that you don't get enough time with your kid, then you finally have her for the weekend, would you spend the time texting with guys from your fathers' group? He isn't interested in actually connecting with her. Well, that is, except when he suddenly wants her to be his girlfriend."

"Say what?"

"Oh, you haven't heard about that part, eh? Like that he tells her she needs to lose weight, that the boys aren't gonna want her if she gets heavy? At ten years old, for God's sake. And he probably hasn't mentioned that she complains that he hugs her for too long and won't let her go when she pulls away. And that not too long ago he asked her if she's starting to get breasts yet. So, yeah, he either ignores her or flirts with her."

"How much of this stuff have you actually heard Brandi talk about?"

"This part, none that I can remember. But, what, Lauren is making this stuff up? She was completely baffled by it. She'd say, like, 'Why can't he just get himself a girlfriend and let our little girl be a little girl?' He wanted her to grow up too fast."

"Brandi ever reluctant to go on her weekends with him?"

"Definitely. That part I did hear straight from her. Although, to be honest, there were also times she'd be eager to go, especially if she and her mom had been fighting or Kelly had promised some special thing they were going to do together. One time it was that they were going out the next day to choose a kitten for his house and it would be her kitten. That one never happened, of course. I forget what his excuse was."

"If Lauren was such a good mom and Kelly was so bad, why were Brandi and Lauren fighting so much?"

Sofia paused for a moment, taking a breath. "The last seven or eight months before they disappeared, everything was escalating. Brandi's behavior was getting out of control, her mouth was getting like a fifteen-year-old's. She would say stuff like, 'F you Mom, I'm gonna go live at Dad's, he says I can if I want.' But at the same time she was getting more upset about having to go over there. It got hard to make sense of it all."

"Other people have told me how much Brandi was changing… "

"Yeah, and she was losing weight, and she's a thin kid to begin with."

"You mean, like…"

"Starving herself? At times it seemed like that. Or maybe it was her anxiety, but either way she wasn't eating so much. By the time they disappeared, she was kind of tiny."

"But you never heard anything about Lauren planning to take off with her?"

"No, not that she meant seriously. The only thing I can think of is, maybe a month before they disappeared, she was crying at my house one day—Lauren, not Brandi—and saying that she couldn't talk about it. That was the first time she ever had something going on that she wouldn't explain to me."

"The thing she couldn't say was that she was getting ready to run?"

"Maybe. Or maybe she meant the *reason* for her running was what she couldn't say."

Another connection happened in Carrie's frayed mind, though she couldn't figure out what it was; it remained just out of reach.

"One last thing and then I gotta call it a night, I haven't slept since God knows when. What did you mean about Corinne Fletcher being in a 'camp'?"

Madsen hesitated. "You'd be here all night. But the thumbnail is that the people who specialize in divorce—the judges, the lawyers, the evaluators—they're all part of a culture that says that both parents cause a divorce, that it's always a *dynamic* between two people. They're not willing to believe that a guy could just turn out to be an abusive asshole. So they're always making the mom to blame for 'setting off' the guy's behavior. And they take that thinking into their work with kids, just seeing them as 'caught in the middle,' like it could never be that they have a parent who's an abuser."

Carrie hoped that with some sleep she'd be able to make sense of all this.

She prepared to say good night to Madsen and focus on driving home safely. As a parting shot, she asked whether Sofia thought any other friends of Lauren's might be willing to talk to her; if she could back up what Sofia had described that evening, she'd have a hell of a story.

"Well, there's Delta Evans. And Lauren's friend Rhapsody. Those were the people that the police thought knew the most. I don't know if they'll want to say anything."

"I have contact information for Delta." Carrie didn't reveal that she'd already spoken with her. "But who's this Rhapsody?"

"She's a student who gave Lauren a law school tour at the University of Akron. I guess they hit it off and became friends."

Holy shit.

Kelly never mentioned this detail, and he has to have heard it back when his pipeline was telling him everything. But then, he would have had no clue what it meant.

"Um… you think I could speak with her?"

Madsen said she'd see what she could do about putting them in touch.

CHAPTER 25

The Alliance for Child Rights called an emergency meeting in the back corner of a pool room during Thursday's lunch hour to plan a picket for Friday afternoon. Percy arrived twenty minutes late, by design, and pretended to be baffled by the whole issue, "but you guys were nice to me the other day, so I want to help out if I can." True to his earlier persona, he was a lost young man. The group set itself directly to fortifying him.

Two of the men present, Van and Dexter, were new to Percy but evidently long-time members of ACR, judging by how pleased the other guys were to see them. The two made comments that indicated extensive involvement in each other's lives; perhaps they played together on a softball team or attended the same church. They also proved more militant than anyone else present, with the possible exception of Holsheen himself, and rarely spoke of "women" or "mothers," preferring exclusive use of "the bitches" and "the whores." At times their body language seemed to draw Holsheen's second-in-command, Mark Chambliss, into a trio with them.

In contrast to Carrie's description of the women's group in Pittsburgh as a thorough mix of races, ACR was today, as before, unrelievedly white.

Although the focus of the meeting was on making Kelly Harbison their *cause célèbre,* Percy asked if he could get "a few quick minutes of advice" about his case. "Things haven't been going so good. I guess my three-year-old has been saying he doesn't want to see me. I don't get it, he seems so close when we're together."

Percy received an earful about what the men referred to as "Parental Alienation Syndrome." It appeared he'd stumbled into one of the group's central preoccupations; every man in the room was dying to contribute an illustration of ways in which his kids had been turned against him.

When the details for the next day's march had been ironed out, the members began to disperse. A couple of guys stayed after, interested in giving Percy support and advice, but Holsheen hurried them along; it seemed he considered the newcomer his special project. The departing men agreed that they'd meet back at The Taproom for beers at the end of the workday, then Percy and Holsheen remained alone.

Leaning into his mousy nature, Percy said, "Uh, it was good meeting Dexter and Van, those guys have a lot of energy. They kinda scare me, though."

Holsheen laughed and gave Percy a fatherly pat on the shoulder. "Those guys are completely on our side, that's what counts. You wouldn't wanna have them against you, but that's someone else's problem."

Percy tried to joke along. "Like they're in a militia or something?"

Holsheen ignored the comment, and went straight into a rant on Parental Alienation and how mothers manipulate kids into accusing the father of child abuse or domestic violence.

Percy resisted; he expressed doubts that his ex was on some kind of campaign against him, she was just unstable and drinking too much. But, with visible reluctance, he gradually fell under Holsheen's influence; the group leader's own kids had been resoundingly poisoned against him even though he was a loving and responsible father, as his own dad had been before him.

By the time Holsheen wrapped up their little bonding session, Percy was showing the first signs of girding himself. This group was going to help him find his balls.

As they headed out of the building, the group's ringleader indicated that he needed to go home after work and wouldn't be joining the guys meeting later for drinks.

"I'm not much of a drinker myself," replied Percy. But as he walked to his car he found himself wanting to grab the chance to observe casual social interactions in the group. And with the boss not present. He'd have to work things out so he could return to Canton in a few hours.

~

Wisneski and Ledbetter stalled until early afternoon before responding to Lauren's email from the night before, strategically fueling her anxiety and anticipation. When the time came they wanted the mom to leap madly for the bait, too desperate to think it over as carefully as she should.

Hi Lauren:

I'm nervous, I've never been involved in something this big. I know it doesn't have anything to do with me really, it must be a thousand times harder for you and Brandi.

Brandi says they won't let her tell the address where she's been staying. They're going to take her to another house to meet you, in Beaumont, Texas. They'll give me the exact address for you tomorrow afternoon. They'll make certain no one follows them to the address, but to be on the safe side they said you shouldn't arrive until after dark tomorrow, and of course be sure you're not followed either. I know this is obvious, but I'm just saying what they told me to say. Go around the house to the back door and knock, but not too loudly, and they'll let you in.

They said you're welcome to stay the night so you and Brandi can rest up and leave early in the morning, though it'll just be mats on the floor to sleep on. Or they can drive you somewhere if you prefer, but in that case they want to go right away, not wait until morning, because they don't want to be seen with you in daylight.

They'll meet you there tomorrow night. I'll send the address the second they give it to me.

Be careful, stay safe, I love you both so much.

Sofia

Ledbetter and Wisneski wanted to be at the scene the next night, but federal agents gave a definitive no. The address was a house the FBI used for various purposes, so they weren't even willing to tell the detectives the precise location; and for that reason they would be the ones to send Lauren her final instructions, including the address, the next day. Ledbetter turned the password to the Protonmail account over to an agent.

A middle-aged couple earned a salary to live in the house and conduct business designed to look as normal as possible, leaving in the morning to go to "work," shopping for groceries, digging in the garden. The only difference from, say, living on a trust fund was that they had to abruptly vacate the house, sometimes for a week or more, whenever the FBI gave them marching orders.

~

Sofia Madsen succeeded in arranging a meeting between Carrie and Rhapsody, set for 2:00 that afternoon in Akron. It was not easy to do. "Sounds like Rhapsody hates you," Sofia said, curiosity in her tone. "She said your articles are very biased."

Carrie chose not to mention that there was an additional source of resentment.

The reporter now sat waiting in the appointed coffee shop, having come early to make sure they wouldn't miss each other.

Rhapsody arrived punctually. Carrie was startled by how beautiful she was; she'd pictured an underworld of shadowy figures with pockmarked faces and emaciated, skeletal forms. The assistant kidnapper she was greeting had beaded cornrows in long dark hair, shiny dark skin, and cheekbones to die for. Carrie felt outclassed in a way that she hadn't around TV news anchors, or even around her boy Gavin who came from the most upper-class town in western Pennsylvania.

The law student made no show of hiding her hostility. "I know who you are," she said icily. "I of course couldn't reveal that to Sofia Madsen."

Carrie dropped all pretense. "So you've talked to Amy about me."

No response.

"Listen, those folks are pissed, and I get why. But have you followed my articles? I didn't blow their cover. I'm a reporter, not the FBI."

"Yeah, and you'll do anything to get a good story."

"Okay, yeah, that's kind of my job. But I haven't burned anybody and don't plan to."

"You've already made Lauren look like a criminal, and that makes anyone who helps her look like a criminal."

"Listen, Kelly and the people on his side are quoted in my articles because they're the only people who will talk to me. No one who supports Lauren has been willing to tell me squat until *yesterday,* for God's sake, when Sofia finally gave me a little insight into why Lauren ran."

Though then she remembered that Delta Evans had tried to tell her several days earlier but Carrie had analyzed her comments to death.

More silence from Rhapsody.

Carrie plunged on. "Look, I'm from the wrong side of the tracks down near Morriston, the cops hate us and we hate them, and our feelings about judges are pretty much the same. I get it that things are fucked up in high places."

Rhapsody's belligerence went down one small notch though her personality, unlike her outfit, remained unadorned. "I can't believe what you pulled on the people in Pennsylvania. Now we're supposed to believe that you're suddenly a friend to abused women?"

"Sofia was the first person to give me a clue about why Brandi's been acting so strange the past year. I've had nothing to go on."

"Well, duh. Why the hell do you think Brandi is out there on her own instead of coming back?"

Carrie was confused. "What do you mean, 'out on her own'?"

"You haven't heard? She ran away Sunday from the guy she was traveling with. Police have known about it since that night."

"She's not with the kidnapper guy, the tall man?"

"No, and she's not with Lauren either. She's traveling solo."

"Who's she with?"

"The police don't know that."

"Did they catch the tall man?"

"No, but they know he doesn't have Brandi."

"How can you say for sure what the police know? Are you just guessing?"

Rhapsody scowled. "You've got some attitude, girl. I guess it shouldn't surprise me, you're a bigwig now."

Carrie was done placating, for better or worse. Her sense of awe at this beautiful law student hadn't vanished, but deeper aspects of her nature grabbed the wheel. "You go to law school, you've gotta know that reporters can't just go around believing whatever they're told. Of course I'm gonna ask you where you get your information. You don't want to tell me, that's fine, but it's my job to ask."

Now Rhapsody was really pissed. But she also seemed to register Carrie for the first time, as if she'd been talking to an imaginary presence until now. Her eyes narrowed. "I'm doing you a favor by talking to you," she said.

"No you're not. We both have reasons for being here."

A stand-off ensued, both of them making occasional brief eye contact and then looking away. Carrie finally broke the silence. "You gotten toweled off enough? Let's start round two. I'm ready."

Rhapsody almost smiled, maybe. "Any black folk where you grew up?" she asked.

"Hardly at all in Mormon Valley. Almost a hundred percent white trash. Black kids and immigrants live in Huntington, opposite side of Morriston. We all met up at the regional high school, otherwise we never would've known they existed, and same for them with us."

"How'd you get along?" A little smirk.

Carrie rolled with it. "Like shit. But after a year or so you start to realize you've got more in common with each other than with the snots from Round Hill Estates. A lot of the girls made friends with each other eventually. The boys kind of stayed enemies, but not all of them, it got better even with them. I had a boyfriend who was Dominican for a while, I caught a lot of shit about it, but nothing too serious. That kid was no-joke good looking, I would've been willing to deal with more shit than I did."

"What happened to him?"

"He dumped me for a girl who was thinner and not so mouthy."

This exchange remained stiff, neither woman dropped her guard. But it served its purpose; they were able to make something of a fresh start.

Rhapsody was the one to pick up the thread. "I can't tell you how I'm getting my information about the cops."

"Okay, fair enough. So what do you make of Brandi traveling on her own? The police said they saw signs that Lauren and Brandi weren't getting along in hiding. You'd think if Brandi got away she'd go straight to the police and ask to go home, not take off in the other direction."

Rhapsody took an audible breath, then said, "Lauren's been missing for three weeks."

"I'm well aware of that. Your point being…"

"No. I mean *really* missing. Since the beginning. A man who was going to be their first guide arrived at their house that Friday night. Four o'clock Saturday morning, strictly speaking. Everything had been planned and set. They were going to get up at three a.m., have breakfast, make their final preparations, and be ready to leave when he arrived. Only, when he came in the door the house was empty; they'd already gone. Something happened that made Lauren and Brandi leave before he got there."

The impeccable house except for the storm-tossed bedrooms and a few last dishes in the sink; Carrie suddenly understood what she'd seen.

Her mind raced. "She had some way to get in touch with her planned helpers?"

"Yes. But she never did."

"Someone persuaded her not to trust you?"

"I'm not part of this. I just introduce people."

"Point taken." It was a game. But Carrie got that it was an important one.

"So that's one possibility, that this other person lied to her and got her to turn against her helpers. Maybe he told her the network was fake and they hold people for ransom, God alone knows what he may have gotten her to believe."

"This mystery man got them out of the house fast—their bedrooms were a mess."

"He either held a gun on them, or he played that he was on their side and told them it was an emergency."

Carrie breathed, taking it in. "That would explain some things... The police and FBI haven't caught any sight of Lauren. The closest they've come is a pile of her stuff they found in some bushes a few days ago. Looked to have fallen out of her bag."

"Yeah, that was in the news."

They were quiet for a time. Then Carrie said, "This is huge. Can I write it?"

"It's not up to me. The people in question don't trust you, for good reason. They want my opinion on whether it's wise to put this information in your hands, but the decision will be theirs."

"Rhapsody, I'm seriously not gonna fuck with you. Are they worried the police will put the squeeze on me to reveal who you people—sorry, those people—are?"

"There are starting to be legal cases where reporters are being forced by courts to reveal their sources. I wrote a paper about it last year. That blanket protection that everyone thinks journalists have doesn't exist anymore."

"That's fucked up," Carrie said.

Rhapsody nodded. "The other concern is that you're going to take this story and make it look like a ridiculous invention on their part, use it to make them look bad."

"Well, tell them that their version fits a few things that I know. In fact it makes more sense than any explanation that's been put out there so far."

After a pause, the future lawyer said, "Okay." Maybe Rhapsody would put in a plug for the network to grant permission.

Carrie decided to play another card. "The truth is, the police do know something about what Lauren's doing. They just don't know where she is."

It was Rhapsody's turn to be caught off guard. "Excuse me?"

"I've been talking with someone who keeps in touch with Lauren. I can't say who it is. But that person told me that Lauren and Brandi almost succeeded in getting out of the country."

Rhapsody looked shocked, then doubtful. "Why would she keep in touch with someone else and not the network?"

"You said it yourself, maybe this guy got her not to trust the network, to be afraid of them."

The law student looked lost in thought.

"So no one in the network has any idea who this guy is that Brandi was traveling with?"

"No clue."

"Kelly was told that the tall man was known inside of fathers' organizations, that he used to help fathers track down kidnapped kids but he switched sides. They say he's a traitor, that mothers offered him more money."

Rhapsody scowled. "Why would you believe anything he tells you? And the last part is a joke; where are mothers going to get money from? They have way less money post-separation than men do, for at least the first two years. Look it up. A lot of why mothers are getting creamed in family court has to do with who can afford an expensive battle, pay thousands of dollars for discovery and evaluations, tens of thousands for expert witnesses, you name it."

"You have a guess who the guy is?"

"Somebody that Kelly Harbison hired to kidnap Lauren and Brandi."

Carrie scrunched up her face. "Come on. You're telling me this guy just happens to come and kidnap them the very same night your people were going to leave with her?"

"No, I'm not telling you he 'just happens' to." The law student was pissed again.

"Then what? He, like, had them under surveillance?"

"Exactly."

"You're serious?"

"I gather that, along with your other ignorance on these issues, you're not up on how common it's become for abusers to use high-tech monitoring of their victims. They now can track every move the woman makes, listen to her phone calls, read all her texts. They can even know keystroke-for-keystroke—I'm not exaggerating—exactly what she's done on her laptop or phone, read all her emails, know every website she's visited."

It took a lot to throw Carrie off but Rhapsody had succeeded. "Okay... How do I learn more about this?"

"Do a search for 'high-tech surveillance and domestic violence.' You'll get pages and pages of hits—including some famous cases."

Carrie was quiet for a while, pieces once again rearranging themselves in her brain. "That would explain why Brandi isn't coming home... Is she surviving on her own somehow? Or did she find her mother?"

"Neither. She has help." These words were accompanied by a stern tightening of her face; Carrie was to ask nothing further along that line.

"All right... So, what are you free to tell me about Brandi and Kelly?"

Rhapsody looked hard at Carrie, calculating trust. She then spoke haltingly, choosing her words phrase by phrase. "Brandi was coming home from contact with her father increasingly disturbed, and acting more and more aggressive towards her mom. She started saying she wanted to kill herself. Telling her mother she hated her. Not eating. Lauren took these concerns to the court multiple times, but the judge ruled that her concerns had no basis, that Brandi's tensions were caused by Lauren's own inability to get past her resentments towards Kelly. The solution was that she needed to stop trying to turn Brandi against her father."

"There's nothing about any of this in the court documents."

"You read the whole file at the courthouse?"

"No, Kelly gave me copies of all the documents."

"That may be your answer."

Carrie nodded slowly. After a breath, she asked, "You got time to help me out with one more thing?"

Rhapsody told her to go ahead.

"Not too long ago, I read what happened to Katie Tagle. To her baby. And I thought, well, this is some nowhere county in California, I pictured one of those wild-west places where you wander into town and get shot. But I've started learning about cases from all over the country. And now you're telling me the same shit is happening right here, that Lauren got completely blown off by the court."

"Law journals have been publishing articles about the problem for years. Law students know that this stuff is happening because they study cases and they intern with lawyers. It's going on all over the place."

"But there's this Fathers Rights movement all over the country, they're saying they're the ones getting burned. Are the family courts just screwing everybody?"

"You just said you've looked into cases besides Katie Tagle's, right?"

"Not a ton, but a decent number, between me and this guy I work with." It struck her she'd gone a long time without thinking about Gavin.

"And how many cases have you found, when you really check it out, where the court sided with the mother while she was abusing the father or the kids? Sided with her for no reason, ignored all the evidence? And say, worst-case scenario, the kids ended up dead."

Carrie was reluctant to concede the point. "The worst cases we found were pretty much against the mom. Yeah, almost all of them. But I'm new to researching this, I could be missing a lot."

"Research it for years—I have—and you're still going to find that the most serious outrages by family courts are almost all being done to mothers. But you have to explore the cases thoroughly, you can't go by surface impressions. And you can't go by what the court-appointed evaluators concluded—they're part of the same sick system."

Carrie was gripped by a powerful urge for a cigarette but didn't have any. Instead she took a couple of slow, deep breaths through pursed lips, creating an approximation. "Then why does everyone think it's the other way around?"

"The fathers—the abusers I should say—are better organized. The mothers are too busy and broke and traumatized to be out there running mothers' organizations. The fathers have way more money to pay fancy evaluators to get the answers they want. Plus they're scary; abusers intimidate people. Look, these aren't just any fathers. You want to see who comes to the Fathers Rights movement, read their websites. They're specifically recruiting men who have been accused of abuse, or who are bitter about paying child support."

"But mothers win ninety-five percent of contested custodies."

Rhapsody emitted a disgusted half-cough. "You heard that from Fathers Rights literature, right? Mothers win ninety-five percent of *uncontested* custodies—because most responsible dads recognize that kids are best off with the parent who's been their primary caretaker. But in contested cases, mothers lose more often than they win. That's been true since the 1980s, when the big shift happened in the courts. And remember, mothers are still almost always the primary caretakers, even today."

Carrie paused before trying one more salvo, her arsenal almost empty. "What about all these guys who've had false accusations against them so they can't see their kids?"

"Investigate those cases. You're going to be amazed what you find when you look at the evidence. But don't take my word for it; do your work."

Carrie nodded slowly, thoughtfully, and then mustered a sort of smile. "Challenge accepted," she said.

She left with unmistakable instructions about what she could write and what she couldn't, at least until Rhapsody conferred with the network.

~

The ACR guys sat around a table at The Taproom, watching an Indians game and ignoring each other's comments unless they were about the baseball action, in which case they were met with either enthusiastic agreement or combative retorts. Most men from the lunchtime meeting were there, minus only Holsheen, Dexter, and Van. The fathers were gruffly welcoming to Percy, two of them sliding over to make space while a third grabbed a chair for him from another table.

Percy pretended to know little about baseball, not a man's man. (And he truly wasn't all that interested.) He was thus left with little he could say for almost an hour, until the home team fell six runs behind and the conversation finally drifted onto other subjects.

After going through their usual warmup paces (women who view them as cash registers, children who've been turned against them), the group drifted to speculating about the disappearance of one of their stalwarts. Not that Denny Arbeitman was missing in any serious way; he'd just abruptly stopped coming to meetings and stopped returning anyone's texts or email announcements.

Percy let theories fly for a few minutes about where Denny had gone before asking dimly, "Was he, like, on the news or something? I feel like I've heard his name."

The men looked at each other, but all shook their heads. Chambliss said, "He came to two or three of our pickets but there weren't any TV reporters there those times. We would have steered him away from the cameras anyhow, you never know what's gonna be the next thing out of Denny's mouth."

Percy scrunched up his eyes, hoping to look vaguely stupid. "Anybody got a picture of him? I swear I know him for some reason." All present reached for their phones and started flipping through their archives. Terry handed his phone over to Percy. "Here's one from a rally we had at the courthouse. Denny was wrecking the mood that day, he kept clowning around. And he's the one who would always tell us we weren't serious enough about things! So I took a picture of him being a goofball to stick in his face the next time he started lecturing us."

Percy studied the image minutely, committing it to memory, then shook his head. "Nope, doesn't look familiar at all. I wonder who I'm thinking of."

Chip said, "I bet Denny took to the hills like he said he was going to."

The response from Chambliss was, "Whatever gets him away from here."

Percy wanted to ask what this was all about but didn't dare. He let his face go blank and vapidly turned back toward the game. And, always the good boy, he declared shortly after ten o'clock that he'd better get home and get a good night's rest.

The guys ribbed him. "Oh, you got some lady waiting in bed for you, eh killer?" and, "Sure, after drinking a whole half a beer like that, you probably need to go sleep it off." He gave an embarrassed grin, eyes a little cast down, and said, "Well, see you at the next meeting, I guess. Don't think I'll make it for the rally tomorrow."

Chambliss, filling Holsheen's shoes, grabbed Percy's hand and shook it heartily. "Oh, you'll keep coming, we've seen enough fathers in your kind of situation. Good to see you again, kid."

~

Gavin sat in his car reflecting before pulling out into traffic. He was intrigued by the phrase "took to the hills," especially because the man in the picture had been white and extraordinarily tall.

~

Gavin and Carrie sat in an ice cream parlor in Morriston, open until midnight. Carrie had little appetite, her insides consuming themselves. She occasionally took a small cool mouthful of her single scoop of coffee ice cream in a dish and let it melt in her mouth, watching distractedly as Gavin worked his way through a banana split.

They had each delivered their big news, Carrie that Lauren had disappeared from the underground and that Brandi was now running on her own, Gavin about the strikingly tall white guy, Denny, who had disappeared not only from attendance at meetings and rallies of the Alliance for Child Rights but from all contact with anyone.

Carrie sat trying to fit the pieces together.

"Maybe what Kelly told me was true, about Tall Guy starting on the fathers' side but turning traitor. Maybe Denny took off to go work for mothers."

Gavin made a clicking sound with his mouth. "But if Kelly knows who he is, why would he be pretending not to? He'd be so psyched to blow the whistle on whoever's aiding Lauren."

She licked a thin coating of ice cream off her spoon. At the rate she was going, her scoop would be a puddle before she finished it. "Maybe the guy has some hold on Kelly, a secret from his past or something. Or maybe he threatened to kill Brandi if Kelly reveals who he is."

"If it was a threat to harm Brandi, then as soon as Kelly finds out she's escaped— which could happen any moment—he'll expose the guy."

Carrie held her spoon in the air as if getting ready to cast a spell with a wand. "But why would Lauren switch to this lone wolf when she had a well-organized group lined up behind her? And once the shooting happened in Athens, she has to have known she was with a crazy man. So you'd think she'd at least get back in touch with the network at that point."

"Maybe Tall Guy wasn't the shooter. Maybe he was their rescuer after their initial helper turned out to be insane."

That theory left as many questions as any of the others did.

"Rhapsody thinks Kelly had Lauren under surveillance and found out she was getting ready to flee with Brandi. So he hired Tall Guy to kidnap them first, taking advantage of the fact that they would appear to have left by choice."

Gavin gave a little shake of his head. "Have them kidnapped for what purpose? To demand ransom from himself?"

Neither of them had an answer to that one. Maybe Rhapsody did.

Carrie was itching for Gavin to stick his nose right back into the Alliance for Child Rights. "How about you invent some crisis, totally unexpected, that just happened between Percy and his ex? Like she just pulled something even worse than before and he needs help with it. So that you can get more time talking to this deputy guy, or Holsheen himself."

"It's way too soon. These guys are always on guard, it's how they live. If my drama ramps up right after I've joined the group, they're gonna smell a rat."

"But they're gonna think Percy is too pathetic to be conniving."

He shook his head. "Let's not wreck this, we could learn a ton if we play it cool."

Carrie poked further at her dish, seeking a channel for her impatience. She was geared up to start getting irritated at Gavin, but he hadn't said anything wrong. Maybe she kind of wished he would.

There was a better way to work out her tension. The problem was she couldn't figure out where it might happen. She was not a fan of lovemaking in the car, it felt very high school to her, a mental return to times of hurried sex with guys who came as soon as you touched them and then considered it a successful evening, or maybe an embarrassing one, but either way they were in a hurry to move on. Fifteen-year-old boys seemed to think they had only one useful body part, so once that one had popped back down into its hovel it was all over, for better or worse. And for Carrie that had usually meant for worse.

But no other option came to mind. So she recommended they go for a drive in her car, which would at least put him in the passenger seat, free from interference by the steering wheel. Thus when she found an adequately remote place to park she was able to climb right over, straddle him where he was, and start kissing his beautiful mouth, which she needed even more badly than she needed to slip him inside of her, though both mattered.

CHAPTER 26

The lead story in *The Morriston Chronicle* was once again under Carrie Green's byline. She claimed to have spoken with people involved in planning Lauren Harbison's flight with her daughter. Those people in turn were asserting that Lauren and Brandi had left with someone else's assistance, or had both been kidnapped, but that in any event at no point had they traveled with anyone from the network that had been put into place to guide their escape.

The report created a minor sensation despite being believed by almost no one. Law enforcement officials were openly derisive of the claim; as the State Highway Patrol spokesperson said publicly that morning, "It's like hearing a man accused of a murder say, 'Yeah, I did pull out a gun to shoot my boss that day, but by coincidence someone else shot him first.'"

~

By Friday morning neither law enforcement in Louisiana nor the FBI had uncovered any trace of Tall Guy. Nor did they have any idea where Brandi or Lauren had gone. Agent Zink decreed that it was time to let the media and public know that Brandi was no longer with her original kidnappers; public eyes are valuable but not if everyone's looking for the wrong thing. The official stand would be that Brandi had most likely been threatened with harm or death, or the same to one of her parents, if she came forward.

Kelly Harbison's fragile condition was no longer a reason to withhold this information. He had been taken out of the ICU on Tuesday and released from the hospital on Thursday, though with strict instructions for monitoring the risk of infection for several more days. It was assumed he now could withstand the shock of knowing Brandi was deliberately staying away from help.

Wisneski and Tobias met privately to assess where they stood. Their leak appeared to have stopped leaking though they didn't know why; no police secrets had turned up in Green's stories for many days. Her article that morning was a source of distress to Wisneski nonetheless. "Are we supposed to believe that this kid has somehow gotten the inside track on an underground kidnapping network? Don't you think she's just making the whole story up, with her supposed sources?"

"I wouldn't put it past her," the chief said. "She's ambition on steroids. But she's also become the go-to reporter on this issue, as ridiculous as that sounds; so maybe a network did decide to contact her."

Wisneski swore in disgust.

Last on her agenda, but most important, was Shane Kresge. "I can't keep him on the team any longer, Chief. He does okay as long as I tell him precisely what to do, but the minute I need him to be capable of thinking for himself he's off down the garden path. And he's gotten so cranky, he can't take a joke anymore, he disagrees about every little thing,. He's negative for the sake of being negative."

Tobias took a few moments to collect his thoughts, so Wisneski threw another log on the fire. "The biggest problem is that tension's getting bad between him and Ledbetter. She's not as patient as I am, his sniping is getting to her and she's starting to bite back. I don't need it."

He gazed off into the middle distance as if adding a column of numbers in his head. "You know anything about his life outside of here? Marital problems, elderly parents, health issues?"

"No idea."

The chief gave in with reluctance. "All right, I'll find different work to move him into, something he'd see as a step up not a punishment. But first I have to take a shot at getting him to open up about personal issues, that's my job." Tobias' voice changed a little. "In return, you need to throw him a bone."

"Such as?"

"He's convinced that one of you should talk to the Stolnik kid again. Ledbetter was pissed about it, like it's a waste of her time, and it probably is. But I want you to go to the kid's house yourself. That will put me in a position to say to Shane, 'This change in your role has nothing to do with the job you're doing, look, they even used your idea about interviewing the girl again.'"

Wisneski nodded. "All right, if it gets me rid of him, it's a deal."

Tobias winced, always the politician. "So much for diplomatic language, Detective. Better hope we're not being recorded."

~

Percy ended up, without enthusiasm, driving all the way from Pittsburgh back to Canton to join the ACR picket line that afternoon. Carrie hadn't succeeded in pressuring him into inventing a crisis that might get him Nathaniel Holsheen's ear, but had laid on enough guilt to get him out of his newspaper's building and behind the wheel of his car. He joined the other guys on the sidewalk, where some of them stood still with signs while others paced around in a large circle. He didn't have to pretend not to want to be there, it was real.

As the rally wound down the men got to hanging around in three or four small groups, drinking coffee while complaining about the ex-wife and laughing at off-color jokes. Percy became the focus of the three guys he was huddled with, out to toughen him up. He was wondering how to subtly change the subject to Kelly Harbison, and it occurred to him to use a near-truth: he mentioned casually, sheepishly, that he'd recently been out on a couple of dates with a girl from East Liverpool, a cutie named Jenny (the first name to pop into his head) that he'd met in a pizza shop where she worked.

His unskillful casting of bait toward that corner of Ohio worked, though not in the way he'd expected. A guy named Reilly said, "East Liverpool? No shit? What were you doing there? That's where my girlfriend is. I mean, that's where she works, she doesn't actually live there."

"She works in the pizza shop?" Percy asked incredulously, afraid that his fiction about Jenny the pizza shop worker was about to unravel and blow his entire cover off with it.

"No, but in that town. That place is friggin' small, wouldn't you say? It's an okay place, though. She's a cop there."

"Oh," said Percy, allowing the breath he'd held in to escape. Then, genuinely confused, he said, "That's who you're fighting for custody with?"

"No, no, I'm not talking about the whore. My new girl's nothing like the ex-wife, she's great. And she loves my kids, they get along with her better than their mom, for real. My girl sees what I'm going through with the court, she's as pissed about it as I am."

"Isn't that the department that's handling that kidnapping?" Percy asked, trying to sound as uncertain as possible.

Reilly winked at him with a little smile, which Percy pretended to be confused by. He then immediately changed the subject to a mixed martial arts fight coming up that night that he had money down on. Banter started flying back and forth about the stupidity of Reilly's bet, and surrounding fathers started drifting into one big group, analyzing the upcoming bout. Several new bets resulted.

~

Wisneski began what was for Gabbi Stolnik a replay of the scene from two weeks earlier, seated nervously in her favorite kitchen chair with a cop once again facing her across the table. Three things were different this time: her dad was out in the yard, her mom wasn't even home, and the officer was humorous and friendly.

Wisneski decided to approach the awkwardness head on. Deliberately introducing herself as "Janet," she went on to say, "Kids always hate talking to cops, like they're gonna get in bad trouble. It's the same for adults. Like when they see a cop driving behind them their heart immediately starts to race, even though they're not doing anything wrong."

Gabbi nodded tensely.

The detective went on. "I'm only here to help find Brandi and bring her home safe. Nothing else you say will even go in my notes. You tell me your best friend just robbed the TD Bank, I'm gonna pretend I didn't even hear it."

That elicited a little laugh.

"Now, Annika was the one who talked to you last time. She makes kids extra nervous, she doesn't mean to, that's just the way it is. Did you feel that way?" *Give the kid a sense that everything is okay to talk about, even to badmouth cops.*

"Yeah, I guess, a little," the girl answered uncomfortably. "You seem a little easier to talk to."

"I'm *way* easier to talk to," Wisneski said, succeeding in getting another laugh. Then she pulled a cold Cherry Coke out of a cloth bag she'd carried in. "Care for a soda?"

Gabbi looked around a little nervously, and Wisneski said, "Don't worry, no one's gonna know about the soda either." The girl accepted the can, popped it open, and took a drink.

It was like meeting with a stoolie in a bar and plying him with a couple of cocktails to loosen his tongue.

Kids were now deep into the school year. The detective got Gabbi talking about the huge change involved in starting middle school. She kept it light, including surprising Gabbi a couple of times with slightly unprofessional comments that made the girl giggle, including one about looking around to see which boys had the nicest buns.

By the time Wisneski started to lead Gabbi toward sensitive ground, her nervousness had subsided. The detective passed the girl a second soda, took a sip from her own, and then, tossing off words as though discussing a sitcom from the night before, said, "Annika mentioned that there were parts of Brandi's strange behavior that you weren't comfortable talking about."

Gabbi nodded.

In a conspiratorial tone, Wisneski said, "Let's go into it. Believe it or not, I need to know everything there is to know about her. The stranger the better."

The girl shook her head. "It's gross stuff. Not the kind of thing you talk about."

"Good girl, Gabbi. Except it's different when you're talking to a detective. Now you're supposed to go ahead and say all that stuff you shouldn't say the rest of the time."

"You mean, say out loud the gross stuff she said?"

"That's right. Or, if you can't stand to say it, write it down on a piece of paper for me."

This turned out to be a brilliant stroke.

Gabbi thought for a while. Finally she said, "How about I write it down but you don't read it until you're gone?"

It seemed they were entering territory the girl found severely embarrassing, beyond even what Wisneski had imagined.

"It's a deal. I won't read it until I'm back at my desk at the station."

Gabbi sat writing for a surprisingly long time; whatever the girl was feeling so shame-faced about, she apparently couldn't wait to go over every detail now that she had the opportunity.

~

Wisneski regretted the waste of a big chunk of her afternoon, but looked forward to being able to get on with the investigation without the irritation of dealing with Kresge. Gabbi Stolnik seemed like a sweet kid; she hoped middle school didn't harden the girl too much, those can be some rough years.

As she'd promised, Wisneski waited until she was seated in her office with the door closed, then flattened out the piece of notebook paper that Gabbi had scrawled upon nervously before meticulously folding it into eighths.

> Brandi started wanting to talk about sex all the time, and look at pictures. She's not the only girl in my grade like that, but it's like a bigger deal with her, and the pictures were gross. She kept asking if she could kiss me, and one time I let her and she stuck her tongue in my mouth, it was disgusting, so weird. You promised not to tell my parents any of this, I would die if they knew. Then one day she wanted to take a shower together so we did, no big deal, I shower with friends, but she stuck her finger up inside herself, and then asked if I would do that to her, which I said no, then she said well could she do it to me, and I said I was cold and needed to get out of the shower. That's still not even the weirdest thing. This other time she asked me if my dad has a big—well, you know. I said how would I know? And she said just look and find out and tell her. So after that I stopped hanging out with her, it was too weird.

"Jesus in heaven!" Wisneski sputtered. She exploded out of her padded rolling desk chair and bolted down the hall toward the chief's office. He was at his desk but put up a finger to signal her that he was on the phone. The detective waited in the doorway, which Tobias would know meant something big was up.

When he finished talking and put the phone in its cradle, she said to him, "I have to use my least favorite phrase in the English language: Kresge was right."

~

Gavin was not about to drive home to Pittsburgh without making a stop in Morriston or Middle Beaver or wherever Carrie happened to be. He was still feeling the glow from making it with her in her car the night before, still a little dizzy trying to understand her, the way she could tell him he was full of shit but then start stroking the inside of his thigh, or the way she'd seem unsure of herself and then suddenly be unstoppable. He couldn't get the currents to mesh.

Carrie was frantically writing an article when he called. He'd have to come to see her at the family house, even though her mom and a sibling or three were around.

By the time he arrived she'd submitted a draft to Vinestri and was waiting for the edits to come back. She kissed him with less intensity than he was hoping for, off somewhere else.

"I come bearing news," he said. She raised her eyebrows but he insisted that she find a beer for him first, *quid pro quo.* "I've been hanging around a bar pretending I can't handle my alcohol and after all that excellent acting I need a drink."

With Gavin in mind she'd bought a six of Black Horse Ale, or rather paid Francesca to get it. She slowly drank one herself, thinking how much happier she would have been with a PBR.

Gavin took a couple of deep draughts. "So, one of the ACR guys let it slip tonight that his new girlfriend, this 'hot ticket' he's so proud of himself about, such a contrast to the old bitch, etcetera, is a cop. Get this, for East Liverpool PD." Carrie cocked her head, alert. "And, according to him, she's a full-on believer in the Fathers Rights cause."

She leaned back against the refrigerator, eyes wide, then lurched forward. "Holy shit," she said, "Kelly really does have a mole, it's not his hacker friend!" Her mind raced. "What's the lady's name?"

"He referred to her as Arielle."

Carrie grabbed her phone hard, as if to keep it from escaping, and started punching with her thumbs. She held it to her ear, waited, then launched abruptly into speaking. "We've got some shit to talk about. Are you working?… Eight o'clock?? No way to slip out before that?… All right, where can we talk?… Listen, I just found out who my police department leak is—it's Arielle Mason… No, I'm not betraying a source, I wasn't getting it from her directly. And since when do you care about that anyhow? Get this, though: she's connected to the ACR group in Canton. In other words, Holsheen has known your every move the entire time… Okay, I'll see you then. Make sure no one follows you."

The last line was a joke.

Gavin gave her an inquisitive look after she hung up.

Carrie affected a superior smirk. "What, don't you have a secret buddy in the police department? The rest of us all do."

"Was that Kresge?" She nodded yes. "Why did you just give your pipeline away? No more inside scoop for you, Miss Maverick."

"She had already stopped leaking to Kelly, maybe she got scared. But I'm sure she's still spilling it all to her boyfriend, and I don't want everything the cops find out about Lauren and Brandi getting instantly passed to a bunch of scary dudes in Canton."

"Oh, now they're scary dudes to you? That was fast. I thought they were wounded fathers."

Carrie made her *up yours* face. "You've just informed me that Holsheen's been totally bullshitting this whole time, to the cops and then to you."

"No I didn't. What are you talking about?"

Carrie felt the typical dynamic of their conversations shift into reverse. "Come on, Gavin. He's been claiming that their ACR group has no connection to Kelly, that they don't even like each other. But a guy in his group has a girlfriend who just happens to keep Kelly up on everything the cops are doing? Holsheen and his group are up to their asses in this thing."

That thought connected another dot in her mind. "That mini-feud between them, the whole 'Harbison thinks the Fathers' Rights guys are too extreme' thing? He and Holsheen just cooked that up to keep the cops from connecting the kidnapping to ACR. I'll bet you any amount you want that Kelly used to go to meetings up there, only now they're all brain damaged and can't remember ever having met him."

Gavin was silent for a minute, thinking.

And then Carrie's face contorted into shock as if she'd just touched a live wire sticking out of the wall. Even her hair appeared to electrify, her eyes barely managing to hold to their moorings. "Oh my God," she blurted out. "They must be holding Lauren somewhere! Holy shit! And your Denny person is the tall man for sure!"

~

Kresge was the last to arrive for yet another emergency team meeting. He took only two steps into the room, then said to Wisneski, "I need to speak with you for a moment."

"Go right ahead," the detective said.

He motioned with his head to indicate that it needed to happen outside. She made an exasperated face, then remembered that the time for constant annoyance at Kresge had passed. She pulled herself into a semblance of professionalism and exited the room.

"Our leak has been found," Kresge said. "And she's in there."

Wisneski took a slow, deep breath, governing herself. "Shane, I know it's been a rough time, and we've all made some mistakes. Now let's bury the hatchet."

"I'm not talking about Ledbetter."

There was only one other "she," because Martinez hadn't arrived yet. "You mean Arielle? Don't be ridiculous."

"Yeah, well, you may get tired of saying that to me and having me turn out to be right. And we need to move cautiously, she's connected to some violent guys. The deal is, it turns out Mason's boyfriend is part of Nathaniel Holsheen's little army up in Canton. And it looks like she's become part of their team, you might call it Kelly's Boys Plus One Girl."

Wisneski stared, dumbfounded. "Shane, where are you getting this from?"

"A reporter who's been investigating Holsheen's group."

"Jesus, you mean the Green kid?"

He rolled his eyes. "What, like Green's going to reveal her own source to me? No, the information is from a reporter for a Pittsburgh paper, a guy who's been looking into that Alliance for Child Rights group that's been in the news."

"Care to tell me his name, or how you know this?"

He couldn't tell her, but he also wasn't sure how he'd duck it. "Look, can we just come back to that? If you've got some big news to spill at this meeting, and I assume you do since you told us to get over here instantly, you need to get Mason out of the room first unless you'd like the Fathers Rights guys to know every word you say."

Wisneski covered her eyes with her hand for a moment. If Arielle was the leak, that would explain a lot. In fact, suddenly it was the only thing that made sense.

"You will never cease to be a pain in my ass, Kresge," Wisneski griped.

"I aim to please, ma'am."

The detective shook her head to herself, then said, "Go on in, I'll be a couple minutes behind you." Then she stood in the hallway thinking fast, making up supposed facts she could share in the meeting that would create a huge stir up at ACR when Mason leaked the details to them. And then they'd have proof against Mason and could fire her ass.

And, as quickly, she knew she was overreacting; the next steps would have to be carefully planned between her, Ledbetter, and the chief. Better to just find a way to get her out of the meeting.

She poked her head in the room and called Kresge back out. "Listen, here's what we're doing. You need to go in there and tell everybody that you took me out of the room to give me news of a death in my family. Tell them I'm heading right home, the meeting is canceled. I'm gonna leave the station to make it believable. As soon as the coast is clear, you find Ledbetter and Martinez and take them to Tobias's office, and you all get on a conference call with me."

"Those instructions are awfully complicated, Detective," Kresge said. "You sure I can handle it?"

Wisneski gave him the finger, ordered him to get back in the room and look sad, and hurried off.

~

Half an hour later she was home and the newly reduced membership of the investigative team had gathered surreptitiously in the chief's office. All present took a deep breath and the detective, her voice filling the room by speaker-phone, dived into describing the new interview with Gabbi Stolnik. She finished by reading aloud the girl's handwritten testimony.

Martinez was cautious. "I know this stuff sounds very weird, but we need to consult a psychologist in case the things Brandi was doing aren't that far off the chart."

Wisneski's gut clenched; but the Sergeant was right, they weren't experts in this area. The Morriston department had an officer, Angel Cordero, who specialized in investigating sex crimes against kids; she'd ask him for a consultation.

Suddenly there was greater significance to the steady stream of boyfriends that Lauren was known to have had since her divorce. Maybe Brandi had been the one who wanted to flee, because of one of these men. But then why wouldn't Lauren just keep the guy away?

Perhaps they were dealing with a violent man. Maybe they had both needed to go into hiding from him.

The team hadn't done well to date at tracking down information about Lauren's many paramours. They were going to have to get back on it, squeezing facts from stones if necessary.

~

Gavin said he'd drive to Morriston and plant himself in a coffee shop until Carrie was finished with her rendezvous with Kresge.

She and the cop met at the kiosk for a hiking trail. Her co-conspirator, now out of uniform, walked toward her wearing sunglasses though it was late in the day and cloudy.

"A frog has five fingers," Carrie said, deliberately looking away from him.

"Three men in a tub," the off-duty officer responded.

This exchange exhausted his capacity for humor. "I know you've got news for me, but it can't top what I'm about to tell you," he said, deadly earnest.

"Okay, then you first. You already know the headline of mine anyhow."

Kresge quoted, as close to word-for-word as he could remember, the handwritten revelations handed to Detective Wisneski by Brandi's young friend—or rather, former friend—Gabbi Stolnik. Then he said, "You can't make this stuff up."

Carrie felt ill. "When I said about sexual stuff, I wasn't thinking along these lines at all."

"I hope not," he said. Then: "If this is too personal just tell me, but when you were in fifth grade, did girls do shit like this? I mean, I know times have changed, but…"

"No. Girls said stuff, they didn't do stuff. Oh, there were some girls who kissed boys, a few who kissed other girls. But no, nobody was sticking things up herself in front of people, or asking other girls could she do that to them. Nobody was asking for updates on the dicks of other girls' dads. No wonder Gabbi couldn't bring herself to talk about it."

"What do you make of it?"

"Maybe someone was preying on her."

"We're gonna get serious now about tracking down Lauren's many boyfriends."

"Yeah, well, it turns out they don't exist, except maybe two." She filled Kresge in on that aspect of her conversation with Sofia Madsen.

"Then are you thinking what I'm thinking?" Kresge asked.

"Well, Brandi wasn't asking Gabbi about the dicks of boys at school, or gym coaches, or priests, was she? She asked about Gabbi's dad. And now Brandi's going crazy trying to not come home to her father?"

Kresge dug at the ground with his foot, as if hoping to tunnel his way out of the case. "I'm not gonna say 'I told you so' to anyone, but I hated this guy's guts from the very beginning."

"You're not gonna say it but you just did."

"I wasn't talking about you. Although I don't get why you ever liked the guy."

"Yeah, well, I felt bad for him." Kresge made a disgusted face at her. "Okay, so I was stupid. Throw it in my face for years if you want. What do we do now?" She felt as though marbles were spinning down a funnel into her brain, her understanding gradually coming together. "Lauren's in danger somewhere. We have to move fast."

She proceeded to tell him about the picture of the very tall ACR guy that Gavin had been shown. "The guy's been mysteriously missing since, like, a week or two before Lauren and Brandi disappeared. Now you have Mason connecting Kelly to ACR. It all starts to add up."

Kresge nodded. "Because of Mason, the cops are gonna be all over those ACR guys first thing in the morning, pulling people out of bed if they have to. Everybody's ripshit about them using Mason to watch us."

"How can the cops know who's in the group? Holsheen will stonewall them."

"We've got TV and newspaper stories about the group's events, we can show pictures around town, hell, around the courthouse, and get names. We'll be turning up the heat fast. And the Canton department will be dying to help us. You pull that kind of shit on the cops and we circle the wagons."

"Tell your people to see what they can find out about this guy Denny. Don't say it came from me."

"Right, Green, like I'm going to tell them anything comes from you."

A new thought caused Carrie's gut to clench. "The ACR guys are gonna put it together fast that Gavin's the reason why Mason got exposed. He's out of time to see whether he can find anything else out—like where Lauren is being held."

It was tonight or never.

~

The coffee shop in Morriston was getting more crowded, not less so, as the hour got later. *There must be nothing going on in this town if everyone's heading here,* Gavin thought. *Not exactly an exciting nightspot.*

Carrie came in the door and motioned to Gavin to come outside with her. They walked a few shop doors away to put some distance between them and the surrounding ears.

"It's too soon to say for sure, but it's looking like Brandi was being molested. Turns out she dropped some broad hints. Plus she'd been coming apart for like a year. The whole picture is making more sense all the time."

"Some teacher or priest or something?"

"Who knows. But I'm thinking her father."

"You've got to be kidding."

She explained why her suspicions were leaning in that direction.

"The police going after him?" Gavin asked.

"They don't have nearly enough on him yet. But, anyhow, they're focused on Lauren's supposed boyfriends."

"That's so messed up. Poor kid."

"It's fucking awful." Carrie looked around, anxious that in her agitation her voice had gotten ramped up and audible to anyone nearby.

Gavin was shaking his head, then put his hands out as if ready to catch a basketball falling from the sky. "Jesus, Carrie. There's a serious lesson in here."

She went on all-points alert.

"What the *hell* are you talking about, Gavin?"

Her young paramour was oblivious to the bright flashing lights and warning sirens. He leaned back a little. "It's about not overgeneralizing based on your own experience."

He might as well have been speaking Thai. Carrie was ready to choke him. "Will you just say what you fucking mean already?"

"You insisted on seeing Harbison as one of the characters from your Valley over there, ornery but ultimately manageable, maybe even lovable. I've been trying to tell you that he's bad news. Sounds like Kresge saw it too."

Carrie didn't know whether to scream, cry, or kick him in the nuts. She could feel hot tears coming but was determined not to go down that road in the middle of a busy Friday night in downtown Morriston (such as it was). She stared furiously at him, a string of words going through her mind, none of them exactly right, and feeling that if she said the wrong thing he would in some way win.

What came out was, "I'm so fucking done with this shit."

She then swung into motion, cutting fast around him as if he might try to tackle her, and steamed down the sidewalk in the direction of her car. She half expected him to run after her, she was ready to elbow him hard in the gut if he put a hand on her shoulder, but he stood still and watched her go, or so it seemed anyhow, she couldn't say for sure because she wouldn't allow herself to look back.

She peeled out, tires spinning, and headed straight in the direction of Middle Beaver. But she realized she wasn't ready to go home yet, and pulled onto a residential street still in Morriston and parked the car.

This was the story of her life; nothing was ever allowed to be good and just stay good. It was like building an elaborately cool castle at the beach and knowing that some bully had to come along soon to blast it into dust. If she was super excited about winning a footrace, one of her siblings had to say something about what lame kids she was running against that day. If she had a cute boyfriend, some "friend" of hers had to tell her that he'd been seen kissing another girl while she was at her convenience store job. If she got a good grade, someone had to say it was the easiest class in the school.

Gavin was too cool, too smart, too sexy. Of course he had to also be a stuck-up, insensitive dickhead, that's how things worked. He could go to hell and never come back.

Except first she needed him to go back up to Canton.

Lauren was in some kidnapper's custody, that had to be why she was never appearing and why Brandi couldn't get to her. And the key to her whereabouts had to be with those guys in Holsheen's group, or in the network of vine-like, strangling tentacles that Carrie pictured growing out from that group and—to hear Kelly tell it—extending across the continent.

Gavin had to go up there tonight, before the cops arrived en masse in the morning. He had to invent an emergency. Tomorrow would be too late.

She had a text from him. "I'm sorry. Can we talk?"

She wrote back, "Okay, but not 'til tomorrow. Tonight we gotta do business. Call you in a minute."

First she had to pull her head together.

~

When he answered her call, she went straight to what she wanted him to do. "Tonight's our last chance to pull information out of the ACR guys. First thing tomorrow they're gonna have a dozen cops up their butts, turns out police don't take well to being spied on."

"What do you want me to do about it tonight?"

"Percy needs to have an emergency. Call them up and tell them about some terrible new thing your 'wife' just did, suddenly it's way worse than you thought. See if they'll try to convince you to take your kids and run, maybe they'll take you to their secret hideout."

"I'm gonna end up dead, Carrie."

"Hey, at least you'll die doing something useful."

~

Wisneski's phone signal sounded an hour after dark. The text was from the station, telling her that the FBI was trying to reach her. It had to be news from Louisiana; that night the trap had been set and, with luck, had sprung. Hands trembling with excitement, she punched her thumbs at her phone, several times having to make backspaces and corrections from trying to go too fast.

Agent Zink, of the Ohio headquarters but currently just outside of Baton Rouge, picked up. "We didn't catch Lauren, I'm afraid," she said quickly, knowing that Wisneski would be on tenterhooks waiting to know. "We snagged different animals in the trap instead."

The FBI had set up operations in the undercover house after dark on Thursday night. At three o'clock Friday afternoon, using Sofia's Protonmail account, they forwarded the house's address to Lauren: 1172 Lumberton St. in Beaumont. Since she'd been instructed to get to the Baton Rouge area by that morning, she'd now have more than enough time to collect herself and get to the house a little after dark.

FBI sentinels were scattered on nearby streets all afternoon, posing as cable service installers, landscaping crews, house painters. None of them caught any sign of Lauren Harbison, nor did they see Tall Guy. Amongst the various pedestrians in the residential area they did observe one man who, though not especially tall, seemed like he might be attempting to conceal his face; he wore a sweater with a high collar on a day that wasn't chilly—this was September in Texas—and sunglasses. He disappeared from one agent's view before entering the next one's realm; it seemed he must have entered one of the houses.

About a half hour after full darkness, a woman appeared in the backyard of the Lumberton Street address. She didn't knock at the door, but instead stayed well back at the rear periphery of the property, hard to make out in the dark amid the tall trees and bushy shrubs. "Hello? Hello?" she called out, then again louder, approaching a volume that neighbors would be likely to notice.

The feds did not want neighbors to be drawn by curiosity about the noise in a way that could force the shutdown of the operation. So an agent inside the house appeared carefully at the back door, wary of being shot at—especially given the Athens event —and whispered loudly, "Shhh, shhhh. If anybody hears you, we'll have to run."

The woman responded in a similar long-distance whisper. "I'm scared to go over there, I can't trust you. Just send Brandi out to me. Brandi darling, can you hear me? Come on sweetie!"

The agent rasped out, "Okay, we understand. But we've got to be able to see you, Lauren, before we send Brandi out. Come out into the light just a little just so we can know it's you."

The woman moved forward two or three steps. She did look like Lauren. But the agent was not seeing her well enough to feel sure; he stalled, waiting to see if she'd move further from the darkness of the trees. Agents that were hidden behind her in the bushes could have grabbed her at this point, whether she was Lauren or not; but that would mean any accomplices—which could include the real Lauren if this woman wasn't her—would get warned by the tumult and make a run for it.

"I'm not coming any closer," the woman said, "unless you at least show me Brandi. Just have her wave at me, I need to see you really have her."

The agent took a deep breath, buying time. But suddenly pandemonium broke out anyhow, not where the woman was but in the even deeper darkness further behind the house, apparently on the other side of a broken-down fence that ran (or more like limped) across the back line of the property. In reaction to the racket, the mystery woman dove sideways into the bushes.

The agent heard a chaos of yells, grunts, fists, and scrambling, appearing to come from two directions as if through stereo speakers. Then, just as abruptly, everything on both channels went quiet. In another two seconds a male voice called out loudly, "We've got him!" Sounding almost like an echo, another man yelled back, "Got her too!" The agents involved in the takedowns froze where they were, while others swept the surrounding area to make sure no additional accomplices were hidden and dangerous.

Five minutes later the "all clear" call went out.

The two individuals in custody had to be the only ones involved; the surrounding area was crawling with agents who, even if they failed to catch an escapee, would have at least heard the person fleeing.

The female was unknown to them, and on close inspection turned out not to look that much like Lauren, though she'd tried.

"The male they recognized perfectly," Agent Zink said. "It was Kelly Harbison."

"Oh, shit," Wisneski replied. The man was omnipresent.

~

Percy was on the phone with Holsheen, explaining that he'd just found out that his wife was prostituting, that she was doing business right out of her house and sometimes even when the kids were home. He was freaked out in his snively, helpless way, especially about the three-year-old. The baby he figured would hardly even know what was going on.

Holsheen responded curtly, "Listen, I feel bad for you." His voice was a regular summer wind of warmth and compassion all right. "But my role is organizing the group. We're changing this screwed up, anti-father system. I can't help with guys' particular situations, that's not my place."

Percy pressed on, desperate. The group's leader finally and impatiently told him to call Mark Chambliss. Then he said he had to go.

Oh yeah, Holsheen cares so much about kids. Jesus.

~

Chambliss was friendlier than Holsheen, though in a politician-patting-you-on-the-back kind of style. When Percy laid out his story, Chambliss said, "Hey, I really feel for you kid." You could almost believe he did. "You got anything you can show in court? If so, they'll give you an emergency hearing on Monday."

"Oh dear, Monday? That's far. Uh, okay. I'm not sure I can convince the court, the only time I went in there they didn't seem to like me too much. I found out about the prostituting from my ex's own sister. But she's not going to stand up in court and say that, their parents would kill her. My kids' grandparents. Those people are a piece of work themselves, that's another story."

Percy hadn't planned this last part; he was discovering improvisational talents he didn't know he possessed.

"Get her to put something in writing, an affidavit. She'll do that much?"

"Uh, geez, maybe. Don't know. But what, I leave my kids there all weekend? Isn't there some emergency judge on the phone or something?" Percy knew the answer to his own question; women (or men) in physical danger could get emergency restraining orders, but beyond that judges weren't on call.

"Nope," Chambliss replied. "You can call CPS, but I can tell you, they don't suddenly pull kids out of the house on the weekend unless it's life or death. If I was you, I'd just go pick up your kids and hide out for the weekend. Then you go to court on Monday, good chance the judge will be understanding. You got your kids this weekend?"

"Yeah, I get them at eight o'clock tonight, soon. But I'm supposed to bring them back at five tomorrow afternoon, because of the baby."

"Just hang on to them, it'll be okay. It's not like it's kidnapping or anything if you're just a couple days late bringing the kids home from your parenting time. I think the judges up in Akron will be sympathetic if it's about prostitution. They'll want her to prove she's not doing that."

Chambliss was saying that if Percy accused his ex of something, the court would consider it her job to establish her innocence, not his job to prove her guilt. It was a departure from the group's mantra about judges never listening to fathers.

"I don't know," Percy whined, doing his milquetoast thing. "She'll just bring the cops right to my house and make me give the kids back."

"Well, of course, that's why you stay somewhere else. Take 'em to a hotel, kids get all excited for a night in a hotel, it's a big deal to them. I did that a few times with my kids, they loved it."

"Yeah, but, you know, I don't think that would work out so great with the baby, and if she's crying, my boy won't be able to sleep, he needs to be a little distance away from the noise, you know, sleep in a different part of the apartment or whatever. I think I should just forget it, I don't really have any place to go."

This was the crux. Percy crossed his fingers hard.

There was quiet for a while.

Then Chambliss said, with a breath, "Listen, there's a couple guys in our fathers group that have a camp out in the woods, a training camp."

"A sports training thing?" Percy asked.

Chambliss sputtered a little. "I just meant a camp, I didn't mean a training camp, I was thinking of my kid's football team. So maybe those guys would be willing to take you up to their spot. Listen, though, this place is their getaway, they won't even let you see the way there, you'll have to wear a blindfold. Think you can make up something with your kids where they think the blindfolds are a game?"

"Well, uh, yeah, I guess so." These guys certainly did take themselves seriously.

"All right. No promises, but I'll see if I can set something up. If it's a go, I'll tell you where you'll get picked up."

Percy needed to drag his feet, as he would. "Geez, I dunno. Isn't it going to get used against me if I do this?"

"I don't think so," Holsheen's deputy said. "I think it'll show how much you care about your kids."

~

Percy now faced the same challenge that Maria had been up against when it came time to flee: he lacked actual children. If only there were places to rent kids. He called Carrie to point out the problem.

Her mind was in sixth gear, she'd been upshifting for hours. "Okay, here's what you do," she said, sounding amphetamine-riddled. "You tell them you couldn't get the three-year-old, he's sick or something. You only have the baby. Tell them you put the baby to sleep with a little alcohol so it wouldn't scream. You bring a doll, it's pretty tightly wrapped up in all kinds of stuff, nights are starting to be a little cool now, it'll be dark. These aren't the kinds of guys who are gonna look that closely at your baby, are they?"

"Carrie, that's ridiculous. First of all, a real baby's a lot bigger than a doll. Second, as soon as they notice, it's over, plus they'll kick the shit out of me."

"Some people have those big porcelain dolls that look crazy real, I'll hunt you up one of those. Call you back soon."

And she was gone.

Gavin relaxed. In a few minutes Carrie would come to her senses and he wouldn't have to go through with this mission, at best humiliating and at worst suicidal.

~

Kelly Harbison was placed under arrest and rushed to the hospital. His internal organs were not nearly in shape yet for being tackled by FBI agents; he was in excruciating pain and his life was potentially back in danger. The agents preferred that he not die until they got the chance to find out what the hell he'd been doing there.

A half hour later Wisneski, who shared interests with the federal agents, was relieved to hear that hospital personnel had succeeded in stabilizing the patient. The next day was certain to be an interesting one.

The bizarre possibility now confronted the detective that Lauren and Kelly Harbison were in league together. Working toward what, she couldn't imagine.

~

Chambliss called at 9:45. "You got your kids?"

Percy's speech was stuttered. "Yeah, well, kinda. I got the kids from my ex at eight o'clock, like I was supposed to. She was drunk and there was a man parking in front of her house as I put the kids in the car. It makes me queasy. But I still don't think I should keep them tomorrow."

"Buck up, kid, it's gonna be okay."

"But I need to finish telling you. Part way home the three-year-old starts crying and saying that his Mommy slapped him for being sick, he was telling Mommy his belly hurt but Mommy told him to shut up and get ready to go. And then when I got the kids in my house, he threw up."

"Can the three-year-old stay over someone else's house?"

Percy had been ready with the same idea, but even better that it came from Chambliss. "Yeah, I got a friend who Brandon likes a lot, I guess I could take him over to her house. Hard to put him in the car again when he's so sick, but yeah, I could… But I don't want to get my friend in trouble."

Chambliss was losing patience. "How you gonna get her in trouble when she doesn't even know what's happening? Don't even tell her you're not coming back tomorrow, tell her you'll come by for the kid in the morning. Tell her it's just so he doesn't get the baby sick."

"I just stick her with my kid all weekend?"

"Jesus, fella. All right, here's what we do. Tomorrow morning you call her, tell her that now you're puking too, you've caught the stomach bug yourself. Buy us a few more hours. Then we'll drive you down there to pick up the three-year-old, or we'll think of something. It'll work out. Look, we know how to handle these situations, we weren't born yesterday."

"God, I don't know…"

Chambliss reached the end of his rope. "Grow a pair kid. You need to meet us by midnight." And he provided a set of GPS coordinates.

~

While Carrie looked for a big doll, Gavin went hunting for a voice for it, no longer entirely hoping to fail, though still mostly. A tiny seed of thrill at the chase had germinated.

He began by calling Sunni to see if she was still in touch with anyone from the theater crowd from high school. And, consistent with the fact that everyone adored her, she did have contacts for him to try.

The clock was racing ahead, however. Gavin needed to get on the road, every minute counted since he supposedly lived in Akron but in reality had to make the drive all the way from Pittsburgh to Canton. He blamed the delay on his friend, saying she wasn't available to take his three-year-old for another hour because she was away from her house.

Sunni succeeded before Gavin did. "I reached Willard Malcomb," she reported at 10:05, "that nerd who loved to do tech for all the shows, remember him? He's a totally cool guy now, you wouldn't recognize him, he got into hallucinogens or something. Anyhow, he did the sound for a play where a bunch of baby noises had to come out of a stroller, and he's still got this little box with three or four different little cries or coos in it. Each time you push the little button you get the next cry in the sequence. He says you can go pick it up from him. And guess what, he's got the baby to go with it, a big one he said, real-baby size instead of doll size, to make it visible from the audience. Perfect for the drama you're starring in tonight."

"Wait, so when it gets to the end of the four sounds or whatever, it starts over again at the beginning?"

"Yeah, so only push it four times, dimwit, spread them out. Or if the guys you're with are talking to each other they're not gonna notice the details, you can go up to five or six."

Sunni's excitement about Gavin's dangerous adventure was not making him feel loved. "You can't wait for me to go off and die, can you?" he whined.

"Hey," Sunni said, "grow a pair."

~

Gavin checked in with Carrie a few minutes past 10:30. He had found his way to Willard's home, clear across the other side of Pittsburgh but fortunately pretty much in the direction Percy needed to go. The museum-like interior of the house looked like the work of a curator with a split personality; three laptops, stacks of stereo equipment, tangled wires, and meters with flashing displays were in a hodgepodge with swollen mannequin heads, colorful costumes on racks, and fanciful wigs.

"Theater's still my thing," he said, looking only vaguely embarrassed as Gavin perused the array. "But I don't do sound and lights so much anymore, I prefer the creative side now, costumes and scenery, even hairdos."

The room did give a vibe of being influenced by psilocybin; Gavin hoped that Willard's technical abilities hadn't been compromised.

Willard was especially proud of the doll. "I did a little additional sewing on it while I was waiting for you." He showed Gavin the new stitching. "It now contains a GPS." He handed over a matchbox-sized black unit. "Give this unit to your girlfriend, and she'll always know where the doll is."

Gavin might never be seen again, but they'd be able to recover the doll.

"And if the unit in the doll is squeezed hard, the one your girlfriend has will make a warning sound. So if you need help, grab the doll hard around the waist."

Willard Malcomb was a regular Q. Gavin was no Bond, however.

He was now flying down the highway toward Ohio, running on undiluted adrenalin and a joint of Pineapple Trainwreck. Fueling him even more potently was his infatuation with Carrie and his awareness that a couple of hours earlier he'd blown it with her once again. It added up to a roiling inner turmoil that bordered on psychosis.

"I can't talk and drive right now," Gavin said breathlessly into his phone. "I have to haul ass. Meet me in Morriston so I can give you Willard's little black box."

~

Carrie and Gavin had agreed that, once he was fully equipped and on the road, she would call Kresge and get him to alert the police.

She woke Kresge up. He'd been accustomed for years to staying awake past midnight and sleeping much of the morning away, but during the investigation he'd undergone a major change in habits now that he usually had to get to the station by 8:00 in the morning.

The call caught him in the hallucinatory realm half way between waking and sleeping. "Jesus Christ, Green," he slurred. "What the hell?"

Carrie filled him in on their latest maneuvers.

The officer was not impressed. "You're out of your mind. You children need to let the grown-ups handle the bad guys." His words became distinct from each other; he had come alert. "This isn't a sandbox, Green. That boy is gonna get himself offed."

"Yeah, that's what he keeps griping. He'll be all right."

"You're a hard-ass, kid. You should become a cop."

"Over my dead body."

She tried to persuade him to call the station and request officers to follow Gavin and his gentleman friends. Staying well back and out of sight, of course.

Kresge laughed. "And how shall I convince them to do this? You want me to tell them these men are accessories to the abduction of a talking doll?"

Carrie's heart was racing. "Your people don't have to get involved! All they gotta do is see where the vehicle parks, then they can go home and live to fight another day. They can start checking the area out tomorrow in the daylight."

"Why would they go through that? Isn't your boy's GPS gonna record the whole route they take?"

"Yes, but we don't know that he's gonna get home with that thing, he might have to drop the doll and run at any moment. That's what he's planning to do anyhow, as soon as they park; he's gonna say he has to pee and then disappear into the woods. He obviously can't spend the night with them with a fake baby."

"So I should tell my department that, based on nothing but your intuition, you think Lauren is being held up in those woods somewhere? Plus it's out of our jurisdiction, we'd have to get the Highway Patrol on it."

"All right, then," she said, desperate, "you follow him. He could have to be rescued any moment. And even if it all works, he's going to need a ride back down here."

Kresge groaned impatiently "I'd have to take my own vehicle, I can't check out a cruiser when I'm not on duty. And that means no tracking equipment. So if I'm gonna follow him, you might as well do it instead."

"All right then, I'll go after them myself." She was bluffing; it was bound to pique Kresge's manhood to know he was letting a twenty-year-old girl head off into the dark against the Evil Hill Gang.

But the officer replied, "That's an excellent idea. That way when I wake up in the morning, I'll still have a job."

So much for his manhood.

~

The men did indeed take themselves very seriously. First, they wanted Percy to park his car at a specified location and then walk two blocks forward and one block to the right. At that corner, he was greeted by an unfamiliar man who said, "Hello, Percy," and demanded his telephone. Percy handed his burner over. The man then gave Percy directions for another few minutes of walking on his own. Half a block short of that destination, another strange man stepped out of an entryway to a building and blocked his path. "Right here, Percy," he said, and led him around the corner to a car. The man who had taken Percy's cell phone now reappeared; it turned out he was their driver for the night.

Evidently they fancied themselves a militia, or secret agents, or something. Their behavior could have appeared comical but to Percy it felt like stepping into someone's violent fantasy. His fear sharpened.

Chambliss was in the vehicle, seated in the back. One of the two men opened the opposite rear door and motioned to Percy to climb in next to Chambliss.

"Sorry about all that," Chambliss said, not sounding at all sorry, more like angry, as if Percy were the cause of it all. "Some of these custody-mad moms hire private detectives and they're up on all the latest technology."

Percy could barely hear what Chambliss was saying because of the ringing in his brain. He'd assumed all along, for no reason, that he'd be sitting alone in the back of a car or a van; it had never occurred to him that someone might be riding right next to him. How long could it possibly take before it became obvious to Chambliss that Percy did not have a baby wrapped up in the little blanket in his arms? His fear shot higher.

No director was present to warn him against overacting, a common pitfall among amateur actors and amateur con men. Percy used his hand tucked under the doll to make it seem like the baby was squirming, which would have been good if he'd left it at that. But he proceeded to nervously push the button that elicited sounds, receiving the questionable reward of a half-squeal, half-sigh that was too loud, more like what might erupt from the offspring of, say, a harbor seal.

"I gave her wine to knock her out," he said, "we won't have any problems."

His anxiety was misplaced; he was in a group of men whose relationships with their children revolved around the needs and feelings of the father, and true to form they didn't seem to register the baby's odd vocal power. (Or perhaps they were asking themselves, *How did this shrinking violet punk produce a baby with such powerful lungs? Why couldn't I do that? Is this wimp secretly really hung?*)

Thinking he needed to divert their attention, he said in an exaggeratedly shaky voice, "Maybe we should go back."

Chambliss leered at him. "Too late, kid," he said, "suck it up."

Percy reverted to feeling as though mafia hitmen were taking him out to a remote meadow, where he'd be garroted and then set in fresh concrete.

"Time for real darkness," the deputy added, and he pulled out a dark strip of wide cloth, leaned across, and brusquely blindfolded Percy.

It appeared that this act was carried out at a preset spot, because as soon as Chambliss's knot was complete the driver accelerated and took them through an extended series of nausea-inducing twists and turns. Percy lost all sense of direction, not that he'd had much compass sense before the stunt driving began. "I need to pee," Percy said, desperate to get out of the car before he puked, and forgetting that he needed to hold his urine for the last step in the plan once their final parking spot was established.

"We're almost there, boy," the large man in the passenger seat declared, the first words from the front of the car since they'd pulled out onto the street in Canton. "Hey," he added, "I love babies, give me a turn holding the baby. Here, pass her up."

The guy looked and sounded like a talking rattlesnake head. No father in his right mind would let this viper near an egg, much less a live baby.

Percy didn't have a live baby, he reminded himself, but there was no relief in this fact. "Uh, um, soon as we're out of the car you can hold her, okay?" His stuttering was genuine.

The passenger-seat guy started laughing. "I'm just kidding, kid, lighten up. You don't gotta pass me the baby."

Percy's heart rate slowed a few beats per second. He was sucking air but tried to make it quiet.

Chambliss read that something was up. "Wait, is there something wrong with the baby? Is she sick or autistic or something?"

"She's fine, she's just sedated," Percy protested. "But *I'm* sick. I'm gonna throw up." He panicked and started, irrationally, trying to open his door, even though the car was still moving right along.

Chambliss grabbed Percy's arm and yanked his hand off the door handle. "Cut that out kid!" he yelled. "You'll get us all killed! What's the matter with you??"

But in leaning into Percy to grab him away from the door, Chambliss had bumped hard against the bundle in Percy's arm, and it had not moved or reacted in any way, not a sound. Percy groped for the baby-talk button but couldn't make contact with it.

Chambliss yelled fiercely at the driver, "Stop the car right now! Pull over here! This guy is holding a fucking doll!!" He pulled hard on the little bundle while Percy squeezed it with all his might, succeeded in yanking it away and slamming it down on the floor of the back seat, and latched tightly on to Percy's left arm. Percy prayed that he'd squeezed the doll hard enough to activate the panic button.

The car screeched to the side of the road. Both men in front hopped out of their doors, ran to Percy's side of the car, yanked him out, and threw him to the ground. Chambliss came piling out right after Percy and instantly was kicking him hard in the side with his boot.

"You're about to fucking die, kid!!" he yelled, booming like a whole bank of concert loudspeakers. "Say goodbye to this world!! Goodbye to anyone who knew you, they'll never even find your body kid!"

All three men were beating and kicking him in the side and gut, in the shoulders, in the head. He was rolling around on the ground trying to move away from them, but each time he lifted himself up massive arms bashed him back down to earth. Gavin (Percy had ceased to exist) had never endured such bone-breaking pain in his life, as if his skull were being smashed with iron bars and his gut rammed with a telephone pole.

He could feel unconsciousness closing slowly in, and he longed for it. As the sound and lights faded the men continued to bellow at him, strange collections of words he could make no sense of, except for the part about his grave. Then there were explosions.

He drifted painlessly off into a dream. He imagined a girl next to him. Next to her was a blue ghost, his guide to the next world. It all seemed familiar; he'd heard about the soothing tepid breezes, angelic music, flashes of vivid memory, and a warm glowing amber light that come to accompany you when you die.

CHAPTER 27

Gavin's body looked as though it had been worked over with a rack of baseball bats and an assortment of saw blades. His skull had gushed blood, there were five different deep gashes in his cranial skin. His head was one huge bandage. There was a fracture in his skull and his head bones were deeply bruised; the next kick would have been the fatal one. His cheeks were swollen big as lemons, his eyes could see but he might as well have been peering between slats of a Venetian blind, the world existed only in small, selected horizontal slices.

Carrie sat on the side of the hospital bed, holding his bandaged hand. Talking to men who'd nearly been killed had become a recurring aspect of her life as a reporter; maybe she'd become a war correspondent one day.

Gavin's speech was slow and slurred as if he were on a couple of hefty Quaaludes, or was recounting a nightmare he'd just woken from. "I've never seen such scary men in my life. Even when they smile it looks like they can't wait to hurt you. They're like... supervillains."

He left extraordinarily long pauses; she wasn't always sure whether he intended to continue or was done for the day.

"I thought one guy, maybe two at the most, would be driving me. What did they need three guys for?... Chambliss ends up sitting right next to me in the back. How long could it take someone two feet from me to figure out I'm not holding a baby?"

Then came a pause so long that Carrie finally gave a gentle prod. "Remember anything else?"

He breathed deeply but with a skeletal rattle, like a lifetime three-pack-a-day smoker who was in the hospital to say his farewells. Those gorillas must have kicked the lining right off his lungs.

"You have any weed?" he asked.

"It would have to be edibles, Gavin. You can't smoke in a hospital."

"'Kay... Got any?"

"No. I'll see what I can do for later. But I don't think your mouth's gonna work for a while, your jaw's the size of a melon. I'd have to push mashed brownies into it like feeding a four-month-old."

"S'all right," he slurred. "With a li'l applesauce."

God how she loved him when his ego wasn't attached to a chariot.

"I gotta go back to sleep," he said, his voice even softer than before.

"That's fine. Sleep to your heart's content. But first you gotta finish telling me what happened."

He was quiet, teetering between wake and sleep. "Dunno much. I got scared, tried to open the door, said I needed to puke. Chambliss grabbed me, then started screaming about the doll. Then it all goes pretty dark. Lots of kicks or punches, I couldn't tell, ribs and head, it killed, like being hit by bricks. It's a dream world after that. Squealing brakes maybe, maybe gunfire. Then I thought I saw you near me, so I knew I was dying. The Grim Reaper was there too, in like a blue uniform... Does death wear a uniform?"

"There was a guy there helping me. His clothes were blue. Not a uniform though."

"Who was he?"

"We'll talk about that later, Gavin. No one you know. Get some sleep."

In seconds his breath had gone regular and loud.

~

The mysterious man who'd been with her at the scene was Shane Kresge; he'd been unable to get back to sleep and so finally consented to ride along. He was indeed wearing an old police uniform, though he wasn't supposed to be. Carrie would need to wave her wand and alter that portion of Gavin's memory.

~

Wisneski, Ledbetter, and Kresge met at the station, Chief Tobias joining on speakerphone. Sergeant Martinez could not extricate herself from preparations for her daughter's birthday party. Officer Mason was left out of the loop, as she would be for however long they found it useful to conceal the fact that they were onto her. Then she'd be suspended, investigated, and fired.

Wisneski had lost her ability to hide how sleep-deprived she felt. "Carrie Green, everybody's favorite muckraker, called 911 around one o'clock in the morning, reporting that a friend of hers had been badly beaten, looked at risk of dying, was lying by the side of the road. She was calling from a remote area outside of Baltic, not a place you're likely to have heard of, down toward Coshocton if that means anything to you. One of the parts of the state with the least cell phone coverage, but she was lucky and got enough signal to get through. Oak Valley Road it's called.

"So next, Highway Patrol troopers locate Green at Union Hospital in Dover where the ambulance has transported her friend, he's getting emergency care, alive by a thread. She says his name is Gavin Neal, a journalist from Pittsburgh she works with sometimes. She says he's been investigating Holsheen's Fathers Rights group in Canton—Arielle Mason's boys—pretending to join them. He finds out a few of them have a secret camp up in the hills and he's trying to get them to take him there; get this, he thinks they have Lauren Harbison imprisoned there.

"Green and a guy she knows are tracking him in her car but staying well back out of sight. So she gets a panic signal from Neal, she pumps the gas up to full speed to catch up to the car he's in. She comes in honking loud to scare them, the man she brought along hops out of the car yelling and pointing a gun at them. The three guys pile into their vehicle and screech off, Green can't pursue because she has to attend to Neal who's been beaten to a pulp, he's muttering, not saying anything sensible. Ambulance takes almost fifteen minutes to get there, she's petrified that her friend is going to die any second but the EMT's arrive in time to stabilize him and cart him off."

Kresge asked, "Who's this man she was with who scared off the bad guys?"

"Green won't tell. She says he has a history of legal problems and doesn't want it known he was involved in this confrontation. She brought him along as muscle."

"Any way we can make her tell us who he was?"

"No, how are we gonna do that?"

"That kid lies like a con artist. I'd give you odds there's some bigger reason why she's hiding his name."

"That is what you would think, Shane," Ledbetter said.

The fact that he'd recently been right about some key things evidently hadn't improved his standing. He chose to ignore her. "Any description of the vehicle?"

"Better than that. Her man-friend snapped a photo of the car as it sped away, so we may get a license plate, Green says the getaway car was lit up pretty good in her headlights as it peeled out. She's checking now to find out how the shot came out and get him to send it to her."

"Fast-thinking guy," Kresge said.

"Well, we'll see. For all we know he grabbed his phone and faced it the wrong way, we'll get a great close-up of him."

No, he'd faced it the right way. In fact the picture had come out surprisingly clear.

"Well," he said, "if her 'friend' pointed it backwards, at least we'll know his identity."

Twenty minutes later the state police were in contact; they'd gotten the photo from Ms. Green and had a make, model, and plate number for the vehicle. They were swinging into action and wanted Wisneski or Ledbetter, both if possible, to head to Baltic to work with them.

"Damn," said Kresge. "They didn't ask for me?"

~

Camille Storm-Petersen was dying to get home, the end of another interminable EMT shift. Today she had the additional burden of an aching back and burning shoulders; three times in the past twelve hours she'd ended up helping to carry or drag large and overweight men, who would have felt like boulders even without the unnecessary pounds, during rescues. She hoped she'd still have a spine left when she reached middle age.

A girl who looked even younger than Camille approached her as she was about to open the hospital door and head for freedom. "Hi," the girl said, sticking out a business-like hand. "I'm Carrie Green, I'm a reporter down in Morriston. Gavin Neal is a guy I work with. The desk told me I might catch you at the end of your shift."

"Oh, you were there at the scene last night, weren't you?" she asked in a strong working-class British accent.

"Yeah, I'm the person who found him and called 911. Long story."

"Well, I'm not supposed to discuss his condition, only doctors are allowed to say what might a' caused what."

"Yeah, sure, that's not what I... I just want to know if he said anything. I just talked to him, he hardly remembers what happened. Did he tell you any of it?"

"Oh, God no. He was in la-la land. Every few minutes we're supposed to ask certain things, his name, does he know what day it is, does he know who we are. He had no idea of anything, except that his name was Gavin. Mostly he seemed to not even hear the questions, though once he said he was from Pittsburgh."

"Was there anything else? Even just babbling? Nonsense words?"

Storm-Petersen thought hard. "The guy looked as if he'd been put through a wood chipper. It was upsetting even for me, and in my job that's saying something... I can remember him mumbling, but we couldn't catch any words really... Oh, one time he said his parents had tons of money, we didn't have to worry about getting paid for the rescue. We got a bit of a laugh out of that one, really... Oh yeah, another thing, he kept saying, 'The bitch, the bitch, the bitch.' Per'aps he thought some girl set him up for this to 'appen..."

"Yeah, could be," said Carrie. She felt like banging her head against the cinder block wall.

"Oh, I just remembered one more line from him, actually: 'Room enough for me and her.' He repeated that phrase two or three times."

"Huh? You sure you heard it right?"

"No, he was mumbling. For all I know he was saying, 'Moon enough to meander'—would've made as much sense. But for whatever it's worth, one of the other EMT's also heard it as 'room enough for me and her.'"

Carrie hoped he hadn't been talking about meeting her in heaven. Especially since it wasn't looking like she'd be allowed in.

~

Kelly Harbison was booked on fraud charges, as he had bilked Sofia Madsen out of some $3000 in total. Charges were soon added for interfering with a police investigation, conspiracy, and crossing state lines for these purposes. Law enforcement wanted a tight hold on him.

Police were not granted access to Kelly that morning, due to the possibility that his bullet wounds might still rupture from the takedown and cause internal bleeding. By mid-afternoon the time of greatest risk had passed, however, and the medical staff, understanding the urgency of the matter, allowed them in.

Harbison was, predictably, furious to hear about the fraud charge. "How can you charge me with fraud when Madsen was committing a crime? She was abetting a kidnapper!"

FBI Agent Xavier Rollins replied, "No, she wasn't."

"What do you mean she wasn't?"

"She *thought* she was. But since she wasn't truly communicating with Lauren or sending her money, she accidentally did nothing illegal."

Harbison rolled his eyes.

Rollins continued. "We recommend you start explaining what you've been up to."

"No thanks. I'm sure you can figure it out for yourself."

"You've been impersonating Lauren Harbison to Sofia Madsen since just four days after your ex-wife disappeared."

"I had a right to see if I could find out what Sofia knew about where Lauren was. Like if Sofia would write, 'Are you still in Phoenix?' or whatever."

"Your emails to Sofia didn't make a single effort to learn what she knew."

"That would have just given me away. Better to wait and see what she would drop."

"And two weeks later, when Sofia hasn't revealed anything, you're still not making any effort to get her to reveal secrets? You're getting money from her instead? We're not stupid, Mr. Harbison. Try telling us what you were really up to. Besides bilking Madsen for money, of course."

"Trying to find my daughter, since law enforcement obviously wasn't going to find her."

"Actually, you interfered with our ability to find her, which you're also going to be charged with, by impersonating her mother. And only four days after they disappeared, it was already 'obvious' that we weren't going to find them? Plus you were remarkably confident that Sofia wouldn't have already heard from Lauren, since if she had she would have known your emails were faked."

At this moment the interview was interrupted by an urgent call, informing the agents of new developments regarding the morning's other prisoner: the woman who had impersonated Lauren Harbison.

~

Her name was Mimi Lafayette, which sounded like an alias but turned out to be bona fide. She refused to say how she knew Kelly Harbison.

Had Kelly paid her to do this?

No, she just wanted to help him get his kid back safely.

If they knew the kidnappers were in that home, why not send law enforcement?

Kelly had explained to her that law enforcement had made lots of mistakes on this case and he was afraid they'd send in a SWAT team or something and his daughter would get killed in the crossfire.

Had she ever heard of professionals whose specialty is dealing with hostage-takers, nationally-famous negotiators like Chris Voss, for example? Did it ever occur to her that the FBI would use the top people in this role?

No, she didn't know anything about that. Kelly is a good man, she trusted what he was telling her, that if she could look like Lauren in the darkness the girl would be sent out to them.

Why was Kelly carrying a gun?

In case he was caught by surprise by any of the kidnappers and had to defend himself.

At this juncture the agents tightened the screws. They informed Ms. Lafayette that she was being charged with a litany of felonies including attempted kidnapping, impersonation, conspiracy to kidnap, interference with an investigation; and, due to the kicks and punches she'd thrown as they were arresting her, assaulting a federal agent. (In reality, the woman had put up no resistance at all; agents had grabbed her from behind in the darkness and she instantly cried out and collapsed.) She was looking at spending much of the remainder of her life in jail.

Lafayette caved easily, disappointing the agents who'd geared up for the battle. She spilled out that she was the new wife of a member of a Fathers Rights group in Houston. It was heartrending to hear the men's stories, how the mothers poisoned the kids' minds against their dads. Her husband's ex was doing that stuff to him. The kids were even refusing to come on visits with him, and he loved them so much.

"Get on with it, ma'am," the agent insisted.

Okay, so, a call had come to her husband through a network of national contacts starting in Ohio, asking for help getting a kidnapped girl back, this man needed a woman who could help him. An arrangement was made for Mimi and her husband to meet Kelly Harbison at a sandwich joint in Houston. Hearing his story melted them inside. When he then explained what he needed Mimi to do, it sounded like something she'd be proud to be part of.

Kelly paid them five-hundred dollars. He insisted there was nothing illegal about tricking kidnappers into giving up a child, he was only offering money because there was some risk involved if the kidnappers should turn violent.

And Mimi's husband reassured her that nothing like that would happen, what would be in it for the kidnappers to start something?

The agent thought her husband sounded like a helluva guy, gluing his eyes to that $500 and convincing himself that any bullets that flew would miss his new young wife.

~

Armed with this update on Ms. Lafayette's loosened tongue, the agents at the hospital threatened Kelly with a similar litany of criminal charges. He was unimpressed, however. "You idiots won't even be able to make the fraud charges stick, much less these other inventions."

The agents were surprised upon checking Harbison's record to see that not only had he never been in jail, he'd never even been charged with a crime. They were accustomed to encountering his level of smug entitlement among the heads of organized crime families and other hardened career criminals, not from some random Joe.

Rollins and his partner smiled derisively at Harbison. "I gather you have no idea how miserable the U.S. Attorney's Office can make your life when it chooses to."

Harbison returned his own disparaging laugh. "You guys didn't come up with Lauren or her henchman, so you want a scratching post to take your failure out on."

This statement pissed the agents off, partly due to its accuracy. Their irritation was not destined to work in Kelly's interests, however.

~

When Gavin rose back to consciousness, more than three hours later, Carrie managed to get in to see him again. He looked even worse than he had earlier, and was unable to come up with the faintest idea of what "room enough for me and her" might have meant. It sounded to him like a line from a pop song; maybe Tyler the Creator could interpret it. He said this with no smile, not yet physically capable of producing one.

As for his reported moans of "the bitch, the bitch, the bitch," Carrie opted not to mention those; it wasn't like she needed any assistance interpreting them.

~

The license plate on the getaway vehicle in Baltic was a dead end—it turned out to be for a tractor and long out of date, from a farm a hundred miles away.

State troopers visited Gavin's hospital room in the mid-afternoon. He could think and talk but was exhausted and heavily medicated. His memory of the assault remained little better than blank. His longer-term memory seemed more or less normal, though, and he gave troopers several names that he remembered from the ACR gatherings he'd attended. He also said that Mark Chambliss was by far the most influential group member after Holsheen.

The OSHP was able to rapidly track down Chambliss's address, and troopers were dispatched. They found Chambliss's kids home, two teenagers and a ten-year-old, all boys. The boys told troopers that their dad had custody of them and they only saw their mom once in a while. They went on to say that Chambliss had been gone when they woke up this morning and they weren't sure whether he had ever come home after he went out late the night before. "He said he had an emergency involving his fathers' group," the ten-year-old said.

The troopers asked the boys whether their mom knew that their father was MIA. The three looked uncomfortable. Again it was the youngest who spoke. "Our dad gets mad if we call our mom. And she'll make a big deal that he left us alone here, that's how she is, and he'd know we called. It's okay, we'll just wait until he gets back."

The teen boys were making faces at their little brother, indicating that he was saying too much. "What he said isn't even true," the middle boy protested, "We can call her whenever we want. Don't listen to him."

But when the trooper offered his phone, saying, "How about calling her now, then?" the teen squirmed and said, "Everything's fine, why would I call her?"

And when the trooper said that the state police would need to contact their mom right away to tell her that the father had not been at the house for several hours and might not have been there overnight, the oldest boy said, "You don't know my parents. My mom is going to get totally hysterical, and then our dad is gonna take it out on us. I'm fifteen, my brothers are fine with me here, just leave our mom out of it."

Troopers remained at the house until the mother could be contacted. By the time she was able to arrive to pick up the boys another hour had elapsed, and there was still no sign of Chambliss.

~

The area where Gavin had been found was sparsely populated for miles in every direction. Much of the expanse was state forest land, and other large tracts belonged to logging companies. There were several dozen private parcels scattered through these twenty square miles, some of them belonging to people who lived remotely and had not built on them yet; the population density was the lowest in the state. If you wanted to create and train a militia, or hide a hostage, this would be the place to do it.

As expected, troopers learned little of interest that day as they visited home after home in the hills. Almost everyone they spoke with reported having heard periods of gunfire over the years, their fingers indicating every possible direction the noise came from. One woman put it, "Eight-year-olds get turned loose in these hills to go out in their back woods and shoot. There's so much weapons fire out here it's surprising the animals haven't learned to shoot back."

They showed residents a photograph of Mark Chambliss they'd located from news stories about ACR, but the face meant nothing to anyone.

With one exception. A resident named Jerome Zeiger had shown a flicker of recognition before stating with exaggerated certainty that he'd never seen the man in the picture before. Troopers had wandered some on Zeiger's property, but observed nothing other than vast beautiful stands of beech, hickory, and oak.

~

Annika Ledbetter lay in bed, exhausted but awake, unable to quiet her mind. Her thoughts would move along one of the threads from the case, she would tell herself to stop it and go to sleep, and her thoughts would just switch to following a different one.

She found herself wandering back through the early phase of the investigation: the gradual forming of their theories and suspicions, Kelly's explosion when he heard about the Athens shooting, their efforts to get Sofia Madsen to talk, Annika's interview with Dr. Kinzer, the custody evaluator.

And then it hit her. She grabbed her phone. As soon as Wisneski answered, she blurted out to her, "Dr. Kinzer knew something about this!"

"Hello?" Wisneski responded, shaken from sleep and mystified. "Care to explain?"

"I didn't make anything of it at the time, I thought he was getting two different cases confused. He knew I was there about the Harbison case, but he didn't know that Lauren and Brandi were missing until I told him. He looked startled, which you'd expect, except what he said was, 'Oh, I thought you were going to ask about—' and then he suddenly clamped his mouth shut and said never mind."

"It could have been a million things," Wisneski cautioned, wary as usual of people lashing themselves to theories.

"It's too much of a coincidence, Janet. He was super cagey and strict about confidentiality at first, but as soon as he knew it was about a kidnapping, those rules pretty much disappeared."

"Maybe because a kidnapping is an emergency?"

"That's what I thought at the time. But I play it back in my head now, it's like he couldn't wait to say bad things about Lauren, yet none of it was in any way useful to catching her so why break confidentiality for that? And now I'm realizing how relieved he was that I wasn't asking about this other mystery issue."

"All right, we'll try to track him down tomorrow."

"One more thing. Since he obviously despised Lauren, he would have loved anything that cast suspicion on her boyfriends. So why does he choose to bury this?"

Neither detective could miss the implications.

CHAPTER 28

Janet Wisneski sat in the office of Dr. Robert Kinzer, occupying the same chair that had been Ledbetter's three weeks earlier. She had received quite an education over the past seventy-two hours regarding matters she'd known little about before, and now was eager to apply what she'd learned.

The detective engaged the psychologist in some humorous repartee, then proceeded to go into questions that Ledbetter had already covered with him. She was just there to review a few points from that discussion, looking for small details that might have been missed. They'd be finished in short order.

The stage-setting seemed to be working, the psychologist relaxed and comfortable. Wisneski asked him questions from a list she was holding (a blank piece of paper). She checked imaginary items off as she went as if following a mandatory protocol she was bored by.

Then, in the same rote-sounding way that she'd asked the previous five or six questions, she tossed out, "Were there ever any concerns that Brandi might be a victim of sexual abuse by an adult?"

"No, of course not," Kinzer said, his throat tightening audibly. "That would have required great care and detailed evaluation." The detective was gratified to see she'd succeeded in startling him.

"So Brandi never made any statements to you that pointed in such a direction?" Wisneski kept her eyes on her paper, as if just going through obligatory motions and not much interested in the answer.

"No," the evaluator responded, his voice turning mechanical, as if matching the tone of the detective's question, "certainly not."

Wisneski kept her eyes down and her tone neutral, but opened the bomb bay. "We're concerned because we now have reports that Brandi was trying to stick her fingers in her friends' vaginas, encouraging friends to do the same to her, and asking questions about their fathers' penises. She was shocking other children and losing friends over these behaviors."

The detective was exaggerating a bit. The Stolnik girl had been the only one to talk, though there'd been hints and rumbles from two other girls.

Kinzer sat cast in stone. His manner went from chatty to authoritative and from soft to superior. "Well, I gather you were told this by Lauren Harbison, which would fit her pathology well, as our evaluation and testing demonstrated. Or by people who heard it from her."

"No, children were our direct sources in this case, not their parents."

Kinzer grew taller in his chair, leaning back so as to get a better view down his nose at the ignorant public. If he had a beard he would have stroked it. "Lay people are unaware of the impact it has on a child when her mother becomes preoccupied with the belief that the girl is being sexually abused. The child, predictably, starts to wonder about the acts that her mother is repeatedly grilling her about, 'Did someone do this to you, did someone do that to you?' The child is upset by those images but also curious about them. Children desire mastery and control, and the most direct way to gain a sense of control over these allegations is to act them out. And that's where you might find a child trying to experiment with friends."

Wisneski's curiosity was piqued. "Well, then, is there ever a bona fide sexual abuse case?"

Kinzer seemed startled again. "Of course there is. Sexual abuse does occur, and is very serious… Perhaps I'm not understanding your question."

"Well, according to you, all behaviors by a child, all statements by a child, can be dismissed as having been planted by a parent's preoccupation So then, how would you ever conclude that a child—or a parent the child discloses to, for that matter—was telling the truth?"

"Oh, there are many ways. Sometimes there's physical evidence, found by a properly conducted medical exam. Sometimes the accused individual fits the profile of a pedophile: an isolated, lonely individual, not capable of successful adult relationships, often a victim of sexual abuse during his own childhood. Sometimes the perpetrator confesses. Sometimes you have parents who are appropriately measured in their responses, not hysterics about sexual issues. But the circumstances are important also; sexual abuse allegations that arise in the midst of a custody battle are known to have a very low rate of reliability."

"Could you tell me the names of the studies showing that these offenders are always social rejects? Or showing this low rate of reliability of sexual abuse reports during custody battles?"

"Of course."

She waited. "Well?"

"Oh, not off the top of my head. I'll get them to you."

"It's interesting, because the only large-scale study we've been able to locate indicates that, even during custody disputes, a majority of sexual abuse allegations are proven true when they're investigated by professionals who aren't working for either side."

"People can make a study say whatever they want it to say," said Dr. Kinzer from far above.

"True. Just as people can choose to ignore well-performed ones." She went on quickly, her strategy to keep feeding the flames. "You said that Lauren had this pattern of constantly grilling Brandi about possible acts of sexual abuse. How do you know she had this pattern?"

"I said nothing about such a pattern, this case is confidential. I was talking in generalities, about dynamics in these kinds of cases."

There it was again, that confidentiality wall that kept appearing and disappearing at convenient times.

"Would you agree that a caring parent whose child discloses being sexually abused would tend to get upset at that news?"

"Upset? Naturally."

"Yet you're saying that a parent who becomes, in your words, 'preoccupied' with the abuse, is a sign of a false allegation. It's not clear how you think a parent *should* respond."

"Calmly, objectively."

"Ah, like a trained clinician."

"Detective, I would be out of place if I told you how to be a police officer, would I not? So perhaps you should leave psychology to the psychologists."

Wisneski smiled broadly and derisively, hoping to irritate the evaluator further, driving him to make a mistake. "One more question. When Detective Ledbetter informed you that Lauren and Brandi were missing, you said"—and this time Wisneski genuinely quoted from the material in front of her—"'Oh, I thought you were here to ask about allegations of— Well, I can't actually tell you what allegations I thought you were here about.' Do you remember that part of the interview?"

Kinzer hesitated just long enough for Wisneski to detect it. Then he said, ever so smoothly, "I couldn't discuss that at the time and I can't discuss it now. But I assure you it was not sexual in nature."

"So you had heard neither from Brandi nor from Lauren that Brandi was being sexually touched by someone?"

"As I've told you several times, I am not at liberty to discuss specific statements. But Lauren Harbison is a person of low credibility, she made many statements that didn't hold up to examination. She exhibited symptoms consistent with a woman who would kidnap her child, and she saw her ex-husband as the devil incarnate, which anyone who interviewed and assessed him, as our team did, could see he was not."

Bingo; Lauren had indeed told him. And he'd chosen to bury it. If only they could get their hands on that impounded evaluation.

Wisneski got to her feet. "I wonder if your view will be influenced at all by the fact that Mr. Harbison is currently imprisoned in Texas facing charges for multiple felonies, and furthermore is expected to be charged in Louisiana for reckless endangerment of his daughter Brandi. None of these charges came from Lauren Harbison—obviously, since she's still missing—nor do they have anything to do with past statements by her."

Kinzer did not respond, finally stuck for a comeback. The detective wished him a good day and made her exit.

~

The interview with Dr. Kinzer would have taken a different direction three days earlier. Wisneski owed her familiarity with the underlying issues to Angel Cordero, the Morriston police officer who specialized in investigating sexual crimes against children. Cordero had given her a tutorial more than two hours long, profoundly generous with his weekend time as crusaders for children so often are. Cordero had prepared her for the raft of strategies employed by forensic psychologists to discredit children's disclosures of sexual abuse. He'd informed her, among a stream of other points, that medical findings in sexually abused children are rare—even in cases where the perpetrator confesses. Kinzer and his Children In the Law outfit had invented a set of criteria that no child could meet.

Wisneski perhaps lacked justification for being so condemning toward him, given where she had stood on the Harbison case only a few days earlier.

But Gabbi Stolnik's letter had caused a sea change in her outlook; she now had the fury and determination typical of recent converts.

~

Kelly Harbison's bail was set at $20,000. Prosecutors pressed for a higher figure, but the accused had no criminal record and was not accused of acts of violence (the possible charge in Louisiana still pending), and thus there was little basis to argue that he was dangerous or a flight risk. Neither did they have proof to offer that Kelly knew where Lauren Harbison was being held, the words, "but it's obvious to everyone, Your Honor," not constituting a legal argument.

He was able to pay the bond by mid-afternoon. His case was referred to both federal and state probation departments in Ohio, and he was told that he could fly home to Ohio as long as he reported to probation in that state the very next morning. He agreed. He appeared, to those familiar with his reputation, noticeably subdued. Perhaps the reality of federal charges was sinking in.

He was not yet medically cleared to fly, but the terms of his release said nothing about following the doctor's admonitions.

~

Kelly arrived back at his Irondale, Ohio house in the early evening. A crowd of journalists was out in front when he got there. He waved them away and refused to answer questions as he walked into his house, and neither answered his phone nor responded to knocks at the door over the next hour. Eventually the reporters present agreed that it was time to call Carrie Green and tell her Kelly was here; they weren't happy to hand the story to her yet again but anything she got they would get soon after, which would be better than having no story at all.

Kelly picked up when Carrie called. He sounded weak but it was hard to know what that meant, as cued as he always was into his audience's sympathy. Carrie expressed how glad she was to hear that he'd gotten through it all okay, a necessary pretense. But she moved into business without much delay. "How does it feel to know that Brandi has escaped the tall guy?" she asked.

Instead of answering her question, he growled, "You made those criminals who helped Lauren kidnap Brandy sound like a bunch of caring do-gooders. You finally showed your true colors, as I figured you would."

Carrie no longer felt drawn to do the sparring dance with him and was tempted to tell him to go to hell, but self-interest won out. "Everybody on both sides hates me, Kelly, but all I do is write whatever they say to me. I'm here again if there's a message you'd like to get out there." She felt some revulsion at her own words, but it was her job to get Kelly to talk.

"Well, here's what you can tell your adoring fans," he said bitterly. "If people want me to be happy that Brandi's escaped, sorry, but I can't do that when I have no idea what's happening to her. Chester must have other thugs working for him and Brandi's too scared to defy them. I know she'd be here with me unless she feared for her life."

"Why were you in such a hurry to come back to Ohio when Brandi is still down south as far as anyone knows?"

"I have to be home to take care of my health. I almost died trying to set her free."

Great lines for her article. Total bullshit, but still.

And, immediately following that thought, the real reason why Kelly had rushed home dawned on her. She needed to get right off the phone. "Thank you for taking the time to talk to me," she said, without sincerity. "Feel better."

~

Carrie's first thought was to try to position herself somewhere in Kelly's neighborhood. But she realized that when Kelly decided to head out of his house—and she was convinced that it was when, not if—he would be impossible to follow; he lived in an area of long unbroken residential streets and slow county roads where anyone tailing on a Sunday evening would stick out like a black tooth.

The only alternative was to hope she was guessing right, that he would go looking for Holsheen or Chambliss. And the latter he wasn't going to find any time soon. So she contacted Kresge, who in a matter of minutes was able to get her Holsheen's address.

~

Holsheen came out of his house at close to ten that night. He looked around, then got in his car and pulled out of his driveway.

Carrie had never attempted to follow someone. To add to the challenge, her quarry was conscious of the possibility of being watched. He drove three blocks, paused for an oddly long time at an intersection with no Stop sign, looking left and right and checking his rearview mirror, then made a left followed by a quick right.

She was on the phone with Kresge, a few blocks away in his private vehicle. He was able to pick up Holsheen's car by aiming for the main drag and guessing roughly where he would come out. He then proceeded to guess wrong about which way Holsheen would go next, and a sudden U-turn would have made him obvious, but he told Carrie where he was and she was able to pick the trail up again. Even on the thoroughfare there was little traffic, however, so she had to stay far enough back to keep from being spotted. Before long she had lost him again.

That could have ended their evening. But Kresge got lucky while driving around; he spotted Holsheen moving fast down the sidewalk on foot, evidently having left his car somewhere nearby. Kresge drove on past, turned a couple of corners, parked, and went racing back on foot. He didn't have to worry about Holsheen recognizing him as they'd never met; with some caution he might be able to get fairly close.

Except then he suddenly detected Kelly Harbison walking toward Holsheen from a half-block away. Harbison knew Kresge's face well. So the off-duty officer had to abruptly jaywalk across the street and continue off in the opposite direction as if hurrying somewhere.

As soon as he was out of sight he called Carrie and, speaking as softly as he could and still be heard, told her how to find the two men. She hurried in their direction carefully, on edge.

The challenge became still greater. The oddly matched investigative team had assumed that the men would talk in a bar or restaurant where it might be possible for one of them to slip unnoticed into nearby seats and overhear their conversation. Toward that end, Carrie had created a new alter ego, as distinct as Maria had been and even harder to recognize, her hair spiked up, black lipstick and black eyes, with a pair of gigantic plastic-rimmed glasses reminiscent of 1970s Elton John.

Kresge wasn't sold on her costume strategy; looking as different as possible was wise, but not by looking so teenage and ghoulish as to invite people to stare at her, which could lead them to notice the resemblance.

To Carrie's credit she adopted a matching personality, chewing a large wad of gum, walking clumsily, and waving her head around as if her neck muscles had never developed. Kresge found her annoying to look at and hoped everyone else would too.

But that all stopped mattering; it looked like the men were planning to hold their meeting outdoors. And the goth girl was in no position to be a subtle figure following them down the almost empty streets. So Kresge watched, but from well away. After another three-block walk, the men took seats on a bench in a small, sparse park where they could easily watch their periphery and be sure there were no eavesdroppers.

Desperate to hear the conversation that would ensue between Kelly and Holsheen, Carrie was forced to take her theatrics to a new level. She walked around the block, then came into view staggering at the opposite edge of the park from where the men sat. She wobbled in hopeless drunkenness (while carefully avoiding turning her face in their direction) and proceeded to collapse face-first onto a plot of grass as if she had lost consciousness. She heard distant humorless laughs, then the men appeared to ignore her.

~

Her acting experience was nil, but she was drawing upon real life; in her teens she had passed out in more or less this way on three different occasions, though never by design. One time the strange lawn she passed out on turned out to belong to Scoop's school teacher, with resulting acute embarrassment for Carrie, Scoop, and their parents. She'd been grounded until her parents couldn't stand to have her around the house anymore.

Prone now in her drunken stupor she was able to make out only occasional portions of what was said; though that was still better than she had any right to expect, given the guesswork and ineptitude she'd brought to the endeavor.

The scattered and short tidbits she could hear well came when the men raised their voices; but these also seemed likely to be among the most important exchanges.

Kelly: If I find him, I'll kill him.
Holsheen: Be my guest. But you won't find him.

Kelly: You got me into this situation, you'd better fix it.
Holsheen: You got yourself into it.

Fairly soon after the last bit:

Kelly: You seriously want me to believe you have no idea where she is??
Holsheen: Calm down, shithead, you're loud!

Kelly: The kid is totally brainwashed.
Holsheen: So you're free now to help her see reality again.
Kelly: Fuck you, Nat.

Holsheen:	Is there a fee attached?
Kelly:	Of course there is. And you know the answers to your own questions, I'm not stupid.
Holsheen:	I'm the one who found that address out for you, you bastard!

And, noticeably louder:

Kelly:	You know everything that goes on around here! You think I'm gonna buy it that suddenly you don't? Why don't you tell me what your people want and get it over with?
Holsheen:	If I'd known you were such an asshole I never would have been there for you. You don't want to believe me, go fuck yourself.

Kelly:	I'm not kidding, Holsheen, I'll fucking kill you!
Holsheen:	Don't make me laugh. The one who'll end up dead is you.

At this point Carrie knew she'd better make her move; the escalating rage was about to blow the men in separate directions and the whole point was to catch them together. She began to mutter slurred nonsense syllables, stood up shakily, fell back down, got up again, and walked, just barely managing to remain upright, obliquely across the grass expanse as if to cut across and leave the park. She bumped intentionally into the park's only other bench, then swore in the crassest way she knew how to do, giving her great pleasure.

Then, as if from nowhere, she took five fast steps toward the men and was suddenly facing them and snapping pictures with her phone.

Holsheen flew off the bench toward her and tackled her. But as he grabbed her phone away from her, Kresge rocketed out of the darkness, shouting, "Keep your fucking hands off of her!" and pointing a gun.

Holsheen let go and backed away, his eyes glued to the weapon, and was caught by surprise as Carrie launched herself at him and snatched her phone back. Holsheen was just deciding to take the risk of being shot in order to grab it again—he didn't believe the guy would go through with firing—when Harbison yelled, "That's a cop, Nat! East Liverpool cop!"

Holsheen had the sickening thought that he'd been caught in an undercover operation related to the kidnapping. In a sense this was true, though not in the way he assumed. He continued to back carefully away. When Kresge made no move to grab him, he turned slowly, forcing himself not to run, and left the park.

Carrie was well away by then, having sprinted across the street and, with something like a dive, disappeared into a row of shrubbery. It took her a while to take in that Holsheen was no longer after her.

Harbison remained frozen in place on the park bench, an expression glued to his face that would have been hard for Kresge to describe. His features were contorted in one of the more pained and stunned configurations the young officer had ever witnessed.

~

When, close to an hour later, Kelly drove back up his street, he saw that there were three police cars in front of his house and several officers standing outside. He quickly turned his car around, but just as quickly found his way cut off by an unmarked vehicle that had been parked half way down the block from his house.

"What the hell is this?" he barked.

The officer got out of his vehicle but stayed well away from Kelly's car window and watched him vigilantly. "We're waiting on a search warrant for your house, car, and person. While we wait, you cannot enter the home."

"Fuck you all. Okay, get out of my way, I'll go to a motel."

"I'm sorry sir, but you can't leave or go out of our sight. And you won't be able to use your phone unless an officer is standing right next to you and watching you do it."

"What the hell is all of this about?"

The officers refused to respond.

In another half hour, more police officers drove up the street, this time bearing a signed warrant. Kelly was searched and his phone confiscated, the contents of his car were riffled, removed, and bagged. Officers exited his house with his extensive collection of computer equipment, his old phones, and more.

After a brief period of furiously watching the search crew go in an out, Kelly asked if he could leave. He was told he was free to go, since they were done searching his person, but would not be able to take his car. They offered to call him a cab, which he would have been wise to accept since he lived an hour's walk from the nearest lodging, but he stormed off.

CHAPTER 29

Gavin slept heavily for two days. The doctor, caught by Carrie for a brief moment early Monday afternoon, explained that this was a good sign; when patients start to heal their sleep often becomes deeper and less disturbed. Given the severity of the young man's trauma, he would probably sleep most of the time for days to come.

The patient stirred a few times during the night on Monday but never came fully awake, not least because of soporific medications continuing to drip into him. But around 6:30 Tuesday morning he opened his eyes, and found he could make sense of the room around him for the first time since his arrival in the middle of the night three days earlier. He remembered nothing distinct about the days he'd spent in that bed, unaware for example that he'd spoken quite a bit on Saturday though not again since.

He perceived what at first seemed to be a messy pile of clothing on a chair, such as he would often wake to in his room at home. But as his eyes came into focus he made out that the items weren't familiar to him, though neither were they hospital attire. Then he realized there was a person *in* the garments: Carrie Green, asleep in the chair.

"Hi there, Carrie," he squeaked out.

She awoke and was instantly wide-eyed. "Morning, Gavin."

He was glad she was there. He supposed his parents must be around somewhere also.

"When did you get here? Did you just stop by for a place to nap?"

"I've been here all night. I would never leave your side."

"Yeah, except I woke up at least three times during the night and you weren't here. Something beeps or slams in this building every twenty minutes. Not counting the things that never stop beeping."

"Your mother went out to look for food for her and your dad, and she said I could sit in while she was gone."

"She chose a real stalwart to leave in charge during her absence."

"I was up all night chasing bad guys. And, by the way, there's no question anymore that Kelly's one of the bad guys. So if it'll help your recovery to rub my nose in it, you can get started right away."

She spun out the previous night's adventure for him in all its Indiana Jones glory. His response was that it was a miracle she and Kresge weren't both dead.

"I couldn't agree with you more," she replied cheerfully, as if he'd said something completely different, "it was one of the great reporting coups of all time."

Indeed, the drama at the *Morriston Chronicle* had reached a level the previous night not seen there since the end of the Second World War. The paper was still printed in-house; it had one of what were believed to be fewer than ten flexographic presses still operating in the country. They had literally halted the printing in mid-stream, leading to a heated middle-of-the-night debate about whether this had ever happened before or whether "stop the presses" had heretofore been strictly a figure of speech.

Because once the editors saw Carrie's candid park shots, there simply had to be a new front page.

Naturally, neither Holsheen nor Harbison chose to make himself available by phone during the night; but in this case their refusal to comment just made the article more sensational. Not that there was anything they could have said. How exactly were two men who professed not to know each other, and in fact to disapprove of each other's actions, going to explain their midnight meeting in the city darkness, working carefully (though not carefully enough) to keep from being heard or seen?

Carrie wondered why Holsheen had even consented to the rendezvous. Kelly must have concealed his real agenda.

Gavin asked blurrily why Kelly would think Holsheen had something to do with the kidnapping. Carrie squinted at him; his brain wasn't working that well yet. "Gavin, Denny Arbeitman is clearly Tall Guy, but he's not a traitor who switched to the mothers' side; if that had been true, Kelly would have been dying to tell the police his real name. I was stupid to ever buy his story about the supposed Chester. He made all that shit up to cover his own ass."

"To cover up what?"

"Geez, they really bashed the hell out of your poor head, didn't they?"

He groaned and was quiet. Then he said, "I've never felt one-tenth that much pain before in my life. I thought for sure I was dead. I don't get how a skull can withstand that."

"It can't. Your skull's fractured."

"Yeah? Well, I should think so... How come I'm alive?"

"Honestly? The doctors say it's because me and Kresge showed up. They told me the next kick would have been the last one." She winced, knowing she'd said too much. "Anyhow, you're okay now, and they're keeping a constant eye out to make sure your brain's not swelling... Though I told them they don't need to worry about it, it swells up all the time."

He managed to glare at her. "All right, so what were you saying?"

"There's only one possible explanation: Kelly's covering for him because he's the one who hired him."

"But Kelly went in that house in Louisiana trying to kill him."

"Maybe Denny wouldn't give Brandi back and started demanding ransom. It turns out Kelly's been trying to bilk Sofia Madsen for thousands of dollars, maybe he suddenly needed it to pay Denny; why else would he be doing that? Whatever was going on, Kelly didn't want police to catch Denny and have Denny spill the beans, so he tracks Denny down himself and tries to kill him. Only Kelly gets his guts shot out instead."

"Where's Lauren?"

"Dunno, but Brandi must be trying to get back to her."

"Accomplices of Denny's still got Lauren?"

"That's what I'm thinking. The guys who beat you up, for example."

"What do you think the original plan was, like, what was the kidnapper supposed to do with Lauren?"

"My guess? He was supposed to set it up for Lauren to get caught for kidnapping Brandi. Somehow Kelly got wind that Lauren was about to run— that's what Rhapsody said, and I think she's right—so he and Denny hatch a plan where Denny arrives at Lauren's house that night and poses as one of the people helping her run. After a day or two in hiding with them, Denny was supposed to drop a dime on Lauren and disappear himself. Lauren goes up for kidnapping, Kelly gets Brandi, no more child support to pay, in the public's eye he's the loving father there for his daughter whose mother abandoned her. But instead, Denny decides to hang on to Brandi so that he can demand a lot more money from Kelly than what they'd agreed to. And hanging onto Brandi means he has to hold onto Lauren too. With some help, no doubt."

Gavin was quiet for a long time, enough to make Carrie wonder if he'd fallen back to sleep. "If only I hadn't panicked and tried to get out of the car, we might know where to look… We've got to keep trying…" His voice started to drift away.

"I'm afraid it ain't 'we' anytime soon. You're going nowhere."

He gave a sort of laugh, sad-sounding.

"You better go back to sleep," she said. He seemed already half way there. "They'll kick me out in a minute anyhow. They said no talking about anything stressful, I've already fucked up completely."

He nodded with his eyes closed. Then he opened them a slit and said, "I care about you, Carrie. There's no one quite like you."

"I care about you, too." There was more to be said, but this wasn't the time to go into it.

"And for real, I'm not blaming you for what happened. I'm an idiot, trying to be a movie hero. You didn't make me do it."

Carrie, guilt still heavy upon her, said, "Well, you had a different outlook while they were rescuing you that night."

"Huh?"

"I talked to one of your EMT's, this British girl Camille. She told me that during the ambulance ride you kept saying, 'The bitch, the bitch, the bitch'… I get it, you had every right." She wished she could disappear.

Gavin's face wrinkled up, and his eyes came more open. "She sure that was me?"

"Well, they generally just save one person's life at a time, so, yeah, she's pretty sure."

"That doesn't sound like me."

"You weren't exactly yourself, Gavin."

This time he didn't laugh. He had come fully back awake. "What I mean is, that's just not my word. It's sexist and stupid. If I'd wanted to put the blame on you, I would have said more like, 'That fucking manipulator,' or 'That girl would kill to get ahead,' or something."

"Awesome," Carrie said darkly. "I feel so much better now."

Gavin ignored her. And, oddly, he started repeating the words "the bitch, the bitch, the bitch" to himself, like a mantra. And it appeared to work like one; he drifted off into a sort of trance, and almost a minute later was still chanting.

"That ain't Sanskrit," Carrie protested. "Stop it already."

But he kept on. At one point he hesitated, muttering, "It meant something… I was referring to… Damn, what was it?" Then he went back to chanting.

"Wait!" he suddenly blurted out. "What was that line you asked me about before? The other thing the EMT said I mumbled?"

"'Room enough for me and her.'"

"Yeah, yeah… 'Room enough for you and the bitch', that's what somebody said. What the hell did that guy mean?" He lay quietly for another extended period, occasionally breaking the silence with more recitations.

Then he sat up, eyes suddenly big. "They told me they were gonna kill me. It just came back to me." His voice had turned crisp, not the low rasp he'd been speaking in that morning. "And they meant it. I've never been so petrified in my life."

Carrie was watching the door, expecting the nurse to pop in any minute. If anybody got killed right now it would be Carrie, given a death sentence by a furious nurse defending her patient's life.

He was quiet again, eyes closed. She battled the temptation to ask him a question, to press him to continue. But her conscience won over in a rare victory. "Get some sleep, Gavin. I'll come back later today and we can—"

"Shhhh," he cut her off. Carrie waited, watching him intently.

At that moment the nurse did come through the door. Carrie put her finger across her lips to ask for quiet, as if Gavin had just fallen back to sleep. The older woman, clad in blue scrubs, nodded and moved slowly toward the monitors she needed to check.

Gavin started to speak again, eyes closed, as though mumbling in his sleep. "'You're gonna share that bitch's grave, there's room for both of you.' That's what they said right before I died."

The nurse looked up, a little startled. Then she smiled at Carrie with crinkling eyes, sharing in the humor of the patient's delirious dream. She punched a few more keys and scribbled more numbers on a clipboard, then noticed that Carrie was watching her boyfriend sleep rather than leaving. "Young love," she whispered with a grin. "Don't worry, he gonna be okay now. His numbers been good almost forty-eight hours."

"Who is that?" Gavin said, half opening his eyes but not moving his head.

The nurse took a step over, concerned that she'd woken him. Gavin glanced at her, then back at Carrie. "It sounds like they know where she's buried," he said softly, exhausted. "That's not good news."

"No, it isn't." Carrie couldn't even begin to take it in. "But maybe it means that Brandi can come out of hiding."

"Yeah," he replied. Then he was gone into sleep.

The nurse stood with her brow furled, her intent gaze moving back and forth between the two of them, pondering this peculiar conversation. The young man appeared to use a secret language to communicate with his girlfriend from the realm beyond consciousness.

~

Carrie walked out the main doors of Union Hospital and crossed to a small copse of trees that divided two sections of the parking lot. She leaned her back against the trunk of a pine tree and took long, deep breaths, looking around at the sunlight filtering down through the fronds of needles. She had never lain down that night, her only sleep the half hour she'd dozed in the plastic chair in Gavin's hospital room that morning, her head leaning against the wall.

The center of her body was consumed with the revelation that those guys had truly meant to kill Gavin, that in fact there hadn't been the slightest doubt in their minds that they would go through with it. Otherwise they would never have risked mentioning Lauren's grave to him.

And, even worse than Gavin's close call: Lauren Harbison was almost certainly dead. The mom had drifted ethereally in the background of Carrie's rise as a reporter, a goddess in her power and invisibility. Mysteries had been sprouting from the earth in every direction, Lauren the unseen force behind it all, generating seismic activity from the deepest levels.

Only she hadn't been.

And poor Brandi, who'd been fighting all this time to get back to Mom.

~

"Lauren Harbison is buried somewhere up in those hills," Carrie blurted out the instant Kresge picked up his phone. "Your people were looking for the wrong thing. You don't need a helicopter, you need fucking cadaver dogs." She told him what Gavin had remembered.

Kresge was quiet, then reminded her grimly that they needed to stick to pretending that the two of them barely knew each other. "You have to call down to the station and report this. As far as anyone in my department is concerned, I've been sitting at home drinking beer and watching television since the end of my shift on Sunday because I had the last two days off and there's nothing else going on in my life."

Carrie said, "Jesus Christ, Shane!" It was the first time she'd ever called him by that name. But he was right, the report had to come from her.

~

Wisneski was on her living room couch, having feasted on a breakfast of eggs and french toast that her husband had made for her and the kids, letting her aching body and mind recover from the recent spate of twelve and fourteen-hour days. Soon the kids would be off to school, and then she was taking at least half of the day off from work to rest and spend time with her beloved life partner, who had called in sick to his job for the occasion.

So when she heard her "urgent department call" ringtone she felt like bursting into tears, and certainly would have had her children not been in the room. "This can't be," she wailed at Ian as she reached for the phone. "Tell me this call isn't happening."

The news turned out to be even worse than she thought, both for the victims of the loss and for what it meant about the detective's time with her husband.

~

Towards the end of the afternoon on Monday, nearly three days after the attempt to kill Gavin Neal, investigators for the state police had found a connection between the Alliance for Child Rights and Jerome Zeiger. A divorcing father named Chip, who was an occasional ACR participant, had mentioned to troopers that a few men from the group sometimes went out hiking in remote woods that belonged to an acquaintance of one of the members. He didn't know who had joined these hikes, he never had, but he remembered the name of the property owner who'd given them permission to be in his woods. It was Zeiger.

Tuesday afternoon, thanks to a call to police from journalist Carrie Green, a large crew arrived at Zeiger's house with dogs. His property was at least a half mile wide and almost a full mile deep, hickory, ash, beech, and oak in large expanses, and a smaller number of areas dominated by pine.

The crew dispersed with two-way radios, looking for signs of disturbed land. Any time searchers found indications of footsteps or trampled vegetation one of the dogs was led by its civilian handler to that area. The work was painstaking and slow.

Dusk was gathering, and the site commander was close to suspending operations for the night, when one of the dogs alerted energetically, the first strong reaction the crew had gotten from the three canines that day. The shepherd was in an area free of signs of human traffic, an odd place for her to smell something.

Crime scene investigators had to take pictures and gather samples before digging could begin. An hour later, with the area flooded by battery-powered bulbs on metal stands, the crew steeled themselves for the arduous work of uprooting a thick collection of mountain laurel, barberry, and sumac bushes, likely facing hours of fighting through dense roots before being able to even begin digging. And it all seemed pointless; nothing could have been recently buried here.

But, bizarrely, the little grove turned out to have the quality of stage scenery. Bushes they prepared to do battle with popped out into their hands with a minimal tug. Thick tufts of grass turned out to be rolls of sod, laid out in rows as if on an athletic field. Saplings as tall as three or four feet, a half-dozen of them, had been transplanted into the ground and relinquished their positions without a fight. The landscapers, so to speak, had performed a thorough and aesthetic job of set creation; the search party was looking for areas pounded with footprints and scatted with broken branches, not these dense bushes, thick grass, and thriving small trees. If not for the dog they would have paid no attention to this spot.

Once the copse was cleared of transplants, the excavation began. The shepherd couldn't wait to see what the crew would find; she could tell it would be one of her proudest discoveries, the kind she'd wish to could carry home in her muzzle and present to her owner.

The item would turn out to be too large for that.

The body was buried horizontally, with no box, at a depth of over seven feet. To dig a hole that size must have taken three or four strong men many hours, perhaps a full day, especially with the constant removing of rocks.

Redigging it, however, was fast work in the well-softened earth. Adding Gavin Neal to the hole would have taken his assailants only minor effort.

The wild burial site had been crafted to ensure that the body would never be found. Only a series of the most unlikely events had thwarted the plan.

CHAPTER 30

Sofia Madsen got her kids onto their school buses, dragged her tired rear end into the auto shop, greeted Jeremy with genuine happiness to see him after another strange and stressful weekend, and began her five-day-a-week protocol for opening the office: switching on the desk computer, tidying the waiting area coffee table strewn with magazines and newspapers, and walking into the corner to switch on the television. Sofia hated having the TV on all day, she would have almost preferred a mosquito buzzing in her ear, but customers expected the screen to stare at while they waited.

The sound and picture came on, the TV as always set to go first to the morning news. The anchors were chatting and cracking weak jokes, the female anchor was dressed in a shade of overwhelming pastel orange-pink, the news was about a lawsuit regarding the hotel development plan for downtown Morriston. In short, all was normal.

A game show always began at nine. But at two minutes past the hour, the news crew was suddenly back on the screen: Lauren Harbison, believed to have abducted her daughter Brandi a month earlier, had been found dead in Baltic, Ohio in the middle of the night. The newspeople reported that she'd been buried in a forest there "for not less than two weeks," and the Medical Examiner was speculating that it was closer to three or four, her full exam not yet complete.

Sofia gasped and ran out of the shop like a bullet to her car, made sure the windows were closed, and burst into loud sobs.

Jeremy hurried in from the shop floor to see what had happened. As soon as he took in what the newscasters were talking about, he had his answer. He grimly reached for the phone to try to reach his fill-in front desk help, knowing it would likely be days before Sofia returned.

~

In the early afternoon, with her children still due to be at school for more than an hour, Sofia received a call from an unfamiliar number. She chose to answer but braced herself to hang up instantly if it was media.

"Ms. Madsen?" said the male voice.

"This is Sofia," she said, her finger poised to hit the red phone icon. A telemarketer trying to sell a cable service plan might enrage her even more than a call from a TV station. She was ready to kill.

The man's voice was kind, though, and polite and sad. "I'm sorry, ma'am, I can't tell you my name, but I have a message for you from Brandi Harbison. She wants to know if she can come to stay with you. To live, she means. And if that's not possible for you, could she stay a week or two until she can make other arrangements."

All Sofia could muster at first was, "Oh, my God."

"Yes, we understand that it's a big decision. We don't need to know right away; Brandi can stay where she is currently."

"No, no, of course!"

"I'm sorry, ma'am?"

Sofia tried to think in a straight line. "I mean, of course Brandi can stay here. Live here, I mean, absolutely, I don't have to think about that, are you kidding? Oh, Lord, Brandi... We'll get her the moment she's ready to come, just tell me where to pick her up. Please send her my love. I— can't even imagine what this is like for her."

"Well, she's kind of strangely okay so far. I don't think it's real to her yet... I'm not sure exactly how soon Brandi will be ready to go to your place, she's still afraid to come out of hiding, her father wasn't kept in custody long. But she wants badly to be with you, she says you're like her aunt and your kids are like cousins. So we're trying to figure out safety for her... We'll be in touch very soon."

And he was gone.

~

The investigative team's somber morning meeting started slowly. Their villain had turned out to be the victim. They were sad for both mother and daughter, and frustrated that it was too late for Lauren to tell them what had happened.

Conversation moved haltingly, with long pauses and stares toward the floor. They were all hardened individuals but feeling this one, not least because their mission had been to save Brandi, and though she was still alive her childhood was gone.

They reviewed what they had on Kelly. It was so much, yet not enough.

One lab finding grabbed their attention: swabs of surfaces at his house had revealed traces of flunitrazepam, the date-rape drug that police believed had been used to secure Brandi's compliance with her mother's decision to flee a month earlier. This was the first physical evidence potentially tying him to the kidnapping.

"But what's the connection?" Martinez wondered. "He supplied it to his hired gun? Who somehow forced Brandi to take it?"

A different possibility occurred to Ledbetter. "Maybe he planted the drug at Lauren's after they'd already been kidnapped—he didn't want anyone to think that Brandi might have been willing, even eager, to run away." If only they could find some evidence to prove he'd been in that home.

The search of Kelly's had not revealed the surveillance equipment they'd hoped to find. Harbison's computer was still being analyzed. Lauren's laptop, which had been seized only a few days after she disappeared, now had to be reanalyzed through a different lens: to find whether spyware had been installed on it. However, the whole point of spyware is how well it hides itself, and they'd been warned that even if the tech crew never found it, that wouldn't guarantee that it wasn't there.

Martinez vented. "Harbison said Lauren fled that house in Louisiana, that she ran out the door with Brandi during the shootout. Another way he tried to make people believe she was alive, like with the emails to Madsen."

The chief said, "But he's got an explanation for everything. Now he'll say that there was a woman with them and he assumed it was Lauren, it's not like he gets to look her over carefully while being fired upon. Everyone knows he's lying, but how we'll prove it is another question."

Carrie Green's article from the previous Friday—containing the claim that Lauren and Brandi had been kidnapped together just hours before the mother and daughter had been scheduled to flee—was looking less and less far-fetched.

~

The three fugitives from the Baltic beating turned themselves in one at a time over the course of the morning. Police had their names, home addresses, and workplaces, so remaining on the lam would have meant never coming home again and never again seeing their children who, they insisted, were the most important thing in their lives. Better to come home having spent three days coordinating their versions of the events and try their luck in the legal system, three respected community members against one preppy punk.

The story the men came up with was that Gavin had begun screaming and threatening to kill them in the car, paranoid ravings accusing them of being part of a bloodthirsty Charles Manson-style cult. He started pounding on the driver and almost caused them to crash into a tree. The reason he'd ended up so badly injured was that he fought like a saber-toothed tiger as they tried to remove him from the vehicle, including thrashing around so much that he kept banging his own head against the roof of the car.

There were a number of ways in which this account did not fit the facts well. But the men would be three clear-headed witnesses against Gavin, who could remember almost nothing regarding the assault.

Mark Chambliss and Dexter Luna made a miscalculation in their decision to turn themselves in, however; they overestimated the strength of character of the man they'd chosen to put behind the wheel that fateful night. By early Wednesday evening, police and prosecutors had already succeeded in getting Van Quisenberry to crack.

The interrogators started by presenting Quisenberry a document that purported to be the Medical Examiner's report, in reality not yet completed, regarding Gavin's injuries. The supposed evaluation was written by a fictitious male doctor; they assumed, correctly, that Quisenberry would have no idea who the local ME was nor that she was a woman.

The document explained that Mr. Neal's injuries could not have been the product of mutual combat. The most definitive "evidence" to support this conclusion was that he had multiple injuries that had been inflicted after he was already unconscious. (This was a particularly inventive part of the report; it isn't possible to prove whether wounds follow a loss of consciousness, though there are ways to identify ones that occur after death.) The interrogator also told Quisenberry that he'd be subject to a minimum of ten years in jail on one charge alone, Multiple Assailants to an Aggravated Assault, a charge unlikely to stick given that no such law existed.

Quisenberry would have done well to get legal representation, as he'd been constantly warned to do if ever arrested; a lawyer would surely have noticed the

ME's surprising change of gender and name, among other curious aspects of the report.

Instead, Quisenberry, so full of bluster and bravado a few days earlier, caved in like a house of cards. Around 7:30 that night he cut a deal to face not more than three years of actual time served, which sounded like a beach vacation after the threats he'd been berated with. Half an hour later he was singing like a nightingale the full details of everything he knew.

His account was that, a little over two years earlier, Kelly Harbison had attended three or four ACR meetings in Canton. He had fit right in; in fact, Kelly and Holsheen had stayed after meetings talking, just the two of them, each time he had come. But about six months ago he abruptly stopped appearing at meetings and never came back. Holsheen reported to the group that he and Kelly had "run into a personality conflict." A couple of group members wanted to know what issues were at stake, but Holsheen had waved his hand at them dismissively. "He's not worth our time and energy," was all they could get out of him.

Van had originally been introduced to ACR by his acquaintances Mark Chambliss and Dexter Luna, who knew he was getting screwed in his divorce. The three of them became good friends, bonding not only regarding fathers' rights issues but also about being sick of immigrants coming to the area and taking everybody's jobs.

The friends used to throw around the notion—outside of ACR meetings—of getting a training camp going in the hills, maybe starting a militia. Another ACR guy, Denny, was occasionally part of these discussions, but he pulled away from them six months or so ago, saying bitterly, "You guys are all talk, it's taken you years just to build that one stupid little 'camouflaged' cabin. You'll be sitting on your asses when the cops come to take your weapons away." A while after that he vanished from ACR meetings altogether. He used to say he was planning to move to Montana and join the war against the government, so they figured he'd finally done it. His big dream was to kill cops.

Holsheen refused to take any part in the camp idea. "Don't bring that shit into our meetings, you'll scare off good group members," he said. He also said he was "sticking to one war at a time," which to him meant the war between fathers and mothers.

Did Van know anything about Lauren Harbison?

Of course, he said, she ran off with Kelly's kid. That's what mothers are like now; they just want the guy's money, they pop down to court and get a divorce easy as buying a newspaper, and they get the kids too.

Did Kelly and Denny know each other?

They probably attended some of the same meetings, he wasn't sure.

Did Kelly ever say anything about wishing his wife would disappear?

Are you kidding? That's the last thing he wanted—unless she could disappear and leave the girl behind, of course. (A little sour-sounding chuckle.) He would have loved that.

Would Van be surprised if Lauren turned up dead?

Not really. She hung out with a lot of bad people, she dated drug addicts and stuff. But he didn't think Kelly would get that lucky. (Another acerbic laugh.)

Actually, they told him, she is dead. Her body has been recovered.

At this point the interrogators watched Quisenberry's reaction carefully. They could find nothing but genuine-seeming surprise in his expression.

Did he know if Chambliss had anything to do with her death?

Yes, he knew for sure he didn't. Chambliss had been with Van steadily since the fight on Friday night, hiding way out near Indiana. He was never out of Van's sight more than, like, half an hour, except when they slept at night. Unless she died out that way? In the middle of the night? (A sick little smile.)

They informed him that Lauren had died between two and four weeks ago. Her body was found by dogs yesterday, buried in a remote part of Jerome Zeiger's property.

Quisenberry's grin vanished like a ghost, replaced by a visible desire to vomit. He wanted to shoot himself for all the unnecessary information he'd just shared, completely irrelevant to meeting the terms of his plea deal. He'd gone blabbing on and on, enjoying the drama of his story and figuring that, as long as he was going to jail for a couple of years, where he would be known as a snitch, why not enjoy the spotlight here while he could?

But now he was going to be known as a snitch to a murder charge. He refused to say another word.

Interrogators took a last try. "Your plea deal doesn't cover the murder of Lauren Harbison, Van. If you know anything about it, you'd better start cooperating so you don't end up in the chair."

But Quisenberry remained far out of reach, as if the injections had already been given.

CHAPTER 31

Gavin wanted to talk about "us." Carrie stalled him off as long as she could, not wanting to go down that path with Gavin still supine on his hospital bed, his skin remaining mostly purple, his body still a mass of lumps, swelled joints, gashes, and missing hair. She feared, in her current state of guilt, being unable to bring herself to say what she needed to.

"I want to be with you," he said, his voice still weak and raspy though he'd gained a little strength over the previous two days. "I want to get along...I don't understand what happens."

Carrie breathed slowly, struggling for words. "I don't know what to tell you, Gavin. Everything's good, and then you suddenly change. You, like, think you're my father or something, except he wasn't like that, so you're a different father."

"I don't change, though, I just say something and you fly off the handle."

Maybe this wasn't such a bad place for this conversation. She wasn't feeling as pissed as she usually got, seeing him in this ocean of white objects, this white world in which he lay helpless; it kept him feeling manageable, she was the parent now and he was the child.

"You don't just say something, Gavin. You start lecturing me, last time you were scolding me like my worst teachers from elementary school. You get totally superior."

He looked a little confused, a potential step in the right direction for a guy who was always too sure of himself. "What do you want me to do, though? You want me to pretend I think you're right when I don't? You say you don't like having people kiss up to you but it seems like, when it's me, you do."

Okay, now her temperature was rising. But she wasn't about to storm out of his hospital room where he lay in pieces. She had to keep thinking, rather than exploding at him as she'd always done before.

And, as she held herself together, something snapped into place; two jigsaw puzzle pieces slid past each other and sat, comfortable and flat, on the tabletop.

For a few moments Carrie was consumed with digesting her own realization. Then she spoke with more weight than normal, as if being interviewed on television (an experience she'd become oddly accustomed to in recent weeks, and in fact had been busy with again the night before). "You think being right is a magic shield that protects you from being a dick. What you don't get is that I stop giving a shit whether you're right or wrong; it stops *mattering* whether you're right or wrong. You can be totally right and a total dick at the same time. But you seem to think those two things can't go together."

"Mutually exclusive," he muttered, mostly to himself.

"Huh?"

"Never mind." Then he was quiet for a while.

"Plus," she finally added, "you conveniently forget the times—and they do happen—when you're so sure you're right and it turns out you're not. Like, you're the one who got me believing all that divorce bullshit. But that's almost beside the point. What matters is you think you're better than I am, you think you're better than my whole neighborhood, like if it was you against everybody in Mormon Valley you'd beat us all."

"I thought you hated Mormon Valley."

"Yeah, well, you hate where you grew up too, remember? I'd rather be from Mormon Valley than Edgeworth Falls. At least I grew up around real people instead of, like, people with magazine covers pasted on for faces."

Gavin said nothing for a long time. Carrie was squirming a little in her seat; she'd gotten more worked up than she meant to, now the awkwardness was making her queasy, like she'd said too much. At the same time, she felt like she'd been wanting to say these things for weeks but hadn't known it.

The boy's eyes were still closed. It had been a while now. Carrie was preparing to say that she should probably head out and let him sleep when he opened his eyes, looked intently at her, and struggled to prop himself up a little.

"I've got to think," he said. For a moment she thought he was telling her to leave, which was going to piss her off even though it was what she wanted to do. But he went on. "You're right, Edgeworth Falls sucks. I don't want to be anything like those people... And I know you're just as smart as I am."

"Smarter." Then she added, "Seriously, you think you know so much more about life than I do, and it's the other way around."

He nodded, though slowly and reluctantly.

Near-death experiences are known to lead to some reevaluation even among the most stubborn of people.

As Carrie walked to her car, it occurred to her that it wasn't even true that she hated Mormon Valley, though she would love to move away for, say, a hundred years. The place was mad complicated, way beyond what a guy like Gavin Neal could possibly understand, born with a silver spoon in his mouth and a bankroll in his diaper.

~

Kelly Harbison, who'd been so embarrassed to have his tears described in the newspaper a few weeks earlier, wept like raindrops running down glass as he talked before television cameras late that morning, appearing for the first time since the discovery of Lauren Harbison's body. "I can't believe the senselessness of this act," he said. "If the kidnapper had wanted ransom to release my daughter and her mother, I would have found a way to come up with any amount he demanded. But no ransom demand ever came. Lauren obviously got involved with some bad elements while kidnapping Brandi, hardly a surprise if you're going to do that kind of thing. Now I'm just praying that nothing has happened to my daughter and that she's back soon."

He declined to answer any questions, saying he was too grief-stricken about Brandi having lost her mother. "And although Lauren and I were divorced, I've always respected her as a person. This is a loss to me personally, not just to my daughter." Then he stepped away from the cameras.

Carrie, watching at the *Chronicle*, was unmoved. Needless to say she was also no longer on the inside track for those headline-making quotations of his. In fact, Kelly had appeared on the Canton TV-5 news the day before, standing in front of his home and telling the reporter, "It's criminally irresponsible that the *Morriston Chronicle* made a teenager their reporter on this story. They never took the danger to my daughter seriously. I complained for weeks about this outrageous choice of reporter and they ignored me. That's how we end up with a stunt like the Green kid just pulled, stalking me as I attempt to find out what's happened to my ten-year-old."

Kelly Harbison could rewrite history as well as an invading army.

~

As soon as darkness fell that night Kelly slipped out of town stealthily, though not enough so. He left carrying only a small bag, exited out the back door of his house, went between other dwellings, followed along rows of trees and shrubs, crossed several streets and passed between more houses, and eventually found a cab almost a mile away which took him west to a motel. Around four in the morning, he left the motel and entered the first of a series of cabs that, over the next four hours, took him south on a circuitous route that eventually delivered him to the Cincinnati airport; he knew that Pittsburgh terminal personnel would have been told to keep an eye out for him. From Cincinnati he embarked for Oklahoma City.

All of these moves were tracked by FBI agents.

Additional agents were positioned to observe his arrival, curious to see where he would head next. He seemed focused, purposeful, almost calm, not at all like a fugitive scrambling for an obscure hiding place. They could have arrested him at any time in violation of both state and federal pre-trial probation, but they preferred to see what deeper holes he could dig for himself, and especially what ring of accomplices he might lead them to.

CHAPTER 32

FBI agents in Oklahoma City watched Kelly Harbison enter an indoor mini-mall, just eight or ten stores but throngs of customers. Two agents followed him in but lost him quickly in the crowds. This was no cause for concern; other agents had the front and back exits from the mall covered, under the assumption that losing him inside could happen easily.

About twenty minutes later, Kelly's distinctive overcoat, narrow-brimmed hat, beat-up khakis, and scuffed lightweight work boots appeared at the back door. Agents followed the man down two blocks of residential streets. He glanced frequently left and right, then abruptly dashed back out to the commercial route.

They were at no risk of being shaken off his trail despite the maneuvers. They watched him enter a café, make an order, and sit at a table with a coffee and Danish. One of the agents, a cute young woman not yet twenty-five years of age, the antithesis of the public image of FBI, walked right in front of the picture window and peered into the café, squinting as if attempting to read the menu on the wall behind the counter. She soon wandered away again, walked into a space between two buildings, and pulled out her radio. "That's not Kelly Harbison," she declared grimly.

In seconds, four agents surrounded the man in the café. They led him out to the street and bombarded him with rapid-fire questions, then took him, quite illegally, to headquarters where he was interrogated for three hours. The fellow acted baffled, but agents weren't buying it for a second. He insisted that he was dressed in a typical outfit for him and it was pure coincidence that he looked like someone they were following. The perfect match of the outfit, down to fine details that would have impressed the Continuity crew at a film production, not to mention the man's similar height and build to Kelly's, left no doubt that the switch had been planned. However, agents could get nothing out of him that day. They would be forced to collect enough dirt on him that they could threaten him with jail in order to scare him into talking; it might take a day or two to assemble the necessary ammunition.

So, with their true prey nowhere to be found, they turned the look-alike loose and set about tailing him.

~

Kelly had in fact stayed put inside the mall men's room, doing an extensive change of outfit and even gluing on a beard, waiting until he felt confident that his double had lured the agents far from the mall. Then he exited back out the main door and headed rapidly in the opposite direction, summoning an Uber.

He was going to find Denny Arbeitman and kill him for what he'd done, no matter how long it took, and screw the risks.

CHAPTER 33

Carrie, Sofia, and Brandi sat in the Madsen's back yard, moving periodically to stay in the sun, the shade cold with autumn now upon them. Brandi stayed close to Sofia and periodically leaned up against her. But Carrie noticed that her body would stiffen while she was talking, she'd move a few inches away and her face would go rigid. At times she sounded like she was reciting from a text, or as if reporting the action on a movie that was passing before her eyes, an observer not a participant. She spoke without much hesitation, though, an odd mix of focus and abstraction to her voice and eyes.

"We were supposed to be picked up at four that morning by a guy named Myles. We were gonna get a few hours' sleep; Mom set an alarm for three o'clock, she would wake me up and we could pack up our last things and have a little breakfast. She said she wished she could carry me to the car and let me stay asleep but it's been, like, four years since she could really carry me.

"So we'd been asleep a couple hours, it was maybe around midnight, we hear this guy come tearing into the house and yelling. He was saying stuff like, 'Myles just got nabbed by the police, Kelly and the police found out the plan, they're on their way over here. Natalie and Gresha'—or some names like that— 'told me to get over here and get you both out of the house before Kelly gets here.'"

"Your room and your mom's room were a mess," Carrie said.

Brandi gave the tiniest nod. "It was crazy. We grabbed our suitcases, tried to grab a couple of things we hadn't packed yet, but he just kept yelling, 'They could be here any second, go, go!' And we ran down and got in his car and he squealed out like a race-car driver.

"This man knew the names of all the people that had been helping Mom with, you know, getting ready to run away. He knew everything about what the plan had been for that night, my mom told me a couple days later that she hadn't doubted him for a second, 'cause how he could know all this stuff? And the first couple of days he seemed okay. One day he and my mom worked together on cutting and dyeing my hair, it was fun, and then my mom got into making me up, which was really cool, she'd always been so anti-makeup.

"But gradually we started to get nervous because it was taking him days to pass us off, we were supposed to be switching to traveling with other people by then.

"So this one night, maybe our third day with him, he took us to some cabin way off in the woods. It was strange, but he said we only had to be there one night and then we'd have people's houses to stay in after that. I could tell my mom was getting set off, something didn't feel right.

"So in the middle of that night, I wake up, and I'm the only one in the cabin. I went and opened the door and they weren't out there. I started yelling like crazy. I couldn't go anywhere, though, I didn't even have a flashlight. And hours went by, I've never waited so long in my life, just there awake in the dark, freaking out. When Denny—I didn't know that was his name—finally came back, it was starting to get a little bit light out. His clothes were all dirty, he looked so tired he could barely stand up. He said, 'I don't know what got into her, she said she was leaving, I said that's crazy, you'll never find your way out of these woods, she said she was supposed to meet some people, I asked her what the hell she was talking about, I'm the one who takes you to meet the next people you're traveling with, but she was all weird. And then she ran off. I've been looking for her for hours. What the hell's the matter with her?' And on like that, except, like, every third word was a swear.

"An hour or two later, when it was finally completely light out, we walked all around there calling out for her and looking for any sign of where she'd gone, but there was nothing. And Denny says, 'We've got to move on to the next spot. I'll talk to the other people as soon as we're down where there's cell service and find out if they can talk her off the ledge.'

"All the days after that he kept being on the phone with people—well, acting like he was anyhow—and he said our network of helpers hadn't heard from my mom and they didn't know why she'd run off. He said he was going to be the one to hide me for a few more days while they all worked on finding her and getting us back together. And we started traveling every day after that."

Carrie asked Brandi if she was trying to alert people during this period, people they drove past for example.

"No. I thought my mom must've had some kind of breakdown, she'd been seeming more and more on the edge the last couple of months before we took off. I thought someone would find her and they'd help her settle down, and then we'd go back to moving where we were gonna live, New Mexico. But more days were going by, so many, and he wasn't passing me off to other people, and I started to realize he was kind of crazy. I didn't know what the hell to think, really. I asked him if I could use his phone to make a call, that I knew a number to try, but he said no, that would be too risky. And that didn't make any sense to me. I started to get it that something bad was happening, that I was like a prisoner. And he was hardly giving me anything to eat, I was starving a lot of the time.

"Then one day he said to me, 'They found your mom, everything's okay, she's back with Myles and those people, police didn't catch her. She'll be able to meet up with us soon.' I can't even tell you how happy I was, all I thought about was being with her again."

And then Brandi was crying and holding tightly onto Sofia. Sofia wrapped her arms around Brandi, but also gave Carrie a surprised look; then Carrie remembered that Sofia had told her that Brandi had been like an automaton, that she hadn't cried at all, that none of the reality seemed to have hit her yet. This was a first.

When Brandi went back to talking, her voice had changed, become dream-like. "A couple more days went by, nothing was changing. I started to not believe him at all, but then I'd get terrified, so I'd go back to believing him and then I wouldn't feel so scared. A couple of times he made me take pills that would get me all spacey, I'd feel like I was walking funny. They made me happier but I hated them anyhow.

"We ended up staying in the basement of a house, that house that was, you know, in Louisiana, except I didn't know where we were, we'd driven so many miles that day. It was awful down in the basement, I just couldn't take it anymore. I started yelling at Denny to let me go, take me back to my mom, calling him a liar, we were yelling back and forth, and then he slapped me hard in the face and I shut up. He's insane.

"In the morning he was listening to, like, a radio-thing that he had, and he suddenly said, 'We're out of here, the police are coming.' That time he was telling the truth. And we start to run through the house and suddenly there's gunshots, someone was trying to kill us, I thought police were shooting. We ran out the back door and between some houses, and it hit me that if I cut off in another direction he wouldn't be able to chase after me. So I turned sharp right behind a hedge and I got away."

"And you found that family?"

"Yeah. I was looking for someplace to hide, but there was nothing. And back when my mom and me were planning the whole thing of running away she said if we ever got separated, or if police came after us, I needed to blend in with other people and call her as soon as I could. So when I saw the family walking along I pretended I was one of them, and went wherever they went. That was my first chance to use a phone."

Sofia and Carrie were startled. "It was? How can that be?"

"Denny made some excuse way back on our first day with him for why I needed to give him my phone, when we still thought he was one of the good guys. Then he never let me have it back. But my mom had made me memorize this help number for if we ever got separated, so that's how I used that Spanish woman's phone to call for help, but I just got a voice mail. An hour or so after that I asked some other people to let me make a call, and that time I got hold of someone, Gresha or something, and she said the closest person who could pick me up lived hours away, I'd have to hide somewhere until morning. Did I want to just go to the police? And I said no, I want my mom. And they said we can't find her, which made, like, zero sense to me. Wouldn't her first phone call be to them after she ran away from that cabin? I got a sick feeling.

"I spent that whole night hiding in some bushes. I even slept for a while, it wasn't cold down in the south even at night. When it was light again, I figured nobody would bother too much about a girl walking along, so I went pretty far, then found that woman at the bus stop and made another call, and I got rescued there, that woman had driven all night from Tennessee to come find me... I'm not allowed to tell you any of those people's names who helped me, or where they live or anything."

Carrie gave a sad smile. "Don't worry, I'm not asking anything like that. The police will, though."

"I'm just gonna say I don't remember, or they didn't tell me, or whatever. I'm not getting any of those people in trouble, they were good to me." And tears flowed from her eyes again.

The three of them sat quietly, trying to believe any of this was real.

"But, about your phone," Carrie said. "Didn't you call your dad a few days after you went missing? He said he talked to you just quickly one morning, then it sounded like someone snatched the phone away from you. But now you're saying you had no phone..."

Brandi looked baffled. "My dad told you this?"

Carrie nodded. "He reported it to the police right away, he was all freaked out. And the cell company confirmed that the call came from your phone."

"My phone?" Brandi grabbed her head with her hands and appeared to be squeezing. After a while she said, in a voice now finally anguished, "Then Denny *was* working for him..." And she leaned into Sofia again and cried, this time long and furiously.

When her sobs finally eased, they sat looking for a long time at the leaves on the trees moving in the wind, behind the branches a painfully dazzling blue sky with only small, wispy clouds to relieve it.

"Why have you come to Sofia's?" Carrie asked, trying to speak in a gentle voice, something she'd never learned to do and wasn't sure she had the hang of.

"I wanted to be home, back in town at least I mean, and be with Sofia and Kiara and Jarred. I've been with strangers ever since the day my mom left that cabin. But I talked with a lawyer—Sofia had me talk to him—and he said there was no way to be sure that my dad wouldn't get me back, he said there was no proof my dad had done anything to me. He said he believed what I was saying but it's up to a judge, not up to him. But now the lawyer said that my dad will be put in prison with no bail if he shows up again, because he ran away, so I don't have to worry about the court making me live with him."

"You're gonna stay living here, then."

"Sofia says I can stay."

Madsen spoke for the first time in a long while. "It's not just that you can stay, I *want* you to stay. And Kiara and Jarred want you to stay." Though in truth her children were anxious about the arrangement; they cared about Brandi like a cousin but found her very difficult, had for more than a year.

Sofia turned to Carrie. "A ten-year-old kid has no rights. Brandi can't choose where to live, it's up to the Ohio Department of Job and Family Services. Barry Shipley talked to them for me, and they said, off the record, that if Brandi's happy here they're unlikely to make her leave. But all they'll say officially is that she can be here temporarily while they do a Home Study about me."

"They put me somewhere else and I won't stay there, I'll run away every night." Brandi's voice was strong now, angry. "They'll give up and let me stay here."

Sofia replied, "They're not going to take a kid out of a home where she's happy," making an effort to sound more certain than she felt.

"You gonna put all this stuff I said in the newspaper?" Brandi asked Carrie.

"I won't say anything you don't want me to."

"I want people to know what happened. That's why Sofia had you come over... And you know what? Go ahead. You can even write the part where I said I'll run away if they put me in a foster home. I don't care."

Carrie shook her head. "No need to go into that. But, you know, once I write this stuff, the TV stations are gonna want to interview you."

"No way! Please! Sofia, I don't have to do that, do I?"

"Of course not, Brandi. Not in a million years."

"I wouldn't do it either in your shoes," Carrie said. Then, "Anything else you want to tell me?"

Brandi shook her head no.

Carrie watched the vast sadness settling back over the girl, a mile-thick layer of volcanic ash that would take a decade to disperse.

"There's a lot more to Brandi's story," Sofia said, "but that's going to stay between me and her."

Carrie struggled for a way to end the afternoon. Every phrase she tried on in her mind sounded like an echo in a gray cement room. Finally, she said, "Your mother obviously loved you like nothing in the world." That couldn't make any difference to Brandi's pain now, but maybe someday it would.

~

That night Carrie spoke briefly with Sofia by phone while putting the finishing touches on her story for the paper. "Do you know whether Brandi believes that Kelly hired Denny to kill her mother?" she asked.

"She's still in a daze," Madsen responded. "You saw it. There's no way she can even begin to take in that possibility on top of everything else."

"What do you think actually happened? Not for my article, just between you and me. Lauren was your best friend, you've got the big picture more than anyone else does."

Sofia sighed audibly and took a long, slow breath before speaking. "The part where Lauren supposedly ran away must have been part of Kelly and Denny's plan all along. They meant for her to never be found. Brandi was supposed to believe—the whole world was supposed to believe—that Lauren decided to run away and never come back, that after escaping with Brandi she changed her mind and decided to run off with some boyfriend and abandon her daughter. It would fit the picture Kelly had drawn of her. Denny would drop Brandi close to a police station, maintaining the impression that he was one of Lauren's helpers, and vanish into hiding. Brandi would be returned to Kelly, he'd never have to pay child support again, he'd have Brandi living with him full time. And he'd be a total hero, the victimized father, the man who was there for his poor daughter."

Carrie felt sick. "The word is that Denny had been wanting to move to Montana since a while back. So it all fits; he could line his pockets with the money Kelly paid him and then vanish out West."

"And Kelly almost got his wish. But what I think happened instead is that Denny realized that if he hung onto Brandi he could soak more money out of Kelly. And then he'd either let her go or, if he could, he'd traffic her and make even more money. I think his plan was to try to get into Mexico with her, they were getting close when she escaped... And whether he succeeded in that part or not, Brandi would have spent the rest of her life believing her mother had left her. Nothing could be worse than that."

That most devastating of outcomes had been averted, thanks to Carrie and Gavin's undercover work. But Carrie couldn't bring herself to feel thankful for anything. She could think only of how logical Sofia's conclusions were about what Kelly's plan had been, the sickening viciousness of it all.

"Did you tell Brandi about the Athens shooting?"

"Yeah. She said Denny was never away from her more than a couple of hours at a time in daylight, hard for him to pull it all off that fast, though I guess it's not impossible. But she also told me about two or three different meetings between him and strange men, he'd leave Brandi in the car with the windows closed and he'd stand a short distance away having these low-voiced meetings with guys."

"That fits too; it turns out Denny's connected to anti-government militia types, the kind who plan to go to war against the cops." Carrie paused. "Okay, last thing, I promise. Do you know if Brandi gets how Kelly found them in Louisiana?"

"She has no idea. Do you know?"

"Fathers Rights guys up here got the address for him. But I don't know how. Somebody Denny trusted must have burned him."

"There was definitely no woman with them at that house, by the way. Brandi said it was just her and Denny running out that kitchen door. She also doesn't know anything about those cards and photos of Lauren's ending up in the bushes in Mississippi, she didn't have those things."

Carrie looked at a calendar. That stuff had been found five or six days after Kelly headed south, a day and a half after it had been in the news that Brandi had been spotted in that town.

She paused and thought for a while, tapping a finger on her thigh, wishing the dark cloud would lift. She had to finish up her article and get some deep, deep sleep.

"Listen, since we're off the record... I fucked some things up on this story, I bought into some shit I shouldn't have. Just have to say that."

Sofia sounded forgiving. "If you want to make up for it, go blow the cover off the custody system, it's so corrupt. Some journalist has been needing to dig that one up for years. Kristen Lombardi tried—she's one of the reporters that broke the clergy-abuse scandal—but when she wrote her first expose of the family courts, that's when she finally got sued. That was like twenty years ago. No reporter's taken it on in a big way since."

"Who knows, maybe I will," Carrie said, though she couldn't imagine it. "And if I get mysteriously killed, you'll know why." Then, not wanting to end it there, she added, "Brandi's lucky to have you."

It sounded so wrong; lucky was the last thing Brandi was. But Sofia seemed to understand, and thanked her.

CHAPTER 34

Sunni was shocked to hear about Gavin's near-death experience. She said she'd head to Pittsburgh to see him as soon as she could, maybe Wednesday in the late afternoon, it depended.

He explained that the worst was past, he expected to be out of the hospital in another four or five days. She started to cry. "It would be so awful to lose you," she said through her tears.

In the closeness of the moment he opened up to her about how strong his feelings were for Carrie, that they were even more powerful than they had been the last time he and Sunni had spoken, though he didn't admit that his desire to be in good with her was what had almost gotten him killed. And he said he was aching to understand why she got so mad at him sometimes. He recounted Carrie's last couple of explosions.

Sunni was quiet for a while, then asked Gavin whether he felt ready to hear what she really thought. He insisted he did. "Listen, you're such a great guy, Gavin, you know I love you, you know a bunch of us do. But no matter how much you hate our dear Edgeworth Falls—and for good reason—it's crept inside you. You don't ever quite come down off this hill that you look down on the world from."

"I don't look down," he said defensively.

"You so totally do, though. Listen, you have a big opportunity here. I love hearing you sounding so crazy about this girl, you've never been like this. And she sounds so cool, I'm psyched to meet her. So don't blow it. All you have to do is stop thinking you're better than her. That isn't asking so much."

He started to say something, but stopped himself.

Before hanging up, Sunni said, "I love you, Gavin. I'm so glad you're okay. I'll get out there to see you soon, for real."

He couldn't remember Sunni ever having told him with such feeling that she loved him, and in this odd mix with hard criticism. He collapsed back on the bed and lay still, trying to take it in.

~

Dr. Stephanie Vaughn's Pittsburgh office was furnished with a plain wooden desk and chairs, a little austere, but the effect was balanced by lush green plants in every corner and in the ample window recesses. She noticed Carrie contemplating it and said, "I don't make enough to have a spiffy office, but I'm fine as long as I get plenty of light. The sun just pours in here."

Vaughn had extra reason to need the sunlight's cheer: her specialty was therapy for children who'd been abused or had witnessed abuse. She spent her days listening to grim stories and helping kids wade through the harm that had been done. Together they searched for an opening the children could crawl through, out of the pile of earth and rocks that had collapsed down upon them.

Her perspective contrasted with many psychologists, as she'd explained to Carrie on the phone three days earlier. First, she believed that children rarely lie about abuse, and in the few cases where they do it's because of intense pressures that have come down on them. She particularly objected to theorists in the divorce arena who said that it's easy to subtly manipulate children into falsely accusing a parent. "You can indeed manipulate a child into doing that," she said, "but there's nothing subtle about it."

Today Vaughn had time to explain the issues in more depth as they sat in the brightness and warmth of her office. "A theory called 'Parental Alienation' has taken over the custody courts in the past twenty years. It's been promoted by fathers accused of abusing women and children, and by psychologists and lawyers working for them. It originated with a psychiatrist named Richard Gardner. Gardner wrote that almost all parental alienators—he put the figure at ninety-five percent—are mothers. In other words, he was on a campaign against mothers from the beginning.

"And here's a view of his you'll find even more remarkable: Gardner wrote that sometimes a girl deliberately uses false sexual abuse allegations against her father to retaliate against him *because he refused her sexual advances toward him!*

He says this in his best-known book, *The Parental Alienation Syndrome,* in a section called 'The Child as Initiator.'"

Carrie put her hands up as if to grab her own face. "No one could take a guy seriously who wrote stuff like that."

"So you'd think," the psychologist replied. "But family courts across the country have attached themselves to his theories. It's gotten to the point now where moms are being slammed by the courts for even believing their children's disclosures."

A few weeks earlier Carrie would have considered Dr. Vaughn off the deep end. But now she and Gavin had reviewed case after case where events had played out just as Vaughn was describing.

"So, if a mother's not supposed to believe her kid, what's the answer for her?"

"There isn't much of one. Sometimes she can get the child evaluated, but sometimes the court orders her not to, believe it or not; I've had more than one of those cases. What's more common, but just as bad, is that the court chooses the evaluator; and typically they use people who are marinated in the divorce profession, that whole culture of denial and mother-blaming."

The young reporter shook her head as if in disbelief. "So the mother gets to a point where there's no way to protect her kids except to run away. And then she's a kidnapper."

"Look, I'm not saying it's okay. But there's nothing more painful a parent can go through than to watch her child doubled up in pain, maybe saying that Dad is getting in her bed and rubbing himself up against her—for real, this has happened with clients of mine. The mother is required to keep sending her kids on visits because the court has chosen, for no good reason, not to believe her and not to listen to the kid. How is a loving parent going to keep sending her kids off every week or two to have this happen to them again? It's inhumane to expect that."

Kelly had perhaps been correct in saying that the family court was responsible for Lauren's decision to flee, though for reasons opposite to what he'd meant.

A doubt continued to nag at Carrie. "I can't see Kelly as a pedophile."

Vaughn nodded. "He probably isn't."

This wasn't the response Carrie expected.

The psychologist clarified. "If it turns out he's been abusing Brandi, that makes him an incest perpetrator, not a pedophile. Those are two completely different groups of offenders. The incest perpetrator isn't usually a loser type, and he typically has normal-looking adult sexual relationships. And he's most likely to offend against girls, while the pedophile is more likely to offend against boys."

Carrie squeezed her eyes shut, as if to drive something out of her brain, then opened them again. "How come nobody ever tells you this shit?"

"Here's one more fact that'll get your attention: men who are violent toward their wives are about six times as likely to be incest perpetrators as other men are. There are multiple studies."

"The courts know about these studies?"

"They should. But if they do, they're choosing to ignore them. They've become the biggest enablers of domestic violence and sexual abuse—don't quote me on that."

Carrie gave a grim smile. Then she asked, "Do you have a sense of why this is going on?"

"Journalists need to go digging and find out. First, follow the money, as they always say. But I think there are other causes also. Come back someday when you have two or three hours to spare, I'll talk your ear off."

A small, humorless laugh was all Carrie could muster.

Her last question, back to specifics, was to ask Vaughn her opinion of Dr. Kinzer.

The therapist replied cautiously. "I don't know him personally," she said, "but I've worked on several cases that his program evaluated. They come to the same conclusion over and over again: the kids' fear or bitterness regarding their dads was caused by the mother's hypervigilance, not by domestic violence or child abuse. They dance around the evidence as though it's dust bunnies on the floor, and call it a 'high-conflict divorce.'"

"And the evidence is there?"

"If you bothered to look, yes, it is. There are things that kids reveal to school teachers. There are threatening texts to Mom from the abuser. There are events witnessed by family friends. All kinds of things."

Such as bloodthirsty short stories, Carrie thought, remembering the Katie Tagle case.

Vaughn added, "When a custody evaluator says, 'It's just her word against his,' it's because they didn't investigate. They just drag out their myths about abuse as an excuse to ignore it."

The therapist had to prepare for her next client. But Carrie had taken in more than she could digest anyhow, so it was just as well to wrap up. The Harbison case had seemed so insane, so extreme. Yet Dr. Vaughn was telling her that it was disturbingly ordinary, part of a huge pattern that needed to be exposed.

Vaughn was now the second person telling her to go blow this national scandal open. If only Carrie were a real reporter, instead of a kid who just stumbled in here by accident.

CHAPTER 35

Carrie, along with Gavin's parents, spent Saturday preparing his apartment: setting him up with a week's worth of food and supplies, rearranging his bedroom to make movement easier, making a schedule of turns for who'd be watching over him. It had not been Carrie's favorite day of life. An entire childhood with these smooth, cultured people would have made her crazy, she'd have ended up chewing on trees like a beaver or scratching her own eyes out with her fingernails.

Or she would have been the next girl to give her parents forty whacks.

His parents weren't at all nasty; in fact they were unrelievedly, torturously polite, pleasant, and generous. She hated them.

Their curiosity to figure out the nature of her relationship with Gavin was palpable, and she took pleasure in doing nothing to help them out of their uncertainty. Why did they have to know exactly what it was? It wasn't like Carrie knew herself.

She met them again on Sunday morning for Gavin's scheduled release from Union Hospital. His parents drove him back to Pittsburgh while Carrie followed behind. The agreement was that she would be the one to stay with him at his apartment until Monday morning. But his dear mother and father stuck around until almost eight o'clock that night, until she felt on the brink of screaming at them to leave. Blessedly, his mother finally got sleepy and they announced they had to go.

Gavin lay on his bed, drained from the trip home. He looked better overall, though. He was still swollen in places, scratches were still visible all over him as if he'd gone running naked through thorn bushes, his skin still had a purple tint if not as much as before. But his injuries were past the grotesque point; they'd gone through a stage of merely looking sad and sickly, then progressed further to being marks of a courageous and significant adventure, and now had healed yet another step to where he simply looked adorable. His reddish marks, his eyes just a little puffier than usual, his hesitant but almost back-to-solid way of walking, had turned sexy. His parents had finally left them alone in his apartment, his housemate was in New York, and Carrie had ideas.

Gavin was quiet for a while, as had become normal for him. Then he asked, "Are you gonna stay over?"

She was sitting next to him where he lay on his bed, intermittently holding his hand. She was caught off guard by her feelings; being kind and affectionate with him had come to feel so natural, so sister-like, during his convalescence, the guy looking for days like a bloated and floating fish, that the question of whether they should remain lovers had felt far away.

"Of course, I wouldn't leave you alone here yet, not overnight," she said.

Maybe they could just be friends. That way she wouldn't have to get wrenched around between adoring the sweet version of Gavin and wanting to rip the head off of the superior-acting one. Although at the moment she was feeling a distinct stirring; if they were gonna be friends, she wanted it to come with benefits.

Gavin looked a little sheepish. "You've been with me a ton at the hospital, and now you did all this work to get this place ready for me to come back, you dealt with my parents non-stop for the last thirty-six hours, that's longer than I can deal with them. I thought…"

"Honestly, I wasn't thinking about it, I just…"

"You've been doing all this out of guilt? I already told you it's not your fault."

"No, no, I wanted to be around…"

He was quiet for a few moments. "I talked to Sunni for a long time yesterday, on the phone. She… is kind of blunt. The two of you should probably meet, especially since she sticks up for you." He laughed a little, she wasn't sure why.

"She does?"

"Yeah. Like I'll tell her things you've said that I didn't understand, and she'll say, 'How could you not understand that?' She says she likes the way you sound and that I'm lucky to be with you. No loyalty from her."

His eyes were beautiful, soulful, and she took his hand again. "Let's just take things slow, okay? And for tonight, could we, like, not try to decide anything? I'm just glad you're okay."

He nodded, and his eyes drooped a little. She was afraid he'd fall asleep, as he very much needed to do.

She leaned over and kissed him gently on the lips. "Does your face hurt to touch?"

"I don't think so, not anymore. No one's been touching it, though." He closed his eyes.

Carrie lay down on the bed and put an arm over him. He shifted his weight toward her a little, so she leaned over and kissed him deliciously for a couple of minutes. She'd been missing his mouth so much. He seemed okay, his tongue moved nicely despite how stiff his face still felt.

Ever so delicately, so as not to hurt him, as if merely a medical attendant getting him ready for sleep, she began to remove his pants. He didn't object.

Then she removed her own, and pressed gently up against him. He seemed to move back toward wakefulness as if only now realizing what she was up to. Next she checked one of his key vital signs with her hand, and the test came back positive.

As a last test of his healing she slowly moved over on top of him, though she continued to support much of her weight on bent arms; and, with a grace and delicacy uncharacteristic of her, started to rub herself against him.

He opened his eyes, though not all the way, made a small wriggle, still some painful spots in his body to avoid, and said, "What happened to what you said about moving slowly?" He wasn't exactly objecting.

"Yeah, I think we should," she answered, kissing his chest a couple of times and then reaching her hand back down. "I'm just trying to get us in the right position first."

AFTERWORD

The following cases that *In Custody* makes reference to are real, with all facts given accurately as they appear in news reports and public documents:

Katie Tagle
Kathryn Sherlock
Hera McLeod
Amy Hunter
Jacqueline Franchetti

The following writers, whose works are mentioned in the book, are also real:

Kristen Lombardi, journalist
Richard Gardner, psychiatrist

The town of Morriston, Ohio and its newspaper are my inventions.

East Liverpool and Middle Beaver are real spots on the map, but my descriptions of those places are entirely fictional.

Pittsburgh is real but is too large to get its feelings hurt.

InCustodyTheNovel.com

ACKNOWLEDGEMENTS

My deepest gratitude for their help with crafting, editing, and producing
this book goes to Wendy White Kniffen, Chip Roughton, and Patty Kelly.
For crucial knowledge and insights into law enforcement procedure, and for
willingness to answer phone calls for months, a million thanks go to retired
police officer Rob Eccleston (who is also one of my all-time favorite baseball
teammates). For encouragement and emotional support during the long process
I send my great appreciation to Teegan Mannion, Patty Kelly, my Shut Up
and Write group from the Lady Killigrew café, my Monday afternoon and
Wednesday noon Peak Living Network support groups (and all my wonderful
PLN allies), John Maher, James Peck, Natalie Goodman, Jenny Goldberg,
Daniel Ritchie, Chip Roughton, Patrice Lenowitz, Fabienne Andrews-Lafont,
Liam Andrews-Bancroft, Flip Rosenberry, and Ann Reynolds. And many thanks
to Alexis and Ana Kumar for their theatrical work.

For musical inspiration (which is my fuel): Rapsody, Eddie Arjun, Doomtree,
Aesop Rock, Little Simz, Branford Marsalis, Laura Veirs.

Printed in Great Britain
by Amazon